There Are Places
I Remember

Stories
By Michael Di Leo

For Stu

CONTENTS

"It's being here now that's important. There's no past and there's no future. Time is a very misleading thing. All there is ever, is the now. We can gain experience from the past, but we can't relive it; and we can hope for the future, but we don't know if there is one."

—George Harrison

"The distinction between the past, present, and future is only a stubbornly persistent illusion."

—Albert Einstein

He wrestled to fall asleep this night, like he had so many nights before. He could never seem to fall asleep easily. Always ceaselessly reviewing the events of the day, yes, but also frustratingly reliving moments from the past. And not always dwelling on the bad times, but also obsessing over—and missing—the good times. The good times that were probably not as good as he remembered. But at night when he tries to drift off, he is reminded, or perhaps even fooled into believing, that things were just a little bit better in the past. If he could only go back, wouldn't that be the greatest dream of all?

Yesterday and Today

(2018)

JIMMY RUSSO SAT QUIETLY in the back of the limo as it sped uptown along Sixth Avenue. As a kid from Brooklyn, he had never gotten comfortable riding in limousines. But the truth was that he had not been on a subway in years, and the thought of going on one now seemed unreal. Not that the subway wasn't safe. He knew the subway was safer now than it had been in decades. But he was a rock star and had been since the early '90s. Since he had attained fame, he hadn't been comfortable being around crowds or in situations where he might be recognized. Not that he didn't enjoy the trappings of fame and fortune. He did. But he preferred to be around other famous people as much as possible. He wasn't proud of this. And deep down, he still considered himself to be a regular guy. He just struggled with being around regular people.

And he supposed that this was the reason he was heading uptown to the appointment. As crazy as the proposition seemed, maybe this was a way to get back in touch with himself, to remember what it was like to just be

Jimmy from the neighborhood. To spend a few hours as a regular person again instead of as rock star Jimmy Russo.

He was the lead singer/songwriter of Purple Crush. Although their two most recent albums had done nothing, they were one of the biggest acts of the '90s, with their first four albums having sold a combined thirty million copies. They still sold out arenas whenever they went on tour. And their greatest-hits CD still sold enough copies, tangible and digital, that he could live quite comfortably on those royalties alone for the rest of his life.

He was also bored and had money to burn. Even with an ex-wife and a hefty monthly alimony payment, he had more money than he knew what to do with. That was why when Zack Tyler—lead guitarist of Suds—had told him about the small company located at 1271 Avenue of the Americas, he had become intrigued. Of course, what this company did seemed unbelievable. Impossible. Really. But Zack swore it was true. It was something only people "in the know" knew about. And you had to have $10 million to even get in the door.

The limousine pulled up at the corner of 50th Street and Sixth. Jimmy got out and looked up at the fifty-story building. Scaffolding ringed the lower floors. He knew that the whole building was going under a renovation. It used to be the Time and Life Building and had been the headquarters of *Time* and *Life* magazines for decades. But *Time* had moved downtown a few years ago, and *Life* no longer existed.

He exited the elevator on the 49th floor and walked down the hall to suite 4932. The sign on the door said *ZTT Corp*. He rang the buzzer and heard the door unlock.

Inside the office was not at all what he expected. It was small and drab. And the receptionist's desk looked old and beat-up. Was this the right place?

"Good morning," said the receptionist. "Mr. Russo, correct?"

"Yes."

"Very good. You are our only appointment today," she said. "Mr. Brandauer will see you now." She motioned to the door behind the desk. "Right through the door," she said.

"Thank you," Jimmy said. He smiled at the receptionist and walked through the door.

As he closed the door behind him, he felt as if he were entering another world. He was in a completely different space. The long hallway had sleek, metallic walls. It looked like something from a James Bond movie. At the end of the hall was an office.

"Welcome, Mr. Russo," said a voice that seemed to come out of the wall. "Please, the office at the end of the hall. Come."

He walked forward and came to the door of the office. The sign on the office door read *Zenith Time Travel Corporation*. He stood in front of the door for a moment and took a breath.

Well, what the hell? he thought.

He had never shied away from taking chances. That's how he became a rock star in the first place. When in doubt, take the plunge, he always said. So, that's what he would do now.

He opened the door and walked into a bare office with a small metal desk, with a Macintosh monitor sitting on top of it. Behind the desk sat a rugged man with slicked jet-black hair and wearing a shiny silver suit.

"Nice to meet you, Mr. Russo," said the man. "I'm Charles Brandauer, director of operations for ZTT."

He motioned for Jimmy to sit. Jimmy lowered himself into the comfortable desk chair in front of Charles Brandauer.

"I'm a big fan," said Brandauer. "I saw Purple Crush at the Garden in '97, I think it was. I wore out my CD of *Cadillac Dreams*. Great album."

"Thank you," Jimmy said.

"So, you've read the contract we sent you?"

"Yes."

"And you understand the process?"

"I think so," said Jimmy. "But why don't you go over it again for me?"

"Of course," said Brandauer.

Jimmy shifted in his seat. He had read exactly what service the Zenith Time Travel Corporation provided. But he wanted to hear Brandauer say the words. It was that incredible.

"So, Mr. Russo," said Brandauer, "it really is simple. The Zenith Time Travel Corporation will transport you back in time—to any one day in recorded history—for a total of three hours on the nose."

"It's that simple?" said Jimmy.

"Well, I wouldn't call it simple, Mr. Russo. I'm not the Science Director of ZTT. But it's simple in as far as our clients are concerned."

"I just take a pill, and…poof?"

"As far as you are concerned, yes."

"And I can go anywhere in recorded human history?" Jimmy asked.

"As far as we know. We've had one client who went back to ancient Egypt. Wanted to see the pyramids being built. That's the earliest to date."

"And I just give you a date and time, sorta like in *Back to the Future*?"

"Yes," said Brandauer. "And a specific time on the date you want to go back to. You have only three hours."

"And then I take the pill, and what, I get transported like, 'Beam me up, Scotty'?"

"Something like that, yes."

"So, I get to be Marty McFly and Captain Kirk, rolled into one?"

"That's an amusing way to look at it, Mr. Russo. But, yes, that's very much what it will be like."

Jimmy sat forward in his chair and thought for a moment. This was insane, wasn't it? Why didn't the whole world know about this? Isn't this the most important invention in human history? And it's hidden in a small office on the 49th floor of the old Time and Life Building? But Zack swore by it. Said he tried it himself.

"You're wondering how this can all be possible, aren't you, Mr. Russo?"

"Well…yes."

"And why this is all so secret?"

"Yes again."

"Well, our founder and his scientists toiled away at this project for many years. Spent millions of dollars—many of those donated by some of the richest people in the world—and have worked to keep the business of this company very discreet. Our client list to date is very small."

"At 10 million a pop, it would have to be," said Jimmy.

"So, have you decided on a date yet?"

"No."

"I'm sure it can be overwhelming. Ten thousand years of human history. How can one choose one three-hour window on one single day within a 10,000-year period?"

"Yes, I guess it's a big decision," said Jimmy. *Fuck yeah, it is*, he thought.

"Take the night. Sleep on it. Give it some thought. Then email me in the morning with your selection."

"OK," said Jimmy. "And then?"

"Once you've given us your date and time, it only takes our technicians a few minutes to map everything out. Then you come back here and take the pill and…"

"Poof?"

"Yes, Mr. Russo. Poof."

"And how do I get back?"

"You don't have to do anything. When your three hours are up…"

" 'Beam me up, Scotty' time," said Jimmy.

"Yes, exactly."

"One more question," said Jimmy. "Why Zenith?"

"Our founder named it after the television set he had as a child."

"Not a bad name. Guess it's a good thing he didn't have an RCA."

Back at his apartment in SoHo, Jimmy poured himself a scotch on the rocks and sat on the couch. He had done some crazy shit in his life. He had gone cliff-diving in Jamaica, driven a Maserati 180 miles per hour at night on Highway 1 in California, taken his clothes off onstage at the Nassau Coliseum, had a foursome with three supermodels, and survived two decades in the rock industry with his sanity mostly intact. But what he was about to embark on made all of that look like schoolboy stuff.

Time travel? He laughed. *Was this for real?*

But how could he pass up the chance? It was like the greatest dare ever, and when had he ever said no to a dare?

But where and when to go? Should he do something that would change the world for the better? Go to 1930s Germany and kill Hitler? Go back to 1963 and kill Lee Harvey Oswald? No, he couldn't kill anyone. Not a chance. Go back to September 11, 2001, and stop the attacks? How the hell would he do that? No, he didn't want to change history. That would be like playing God. Yes, World War II and the Kennedy assassination and 9/11 were all god-awful, but they were part of history and had shaped the world he had grown up in. If those events didn't happen, he would be changing his own life in such a way that it would be like he didn't exist. Or the life that he had lived for fifty years would not have existed. No, he couldn't do anything that drastic.

Maybe he should just go back to some time in his own past before he was famous. Just so he could enjoy being Jimmy again. With no one knowing who he was. Just walk the streets anonymously for three hours. He hadn't been able to do that in twenty-five years.

He sipped his scotch and grabbed the remote on his coffee table and turned on his stereo system. The Beatles' "Tomorrow Never Knows" came on. He had left *Revolver* in the CD player last night. He listened to John Lennon singing about turning off your mind and floating downstream. Yes, this experience that he was about to embark on would certainly be that.

Jimmy took another swig. God, he loved this song. What a voice John Lennon had.

And then it hit him, and a chill went down his spine.

One of the benefits of being a rock star was that you got to meet all your rock 'n' roll heroes. The Beatles were the reason that Jimmy had picked up a guitar in the first place. He had twice met Paul McCartney backstage at Paul's shows, had met Ringo a few times in LA, and even met George once at a party in London a few years before he died in 2001. He would not have become a rock star if not for The Beatles. His mother was a huge Beatles fan, and that's all he listened to as a kid in the '70s. "Day Tripper" was the first song he learned to play on the guitar. He was 13 when John Lennon was murdered in 1980, and it crushed him.

So what if John Lennon didn't die? That would harm no one, right? And it wouldn't massively change history in any way. It would just give John Lennon back to the world. What could possibly be wrong with that? It would give him back to his wife and sons. Hell, The Beatles would probably even get back together at some point! And that would be great for the world. He downed the rest of his scotch. He couldn't think of one bad thing that would happen or change in any significant way if he prevented John Lennon's murder. John would live and go on to make beautiful music for another three decades or so! How could that be bad? And that wouldn't alter world history, right? It would just be a nice thing for the world, and it would be a nice thing for Jimmy. He had never gotten over Lennon's death. No Beatles fan had.

Yes, he would go back to 1980. Walk around as Jimmy from Brooklyn for a couple of hours. Then stop that motherfucker Mark David Chapman from murdering John Lennon.

"December 8th, 1980, Manhattan. 9 p.m." Jimmy said the words calmly and assuredly.

He sat across from Mr. Brandauer with a sense of excitement. In fact, he hadn't felt this excited in years.

"That's a rather nondescript date and time," said Brandauer. "Usually, our clients choose an important place and time in history."

Jimmy was quietly relieved. He was concerned that Brandauer would know the significance of that date. But obviously not. He looked to be around forty years old, so he would be too young to remember Lennon's murder. And assuming he wasn't a Beatles fan, that date would have no meaning for him.

"I have my reasons," said Jimmy.

"Fair enough, Mr. Russo. Just one more thing before we get started. And it's the most important aspect of our service."

"Yes?"

"Under no circumstances are you to interfere in any significant way with any people in 1980. Yes, you can engage in routine or polite conversation. But you are there as an observer only. It is critical that you do nothing that can change or alter history in any way. Yes, walk the streets, go get something to eat. Breathe the air. But do nothing that interferes with any actions of the people of 1980."

Jimmy smiled. *Don't worry*, he thought to himself. *I know exactly what to do. And I'm going to do it.* "Of course not," said Jimmy. "I'm just going to take a leisurely stroll through 1980 Manhattan."

Brandauer smiled. "Very good. Come this way, and we'll get started."

Jimmy stood up to walk out of the office.

"Oh, one more thing," said Brandauer. "Please hand over your cell phone. You can't walk around 1980 with a device that hasn't been invented yet."

"Sure," said Jimmy. He handed Brandauer the phone.

"We'll return it as soon as you get back."

He was led down the hall and into a room marked *Transportation Room*. Inside was a large chair that looked like it belonged in a dentist's office. A technician in a white lab coat asked him to sit in the chair and lie back.

"Just relax," said the technician. "In a minute, you'll be in 1980."

"Just like that?" asked Jimmy.

"Just like that," said the technician. "Just lie back in the chair."

Jimmy took a deep breath and lay down in the chair. "You make it sound so simple."

"It is."

The technician held up a bright red capsule. "Just swallow this, and in a minute, you'll wake up in 1980."

Jimmy took the capsule in his hand. "And what if I wake up in the middle of oncoming traffic on Broadway?"

The technician laughed. "Everything has been carefully calibrated to avoid that, Mr. Russo."

9

Jimmy held the capsule in his hand and looked at it. He thought of what he was about to do. He was going to save John Lennon! In three hours, he would be back in 2018, and John Lennon would be seventy-eight years old and alive. He was euphoric, just thinking about it.

"Mr. Russo?" asked the technician.

"Oh, yes, sorry."

"Are we ready?"

"We're ready."

Jimmy took one last look at the pill, placed it on his tongue, and swallowed.

He woke up a little groggy. It was nighttime, and he was outside, and he was lying on the ground. He looked around and could see immediately that he was in an alley of some kind. The first thing he noticed was the smell. There was an overflowing garbage dumpster a few feet from him. He staggered to his feet. New York City, 1980. The city wasn't as clean back then as it is today, was it? Wait, he meant tomorrow. It wasn't as clean as it would be in thirty-eight years.

He walked out of the alley. He was in Manhattan, but where? He looked to his right and could see an avenue a few hundred feet away. He walked toward it.

As he got to the corner, he could finally read the street signs. He was at the corner of Broadway and 88th Street. He was only sixteen blocks from John Lennon's apartment building, The Dakota!

And, oh God, yes, he was in 1980. He saw a large rust-colored Cadillac Sedan Deville pass by, heading downtown on Broadway. It was a '77 or '78, by the looks of it. God, he used to love those big Cadillacs! His father had always wanted one. Then he saw a Chevy Impala go by. He laughed because, in 1980, that car was considered midsize. In 2018, it would be the biggest car on the road by a mile. He walked past a parked car that looked like a '72 Plymouth Fury. It was as big as a boat and as ugly of a car as he had ever seen. No wonder they didn't make Plymouths anymore.

He walked into a nearby bodega, not because he needed to buy anything, but because he needed to know the time. The radio behind the counter was on. "Another One Bites the Dust" by Queen was playing. Behind the counter was an old white man. Yes, this was 1980 after all. He asked the man for the time.

"Five after nine," the man said.

"Thank you," said Jimmy.

He had about two hours. Lennon was shot around 11 p.m., so he had to get to The Dakota sometime before then. The pit of his stomach was in knots—the same feeling he would always get right before going onstage. But what he was about to do was more important than any performance he had ever done. He was going to save John!

He left the bodega and thought about what John Lennon and all The Beatles had meant to him. Every time he sat down to write a song, he hoped that he could write something that was as good as The Beatles. It never happened. But they always inspired him to keep trying. If someone asked him on Monday what his favorite Beatles album was, he might say *Sgt. Pepper's Lonely Hearts Club Band* or *Abbey Road*. If you asked him the same question on Tuesday, he might say *Revolver* or the *White Album*. He could never decide. They were all so great. Same thing if you asked him who his favorite Beatle was. It was John or Paul. But you would get a different answer depending on what day of the week you asked him. As different as they were, he loved them both so much. So, now he would save John, and one day in the future, Lennon-McCartney, the greatest

11

songwriting duo of the 20th century, would reunite! Or at least they would have the opportunity to do so. An opportunity that Mark David Chapman had so ruthlessly robbed them of.

He headed down Broadway toward The Dakota. He needed to get there around 10:30 p.m. to give himself time to locate Chapman. Which shouldn't be difficult—he reportedly hung out in front of the building all day, waiting to strike. And what would he do when he found him? He would scare him away—just long enough for Lennon to safely enter the building.

He thought of Chapman and how much he hated him. A man who was a Beatles fan like Jimmy. A man who idolized Lennon like Jimmy. It would have been one thing if Lennon had been killed by a mugger or a street thug. But to be killed by a fan? One who traveled all the way from Hawaii for the express purpose of killing him? That's what always made it so tragic. But he was going to change all that. He thought of being back in 2018 in a few hours. The first thing he was going to do would be to grab his iPhone and check for all the new Lennon music that he—and the world—had missed these past thirty-eight years! The thought of it made him dizzy. He had to calm down. Take a deep breath and focus.

He continued walking, soaking up the sights and sounds of 1980. He passed a movie theater on 86th Street. It was playing *Private Benjamin* and *Somewhere in Time*, the Christopher Reeve time-travel movie. He guessed that was apropos, wasn't it?

He walked past a McDonald's and peered through the glass. A Big Mac for $1.29! And nothing but burgers and fries on the menu. Not a McNugget to be found. He hated McNuggets.

At 78th Street, he saw an Irish pub. He didn't want to get to The Dakota too early—just in time would be right. He entered the pub. This way, he could kill some time and have a drink to calm his nerves. He sat at the bar and was surprised at how empty it was. But he had forgotten for a moment that, December 8, 1980, was a Monday. So, even in the city that never sleeps, corner pubs were not that crowded on a Monday night. He ordered a scotch on the rocks and noticed there was a football game playing on the small TV at the corner of the bar. Of course! New England versus Miami. This was the game where Howard Cosell would announce live on the air that Lennon had been murdered!

Jimmy raised his glass and thought to himself, *Not this time, Howard. Not this time!*

Two scotches later, and it was 10:15 p.m. Time to get moving. He still had to walk seven blocks down to 72nd Street and then hang a left and head toward the park. The Dakota was at 72nd and Central Park West. It was about a fifteen-minute walk. That would get him there around 10:30 p.m. Perfect timing.

I'm coming for you, Chapman, you miserable prick!

Fifteen minutes later, Jimmy was on the north side of 72nd Street, heading west. He could see The Dakota coming into view on his left. What a foreboding building! It looked like something out of a horror movie. And something horrible was about to happen. But, no, it wasn't. He was going to change that. Chapman should be there right now, standing in front of the doorman's booth. As Jimmy got closer to the building, he couldn't see anyone at first. But as he got to about a hundred feet away, yes, there he was! It was him! Wearing his long overcoat to conceal the handgun underneath it. And those large '70s-style glasses. Oh God, it was him! And the doorman was right there in his booth. Why didn't the doorman chase him away? Because Chapman had been there all day and was not considered a threat. He was just another obsessed Beatles fan, waiting to catch a glimpse of Lennon.

Jimmy realized that he hadn't thought out exactly what he was going to do at this moment. He kept walking forward, Chapman coming closer into view. Now Jimmy was ten feet from him. Chapman with his back to Jimmy. Looking toward the park. Waiting for the limo that was now carrying Lennon from his recording studio back to The Dakota.

As Jimmy got closer, rage started to build up inside of him.

Without thinking, he yelled, "Chapman!"

Chapman turned around, startled, confused.

"You motherfucker! I know what you're about to do!"

Chapman was wide-eyed and frozen.

"I know there's a gun under your coat," Jimmy yelled, the veins popping out of his neck. "I know what you're planning! I'm going to call the police!"

Chapman looked into Jimmy's crazed eyes for a moment, still startled. And then he bolted across the street like a sprinter. He quickly turned the corner onto Central Park West, heading south, and disappeared from Jimmy's view.

"That's right, you motherfucker. Keep running!" Jimmy yelled. "Go the fuck back to Hawaii!"

Jimmy was out of breath from the yelling and the adrenaline. He slumped over for a moment.

The doorman came out of his booth. He said, "Why don't you move along, buddy, before I call the cops?"

Jimmy turned around and smiled. "Sure thing," he said. "Just give me a minute."

The doorman watched him warily, not sure what to make of this guy who had just scared that Beatles fan away.

Just then a large white Lincoln limousine turned the corner onto 72nd Street. The headlights caught Jimmy's eyes, and he watched the car pull up in front of The Dakota. Jimmy watched in stunned silence as the back door of the limo opened and John and Yoko quietly walked out.

Jimmy smiled, still out of breath from all the excitement, and watched John and Yoko casually walk past the doorman's booth and under the large archway, into The Dakota's courtyard, and disappear from view.

Jimmy started crying. Oh my God, he had done it! John Lennon had just safely entered his apartment building. He lived! John Lennon lived!

He was still crying when the doorman came up to him again and said, "OK, buddy, time to move along now. I mean it. I'll call the cops if you don't leave now."

"No problem," said Jimmy. "I'm leaving now. Tell John I said hi. Tell him I love the new album and can't wait for the next one and the one after that and the one after that."

And then Jimmy wandered back up 72nd Street, still crying, but also laughing. John Lennon was alive! And Jimmy Russo from the neighborhood had saved him.

You done good, Jimmy, he thought to himself. *You done good.*

In a few minutes, he would be back in 2018 with his iPhone in hand and headphones in his ears…

Jimmy awoke, and at first, he wondered if the whole thing had been a dream. He was lying in the chair in the Transportation Room, right back where he started. Had it been a dream?

"Welcome back, Mr. Russo," said the technician. "Feeling OK?"

Jimmy looked up at the technician. "I think so," he said.

"No ill effects?" the technician asked.

"No," said Jimmy as he sat up. "Not at all. In fact, I feel great."

"That's good," said the technician. "Some of our clients feel a little out of sorts when they get back."

Jimmy really did feel great. Relaxed, even. But he was anxious to get his phone. He wanted to look up John Lennon on Wikipedia and read up on what the man had done in the past thirty-eight years.

"Let's bring you down the hall to Mr. Brandauer's office for your exit interview," said the technician.

In Mr. Brandauer's office, Jimmy sat in the guest chair, waiting for Brandauer to enter. He fidgeted, anxiously waiting to get his hands on his phone. His mind raced. He couldn't wait not only to read about Lennon, but also to listen to all the Lennon music that had been made in nearly four decades, music that he had never heard! He was almost giddy with excitement.

"You look well, Mr. Russo," said Brandauer as he entered the office and sat at his desk, facing Jimmy. "Sometimes, our clients look a little sleepy when they return. You look positively chipper in comparison."

"It's true," Jimmy said. "I feel great."

"Wonderful," said Brandauer. "I take it, you had a pleasant time in 1980?"

"Very pleasant," said Jimmy. "I accomplished everything I set out to do."

"That's what we love to hear from our customers."

"This was the best 10 million bucks I've ever spent."

"We love to hear that even more," said Brandauer. "As you are aware, we don't exactly advertise what we do. All our business is garnered by referrals and word of mouth. Be sure to tell your friends."

"I will do that," said Jimmy.

"Well then, we thank you for your business, Mr. Russo," Brandauer said as he stood up and offered his hand to Jimmy.

"And I thank you, Mr. Brandauer," said Jimmy as he took Brandauer's hand.

Mr. Brandauer motioned for the door.

"Wait, one more thing," said Jimmy. "My iPhone."

"Oh, yes, of course," said Brandauer.

He reached into the drawer on his desk and pulled out Jimmy's phone. Brandauer handed Jimmy the phone.

"I'm lost without this," said Jimmy.

In the elevator, Jimmy tried to get reception on the phone, but there was no Wi-Fi. He shook his leg anxiously as he waited for the elevator to descend the forty-nine floors. When the doors finally opened in the lobby, Jimmy raced for the doors leading out onto 50th Street. He quickly opened his phone and saw that he had three bars on the 3G icon. That should be enough.

He immediately went to Google and typed in *John Lennon*. Or at least, he tried to. His hands were shaking so much that he had to type the name three times before he got it right. He then opened the John Lennon Wikipedia page, and his heart leaped with joy when he saw the heading "John Lennon, 1940–present."

He was alive! He had truly done it! John Lennon didn't die in 1980 and was still living in 2018! He didn't know what to read first. So, instead, he scrolled down to the Lennon discography portion of the page and saw albums that he had never heard of! *A Walk in the Park* (1982), *Last Summer in New York City* (1985), *9 Reasons to Dream* (1987). And more albums through the 1990s and 2000s. His latest came out in 2017. Oh, boy, did Jimmy have some listening to catch up on!

He then scrolled through Lennon's history, frantically looking for anything on a Beatles reunion. Surely, with all of them alive, they would have reunited at some point in the past 38 years for something. Even if it was just a one-off concert.

But he didn't see anything! How could that be? He kept scrolling, going back in time from the present back into the 1980s, looking for anything that mentioned a Beatles reunion.

And then he noticed something that made his heart stop. Something about Lennon's biggest No. 1 hit being dedicated to Paul McCartney. He was scrolling so fast that he went past it at first. He scrolled back to a heading called "Yesterday and Today."

It read:

> *"Yesterday and Today" is the #1 song from 1983, written by John Lennon, in honor of his late songwriting partner, Paul McCartney, who was murdered by crazed fan Mark David Chapman in 1982. The song won the 1984 Grammy for Song of the Year and to date is Lennon's highest-selling single of his solo career.*

Jimmy fell to the sidewalk and started to shake. This wasn't possible. This couldn't be true. He looked at the phone again and reread the passage. What the fuck?! He opened the music icon on his phone and chose John Lennon from his library. All the albums that he just read about were on his phone. And then he saw the song "Yesterday and Today."

He started to feel faint. A woman passing on the street stopped to look at him, but when he looked up at her, she saw madness in his eyes and kept walking.

Jimmy tried to clear his head. This had to be a joke of some kind. He kept staring at his phone and then realized he should look up Paul McCartney on Wikipedia. He fumbled with the phone and struggled to type out Paul's name. When he finally got it right, he opened Paul's Wikipedia page. The heading was "Paul McCartney, 1942–1982." And Jimmy collapsed on the sidewalk.

He must have been out only for a few minutes. When he came to, a man was standing over him.

"You OK, buddy?" the man asked.

"Yeah, I'm fine," said Jimmy as he struggled to his feet.

He grabbed his phone and went back to Wikipedia and continued reading, his body quietly shuddering as he did so.

Turns out, Mark David Chapman had traveled to London in May 1982 with the express purpose of killing Paul McCartney, which he did as Paul exited his recording studio. Chapman had purchased the gun on the London black market for $200 shortly after his arrival in London. And now Jimmy remembered an article he had read back in the day shortly after Chapman had killed Lennon. How Chapman had made a list of the celebrities that he was considering killing. Lennon topped the list, followed by Johnny Carson, Elizabeth Taylor...and Paul McCartney. He had chosen Lennon because he lived in an apartment on a Manhattan street, where he was easy to get to, as opposed to the others, who all lived in gated mansions. But of course, Chapman was scared away from Lennon's apartment by Jimmy. The Wikipedia article didn't mention that part, of course. Only Chapman and Jimmy knew that part of the story.

Jimmy stared at the phone and cursed the day he was born and cursed the day he walked into the Zenith Time Travel office. How could he have done this? Brandauer warned him not to mess with anything in 1980! What made him think that he could play God?

He went back to the music icon on his phone and went to Paul McCartney. Sure enough, all the albums Paul had made after 1982 were erased from his phone. Erased from history because of stupid Jimmy Russo from the neighborhood. He had loved Paul's 1997 album *Flaming Pie*, but now he was the only person on earth who knew that album, because it—now—never existed. He slumped to the sidewalk again and started to weep.

Then he went back to John Lennon on his music icon and clicked on the song "Yesterday and Today." He pressed play and listened to his first new John Lennon song in thirty-eight years. And, oh God, it was beautiful. That voice! No one sings "sad" like Lennon.

"*...and since you went away, I dream of yesterday and miss you so today,*" sang John, mourning his friend Paul.

John continued to sing, and Jimmy continued to cry.

"I'm so sorry, Paul," he cried. "I'm so sorry..."

Howling at the Moon

(1969)

BARBARA MILLER CARRIED ANOTHER six-pack of Coca-Cola to the bottom of the driveway and, one by one, dropped each can into the plastic wading pool. The pool was full of large blocks of ice, already melting. It was a hot Sunday, perfect weather for the first block party on Victory Lane, but someone would have to get more ice.

Robbie, her two-year old son, kept jumping into the pool, and Barbara had to keep pulling him out.

"The pool is for drinks today, Robbie, not swimming."

Robbie didn't understand.

"They landed! They landed!"

Barbara turned around to see Mrs. Gayheart running out of her house into the street.

What was she yelling?

"They landed on the moon!" Mrs. Gayheart yelled again. "The lunar module landed."

Everyone in the street cheered. Mr. Krasdale started singing "God Bless America." He was drunk and sounded terrible, but everyone was too excited to care. They had landed on the moon!

Barbara grabbed Robbie and ran into the house. She turned on the TV. Walter Cronkite was talking as grainy images of the lunar module showed on the screen.

Barbara cried. "Look, Robbie. Look," she said, but Robbie wasn't paying attention.

He wanted to jump in the wading pool again.

She heard the toilet flush, and her husband exited the bathroom.

"They landed on the moon!" she told him.

"Holy shit," he said. He ran toward the TV and looked at the grainy images. "Where are they? Did they get out?"

"No," Barbara replied. "Cronkite said it could be hours before they leave the module."

They went outside and rejoined the party. Mike Miller hoisted Robbie onto his shoulders, and Barbara teared up. She had never seen everyone so happy. Bob Krasdale threw his arm around her shoulders and began singing "Fly Me to the Moon." He was no Sinatra, but Barbara didn't mind. He could sing badly all day and night for all she cared. She couldn't remember the last time she had felt such joy.

Later that night, as the block party began fizzling out, Barbara went back into the house and put the TV on. When Neil Armstrong stepped onto the moon's surface, she cried again and ran out of the house to tell her husband. He was sitting on the driveway in a lounger, drinking beer with Bob Krasdale. Upon hearing the news, her husband looked up at the moon and started howling. Bob Krasdale followed suit. Barbara laughed and started howling too. Maybe Neil Armstrong would hear them!

Barbara and her husband slept at ease that night, drunk on Schlitz and excitement for the future.

There were men on the moon!

In the morning, she took Robbie outside and pointed at the moon, faint against the lightening sky. "There are men up there right now," she said. "There are men walking on the moon, Robbie."

Robbie pointed to the moon and said, "Moon." Then he ran into the garden, chasing a fly.

Barbara watched her son light out, then looked up again at the moon. And for a brief moment—after a decade of turmoil and strife, of assassinations and war—Barbara had hope that the future would be a bright one.

The Love You Make

(1970)

"I JUST TALKED TO Mary Gayheart. Joey Barone is home!"

A slight thrill went through Cathy Bishop. She had prayed for the news her mother had just given her. Joey Barone was home! Home! He had made it. Oh, thank God he had made it!

"That's great news, Ma," she said, concealing her joy.

"His parents picked him up from JFK yesterday," her mother said. "Mary saw them when they got home. She said he looked good, not a scratch on him."

Ever since Joey Barone had left last year for his tour of duty in Vietnam, Cathy had worried over his safe return. She prayed for him at night, even said the rosary sometimes. Anything she could to help ensure he would make it home.

Of course, Joey didn't know any of this. When the Bishops moved to Victory Lane in the spring of 1968, Cathy was seventeen, just finishing her junior year of high school. Joey was eighteen, a year ahead of her. Victory Lane was a brand-new development smack dab in the middle of Long

Island, and most of the families were either newlyweds or young couples with toddlers. But not the Bishops and Barones. Cathy's parents were in their early forties. Joey's a little older. He was the only kid on this new block anywhere near her age.

She had instantly developed a crush on him. He had jet-black hair, combed straight back. And he wore it short, unlike most of the kids who were growing their hair out longer and longer. He reminded her of a young Dean Martin.

Of course, Joey didn't pay much attention to her. She didn't think she was bad-looking. She even thought of herself as kind of cute. But she was shy, especially around boys. And Joey was cool. Sort of the strong, silent type. Other than the occasional small talk at the bus stop, they didn't engage much. And even that came to a stop when Joey got a car and stopped taking the bus to school. It was a fading red Chevy Biscayne. She wasn't sure what year, probably a '61 or '62. It was beat-up and rusted, but Joey looked cool in it.

One of her happiest memories was one day when the bus didn't show up in the morning. Joey noticed her standing at the bus stop long after she should have been. So, he wheeled the Chevy around over to the bus stop and asked her if she needed a lift to school. Her heart was racing so much that she almost forgot to say yes. But mostly because of her shyness, the car ride was a quiet one.

When she found out he had been drafted, she hoped he wouldn't be sent to Vietnam. Her friend Mary's older brother had been drafted the year before, and when he was finished with basic, he got sent to West Germany. She had hoped it would be the same for Joey. But he wasn't that lucky. He was going to 'Nam. Before he left, she spotted him on the driveway one day, washing the Biscayne, and she drummed up the courage to walk over to him and wish him luck. He was nice and thanked her, but she could sense his nervousness. It was understandable. She was nervous for him too.

Every night that he was gone, she would pray for him and hope that he was all right. And she would wonder what he might be doing right then. She would see footage of the war on TV every night, and it always looked so horrible. She would look to catch a glimpse of him, but she never did.

There was also that time when *Life* magazine published the photos of every American killed in Vietnam in a one-week span in the spring of 1969. There were 242 photos. Almost everyone looking barely old enough to shave. Her mom had a subscription to *Life*, and when that issue arrived and she saw the cover, she felt so queasy that she almost fainted. Joey's picture couldn't possibly be in there. They all would have heard if something terrible happened, right?

Her father was upset at the magazine editors. "They're just trying to feed the antiwar movement," he said.

He felt that the people protesting the war were traitors.

But Cathy didn't feel that way. The war seemed pointless to her. So what if Vietnam went red? Even though the magazine had scared her, the more she thought about it, she was glad it had shown the pictures. People had to see what the war cost, right?

But now Joey was home and safe. And what did that mean for Cathy? Could she drum up the courage to talk to him? What would she say? Would he even remember her?

Her mother suggested that she bake him some cookies.

That would be OK, right? Something unobtrusive, a nice gesture to say, *Welcome home*. Even a shy person like her should be able to drum up the courage to drop off a tray of cookies.

She didn't know what she might say to him and whether he would care. But she was eighteen now, and it seemed the world was coming apart at the seams. It was time to start living. The poor guy had just spent a year in the hell that was Vietnam. That took real courage. The least she could do was deliver some cookies and make some polite conversation.

Joey's mother was so happy to see Cathy and invited her right in. She called upstairs to Joey and asked him to come down to the kitchen. After some polite pleasantries, the three of them sat at the kitchen table and ate cookies.

Joey was quiet but did manage to say, "The cookies were good."

His mother suggested that the two of them go out and do something. "You've been locked up in this house since you've been home," she said to Joey.

"We could go to the mall," Cathy said.

The Smith Haven Mall had just opened the year before, and Cathy thought it was the most amazing thing ever. Everyone did.

"Yes, the mall. That's a great idea," said Joey's mother.

"It even has a movie theater," said Cathy. "We can go see a movie." She couldn't believe she was being so forward. But she was tired of being timid. It was 1970, and everything in the country and the world seemed to be going to hell, right? Why be afraid? The time for timidity was over.

Even though Joey hadn't said much as they ate cookies and seemed somewhat distant, he agreed to go to the mall with Cathy.

He was quiet still in the Biscayne as they made the short drive to the mall. But when they arrived, he was impressed with it. The sheer size made one take notice. It had a Macy's, a Sears, and an Abraham & Strauss, and about 100 stores or so of every kind in between. They went to the movie theater and caught the 2 p.m. showing of *Airport*. They both thought it was good. It even starred Dean Martin, and Cathy mentioned to Joey that she thought he looked like him.

After the movie, they went to get pizza. Yes, the mall even had restaurants in it!

"Isn't the mall just amazing?" said Cathy as they dug into their slices.

"It is actually pretty impressive," said Joey. "I haven't been gone that long, and it's unbelievable how many things have changed."

Other than the mall opening, things didn't appear any different to Cathy, but she went along with him and said, "I know."

"Do you realize that I think I watched pretty much every Mets game since they debuted in '62 until I went to basic, and then I'm gone a year, and they win the World Series, and I don't see one pitch?"

"I'm sorry," she said. "All anyone talks about since last fall is the Miracle Mets."

"And I missed the Jets winning it all too," he said.

"I'm sorry again," she said. What else was she supposed to say? "You can't turn on the TV these days without seeing Joe Namath on it."

"And I missed it all," he said, shaking his head. "And I missed the fucking moon landing too!" He didn't seem inconsolable, just incredulous.

She didn't know what to say to him. He really did seem to miss a lot of major events when he was gone.

"Can you believe The Beatles broke up?" she said.

"I know," he said. "That's another thing I missed. What happened?"

"Nobody really knows," she said. "Their new album came out, and Paul just quit, and they're fighting with each other, and it's just horrible." She chewed on her slice, trying to hide her nervousness and hoping that she didn't sound like an idiot.

"It's like the world is coming apart at the seams," she said.

"Don't I know it?" he said. "At least the Stones are still together. You like the Stones?"

"Sort of," she said. "But I'll be honest with you, Mick Jagger kind of scares me out a little bit."

"Me too," he said. "That's what makes him cool."

She smiled, and they continued to talk music. Joey hadn't heard *Abbey Road* yet. Another thing he missed while he was away. He agreed that they should listen to it together, and that was the greatest news that Cathy could have heard. Had she not dreamed of sitting in her room with Joey, listening to records?

The next night, he came over after dinner, and they listened to *Abbey Road* in her room. *Joey was in her room.*

He liked the record, especially the side 2 medley. That was her favorite part of the album too. Joey said he would have to go back to the mall and buy a copy of the album for himself and some of the other records he had missed.

"Do they have a record store in the mall?" he asked.

"They have everything at the mall," she replied.

She stopped over at his house the next day at 1 p.m., but his mother said he was still in bed.

"He's been having trouble sleeping," she said. "He finally drifted off a couple of hours ago." She seemed concerned. "Maybe you stop by later?" she said.

But Cathy didn't want to push it, so she decided not to come back that day. She was so excited that she and Joey were "hanging out" now that she didn't stop to think that being back home was probably overwhelming for him. Better to take things slow.

––––––––––

The next day, he stopped by in the afternoon and asked if she wanted to go out that night. Of course she did! Where would they go?

"I don't know," he said. "Maybe take a drive in the Chevy, go get a drink somewhere."

That somewhere ended up being Murphy's Pub, which was in the Pathmark shopping center next to the mall. Cathy had never been to a bar before and didn't know what to drink. Joey ordered a Schlitz draft, so she had the same.

"If there's one thing we did in 'Nam, it was drink a lot of beer," he said.

She hadn't said anything to him about the war because she didn't know what to say, and she didn't know if he wanted to talk about it. But since he brought it up…

"Is it as bad as it looks on TV?" she asked. "The war, I mean."

He took a long gulp from his beer and looked down at the bar. "It's worse," he said.

"I'm sorry. I didn't mean to bring it up," she said.

"No, it's OK," he said. "My parents don't ask me about it. It's like they want to pretend it never happened. Like I was just away at college or something, and now I'm back home."

"Well, if you want to talk about it, I'll listen," she said.

He took another draw from his beer. "I don't want to talk about it. And if I did, I don't think you'd really want to hear what I might have to say."

"OK," she said.

He looked pained, and she didn't want to upset him. She didn't know what to say, so she picked up her beer and sipped it. She didn't like the taste, but she drank it anyway.

"You know, you really are beautiful," he said. "I never noticed that while we were in high school."

She blushed.

"What?" he said.

"I always had a crush on you in high school," she said. "I guess I had one from the first time I saw you when we first moved to Victory Lane. But you never seemed to notice me." She giggled because she was embarrassed to tell him this.

"Well, I guess I see things differently now," he said.

An awkward pause pushed into the conversation. Inside, she was ecstatic that he seemed to like her now. But she really didn't know what to do about it.

"I can't sleep," he said.

"When I stopped by yesterday, your mother told me that you had a rough night."

"Yeah, you could say that," he said. He sipped his beer. "When I was over there, I used to dream about getting back home and sleeping in my bed again. And now I'm home, and I can't sleep. And when I do drift off, I have bad dreams."

"I'm sorry," she said. "It must all be a tough adjustment."

He smiled. "I don't know why I'm telling you this."

"It's OK," she said.

After another pause, he asked if she wanted to take a drive.

"Yes, let's," she said.

They drove in the car and turned onto Middle Country Road, whizzing past the mall. The radio was playing Bob Dylan's "Lay Lady Lay." When

Dylan sang about waiting for the one you love, when he sang about how he was standing in front of you, well, damn, that's exactly how she felt! Did she love Joey? How could she possibly love him when they had just started hanging out together? But, by God, she wanted to be with him. He was hurting, and she wanted to heal him. He was in pain, and she wanted to make it all better. Was that not love?

He turned the car onto Moriches Road and then pulled into a clearing in front of the woods. Behind the woods was Victory Lane.

She didn't know what was going to happen next, but her heart started racing.

"Why don't we go in the back seat?" he said.

Her shyness and her inexperience told her not to go with him. But her heart said yes.

"OK," she said quietly, the word barely leaving her lips.

They stepped out of the car and quickly reentered in the back.

His hand caressed her cheek, and then his fingers gently slid down to her lips. She shuddered. He moved closer and kissed her, softly at first, then harder as she responded. She had long dreamed of this moment, and now it was happening. Years of frustration poured out of her and into his lips as she pressed against him.

They kissed for several minutes, lost in each other, closed off and hidden from the world.

He started to slide his hand between her thighs, and she didn't resist. When it reached the zipper of her jeans and moved downward, she sighed. His fingers lightly rubbed her, and she almost burst out of her skin, shuddering again, but not stopping him. She kissed him harder, and he kissed her back, his fingers never stopping, her body in rapture, her mind euphoric.

She came without warning and without notice and collapsed in his arms. This had never happened to her with another person, and she felt at once embarrassed, elated, and at peace.

He kissed her forehead and held her closely. She wondered what she should do next. Should she touch him down there?

"What about you?" she asked. "Should I…"

She reached her hand between his legs, but he stopped her.

"I'm sorry," she said. "I thought…"

"It's OK," he said. "Things haven't…" He looked down and didn't complete the sentence.

She caressed his head. "What's wrong?"

He hesitated and put his head down.

"Are you OK, Joey?" she asked.

He looked up at her, tears welling in his eyes.

"It's just that…" He hesitated again.

"It's OK," she said. "You can tell me."

"Well, things haven't exactly been working down there, if you know what I mean." He laughed nervously and looked down again, embarrassed to look into her eyes.

"Oh," she said, knowing what he meant, but not knowing what to say.

"Ever since I got home and actually a little before that," he said. "I just can't get the sail up."

Now she was embarrassed. "I understand," she said.

"I think it's all the messed-up shit I saw over there," he said. "It's like something's not right inside of me. I can't sleep, and I can't…you know."

"It's OK. We don't have to do any of that," she said. "Why don't we just hold each other?"

He looked into her eyes for a moment, then put his head on her shoulder. She wrapped her arms around him, and he wept quietly.

"Shhh," she said. "It's OK. It will all be OK."

She held him close and felt warm and at peace. There was nowhere she would rather be than here in this car at this moment, with Joey's head on her shoulder.

The radio was still playing. "Bridge Over Troubled Water" was on. It was always on, wasn't it? Or maybe it just seemed that way. She was kind of sick of the song, even though she knew it was good. Art Garfunkel did have a nice voice. When he sang about easing your mind, Cathy understood.

Yes, Joey, I will ease your mind. Cathy is here now. I will ease your mind.

After a few moments, she heard him quietly snoring. He was finally sleeping. And she was happier than she could ever remember being. All she wanted to do now was to take care of Joey Barone.

———

Cathy's parents were going away for the weekend upstate and were, of course, concerned about leaving her alone. She explained that she would be nineteen in a few weeks, and she could handle herself perfectly well for a couple of days alone. Her older brother lived on his own in the city, and they were fine with that. Why should she be treated differently? Plus, what could possibly happen to her on bucolic Victory Lane?

"Joey will check in on me," she assured them.

"Don't even think that he's going to be here alone in this house with you without us here," her father said.

Cathy blushed. "Dad…"

"Well, I don't want him thinking he can have his way with you because we're not here."

"Oh, Tom," her mother said. "Cathy's not that kind of girl!"

She wasn't, of course. But maybe she could be. Last night in the car had made her see things differently. It was the '70s now, and most kids her age and even younger were certainly more sexually "free" than she was. But she was getting ahead of herself. And Joey was, of course, having issues "down there."

"How is Joey doing, by the way?" her mother asked.

"It's been a hard adjustment for him," Cathy said. "He's had trouble sleeping since he's been home."

"I think all of those guys coming back from there are messed up," her father said. "Did you see that demonstration they had at Columbia on the news? There were soldiers back from the war, throwing their medals on the ground! It was disgraceful! Just disgraceful!"

"That's because the war is wrong, Dad!" Cathy yelled, taking her father aback. "They've earned the right to do whatever they want to do with their medals!"

He looked at his wife. "Do you believe this?" he said to her. "We live in a world where soldiers can throw their medals to the ground, and we're all supposed to be OK with it?"

"Yes, that's the world we live in now, Dad!" Cathy yelled.

Her father shook his head. "Fine," he said. "But I don't want him in this house if I'm not here."

Cathy stormed upstairs. Her father was so pigheaded. But it didn't matter. If she wanted Joey to come over, he was coming over. And if she wanted to lose her virginity to him, well, dammit, that was her decision to make. If Joey was up to it, of course. And that was a big if. What else did this poor boy have to go through?

Her parents left the next morning. Cathy envisioned Joey coming over and her cooking dinner for him and then hanging out, just the two of them, in an empty house, and then…and, well then, whatever happens, happens.

But when she went over to his house around noon, her hopes were dashed.

"I'm sorry, Cathy," his mother said. "He didn't sleep again all night. He only just fell asleep a couple of hours ago."

Cathy could see the anguish on Mrs. Barone's face.

"I'm sorry," Cathy said. "I guess it's going to take some time for him to get back to normal."

"It looks like it," said Mrs. Barone.

"Can you let him know that I stopped by and that he can come over later if he wants?" Cathy said. "I'll just be at home, watching TV."

"I will, Cathy." Mrs. Barone closed the door, and Cathy started walking across the street.

She saw Mrs. Miller playing on her front lawn with her two toddlers, Debbie and Robbie. She sometimes babysat those kids. She was especially enamored with little Robbie. He was so cute. She looked over at the joyous innocence of a young mother playing with her young children, and then she thought of Mrs. Barone, worried sick about her war-scarred boy. The difference was jarring. Here were two mothers, living right across the street from each other, with one enjoying the exuberance of young motherhood, the other tormented by her son's rocky transition back to civilian life.

She waved to Mrs. Miller and the kids. Mrs. Miller waved back.

"Hi, Cathy!" little Robbie yelled.

He was always so happy.

"Hi, Robbie!" she yelled back.

She hoped he wouldn't have to go through what Joey was going through now when he got older. But the way the world was going…

She got home and ate a little lunch before going upstairs and lying on her bed. It was strange, being in the house alone, but it was also liberating. She was in no hurry for her parents to come back.

She wondered if Joey would come over. She hoped he would. Maybe she should ask him to talk about Vietnam. She knew he didn't want to, but maybe that's what he needed to do. Maybe he needed to just get it all out, and then he could start getting back to normal. Maybe that would help him sleep. Either way, she just wanted to be with him.

She decided to listen to some music to pass the time. The Supremes? One of her old Beach Boys records? No, it would have to be The Beatles. *Let It Be* had just come out a few weeks earlier, and it was great. But, no, she would choose *Abbey Road*. That was the one she always went back to.

She put on side two and lay back on her bed. "Here Comes the Sun" came on, and if that song couldn't make her happy, then nothing could.

She had the music on loud enough that she almost didn't hear the doorbell. She jumped up, lowered the volume on the turntable, fixed her hair in the mirror, and ran downstairs.

She could see through the window of the front door that it was Joey. Her dear Joey was awake and had come to see her.

She opened the door and smiled. "Hi," she said.

"Hi," he said. "My mother said you stopped by before."

"Yes, come in," she said.

She ushered him through the door and into the foyer.

"My parents are away for the weekend," she said.

"Cool," he said.

"Let's go upstairs," she said. But he hesitated. "It's OK. We can just talk," she said.

She took his hand, and they walked up the stairs and into her bedroom. He looked around the room, taking in the posters and photos on her walls. Lots of photos of The Beatles, one of JFK, another of Lucille Ball.

"*I Love Lucy* was always my favorite show," he said.

"Mine too," she said. "I always watch the reruns on channel 5."

"I've tried to watch them since I've been home, but I can't get through an episode. It's like something's wrong."

He sat on her bed, and she sat next to him and took his hand.

"The other day, the one where Lucy and Ethel pretend to be Martians was on, and that one was always my favorite, and I sat there, watching it, and I just stared at the TV, waiting to laugh, expecting to laugh…"

He looked down, unable to look her in the eye. "But there was nothing," he said. "I couldn't laugh."

"You've been through so much," she said. "You can't expect things to get back to normal right away."

"That's it though," he said. "I don't think I'm ever going to get back to normal. I don't think I know what normal is anymore."

She wiped the hair that was hanging down from his forehead and kissed him gently on the cheek.

"Do you want to talk to me about it?" she asked. "Maybe that will help."

"I don't even know what I'd say," he said.

"I'm sure you saw some horrible things," she said.

"I did some horrible things too," he said.

"Well, it's not your fault," she said. "It's Nixon's fault."

He chuckled and said, "Fuck Nixon."

"And LBJ's fault," she said.

"Fuck him too," he said.

She pulled him closer and held him tight.

"Thank you for caring," he said.

He put his hands on either side of her cheeks and kissed her. She vigorously responded as he laid her back on the bed. She immediately felt his stiffness on her leg, and she was relieved for him and exhilarated for herself. Joey was a man again, and she was about to become a woman.

When it was over, she lay on her back with Joey resting his head on her chest, snoring away. He was sleeping like a baby. Maybe he couldn't sleep unless he was with her. Maybe she was all that he needed to get back to normal. She dreamed of their life together. Yes, of course they would marry. Wasn't it obvious that they loved each other and needed each other? It was to her. Would they stay on Long Island? Or maybe get a house upstate in the country? What would they do for a living? Surely, as a veteran, Joey could find gainful employment somewhere. And she could type. So she could get a job in an office somewhere—at least until they had kids. A boy and a girl would be perfect.

Her hair stood on end when Joey started screaming.

"Noooooo!" he shrieked. "Noooo!"

She sat up. His eyes were closed, and he was obviously having a nightmare.

He just kept screaming, "No," at the top of his lungs.

She tried to shake him. "Joey, wake up," she said. "Please, Joey, wake up."

She kept shaking him, waiting for his eyes to open. But his eyes stayed shut, and he kept screaming.

"Motherfuckers!" he yelled. "You motherfuckers!"

She shook him harder. "Joey, please, please wake up," she cried.

But nothing happened. It was like he was in a trance. He just kept screaming.

Is this why he couldn't sleep? Is this what happens to him every night? Is this why his mother was so concerned?

She grabbed him by the shoulders and shook him as hard as she could. Tears were now rolling down her face. "Please, Joey, please."

And then his eyes opened. But she could see that he wasn't really there. His eyes locked with hers, and there was no recognition. He grabbed her by the neck and began choking her.

"Noooo," he screamed as he pressed his thumbs into her throat.

She desperately gasped for breath. Her arms flailed wildly. She tried to smack his back, but couldn't reach it with his weight now fully on her. She reached up and started pulling his hair. She pulled as hard as she could. Thank God he had grown his hair a little longer, or there wouldn't be anything to grab.

She was getting no air, and he was not letting up with the choking or the screaming. It was then that she realized that she might soon be dead. Was this her punishment for letting Joey come over? Her punishment for having sex with him? Her father's face flashed before her eyes. He didn't like Joey, and he didn't want him touching his daughter. But even he never envisioned this.

No. It couldn't end like this. She summoned whatever strength she had left and pulled his hair harder. Her forearms and wrists began to ache. Oh God, she needed air! So, she kept pulling and pulling.

He blinked his eyes, and suddenly, Joey was there. Shock registered on his face when he saw Cathy's face. And then he realized that he was choking her and leaped off the bed.

She gulped down the air and grabbed her throat. "Joey..."

He grabbed his pants and threw them on, leaving his underwear and the rest of his clothes on the floor as he ran out of the room, barefoot.

She struggled out of bed and staggered toward the door. "Joey, it's OK," she panted.

She got to the door and looked downstairs to see him exit the front door. She started to run down the stairs after him but then realized that she was naked. She stumbled back into her room to get her clothes, still gasping, still trying to take a full breath of air. From the window, she could now see Joey running across the street and into his house.

She stared out the window for a moment, not knowing what to do. The air started to come fully into her lungs now. What the hell had just happened? What punishment was she being served? How did she go from the best moment of her life to the worst in just minutes?

She collapsed back onto her bed. She looked at her *Laugh-In* wastebasket that was next to her bed, seeing Ruth Buzzi's face staring back at her, and started to cry.

She stared at the ceiling for a while, feeling paralyzed. It had been at least an hour since Joey had run out of the house, and she wondered if she should go across the street to see him. But what would she say or do? Maybe he needed space. Probably he needed a psychiatrist. Something to help him work out his demons. She thought she was that something. And she still hoped that she would be.

She started to drift off, so she didn't notice at first the red flashing lights reflecting off the ceiling. What was it? She got up and noticed the whole room bathed in red light. What was going on outside? She walked to the window and saw an ambulance and a police car in Joey's driveway. Oh, dear God…

She threw on her robe and ran down the stairs and straight out the front door. She saw the front door to Joey's house swing open, and out came two paramedics, wheeling a stretcher. Oh God, it was Joey. Oh God, oh God…

Mrs. Barone came running out of the house behind the stretcher, followed by her husband. She waited impatiently as they loaded her son into the ambulance, and then she climbed in behind the stretcher.

Cathy held her hand to her mouth, frozen in place, standing on her driveway. She noticed Mr. Krasdale, who was a city cop, run across the street. He ran to Mr. Barone, who was talking to the police in front of the squad car.

The ambulance pulled out of the driveway and sped away, heading most likely to Smithtown General. Cathy watched it leave Victory Lane and started to shiver. She saw Mr. Barone get in the squad car, and it quickly drove down the block.

Mr. Krasdale walked back across the street toward his wife. Mrs. Miller was there too. Cathy glanced around the block and saw other people staring toward the Barone house as well, everyone wondering what had happened.

Cathy walked across the Millers' lawn toward where Mr. Krasdale was congregating with Mrs. Krasdale and Mrs. Miller.

When she got close enough, she heard him say, "He tried to kill himself. Hung a belt from the ceiling fan. Damn lucky that Joe walked in on him and pulled him down in time."

Cathy's legs went weak, and she staggered backward. She wisely decided to sit on the grass before she fell on it. *He tried to kill himself...*

Mrs. Miller came over to her. "Cathy, are you all right?" she asked.

Cathy was weeping and didn't answer.

"It's OK," said Mrs. Miller. "I'm sure he's going to be OK."

Cathy looked up at Mrs. Miller. She had big blue eyes that usually made you feel warm and cozy. But right now, those eyes were scared.

"I don't know what to think anymore," said Cathy, sobbing. "I don't know what's going to happen."

Mrs. Miller sat on the grass next to Cathy and put her arm around her. "That damn war," said Mrs. Miller. "That damn war."

Her parents came home the next day. Cathy told them what happened to Joey, but didn't mention anything about his being in the house with her and certainly nothing of the events that led to his suicide attempt.

Her mother tried to console her, but she was beyond soothing. She had never felt grief like this. And fear. Fear for Joey and fear for herself. She kept playing the events of the previous day over and over in her head, trying to make sense of them. But there was no sense to be made. And then the self-pity came. How many women in this world had lost their virginity and then, moments later, their beaus had tried to kill themselves? She almost had to laugh at the absurdity of it all. But then she thought of Joey. None of this was his fault. No one could imagine the things he had been through. She wanted him to be OK, and she wanted to be with him still. They must get past this. They must still have a future together.

Later in the afternoon, her mother noticed the Barones' car driving down the street. "Cathy," she called. "Cathy, I think he's coming home."

Cathy ran down the stairs and peered out the front door. She saw the car pull into the driveway and watched as Mr. Barone helped his son out of the car. She thought he looked OK, but he was walking slowly, his father holding his arm as they walked into the house.

She wanted to run right over there and see him and hold him. She wanted to tell him to not feel any guilt over what he had tried to do to her. He was having an awful nightmare and didn't know what he was doing. She wanted to hold him tight and tell him that everything was going to be all right.

Her mother suggested that she bake him some cookies again and bring them over in the morning.

"Yes, that's a good idea, Mom," she said. "I'll let him get settled and have a good night's sleep and then bring him cookies. He liked them so much the last time. Hopefully, it will cheer him up." She wasn't sure. But it was something to hope for. And she needed hope.

Baking the cookies gave her a purpose and kept her busy. She knew she must stay optimistic. She must believe that everything would work out for her and Joey in the end. Her father came into the kitchen just as she was taking the cookies out of the oven.

"I'm sorry about what happened to your friend," he said. "I know our boys have had a rough time of it over there."

She knew it wasn't easy for him to say that. "Thanks, Dad," she said, and she meant it.

That night, she sat on the couch with her parents, watching TV. Her dad had on *Gunsmoke,* but he changed the channel at 8 p.m. and put on *Laugh-In* for her. But she couldn't pay attention, and not even Ruth Buzzi pounding away at Arte Johnson's head with her pocketbook could make her laugh.

Later, she spent a restless night, hoping that the next day would be better and hoping that Joey would like her cookies and hoping that Joey would be happy to see her. Because if he wasn't, well then, she just didn't know what she was going to do.

"Thank you, Cathy. I'll make sure Joey gets the cookies," Mrs. Barone said. "But he's just not up to seeing anyone right now."

Cathy had come to the Barones' front door, full of hope, but all hope was dashed immediately.

"It's been a rough couple of days for all of us," Mrs. Barone said through tears.

"I understand, Mrs. Barone," said Cathy. "Please tell him that I stopped by and tell him that I am praying for him."

Mrs. Barone choked up and barely got out the words, "I will."

Cathy walked back across the street, bewildered and adrift. She just wanted to see him and talk to him, and then everything would be OK again. If only Mrs. Barone understood.

A few days went by, and there was no sight of Joey. Cathy was beside herself. What was going on? How was he? Should she go over there again?

After a week, she couldn't take it anymore. She rang the Barones' doorbell and waited impatiently for the door to open. Maybe Joey would answer the door. Wouldn't that be great?

But the door opened, and it was Mrs. Barone standing in front of her.

"Sorry to bother you, Mrs. Barone, but I wanted to see how Joey was doing and maybe say hi to him."

"I'm sorry, Cathy, but Joey isn't here," Mrs. Barone said.

Cathy looked at her, puzzled. Where else would he be?

Mrs. Barone choked up, just like the last time. "We had to commit him," she said. "The doctors are worried that he might…well, you know."

Cathy stood there, stunned. Committed?

"He's at a VA hospital in the Bronx," said Mrs. Barone.

Cathy didn't know what to say. "Will he come home soon?"

"Oh, honey, he might never come home," said Mrs. Barone. She started to cry. "It's better if you forget about him."

Mrs. Barone closed the door. Cathy started to gasp. She couldn't catch her breath. She went to her knees.

And then Cathy's mother was there. "Cathy, what happened?"

"They committed him, Mom," she said. "They're worried he might try to kill himself again. He's gone."

"OK, honey," her mom said.

45

"I didn't get a chance to talk to him," Cathy said. "If only I had a chance to talk to him, I could have made everything all right. I could've made everything all right, Ma!"

Her mother took hold of her, and Cathy collapsed in her arms.

They stood there for a few moments on the Barones' porch until Cathy's crying turned to small sobs.

"Let's get you home," her mother said.

They turned toward the house. They saw Mrs. Miller on her lawn with the kids.

"Hi, Cathy," little Robbie blurted out.

Cathy looked at him and, through her tears, said, "Hi, Robbie."

Robbie looked at her, seemingly confused by her crying. His mother grabbed him and his sister and led them back into the house.

That night, Cathy lay in bed, tears still in her eyes. She suddenly wished she were a kid again. It was all so much better then. Being eighteen wasn't turning out the way she had hoped.

She looked at her *Laugh-In* wastepaper basket. She looked at the picture of Ruth Buzzi. *That Raquel Welch is just putting up a big front*, the caption under Ruth's picture read. Ruth Buzzi was far and away her favorite cast member of *Laugh-In*, and that caption always made her laugh. But not this time.

So, she decided to put some music on. She got out of bed and flipped through her albums, looking for something to listen to. But there was no point in sifting through the records. She was going to pick *Abbey Road*, of course.

She put on side 2 and lay back in bed. She stared at the ceiling and listened to the whole side, trying to lose herself, trying to forget, but also trying to remember the last couple of weeks as well. It had all been a dream. And it had all been a nightmare. As the record ended, Paul sang about the love you take being equal to the love you make. But for the first time, she didn't believe it.

Wonderland

(1971)

SANTA LANDED IN A helicopter in the parking lot of the Smith Haven Mall in early December 1971. These were the days long before Black Friday, long before Christmas started before Thanksgiving.

Barbara Miller stood in the parking lot with Robbie and Debbie. As the helicopter prepared to land, she picked Robbie up and held him on her shoulders so he could get a closer look. He was four now and getting a little big for her to pick up like that. But the boy was in awe of the approaching flying machine, and he couldn't see very well with the large crowd of people around them.

"Santa!" he yelled.

The noise was deafening as the copter lowered into a cordoned-off area in front of the Abraham & Strauss department store, which anchored the western tip of the mall. Robbie continued to yell, but his voice and everyone else's were drowned out by the whirring of the helicopter. But soon, the rotors slowed, then stopped.

When Santa emerged, the crowd cheered again. Barbara was afraid Robbie would lose his voice. When she was a kid, Santa wasn't the big thing he had become now. The kids had watched *Rudolph the Red-Nosed Reindeer* the other night and were still talking about it. Tonight, it was *Santa Claus Is Coming to Town* at 8 p.m. There was no TV in the 1940s when she was a kid. Santa was just an image you might see on a poster at the department store. Now he was a rock star, and the kids were his groupies. But she thought it was great. Anything that brought her kids this much joy was OK with her.

After waving to the kids, Santa was whisked inside, where he would wait for the kids to take pictures with him.

That wait was a long one, and Robbie could hardly contain himself. A&S had constructed an elaborate tunnel festooned in a winter wonderland Christmas layout with Christmas trees and reindeer and elves and the like. Robbie and Debbie were in awe. To them, it felt like actually being at the North Pole.

When he finally got to sit on Santa's lap, Robbie was at the ready. Santa dutifully asked him what he wanted for Christmas, and Robbie fired away. An Apollo Moon Rocket. An Apollo Viewmaster. A Slinky. A red baseball glove. A six-shooter from *Wild, Wild West*, his favorite TV show. And lots of green army men.

Debbie was more modest in her wishes. She wanted an Etch-a-Sketch and a *Brady Bunch* lunch box. And the Stay Alive board game if it wasn't too much to ask. She loved the commercial for that game. It always ended with that kid saying, "I'm the sole survivor!"

Santa assured her it wouldn't be a problem. Barbara worried whether she could afford everything her kids wanted. She shouldn't get everything they wanted. But she usually did. She couldn't help spoiling them at Christmas.

As they exited A&S's wonderland, they waltzed into the mall proper and into what Barbara thought was the real wonderland. She couldn't get enough of the mall. When they lived in Queens, she would have to walk to Queens Boulevard to get to where the stores and shops were. In December, it would usually be freezing. It was not an easy way to shop. But at the Smith Haven Mall, all the stores were enclosed in seventy-two-degree comfort. And you could still look up and see the sky through the skylights in the ceiling. It even had a movie theater. She had recently taken the kids to see *Willy Wonka and the Chocolate Factory* there. They loved it so much that when they walked past the theater, Debbie asked if they could see it again. It was playing for two more weeks, followed by the premiere of *Diamonds Are Forever.*

"I don't think your brother wants to see it again, honey," Barbara said.

Robbie had gotten scared near the end of the movie, when Charlie and his grandfather almost got sucked into a giant fan in the ceiling. But Barbara knew she would be coming back in a couple of weeks to see the new Bond movie. Her husband was dying to see it. And she didn't mind watching Sean Connery for two hours.

As they walked toward Barricini Candy, Barbara knew they would be stopping. Barricini had great custard ice cream. She bought vanilla cones with rainbow sprinkles for the kids, and she got chocolate with chocolate sprinkles for herself. Then they walked past the center court, where vendors were selling Christmas ornaments of all kinds. A few weeks back, they had Cleon Jones and Bud Harrelson of the Mets autographing photos. Barbara had waited in line to get hers. But when she brought them home to Robbie, he didn't want them.

"We're Yankees fans, Mom!" he'd said.

She didn't think that would matter to him at his age. But the boy was loyal to his team. He wanted to know when Bobby Murcer might be coming to the mall.

As they continued walking through the mall, Barbara felt joyful, watching all of the other young mothers walking around the shopping paradise. Things were crazy in the country and the world, but she was so happy they had moved here. The craziness of the world didn't seem to reach them here. It was going to be a wonderful place for the kids to grow up in. She could walk around this beautiful, sparkling clean mall forever.

When they passed the Sam Goody record store, Barbara noted two of the albums on display at the entrance—Carole King's *Tapestry* and the Carpenters' *Close to You*. She made a mental note to remind her husband that she wanted the Carpenters album as a Christmas present. She loved the song "We've Only Just Begun." She could listen to that all day. Christine pointed out the new Partridge Family record and asked if she could get that for Christmas too. She had a big crush on David Cassidy.

"We'll see," Barbara said. "Maybe Santa will put it under the tree."

Robbie laughed out loud. "Santa's elves don't make records, Ma!" he said.

They walked for another hour, window shopping, enjoying the festive atmosphere, enjoying the Christmas music playing in the background.

When they had covered all corners of the mall, they exited at the main entrance to walk to the car.

A Salvation Army volunteer held the door open for them and said, "Merry Christmas!"

Barbara said, "Merry Christmas," and pulled a dollar out of her purse and put it in the red pot.

They walked toward the curb.

A young hippie came up to them and handed Barbara a daisy. "Peace," he said.

Barbara took the flower and thanked him. They walked off the curb and toward the lot where the car was parked.

"Why did that lady have a mustache, Mommy?" Robbie asked.

"That wasn't a lady, Robbie. That was a young man."

Robbie laughed. "What?" he said. "But his hair was so long! Why was his hair so long?"

"Because that's the way he likes it, honey," Barbara said.

She took his hand as they neared the car. She looked back at the mall entrance. The young hippie was still handing out daisies to shoppers. Then her eye glanced to the right. Two security guards were talking to a small group of people on the sidewalk. She could see a young man in a Santa hat sitting in a wheelchair. He had long hair and a beard, and her heart skipped a beat when she saw that he had no legs below the knees. The young woman next to him held a sign in her hand. She squinted to see what it said. *Make love, not war.* The security guard was gesturing at them to move along. Barbara froze. It was clear the guard did not want these people bothering anyone. Now it appeared as if the guard was yelling at them. The young man in the wheelchair yelled back. The guard pointed down at him and again gestured at them to leave.

"What's wrong, Mommy?" Debbie asked.

"Nothing, nothing," said Barbara.

She unlocked the car, and they got in.

On the short drive home, Barbara couldn't get the image of the young soldier in the wheelchair and the guards trying to shoo him away out of her head. Did the guards really have to harass the soldier? Was he really bothering anyone?

She pulled onto Victory Lane, all of the warm thoughts from their day at the mall gone.

"We're home! We're home!" said Robbie.

They got out of the car and walked into the house.

"What time is *Santa Claus Is Coming to Town* on, Ma?" Robbie asked.

"Eight o'clock," said Barbara.

"Yay," said Robbie as he ripped his coat off and ran upstairs.

Barbara stared at the Christmas tree in the foyer. The angel on top had the word *Peace* written along its skirt.

She took the daisy that the young hippie had given her and placed it on the tree below the angel. It seemed to her the appropriate thing to do.

"Can I have a snack, Mom?" Debbie yelled from the kitchen.

"Sure, honey," said Barbara.

She walked into her kitchen and took out a package of Chips Ahoy from the pantry. She poured a glass of milk for her daughter and quietly watched her eat her cookies.

"Seventeen days till Christmas!" Christine said.

Barbara smiled. The joy of Christmas was a wonderful thing. But she wondered if the young soldier in the wheelchair could possibly feel the same joy. She couldn't imagine he could.

Maybe she wouldn't be able to keep the miserable reality of the world away from their wonderful new town and their wonderful new mall.

"What's wrong, Mom?" Debbie asked.

"What? Nothing."

"You looked like you were staring into space," said Christine.

"No, I'm fine, honey," said Barbara. "Finish your cookies."

Victory Lap

(1972)

BARBARA MILLER LOVED HOT days like today. A glass of iced tea, some music on the transistor radio, staring at the cloudless blue sky. She couldn't do this as a child in Brooklyn. The stoop was too small, the houses across the street too close. You couldn't really see the sky. But no matter where she looked on Victory Lane, she could always see the sky. She missed Brooklyn, and she missed her old neighborhood—or at least the way it used to be. But she couldn't deny how beautiful Victory Lane was. There was no better place to raise her kids. The Brooklyn of her childhood didn't really exist anymore.

She sipped her tea and listened to the music on the radio. "A Horse with No Name" was playing. She really wasn't sure what the song was about, and it made her feel sad, but in a good way. She liked sad songs. Sometimes, she felt lost in the desert, like the guy in the song.

Robbie burst out of the front door and onto the porch.

"Take it easy, Robbie," she said.

"Can I ride my Big Wheel, Ma?" he asked excitedly.

"OK, but I get to come with you," she said.

"OK, let's go!"

Robbie ran to the garage and yanked open the garage door. Barbara was surprised at her son's strength. But he loved that Big Wheel. Nothing could keep him from it.

Robbie quickly pedaled the Big Wheel out of the garage and tore down the driveway.

"Wait for me!" yelled Barbara. "And stay on the sidewalk!"

She put down her iced tea but took the radio with her as she followed her son down the driveway.

Robbie turned left, and she raced to keep up with him.

"Not so fast, Robbie!" she yelled.

But he was too quick. She watched him ride past the Rosenbergs' house and down the block. She followed him. He skidded out in front of the Marshes' driveway. Then he turned around and pedaled back toward her. He sped up as he got closer, then jammed on his brakes to skid out just in front of his mother.

"Don't worry, Ma. I wasn't going to run you over!"

"Thank you, honey. How about you take a breather? You're sweating."

"OK, but just for a minute," he said.

"Tell me the houses, Robbie," she said.

It was a game Robbie loved. She pointed at the house two doors down.

"Marsh," he said.

"And what was it before that?"

"Bishop!"

She pointed to the next house.

"Rosenberg," he said.

And the next.

"Miller! Us!"

She pointed to the next.

"Krasdale," he said. "I know them all, Ma," he said.

And he was right. He was five now, but he could name all the houses on the block since he was three and a half. The kid had some memory.

Watching her son name the houses made Barbara think again of her street in Brooklyn. Could she remember the names of the houses on her old block? She had a great memory too. There were the LaBarberas next door, and the Rinis after that, and then the Carellos. Who lived in the house after that? She suddenly couldn't remember. How was that possible? She was too young for her memory to be shot. Who lived in the fourth house down from hers? She could see the face of the husband of the older couple who lived there, but for the life of her, she couldn't remember their name.

"Ma, watch this!" Robbie tore down the sidewalk in the Big Wheel back toward their house.

Barbara couldn't get the image of the old man whose name she couldn't remember out of her head. Oh well, she must be getting old herself. She wondered if Robbie would always remember the houses on his block the way he did now. And she strangely pictured him as an old man, trying to remember the street he grew up on. The thought made her shiver for a moment. She hoped he wouldn't be someone like herself, someone prone to lose herself in nostalgia. She was thirty-two years old, and most of her dreams were rooted in the house she grew up even though the dreams took place in the present time. She would have a dream, and her husband or her kids would be in it, but the dream took place on Van Siclen Avenue in Brooklyn. Was that strange? She hadn't been back to the old block in seven or eight years. That last visit upset her because it didn't look right. Something was different, and it bothered her. Only in her memory and in her dreams did the old neighborhood feel right. Dammit, what was the name of that old couple four houses down?

She caught up to Robbie in front of their house.

"What's the matter, Ma?" he asked.

"Always remember where you came from, Robbie," she said. "Remember this street because it will never look or feel this way again." She laughed. "Just don't dwell on it too much, or you'll be dreaming about it the rest of your life."

Her five-year-old son stared at her, confused. "Huh?" he said.

"Nothing," she said. "Mommy gets sad sometimes when she thinks of the old days."

She took his hand. "Let's walk," she said.

He got up from the Big Wheel, and they walked down the street. Barbara still held the radio in her hand. The Harry Nilsson song "Without You" came on.

"My favorite song!" Robbie said.

She looked at the houses on Victory Lane and tried to see them all through his young eyes. Yes, this is the street he will dream about for the rest of his life. She knew he would. He was like her. The Bishops had moved last year when Robbie was four, and he still missed them and didn't understand why they had moved. He couldn't understand why anyone would ever want to leave this street.

Robbie sang along loudly to the Harry Nilsson song. Barbara laughed. Robbie always sang his heart out to this song.

They continued walking on the sidewalk, taking a lap around Victory Lane. Robbie was happy, and Barbara was happy that he was. But she felt a sadness, as was her wont, because she wondered if it was possible for him to ever truly be this happy again.

German Planes

(1973)

ROBBIE MILLER AND BILLY Cohen ran through the woods as fast as they could. They weren't supposed to be in the woods. If either of their mothers knew where they were, they would be in big trouble. But the woods were the best place to play army. And after baseball, army was their favorite game.

Robbie didn't understand why they weren't allowed to play in the woods. The woods literally touched Victory Lane. You could see the back of Billy's house from them.

But Robbie's mom always said something to the effect of, "You don't know who's milling about in those woods."

But they couldn't worry about that now. They were being chased by a German patrol and needed to put some distance between themselves and their Nazi pursuers.

Robbie was especially excited because he was playing with his new Thompson sub-machine gun that his dad had bought for him last week at McCrory's in the mall. It was the coolest toy gun Robbie had ever owned. It was painted in a green camouflage pattern and made the neatest machine gun noise when he pulled the trigger. Billy was using a beat-up Winchester rifle. Robbie had told him that he should use that one only when they played Cowboys and Indians. But Billy wouldn't listen. He loved that Winchester.

Even though America's involvement in the Vietnam War had ended earlier that year, the boys were blissfully unaware of that war's existence. Not many six-year-olds were aware of that war. When they watched war movies on TV, the movies were always about World War II. Nobody was making Vietnam movies yet.

So, it was World War II that they always played at. Robbie loved watching old war movies on TV. *To Hell and Back* with Audie Murphy was his favorite. He never missed that one when it came on. He also loved any war movie with John Wayne in it, like *Back to Bataan* or *The Fighting Seabees*. Just last week, he had been all excited to watch *The Sands of Iwo Jima*. He had it circled in the *TV Guide* and everything. But game 7 of the World Series was on the same day. The game was supposed to be over before the movie started, but it went longer than expected. The Mets and the A's were playing to decide the championship. Robbie and his family were Yankees fans, so Robbie didn't think it would matter if they changed the channel to the John Wayne movie when it started. But Robbie's parents wanted to see the end of the game. When Wayne Garret of the Mets popped up to Bert Campaneris to end the series, Robbie was excited. Now they could put on the movie, which had already started. But then his dad wanted to watch the A's celebration and all of the postgame locker room interviews. Robbie sulked. When his father finally turned the channel to the movie, only thirty minutes were left. Just enough time for Robbie to see John Wayne die at the end, which made him sad. John Wayne died at the end of the *Fighting Seabees* too. He didn't like watching John Wayne get killed.

They reached the edge of the woods and came upon the field. The field was a large, open space with tall grass behind the sump that was at the edge of Victory Lane. On the other side of the field were more woods, and behind those woods was Lancaster Drive. Off to the side was an old house. Robbie's mother told him that that house was built long before Victory Lane and all the other housing developments in the area. No one on Victory Lane even knew who lived there.

They ran out into the tall grass of the field when they heard a plane overhead. Robbie looked up and saw a single-engine plane flying low overhead.

"It's German!" he yelled. "Duck for cover."

He and Billy instantly dived into the tall grass and waited for the plane to pass.

"It's OK," Robbie said. "Looks like he didn't see us."

They had been playing this game for years, which, in their case, meant about 2 years since they were both only six. Robbie knew that World War II had ended years ago and was fully aware that none of the planes overhead were actually German planes looking to drop bombs on them. But Billy didn't know this—at least not when he was four. Now that they were six, Robbie wasn't sure that Billy knew that the planes weren't really trying to kill them. No matter. Billy's ignorance lent some realism to the game and made it more exciting.

As the "German plane" flew on past the field, the boys popped their heads up.

"That was a close one," said Billy.

"It sure was," said Robbie.

"What about the Nazi patrol in the woods?" asked Billy.

"I think we lost them," Robbie said.

They stood up.

Robbie canvassed the field. "Where to now?" he said.

"Why don't we scout out the house?" said Billy. "There could be Nazis there."

"We're not supposed to go there, Billy."

"So what if we go there?" said Billy. "Have we ever seen anyone there? I bet no one even lives there."

So, they walked cautiously toward the back of the house. The house was old and beat-up, not like the new houses on Victory Lane. There was no fence around the back, so they were able to walk right into the backyard.

The grass was long and covered with leaves. A rusty wheelbarrow sat at the side of the house, along with a small patio table that looked like no one had sat at it for years.

Robbie heard a plane overhead. It was a big jet this time. His father had told him that big jets heading east late in the day were usually ones that had taken off from JFK. They were going to places like London or Paris. Well, it was late afternoon, and Robbie didn't know if the plane was heading east or west. But he did know that the big jet would make a good German plane.

So, he yelled, "Hit the dirt, Billy! It's German!"

They both dived for the ground next to the patio table. As the jet flew on by, the boys slowly stood up.

Standing in front of them was a woman holding a baseball bat.

"What the devil are you doing here?" she said.

She spoke with a funny accent and looked haggard and weak, but she scared the hell out of the boys.

"I said, what the devil are you doing here?"

Robbie recognized the accent now. She was English. She sounded just like the English guys in *The Great Escape*.

"We're just playing German planes," said Billy.

"German what?" asked the woman, still holding the bat above their heads.

"German planes," said Robbie. "It's a game. We're pretending it's World War II."

"Pretending?" she said. "I could have you bloody arrested for trespassing."

"Please don't, miss. Please don't," pleaded Billy. He looked at Robbie. "I told you we shouldn't have gone playing in the woods!"

Robbie almost laughed at that. It was Billy's idea to check out the old house, not his. But he was too scared to laugh.

"German planes," she said, shaking her head. She lowered the bat and held it at her side. "Four years of the Blitz, and I get to come to America and watch some little brats make a bloody game out of it."

The boys were too afraid to move as the woman hovered over them. What was she going to do? Should they run? Could she catch them if they did?

"You think World War II is a game?" she said. "You think German planes is a game? Well, I lived through German planes, lads. I lived in London during the war, and real German planes dropped real bombs on us almost every day."

She twirled the bat in her hand. "And real people died," she said.

The boys looked at the bedraggled woman, terror in their eyes.

She must have met an American soldier stationed in England during the war, Robbie thought. He had seen a movie about that. But he put the thought out of his head and focused on the bat.

She lifted the bat over her head.

"Please, miss, we're sorry we came in your backyard. We're sorry," Billy cried.

She stared down at them, her eyes glaring at the boys. Robbie wasn't sure if she was angry or crazy. Maybe she was both.

"Now get on out of here before I give you some!" she said.

The boys didn't need prodding. They tore out of the backyard, through the field, and back into the woods. They trudged through the woods, walked through the backyard of the Gayhearts' house, and onto Victory Lane. They were safe now. Robbie always felt safe on Victory Lane. But it was almost dark, and they would both be in trouble if they didn't go home soon.

"Boy, that lady was scary, wasn't she, Robbie?"

"Yeah, Billy, she was," said Robbie.

Did she really live in England during the war? Did German planes really drop bombs on her? The only other person that Robbie had met who had been in the war was his dad's uncle Thomas. But he never talked about it. Not to Robbie at least.

"See you tomorrow, Robbie," said Billy.

"Yeah, Billy, see you tomorrow."

A plane flew overhead, red lights flashing in the dusk. The boys looked up.

"Is it German, Robbie?" Billy asked.

Robbie stared at the plane and contemplated his answer.

"No, Billy, it's one of ours," he said. "We're safe."

And they were safe. Nothing could touch Robbie Miller or Billy Cohen on Victory Lane. It was their oasis, their shield, a fortress that kept the rest of the world at bay. No German planes or crazy old English ladies or anything else could get them here.

Billy walked down the street toward his house. Robbie walked across the street to his, getting home just before dark. His mom would be happy. He wished he could tell her about the strange English lady in the house

63

beyond the field. But she would get mad that he had been in the woods. So, he would have to keep it to himself. And he'd be left to wonder what it must have been like to see real German bombs dropped from real German planes.

"Life can only be understood backward; but it must be lived forward."

—*Søren Kierkegaard*

The Photograph

(1987—2089)

MAY 1987

TONIGHT WAS GOING TO be a camera night. Whenever the "three amigos" were readying for an epic party or bar night, Cassie Dellesandro made sure to bring her Ricoh 35mm automatic camera. She had become the de facto photographer of the group, always snapping pictures of the gang at all the big parties, the ones that you just had to have pictures of, and always at the ready if something spontaneous happened that needed to be captured on film—like the time Beverly, drunk, tripped and fell face-first into her 20th birthday cake.

The Ricoh had never failed Cassie. It had been dropped more than a few times, and over time, probably a gallon of beer had been spilled on it. But it never failed to take great pictures. And after every night captured on film, the next day would always involve a trip to the one-hour photo to retrieve twenty-four or thirty-six irreplaceable photos of the previous night's frivolities.

There Are Places I Remember

Only a few weeks were left in their college careers, only a few weeks left to take pictures of their wonderful life on campus, only a few weeks left for Cassie and Linda and Barbara to be together before donning their graduation caps and heading off, however reluctantly, into the real world.

Tonight's party, like so many before it, would be at Jimmy's Pub. It was a hole-in-the-wall, typical of so many upstate New York bars. Always a mix of college kids and older locals who lived in the neighborhood or worked in the paper mill down the road. But it was a second home for Cassie and the girls, and she wanted just a few more pictures of them here.

When they arrived, Cassie, as usual, headed for the jukebox. In earlier years, she would throw some quarters in and play songs like "Sweet Caroline" or "So Far Away" by Carole King. The jukebox was loaded with all these great songs from the '70s. But a few months earlier, the bar had gotten a brand-new jukebox that played CDs. None of the girls had a CD player yet. They all still played vinyl and cassettes. But the new jukebox was awesome, even though it mainly had newer music on it. When it first arrived, she kept playing Bruce Hornsby's *The Way It Is* album. But lately, she was only playing U2's *The Joshua Tree*. God, she loved that album. So, she put in three dollars in quarters, and that was enough to play the whole album.

"*Joshua Tree* again?" asked Linda.

"Of course," Cassie replied.

Linda rolled her eyes at her friend, but she loved *The Joshua Tree* too. She just occasionally liked to listen to something else.

The first track came on, and the girls sang their hearts out. Other kids stared at them but otherwise paid them no mind. They were used to the girls singing along with Bono. Tonight was no different.

When the song ended, Linda's throat hurt. "Can we all get a beer?" she asked.

Cassie and Barbara liked that idea, so the three of them sauntered over to the bar and ordered drafts from Nicole, the tattooed bartender who had served them so many beers before. Old Milwaukee, as usual. Fifty cents a draft, same as it was when they were freshmen.

And they drank and laughed and flirted with the guys, then drank and laughed some more. Another night at Jimmy's like so many that had come before. And Cassie took pictures, of course, the Ricoh firing away rapidly.

It was near the end of the night when Barbara realized that Cassie hadn't taken a picture of just the three of them. They had to get one more great picture together at Jimmy's before graduation, and this was probably the last chance.

"Picture, picture!" she yelled. "Just the three of us!"

Cassie immediately grabbed Mike Devlin and enlisted him to operate the camera.

They lined up in front of the bar and put their arms around each other, Barbara and Linda on the ends, Cassie in the middle.

Mike Devlin stood ten feet away and lined up the shot. He looked into the camera and said, "Say big tits."

"Mike!" Cassie yelled. "Knock it off and take the damn picture."

"OK, OK," he said. He lined up the camera again. "Say cheese," he said.

"Cheese," they yelled.

And he snapped the photo. It was exactly 9:47 p.m., May 13, 1987.

MARCH 1990

It was Cassie's second day at her new job. She was a new account manager at Owen/Adams Associates, a public relations firm on 22nd Street, near the Flatiron Building. Her old firm was just a few blocks away on 18th Street.

So, she was in the same neighborhood, which she loved, and still only one subway stop from her apartment on 36th Street. In the summer, she would walk to work. But not in March.

The computer guy set up her computer and phone, and the office manager, Sandy, got her supplied with pens and pads and Post-it Notes. She didn't have a view—her workstation was in the middle of the floor, near the pantry. But the office was pleasant enough. She could definitely see herself coming here every day for the next few years.

After Sandy got her some coffee from the pantry, it was time for Cassie to set up her desk. In her bag were some trinkets from her apartment. These items would make her workstation feel like home.

She reached into the shopping bag she had brought from her apartment and pulled out a vase with fake sunflowers. Then a U2 desk calendar so she could look at Bono whenever she wanted. Then a bottle of hand lotion. Then came the pictures.

First, a small, framed photo of her nephew, Mikey, taken at his first birthday party. Then a larger picture of Cassie and her new boyfriend, Matt, taken only a month before at Live Bait on 23rd Street—where they met. And last but not least, that great photo of her and Barbara and Linda from the last week of college. That one always made her smile. She looked at the digital date in the lower-right corner of the picture—5-13-87. Had it really already been almost three years since they graduated?

My God, we are getting old!

Linda was already married and living in Ohio of all places. Cassie hadn't seen her since the wedding last summer. Barbara was still living upstate. She came down to Manhattan last New Year's Eve so that she and Cassie could ring in the new decade together. She was hoping to come down again in the summer. She had a new boyfriend, too, whom Cassie was dying to meet.

"Looks like you've been here for years," said Sandy as she came up behind Cassie's cubicle.

"Yep, feels just like home," said Cassie.

She then adjusted the college photo so that it would be the first thing that she would see whenever she entered the workstation.

"Nice picture," said Sandy.

"My favorite," said Cassie. "The three amigos."

She realized at that moment that she hadn't spoken to Linda in a couple of months at least. After graduation, they called each other once a week. Then, after about a year, it was every other week. Then, last year, it was once a month. Now, it had been two months. Or was it three?

She stared at the picture and made a mental note to call Linda this weekend.

And she also hadn't spoken to Barbara since early February.

Her phone rang. It was time to get back to work. She could worry about the girls later.

SEPTEMBER 1994

"We're not going to unpack everything this weekend, are we?" asked Matt.

"You know I don't like procrastination, honey," replied Cassie. "The sooner we unpack, the sooner this house will feel like home."

The house was a nice colonial on Long Island, 16 Victory Lane. It was a beautiful, tree-lined street about fifty miles east of Manhattan. It was going to be a bit of a commute for them into the city. The couple who sold the house to them, the Millers, were moving for just that reason. Their kids were grown now and out of the house, and Mr. Miller still worked in the city, and he'd had enough of the commute he had been doing since 1968. They were moving to a condo in Queens. So, now it was time for Cassie and Matt to start their own family. Maybe they would get sick of the commute, too, and sell the house one day when their kids were grown. But that was at least twenty-five years away.

They unpacked their clothes first. Then the kitchen. Then books and CDs and some videotapes in the den. Then assorted boxes to one of the spare bedrooms that they would use as an office. They would deal with the mess in the garage later.

An hour into the office unpacking, Cassie came across the photograph. Now that they had a real home and not a cramped Manhattan apartment, she wanted the photograph displayed prominently. Somewhere where they hung up family photos. Even though she didn't see Linda and Barbara as much as she wanted, she still considered them family.

"I want this to go in the den, next to our wedding photos," said Cassie.

Matt frowned.

"What?" said Cassie.

"I like Barbara and Linda just fine, but mixed in with our family pictures?"

"So?"

Matt had plenty of pictures of him with his college buddies, but not many that were appropriate to hang in the house. But he realized it was pointless to argue with Cassie over this. Pick your battles, right? Cassie loved that picture.

"Nothing, honey," Matt said. "Hang it wherever you please."

"Thank you," she replied. "I will."

Matt usually let it go when it came to anything involving Linda and Barbara. And besides, he was far more concerned with the baseball strike. It was all he talked about. The Yankees were in first place, but now there was talk that the strike wasn't going to end and that they might actually cancel the World Series. It was making him sick. So much so that he didn't care about the photograph or much of anything else in the new house.

So, Cassie hung the photograph in the den, behind the couch, next to one of their wedding photos. It may have seemed out of place where it was, but she liked it there. This way, she could see it every day and feel close to the girls. And it would remind her to give the girls a ring every now and then. And at a time when she lived with the stress of work, a new marriage, and impending motherhood, it would remind her of the most carefree time of her life.

JULY 2002

Cassie sat in the den with Brianna on her lap. Brianna loved looking at the family photos in the room. She also enjoyed naming the people in the photos. It was easy to name her grandparents and her aunts and uncles. But she was also pretty good at naming some of the more distant relatives she wasn't familiar with.

"And what about the people in that one?" Cassie asked, pointing at the photograph.

"That's Mommy," Brianna said, pointing at Cassie. "You had such big hair!"

"And the other two?"

"Linda and Barbara," said Brianna.

"That's right," said Cassie. "You remember Linda, right?"

Brianna looked at the picture and shook her head.

"No?" said Cassie. "You don't remember that time she came to visit a couple of years ago? She played with you and your Barbie dolls?"

Brianna shook her head again.

"I guess you were too young to remember."

When had Cassie spoken to Linda last? It was over the winter, maybe January or February. Cassie asked when Linda thought she might be able to come to New York for a visit. But Linda was reluctant. She didn't feel safe coming to New York after 9/11. Cassie couldn't blame her. Everyone in the tristate area was still on edge, waiting for the next shoe to drop. Cassie herself worried for Matt every day, as he took the train back and forth into the city, then rode on the subway. She couldn't believe how the world had changed overnight. Yes, 2002 was a very scary time. She wasn't used to feeling this way. The news was filled with reports of potential terror attacks, government threat codes—red was imminent, orange was serious, green was good or something like that—and false alarms.

She looked at the photograph and yearned for the innocence of 1987 and longed for her two friends she rarely saw anymore.

"Mommy, I'm hungry," said Brianna.

"OK, let's go to the kitchen."

Cassie looked at the photograph as they got off the couch. Maybe this terror insanity would blow over soon. And then maybe Linda would want to visit. She could only hope.

SEPTEMBER 2012

Matt had been itching to redo the den for years. He wanted a bigger TV and a new couch and love seat. Cassie didn't like change and was content to keep the room as it was. But she had to admit that the furniture was getting a little ratty and could use an upgrade. And a forty-inch TV was kind of small these days. Everybody had a fifty-inch or bigger now.

So, a new set of leather furniture from Macy's now adorned the room. And a shiny new Samsung hung on the wall. This necessitated taking most of the family pictures down and rehanging only a few of them elsewhere in the room.

To Matt, the first photo that should leave the room was the one of Cassie, Linda, and Barbara.

"They're not family," he said.

"They're like family," Cassie replied.

"Like family?" he said. "When was the last time you spoke to either one of them?"

"I talk to them all the time."

"You make comments on each other's posts on Facebook. That hardly counts as talking."

"It's communicating."

But Matt was right. It had been years since she had seen Linda or Barbara, and while the occasional comment or like on Facebook gave the illusion that they were all still connected, it wasn't enough to justify the photograph staying in the den.

"Well, I want to at least hang it in the office," said Cassie. "You know how much I love this picture."

"The office is fine," said Matt.

So, in the office the photograph went. Right on the wall next to the Dell computer monitor. Cassie smiled as she always did when she looked at it. What carefree days those were! And she looked at the date on the picture—5-13-87. Twenty-five years ago. It didn't seem possible.

FEBRUARY 2023

Saying goodbye to the house on Victory Lane was tougher than Cassie thought it would be. Their girls were both out of the house now. Brianna, married and living in New Jersey. Sophia, on her own in Manhattan. So, there was nothing tethering her and Matt to the house anymore, and the girls were OK with Mom and Dad selling the house that they had grown up in. Plus, home prices had been soaring on Long Island since the pandemic started. They were never going to get a better price for the house than now. But this was the house that she and Matt had raised those girls in, and parting with it was like losing a family member. They had lived in the house for twenty-nine years, the longest either one had ever lived in one location.

Now they had moved into a condo in a fifty-five-and-over community fifteen miles closer to the city. Matt was commuting regularly again after working from home during most of the pandemic, so this would make his commute a little bit better while inching them closer to their daughters.

Most of the furniture from Victory Lane was sold. They even held a garage sale before the move to unload as much as their other stuff as they could. Watching a lot of the old stuff go was tough for Cassie. It was like selling a part of her past to strangers, hoping they would cherish it, but knowing they wouldn't and couldn't.

The new condo was much smaller than the old house. Fewer rooms, less wall space, less room for photos on the wall.

The photograph was packed during the move, along with a few other items from the office. When Cassie packed it, she tried to remember the name of the boy who had taken the photograph and was alarmed when she couldn't remember. He was someone they had known well. Someone they had hung out with regularly. Hell, Linda had even hooked up with him a couple of times. And now her mind was blank. What was his goddamn name?

The box the photograph was in went straight to the basement of the condo. There it stayed along with ten other boxes of items that would never be unpacked.

JANUARY 2057

The thought of going through all her parents' stuff had filled Brianna with dread. It had been two weeks since they had buried Mom, and she wished she could delay this further. But Sophia had already put the condo on the market, so they had to go through everything sooner rather than later.

Brianna was sentimental, like her mother. Sophia wasn't burdened by that same sentimentality. She looked at this as a chore and wanted it done as soon as possible.

They spent a whole weekend going through everything. They would each take a couple of pieces of furniture and some kitchenware.

When they got to the basement, they sorted through the memorabilia and the old photographs. Brianna stopped when she came across the photograph.

"Oh my God, do you remember this picture?" she said to her sister.

Sophia looked at the picture. "No."

"Come on. You don't remember this?" Brianna said. "Mom loved this picture. It hung in our den for years."

"Maybe," said Sophia. "Who's in the picture with Mom.?"

"It's her with her college friends," said Brianna. "Barbara and Linda. I remember their names because I used to play a game with Mom where I named all the people in the pictures hanging in the den. Barbara and Linda. One of these girls even came to our house once to visit when we were little. The brunette on the right," she said, pointing at the photograph. "Although I can't remember if she's Barbara or Linda."

Sophia shrugged.

"You really don't remember this picture?" Brianna asked.

"Sorry," said Sophia.

Brianna realized that neither Linda nor Barbara had come to the wake for Mom. Was that because they hadn't heard that she had passed? Or because they also had already passed? Or had they all just lost touch?

Brianna put the photograph aside. She was going to keep it. It was part of her childhood. And Mom looked so young and happy in it. No reason to throw it out.

NOVEMBER 2087

When Brianna passed in the fall of 2087, it fell to her son, Jacob, to go through her things. There was a lot to sort out, as his mother was something of a pack rat. It amazed him how the older generation seemed to have so much stuff. He didn't know anyone who had actual physical photographs anymore, but his mom sure had a bunch. And they were ancient. As he went through them, the photograph caught his eye. It was buried in a box with other photos, but it stood out to him because it had the date on it—5-13-87. The damn thing was 100 years old! He was pretty sure that the girl in the middle was his grandmother. But he had no idea who the other two girls were. His grandmother's cousins maybe?

"Ever seen a picture that's a hundred years old?" he asked his wife.

"No," she said. "What are you going to do with all of them?"

"I don't know," he said. "Throw them out, I guess."

"Don't do that," she said. "Sell them to an antique shop. They love old pictures like that."

That wasn't a bad idea, he thought.

There were a bunch of nice antique shops out east near Greenport. Next time they were out there, they would have to pop into one and see if there was any interest.

JULY 2089

Jasmine always loved going to Greenport. She lived in a somewhat-cramped apartment in the city with her parents, and anytime they ventured out east, it was exciting for her. She just loved being near the water. Yes, it was hot, but not as hot as the city.

She was nine years old and was something of a history buff. That was another reason she liked going to Greenport. There were a lot of antique stores in and around town, and she liked looking at things from the 20th century and the early 21st century.

It was in the third shop that they stopped in that she saw the photograph. She had been looking at some of those old round records that people in the old days played recorded music on. There was one of The Beatles. She had heard of them. One of a guy named Frank Sinatra. She wasn't sure if she had heard of him.

"I think he was a famous singer," her father told her.

Another one was from someone called Pink Floyd. She didn't know who that was, and neither did her father. Then she came across a table with old photographs on it. She was intrigued by these.

"People used to have these old cameras that looked like a box that you would hold in your hand," her father said. "I think you pressed a button, and it took the picture."

"And did the picture come out of the box?"

"I think so," said her father.

There was one that caught her eye because it had a date on it. She picked it up.

"Look, Dad, this one was taken over a hundred years ago," she said.

"That one is definitely old," he said.

She looked at it closely. Three young women were in the picture. They were all pretty and smiling. She couldn't get over how happy they all looked. She wondered if it was taken at a special occasion.

"Who do you think they are, Dad?"

"Who knows, honey? They could be anybody."

She wondered who they might be, and she wondered why they were so happy, and she wondered how this picture had ended up in this little antique shop in Greenport more than a hundred years after it had been taken.

"We're late for lunch," her mother said from the front of the store.

"OK," said her father. He turned to Jasmine and said, "Let's go."

She stared at the photograph for another moment. Something about the faces of those girls pleased her. And those old-fashioned clothes and hairdos! She loved them.

After lunch, as they drove out of town, Jasmine couldn't get the girls in the photograph out of her mind. What had happened to them? Did they live long, happy lives? She hoped so. They were all so young and pretty. She was sure that they had. Would anyone buy the picture? Or would it just stay in the antique shop, gathering dust? She hoped it wouldn't. That would be a sad ending for the happy girls. What an odd thing it was for a photograph of people to outlive the people themselves.

The car headed west back toward the city, and Jasmine fell asleep.

The owner of the antique shop got ready to close up for the night. He wondered how much longer he could stay in business. He had sold some old furniture in recent months. And occasionally, he sold some toys and the occasional vinyl record to a collector. But too many items in the store just ended up sitting on the shelves, never moving, never touched.

He came to the table with the old pictures on it. He hadn't sold one of these in months. People used to like to purchase an old photo to hang in the bar of their beach house or to add some color or kitsch to a room. But not anymore, it seemed.

He decided to load them into a box. He picked up the photograph and barely took notice of the smiling faces of Cassie and Linda and Barbara as he loaded it into a box with the other photographs.

He closed the box and walked it into the back storeroom. In the morning, he would put the box in the dumpster out back.

Then he closed up and went home for the night.

Be Here Now

(1974)

WHEN HIS GRANDFATHER STEPPED on the praying mantis, Robbie Miller and his friends thought it was the coolest—and scariest—thing they had ever seen.

They were at the foot of Robbie's driveway, with Robbie standing with his pals Tommy Krasdale and Billy Cohen, waiting for the bus to take them to kindergarten.

Only it wasn't just the three of them at the bus stop. There was a strange creature on the sidewalk with them. None of them knew it was a praying mantis—they had never seen or heard of one before. All they knew was that the scariest and largest insect they had ever seen was staring up at them.

"It looks like something from a Godzilla movie!" Tommy said.

So, Robbie ran up the driveway and banged on the front door. "Ma, Ma!" he yelled.

His mother came to the door in a panic. "What's the matter?" she cried.

"There's a giant bug on the driveway!"

His mom rolled her eyes, but she opened the front door and trudged down the driveway to the sidewalk to see what the fuss was all about.

Behind his mom, Grandpa Romano followed. He had been visiting for the past week from his house in Queens and was bored—or at least Robbie thought so.

"Wait till you see this, Grandpa!"

When they got to the bottom of the driveway, Robbie's mother peered down at the great insect.

"OK, boys, you can all relax," she said. "It's just a praying mantis."

"But it's the scariest thing I've ever seen," said Robbie.

And before his mother could respond, Grandpa Romano stepped on the mantis with all his might, crushing it. The boys could even hear the poor beast crunch under the old man's foot.

"Dad!" Robbie's mother cried. "What did you do? You're not supposed to kill those!"

"What?" said Grandpa, looking bewildered.

"It was a praying mantis. You don't kill them! They kill all the other bugs and insects!"

"But Robbie and the boys were scared."

Grandpa Romano was born in Italy and had lived there until he was twenty, and even though he had been in America for fifty years, he still spoke with an accent that Tommy and Billy found funny.

"Robbie was scared," he said again.

"It wasn't going to hurt them," his mom said.

She walked back up the driveway and back into the house. Grandpa Romano stared after his daughter in befuddlement. Then he shrugged and scraped the remains of the insect off the bottom of his shoe. Then he winked at the boys and went back in the house.

"That was so cool," said Tommy.

"Yeah, it really was," said Billy.

And Robbie agreed. But he felt bad that his mom had yelled at grandpa.

Grandpa was from the old world, and he did things the old-world way. He saw a threat to his grandson, so he eliminated the threat without hesitation. Coldly, efficiently, he did what he felt needed to be done. What did he care that the praying mantis was a "good" insect?

This is what Robbie was thinking about two years later at Grandpa Romano's wake. Sure, he thought about other things—like how Grandpa would always bring him chocolate cigarettes when he came to visit and how he loved to watch *The Carol Burnett Show* with Robbie. And he would always go over the Yankees box score with Robbie and remind him that Bobby Murcer couldn't hold a candle to Mickey Mantle or Joe DiMaggio.

But as Robbie looked into the casket at his grandpa, it was the praying mantis that he kept thinking about. He wasn't sure why exactly. It was one brief moment of many that he had shared with his grandfather. It was just the way Grandpa had protected him from the great insect that stuck with him. He didn't feel as protected now.

He also didn't like the way Grandpa looked. He just didn't look like himself. He was gaunt, and the skin on his face was taut and sunken. It sort of looked like Grandpa, but not really.

Is this what dead people look like?

Robbie wanted to look away, but couldn't. His mother noticed him staring at the casket and came over.

"You shouldn't be over here," she said.

"It doesn't look like Grandpa, Ma," he said.

"I know, honey," she said. "That's just his body. Grandpa is with God now." She took him by the arm and led him to the back of the room to sit with his sister.

83

Robbie sat down, and his thoughts drifted to the last time he had seen his grandfather. Grandpa was being admitted to the hospital and was sitting in a wheelchair, waiting to be taken to his room. After his sister and his mom gave Grandpa a kiss, Grandpa asked for Robbie to come over to him and give him a hug. But Robbie was afraid. He didn't want to catch whatever illness Grandpa had. His mom explained that cancer wasn't contagious, but Robbie wasn't convinced.

"Please, Robbie, go give your grandfather a hug."

But Robbie shook his head.

"Please, Robbie, please," Grandpa pleaded, holding out his arms, tears rolling down his face.

Robbie didn't budge.

Grandpa was still sobbing when they wheeled him away. Robbie never saw him again. Grandpa was dead a week later.

And now all Robbie wanted was to see Grandpa again. He wanted to watch a Yankees game with him and watch Carol Burnett and eat chocolate cigarettes with him. And he wanted Grandpa to come to the bus stop again and maybe squash another praying mantis.

But none of those things would ever happen again, and even at six years old, he understood that.

He thought of an episode of *Star Trek* that he had watched recently. It was called "The City on the Edge of Forever," and in it, Kirk and Spock travel through time into the past. Robbie wished he could do the same now. Get in a time machine and go back and visit Grandpa. Wouldn't that be something?

Yes, it would, he thought.

He told himself that, one day, he would invent a time machine and go back and visit Grandpa.

84

When he told his mother this a few days later, she told him that this was a sweet sentiment, but that he must learn to not hold on to the past, that it was the present and future that mattered.

"But I want to see Grandpa again," Robbie said.

"I know you do," she said. "I do too. But he's gone. You have your memories of him. But we all have to move forward."

She held Robbie and wasn't sure if what she was saying was right or comforting. She just didn't want her son to be consumed with the fact that he wouldn't see his grandfather again.

"You know Grandpa had a hard time letting go of the past," she said. "He lived fifty years in America, but all he ever wanted to talk about was his childhood in Italy. And he always talked about going back to visit, but he never did. He never seemed to be able to enjoy the present. He always just talked about the old days."

Robbie listened to his mother, her blue eyes teary and red as she spoke to him.

"You have to learn to be here now," she said. "Grandpa never learned that. His head was always in the past."

It was then that Robbie realized that his parents would die someday too. And what would he do when his mother was gone, and he couldn't look into those blue eyes for comfort? But that was long into the future, he hoped.

"Be here now," his mother said.

So, Robbie tried to listen to his mother and "be here now" and not think about the past or the future.

His mother held him in her arms, and for the moment—the "now"—everything was all right.

Passing Showers

(1976)

ROBBIE FELT THE DROPS hitting his Yankees cap as the pitch came toward him. He swung through the drops and smashed the green tennis ball deep to the left—or in this case, the front lawn of the Rosenbergs'. As he rounded first, the skies opened, and heavy rain poured on his head. By the time he reached second base, he could barely see in front of him, but he kept running. He had been playing baseball on this street for years. He didn't need to see to know that third base was right in front of his mailbox. The rain was splashing at his feet now, but he did not slow down. When he crossed the plate, the rest of the guys had already left the field. Victory Lane had become a monsoon.

"This game is over," said Jimmy Roselli. He grabbed his bat and hopped on his bike and pedaled through the deluge toward his house.

Steve Dolan did the same. Robbie was disappointed. He had just homered, and now the game was over? Plus, he loved when it rained on a hot summer day. He didn't mind sitting on the curb, getting drenched.

But he heard his mother yelling from the house, "Robbie, get inside. It's pouring!"

So, Robbie, Billy, and Tommy grabbed their gloves and ran up the driveway and into Robbie's open garage.

"You're all soaked!" Robbie's mother said.

"We're fine, Ma," he said.

"Well, don't go back out there," she said.

"OK, Ma," he said.

She went back in the house, and the boys collapsed onto the garage floor.

"I've never seen rain like this," said Tommy.

The rain was hitting the driveway so hard that the drops splashed three or four inches off the pavement.

"At least you hit your homer before the rain came," Tommy said.

"That's no homer," said Billy. "Jimmy didn't even chase after it after the rain came. At best, it's a ground rule double."

"Is the ball still on the Rosenbergs' lawn?" Robbie asked.

"Yeah," said Tommy.

"That's the end of that ball," said Billy.

He was right. They couldn't play with a real baseball. They would take out a car window if they did that. Sometimes, one of the boys would get a rubber baseball from McCrory's, and those were great. But they didn't last very long. So, most street baseball games on Victory Lane were played with a green Wilson tennis ball. But those couldn't survive a downpour like this. Robbie's homer was the last pitch of that ball.

So, the boys sat at the edge of the garage and watched the rain.

Robbie got up and grabbed the transistor radio his mother kept on the shelf. He turned it on and fumbled with the receiver. Lots of static, but he was finally able to get WNBC to come in. "Silly Love Songs" came on. Everybody liked that one. Then "Don't Go Breaking My Heart" followed.

"Why is Elton John singing with a girl?" Tommy asked.

"Why not?" said Robbie.

Then "Love Will Keep Us Together" played.

"Another duet?" said Tommy.

"It's not a duet, dipshit," said Billy.

"It's the Captain and Tennille," said Tommy.

"But the Captain doesn't sing," said Billy. "So, it's not a duet."

The rain kept falling as the boys listened to the music. Then the theme song from *S.W.A.T.* came on.

"I don't understand why there is a TV theme song on the radio," said Robbie.

"I know. It's not even a good show," said Billy.

"I love that show," said Tommy.

"That's because your father is a cop," said Billy.

"So what? It's a good show," said Tommy.

"They should put the theme to *Happy Days* on the radio," said Billy.

"Oh, I love that song," said Tommy.

"It's OK, but it shouldn't be on the radio," said Robbie.

"You're just saying that because you don't watch *Happy Days*," said Billy.

"I used to," said Robbie.

"How can you not watch *Happy Days*?" Tommy said.

"Because my parents don't watch it," Robbie said.

"Why not?" asked Tommy.

"Because they say the '50s were nothing like they show it on the show," said Robbie. "Look at Potzie and Ralph Malph's hair. The show is supposed to be the 1950s, but they have '70s hair. My mom says it's not realistic."

Tommy laughed. "Who cares about their hair? The show's hilarious."

The *S.W.A.T.* song ended, and the radio went to static. Robbie fumbled with it, but couldn't find a station. Just static.

"It's the rain," said Billy.

Robbie turned off the radio. The boys stared at the rain, still pounding, still splashing.

Next week was the Fourth of July. The bicentennial. It was all anyone was talking about. Mr. Roselli was even down in Virginia to buy fireworks for the celebration. The boys were all excited about it.

"I heard Mr. Roselli is going to get a case of M80s," said Tommy. "That's going to be awesome."

Robbie's parents were excited too. But Robbie's mother was upset that her father wouldn't be here to see it.

"He would have enjoyed a centennial celebration," she said. "We're all lucky to be alive to see one."

Robbie did the math in his head. The next one would be 2076. No, he wouldn't be around for that one, he supposed. That wasn't a comforting thought. Better enjoy this one.

Better enjoy it all, he thought. *Be here now.*

So, he looked out at the rain and remembered how much he liked rainstorms on a hot summer day. "Watch this, boys," he said.

Robbie Miller ran out of the garage and into the pouring rain. He threw up his arms and laughed as the rain pelted his face and soaked his clothes. It felt magnificent. For some reason, his grandfather's face flashed across his mind. Grandpa would have enjoyed this. Robbie wished he could stay in this rain forever.

"Miller, you're crazy!" Billy shouted.

Robbie didn't listen. The rain felt too good.

But the rain stopped as suddenly as it had come. The sun was back, brighter than before. Robbie squinted in the light, his clothes dripping.

Steam rose from the driveway. Tommy and Billy exited the garage and joined Robbie on the driveway.

"Robbie, you're soaked," said Tommy.

"I don't care. It felt good," he said.

"Hey, let's find that ball," said Billy.

Tommy and Billy ran off toward the Rosenbergs' house to look for the tennis ball.

Robbie waited a moment and watched the steam rise from the driveway. He took a breath. He liked the way the driveway smelled after it rained. But he wished that the rain had lasted longer.

"Wait for me," Robbie yelled, and he ran after his friends.

Reggie

(2019)

THOMAS ENTERED THE ELEVATOR of his apartment building on 37th Street, carrying Reggie in his arms. When Reggie was young and vibrant, he had topped out at 57 pounds. But on his last day on this earth, he was down to 41. The vet was just around the corner. Thomas could certainly carry that weight for one block. Reggie couldn't walk that distance now, and Thomas was not going to put him in a dog carrier. No, he wanted Reggie to breathe the outside air, and he wanted to hold him in his arms for a few more minutes. At any other point in Reggie's life, he would never have let Thomas carry him on the street. He would have wanted to make a break for it and explore. But that was then, and this was now. Today, Reggie was content to nestle into Thomas's arms.

Reggie was an English bulldog. The life expectancy of this breed was eight to ten years. But Reggie was a tough son of a bitch and had made it to 11. Thomas couldn't truly bring himself to think about a future without him.

He exited the elevator and walked out onto 37th Street.

A woman passed by and eyed Reggie and said, "How cute," as she walked by.

Thomas looked into Reggie's eyes, and while, yes, he was still adorably cute, he could see the sadness in the dog's eyes. Reggie seemed to know that this was the end.

Thomas thought back to when he first brought Reggie home. The first concern was what to name him. It ended up being a spur-of-the-moment thing. Thomas had had the YES network on, and they were showing an interview from Yankees spring training with special advisor Reggie Jackson. Thomas was a fan of the Mets, not the Yankees. Shouldn't he name the dog after a Met then? His favorite Mets when he was growing up were Tom Seaver and Cleon Jones. He couldn't name him after Tom Seaver because that would essentially be naming the dog after himself. And Cleon did have a nice ring to it, but when he looked into the puppy's eyes, Reggie just seemed to fit.

It wasn't long after Reggie arrived that Thomas lost his job during the Great Recession. So, after a few months of leaving Reggie alone every day when he left for the office, all of a sudden, Thomas and Reggie were home alone together every day. This was an adjustment for Reggie, who had already claimed the apartment as his own. But the months home together cemented their bond.

Thomas thought of his mother, who frequently asked why her son couldn't love a woman as much as he did his dog. Thomas would answer that Reggie was more lovable than most women he met. But Thomas wasn't anti-woman. No, Reggie was just more lovable than people in general, men or women. He never got mad at Reggie. And Reggie loved him unconditionally. He couldn't say that about any person he knew.

His last girlfriend loved Reggie too. More than she loved Thomas, which Thomas fully understood. Reggie had a much more agreeable personality than Thomas did. But Sara couldn't get used to Reggie sleeping in the bed with them. And having sex was difficult. It was done with Reggie in the bed, which certainly didn't add to the mood or ambience. Or it was done with Reggie locked out of the bedroom, as he cried and scratched at the door, which also did nothing to enhance the experience for Sara. And when it was done, Reggie would nestle himself under Thomas's butt. It was his way of letting Sara know that Thomas belonged to him, not her. And Thomas's allowance of Reggie in the bed assuredly let Sara know where Thomas's true allegiance was. When the relationship with Sara ended, Thomas could tell that Reggie didn't miss her.

Thomas crossed the street and could see the vet's office up ahead. He peeked down at Reggie and saw his sad eyes looking back. He had to turn away. Looking into those sad eyes was tearing him apart.

Thomas was amazed at how light and scrawny Reggie had become. It was when Reggie had stopped eating that Thomas knew the end was probably near. If there was one thing Reggie never had a problem with, it was eating. The dog would eat anything. If Thomas dropped a tissue or a napkin on the floor, he had about a second and a half to grab it before Reggie gobbled it up.

He remembered one time when Reggie was a puppy and Thomas was watching the Jets game on a Sunday afternoon. He had gotten an order of wings from the pub down the street and was devouring them with one hand while fending off Reggie with the other. When he finished the wings, he got up to go to the bathroom. But he left the container of chicken wing bones sitting on the coffee table. When he returned from the bathroom, half of the bones were gone, and another was in Reggie's mouth. Thomas looked on the floor for the missing wing bones, but there weren't any. Reggie had swallowed the bones whole! And he wanted more.

Thomas laughed at this memory and continued walking toward the vet office. Reggie sighed in his arms, and Thomas almost lost it.

How do people do this?

Maybe he should turn around now and let nature run its course. But he had to keep going. Reggie was in pain and had been for a while. No, Thomas had to keep walking. He willed himself to look into Reggie's sorrowful eyes.

"It's OK, boy," said Thomas. "It will all be OK soon."

The receptionist in the veterinary office signed him in and asked him to have a seat, saying the doctor would be with him shortly.

Thomas felt his pulse begin to race as he sat down. Part of him wanted the doctor to call him in right away so that this unconscionable experience would be over soon. But the other part of him wanted to sit in that waiting room for as long as possible. That part of him wanted to hold Reggie in his arms forever.

He was having a hard time imagining life without Reggie, a life that would begin for him within the hour. He was a fifty-five-year-old man with no wife or girlfriend or life partner. Reggie was his life partner. To Reggie, Thomas was the world; Thomas was God. What would his life be like when the adoration that Reggie gave him was gone? He knew he wasn't a great person. If he was, someone would have chosen to spend their life with him by now. But to Reggie, he was the greatest person who ever lived. Would his ego be able to handle it when Reggie was gone? Could his soul survive without Reggie's constant expressions of love?

Reggie sighed again in his arms. Thomas held him a little tighter. Reggie loved when Thomas held him. He also always loved sitting on his lap while Thomas watched TV. Thomas watched almost every Jet game in the past 11 years with Reggie in his lap. And how many Sunday nights did Reggie lie on him as Thomas watched *Game of Thrones*? Seven seasons' worth of Sundays.

"Dr. Friedman is ready for you, Mr. Norman," said the receptionist.

Thomas walked zombie-like into the examination room. He and Dr. Friedman exchanged pleasantries—if you could call them pleasantries at such a moment. The doctor explained how he would put an IV in Reggie's leg that would render him unconscious and shortly thereafter stop his heart. He told Thomas that he could hold on to Reggie while the drug was administered. He assured Thomas that Reggie would feel no pain, and he told him that Reggie's eyes might stay open after he had passed. Thomas listened and felt a fuzzy feeling swarming through his body. Was he about to faint? No, he mustn't do that. Reggie was being brave. Thomas must do the same.

Dr. Friedman affixed the IV to Reggie's leg, and the dog shuddered for a moment. Thomas locked eyes with Reggie.

"It's OK, boy. It's OK," he said.

Reggie stared back at him with those expressive eyes Thomas saw that first day at the pet store. And then something changed in Reggie's eyes, and Thomas knew that Reggie was gone. Thomas held him tighter for a moment and kissed Reggie on his head.

"He's gone," said Dr. Friedman.

"I know," said Thomas.

Had there ever been a more horrible moment in Thomas Norman's life? Yes, he had lost his father several years earlier. But he wasn't there when his dad died. He didn't watch the life go out of his eyes.

Thomas left the office and wandered out onto the street. The thought of going back to the apartment terrified him. No, he needed a drink. So, he walked to Slattery's Midtown Pub on 36th Street. He sat at the bar and ordered a beer and a shot.

The bartender asked if Thomas was OK, and Thomas said, "No." The bartender let him be.

Thoughts of Reggie swirled around Thomas's mind, and another shot of whiskey was the medicine that Thomas ordered. But it didn't help. He thought about the time that his dog, Willy, died when he was twelve years old and how he had cried then. But he did not remember it feeling like this. If it had, he would never have gotten a dog in the first place. Another beer was consumed after the shot of whiskey. He didn't really want to drink. But he didn't want to go back to the empty apartment either. So, another beer was consumed.

How did he get here? How did he end up a fifty-five-year-old man, sitting alone in a bar in Manhattan, mourning the loss of a dog? Who would he turn to now? He knew he should be more engaged with people, but the truth was that he didn't much like people. He knew he could never love a person the way he loved Reggie.

An hour later, Thomas opened the door to his apartment. And for the first time in 11 years, Reggie was not there to greet him. Reggie was not there to jump at him and lick his face and wag his stubby little tail. Was there a being on earth that felt greater joy than a dog when his master comes home? That joy was no longer in the apartment. There was only a deafening silence.

Thomas collapsed on the couch, and Reggie was not there to jump into his lap. He looked around the room and saw Reggie's empty daybed. Then a glance into the kitchen, where he saw Reggie's empty bowl sitting on the floor. Should he throw these items out? No, he could not bring himself to do that. Should he save them in case he got another dog? No. There would never be another Reggie. Thomas put his head down and cried.

Later that night, Thomas retired to bed. Obviously, there was no Reggie nestling under his butt, as there had been for the last eleven years, and Thomas had never felt more alone. His bed felt unusually large.

He closed his eyes and tried to sleep. Thomas thought of Reggie's eyes as the IV sent its drugs into Reggie's veins. It reminded him of the last episode of *Game of Thrones*—which Reggie had watched with him, dutifully sitting on his lap—when Jon Snow has plunged the knife into his love, Daenerys, and her eyes looked back at him, just like Reggie's had.

But he quickly shot that thought out of his head. Instead, he thought of Reggie nestled under his butt, snoring like he always did, content and satisfied. And then he had an image of Reggie running free in a field somewhere. It was an odd image to have for a city dog who had never run in a field in his life. But the image made Thomas feel good. Maybe Reggie was off somewhere, running in a field. He smiled to himself. Wouldn't that be nice? He continued the image in his head. Reggie running wild and free off into the distance.

So long, old boy, he thought. *So long...*

The Prowler

(1979)

WHENEVER ROBBIE MILLER NEEDED to think, he always sat in his backyard, under the tall pine tree near the back fence. There were a lot of trees in his backyard, but the tall pine stood out. He had fallen off it a couple of times while trying to climb it when he was younger, and his mother had yelled at him many times over to stop climbing it, but he never listened. But now that he was twelve, climbing it wasn't quite the challenge it used to be. The tree was tall, taller than any other in the yard, and he liked to sit under it and look straight up. He liked the way rays of light streaked down through the tree's branches. And on a bright, sunny day, like today, those streaks looked especially cool.

The summer of 1979 had been great so far. The block party last week had been the best one that Victory Lane had ever seen. At least Robbie thought so. His mother disagreed. Mr. Krasdale had gotten pretty drunk and loud toward the end. But for Robbie, that was part of the fun. Mr. Krasdale was his best friend's dad, and Robbie had seen him drunk and loud many times before. Whenever Mr. Krasdale got drunk, he would sing these old songs that nobody knew, even the other adults. And it always made Robbie crack up. He was so funny when he started singing!

Robbie's team had also won the baseball game that was played among the kids on the block, and for the first time ever, there were fireworks at the end. Fireworks were illegal, of course, but Mr. Roselli had a lot left over from the Fourth of July a few weeks before. He had driven all the way from Long Island to Virginia to get them, like he did every year, and he put on quite a show. Robbie's mother wasn't crazy about that either. She didn't like that Mr. Roselli "blew up the neighborhood" every July. But Mr. Krasdale was a New York City cop, so if the police ever came around, he would talk them into ignoring the fireworks display.

Robbie and his friends had also had a great summer, going to the movies. It started when they saw *Rocky II* the week after school had ended. It was so good. Tommy Krasdale had especially loved it, so much so that after seeing the movie, he went out and bought an Italian horn necklace at the mall. Robbie thought this was pretty silly since Tommy wasn't Italian. But Tommy didn't care. He wanted to be like Rocky. Tommy also didn't walk anymore. He slowly jogged and punched his fists in the air as he moved, the *Rocky* theme obviously playing in his head. A few weeks after that, *Moonraker* came out, and Robbie really loved that one. *Jaws* was back and even helped James Bond thwart the villain's evil plans this time. And just last week, Robbie, Tommy and Billy Cohen were finally able to see *Alien*. It was rated R, and none of them were allowed to see it. But they had told their parents that they were going to see *Moonraker* again. At the theater, they got Joe Roselli—he was 17—to buy their tickets for them.

It had been a hot summer too. And luckily, Billy Cohen's parents had put an in-ground pool in just before summer. So, most days had been spent in Billy's great new pool. It was awesome.

Robbie thought about all these things as he looked up at the pine tree, which always looked so tall and strong and vibrant. He loved this tree. And loved Victory Lane. Nobody lived on a better block than he did.

But the best and most exciting part of the summer of '79 was definitely the prowler. Yes, nothing this exciting had ever happened on Victory Lane.

It had started a few days earlier, when Mrs. Stanley went outside to take the garbage out. The Stanleys lived on the last house on the block, directly in front of the sump. She noticed a car parked at the curb in front of the sump. This startled her. Why would there be a car parked there? No cars ever parked there. Why would they? The fence in front of the sump had a sign on it that read *Curb Your Dog*. And that's the only reason anyone ever went near the sump—to curb their dog. The kids never went near it either because the grass in front of the fence was always covered in dog shit. Certainly no one ever parked there.

When she looked closer at the car, she was startled again when she realized that a man was sitting behind the wheel. The car wasn't running; the headlights were not on. The man was just sitting there. She nervously said hello to him, but as soon as she did, the man started the car and drove away.

Things didn't heat up until two nights later. This time, Mrs. McSorley, who lived directly across the street from Robbie, was out in her yard, watering her garden. The McSorleys' backyard faced the woods, and as it was a little after 9 p.m., it was pretty dark out. But as she watered her tomato plants, she had the fright of her life as she noticed a man in the darkness standing just inside the woods, staring at her. She screamed, dropped the hose, and ran inside the house. Mr. McSorley grabbed a Louisville Slugger from the garage and went out back to investigate, but it was too late. The man was gone.

100

The next night, Mr. Roselli was driving home late and saw a white sedan parked at the curb in front of the Currys' house. It stood out to him because no one really ever parked at the curb on Victory Lane; all of the houses had two-car garages and decent-sized driveways. No reason to park at the curb. And it wasn't until later in the 1980s that many of the families got a third car. In 1979, most of the families had only two cars, and everyone on the block knew which cars belonged to which houses. A new car on the block was a big deal because it didn't happen that often. Mr. Roselli knew that this car didn't belong to anyone who lived on Victory Lane. After he pulled up into his driveway, he walked toward the car, but didn't see anyone in it. He thought nothing more of it and went into his house.

It was the next day, a Saturday, when Mrs. Stanley and Mrs. McSorley were talking and comparing notes on what they had witnessed earlier in the week, and Mrs. Stanley decided to call the police. When the Suffolk County Police squad car arrived a little while later, that's when things really got exciting. Robbie had never seen a police car ever on the block, so this was really getting cool now. Every kid on the block—and there were a lot on Victory Lane—was out and watching as the two police officers interviewed Mrs. Stanley and Mrs. McSorley right there in the middle of the street. All the parents were out there too. Everyone watching and listening.

Turns out, Mrs. Stanley saw a white sedan, an early '70s make, she thought, probably a Chrysler or a Ford. That's when Mr. Roselli piped in and told the police that he had also seen a white sedan, but he was certain that it was a Buick or a Pontiac, a LeSabre or a Bonneville, he told them. Of course, everyone assumed Mr. Roselli was right, as he worked at the Chevy dealership on Jericho Turnpike. He certainly knew more about cars than Mrs. Stanley did.

The cops explained that it sounded like the neighborhood might have a prowler. And, boy, did that sound cool to Robbie. A prowler! It sounded like the title of a good horror movie, *The Prowler*.

"Robbie!" yelled Robbie's mother. "Lunch!"

"OK, Mom," answered Robbie. He was still staring up at the streaks of light coming down through the branches of the pine tree. "Coming."

"I don't know about this sleeping in the Krasdales' backyard tonight," said Robbie's mother as she put the plate in front of him. "Not with this prowler guy out there."

Robbie sat at the kitchen table with his parents and ate his favorite lunch—bologna and American cheese with mayo on Wonder Bread, washed down with orange Hi-C.

"Don't worry, Mom," said Robbie.

Plans had been made a few days before—for him, Tommy, and Billy to spend tonight in Tommy's backyard, sleeping in the Krasdales' camping tent. Robbie had never been camping and had been really looking forward to it. Not that sleeping in a tent in your friend's backyard counted as camping, but it was close enough.

"It's my job to worry," she said. "Who knows what kind of freak this guy is?"

"Mr. Krasdale is a cop. He'll be right inside."

"I still don't like it."

"They'll be fine, hon," said Robbie's father. "Bob Krasdale will be right inside, like he said."

"He'll probably be drunk," she said.

"They'll be fine," said Robbie's father. "We'll be able to see the tent from our living room window. I don't think the prowler is going to come charging into the tent or anything."

"How do you know what that maniac is going to do?"

"Maniac? I think you're overreacting a little."

"Can't you just wait until this whole prowler thing blows over?" said Robbie's mother. "You can do it another time."

But Robbie's mother lost the argument. The night of camping was on. Robbie couldn't wait!

Billy Cohen was going to Pathmark with his mother and had been tasked with picking up all the snacks for the evening. The boys had each chipped in five bucks so Billy could load up on chips, candy bars, and soda.

While he was at the store, Robbie and Tommy decided to lay a trap for Billy. There was a certain evergreen bush on Victory Lane that half of the houses seemed to have on their property. This bush—Robbie didn't know what it was called—grew a hard berry of some kind all over it. The berry— if that's what it was—looked like a chickpea with thorns on it, and this time of year, all of these bushes were covered in this thorny, chickpea-like berry. So, of course, the kids in the neighborhood were always collecting these berries and having berry fights. Billy Cohen even gave this odd berry a name—the gackleberry. No one was sure how Billy had come up with that name, but it sure stuck. The summer of '79 had thus become the summer of gackleberry warfare on Victory Lane, with any kid at any moment vulnerable to a hail of gackleberries from any direction. As Billy was at the supermarket with his mom, Robbie and Tommy grabbed a bucket and scoured the neighborhood, filling the bucket with as many gackleberries as they could. When Billy entered the backyard, he would be hit with a barrage of gackleberries the likes of which Victory Lane had never seen.

After gathering their bucket full of gackleberries, the boys put up the tent with the help of Mr. Krasdale.

"I don't want any shenanigans tonight, boys," said Mr. Krasdale. He looked at his son. "Your mother is going to your aunt's house tonight with your sister. I'll be inside watching *CHIPs* and *Dallas*. I don't want to have to come out here because you guys are getting out of hand. Just stay in the tent and don't make a racket."

Robbie thought it was funny that Mr. Krasdale—this beefy, tough New York cop—liked a show about two pretty-boy LA cops on motorcycles. But Mr. Krasdale liked all the cop shows, even though he would complain throughout every episode about how fake everything was.

"Don't worry, Dad," said Tommy. "We won't make a sound."

Robbie knew that was doubtful, but it was enough for now for Mr. Krasdale.

When Billy Cohen entered the backyard around 8 p.m., carrying his bag of goodies from the supermarket, he was hit with a shower of gackleberries that flew in from two directions. Robbie and Tommy had each taken up position in a different corner of the yard, so Billy was caught in a cross fire that he could not escape. He quickly dropped the grocery bag and took cover behind the patio table, gackleberries whizzing by his head. Ever resourceful, he gathered as many berries as he could and started to hurl them back at his attackers.

Of course, this gackleberry firefight did not happen in silence. The three boys were making enough noise that they could be heard all the way down the block. And they could certainly be heard inside the Krasdale house.

When Mr. Krasdale opened the screen door and stepped onto the back patio, he said, "What the hell is going on?" But before he could get more words out, he was hit in the face with a salvo of gackleberries.

The boys froze. Mr. Krasdale had a known temper. And the sight of multiple gackleberries hitting Mr. Krasdale in the face made their hearts stop.

"Goddammit, that's it!" Mr. Krasdale yelled. "I said, no shenanigans. No shenanigans. And what do I get? Goddamn shenanigans!"

"It was an accident, Dad," pleaded Tommy.

"Everybody, out of the yard," Mr. Krasdale yelled. "Nobody is sleeping in that tent tonight!"

Tommy ran up to his father. "Dad, please, it was an accident. We were just having some fun."

"Goddammit, Tommy, I told you, no shenanigans."

Robbie had to admit, it was becoming increasingly funny to him every time Mr. Krasdale said "shenanigans." It just didn't seem like the type of word that should come out of his mouth. Robbie had to keep from laughing every time he said it. But if he did let out a laugh, that would set off Mr. Krasdale even more.

"Please, Dad," said Tommy, almost in tears now.

The tent party had been weeks in the planning—it would crush Tommy if it were canceled now. Mr. Krasdale saw the tears in his son's eyes and started to soften. He certainly could be a tough, hot-tempered guy, but Robbie knew from experience that he was also a softy at heart.

"If I let you kids stay in the tent tonight, that'd better be it for shenanigans," Mr. Krasdale said.

Robbie stifled a laugh. Why did that word make him want to laugh so much?

"I promise, Dad. I promise," said Tommy, wiping tears from his eyes. "We won't make a sound from here on out."

"Do something constructive for once," Mr. Krasdale said.

"OK," said Tommy.

"I'm going in the house now. Your mother and sister aren't coming home till later. I would like some peace and quiet while I watch TV. Is that too much to ask?"

"Go inside and enjoy your shows. You won't hear any more noise from us."

Mr. Krasdale went inside, and the boys let out a collective sigh of relief. The night in the tent was back on!

Once inside the tent, the boys ripped open the snacks that Billy had brought from the store. Robbie attacked the bag of BBQ Lays while Tommy grabbed the bag of sour cream and onion chips. Billy went straight for the Kit Kats.

"Shouldn't we eat the chips first and the chocolate second?" said Robbie.

"Why?" asked Billy.

"Because the Kit Kats are for dessert."

"Since when is a Kit Kat considered a dessert?"

Robbie and Billy frequently had debates like this. If they weren't arguing over chips and chocolate bars, it was McDonald's versus Burger King, or Billy Joel versus Jackson Browne, or Sean Connery versus Roger Moore—even though Robbie had loved *Moonraker*, he knew it was no *Goldfinger*, but Billy was a Roger Moore kid all the way and wouldn't even watch the old Connery Bonds when ABC would show them on Sunday nights.

Their argument tonight quickly went from Kit Kats to their favorite debate subject—Yankees versus Mets.

"The Yankees lost again last night," said Billy.

"They can't win in Milwaukee," said Robbie. "I don't know what it is about that place, but they just can't win there."

"What are they, ten games out now?" asked Billy.

"Twelve," said Robbie.

Robbie knew that Billy knew exactly how many games behind the Orioles the Yankees were. Billy was just tweaking him.

"Wow, it's twelve now? I guess no playoffs this year, Rob."

"They were fourteen games out last year, and they still caught Boston and won the Series."

"And you really think they're going to do that again?" said Billy.

"If they did it once, they can do it again," argued Robbie.

Deep down, he knew it was a long shot, but you never give up, right? The Yankees were the two-time defending world champions, and they were still the champs until someone dethroned them. Robbie still had hope. But it had been a lousy year so far. They got off to a slow start, then Goose Gossage hurt his thumb during a clubhouse fight with Cliff Johnson, and then they moved Cy Young Award winner Ron Guidry to the bullpen to replace Goose as closer. Nothing had gone right. The only good thing was that the Yankees had traded for Bobby Murcer a few weeks back. Robbie had cried when Murcer was traded after the '74 season. Bobby Murcer and Thurman Munson were Robbie's favorite players when he was little, and he even got them to sign a ball for him at his first Yankees game at the old stadium in '73. And now Bobby and Thurman were back together again.

"And Thurman Munson stinks," said Billy. "And your boy Murcer has done nothing since they got him back."

It was true that Munson was having a lousy year. It was his tenth year as the Yankees catcher, and it looked like age was starting to catch up to him, even though he was only thirty-two. He had hit 6 homers the year before and had only three so far this year. And Billy was right. Murcer hadn't done much of anything since he came back. But why was Robbie letting Billy needle him about the Yankees? Billy's Mets were well on their way to a third-straight last-place finish.

"Munson and Murcer may be struggling a little, but they're ten times better than anyone on the Mets," said Robbie.

"Better than Lee Mazzili?" said Billy.

"Please," said Robbie. "He's a pretty boy with no power."

107

"With a higher average than Munson or Murcer."

"Who cares?" said Robbie. "The Mets suck. They're in last place again. Talk to me when the Mets get anywhere near the World Series."

God, Robbie hated Mets fans!

"Hey, enough arguing about baseball," chimed Tommy. "Let's talk about the prowler."

Robbie had been trying not to think about the prowler. He wanted to have fun tonight. But deep down, they were all thinking about it.

"My mom thinks he must be some kind of sex maniac or something," said Billy.

"So, why is he prowling around Victory Lane?" wondered Robbie.

"Yeah, it's not like he wants to have sex with Mrs. McSorley," said Tommy. "Not even Mr. McSorley wants to have sex with Mrs. McSorley."

The boys all laughed at that one. But it did bring up the question that had been on everyone's mind. Who was the prowler, and what was he doing here? What was he looking for?

"What does your father think, Tommy?" asked Robbie.

Mr. Krasdale was a cop after all.

"He thinks the guy is probably just some pervert, trying to see a naked lady through the window or something."

"Well, he picked the wrong street," said Billy.

They all laughed at that one too.

"Speaking of naked ladies..." said Tommy, as he reached under his sleeping bag. In his hand were three magazines. "How about some *Playboys* for our reading pleasure tonight?"

Robbie's adrenaline—among other things—began to rise at the sight of the magazines. "Where did you get those?" he asked.

"Where do you think?" said Tommy. "From my dad's stash under my parents' bed."

Robbie's only *Playboy*—carefully hidden in a closet in his bedroom, in a box, stuffed in between Yankees yearbooks—was given to him by Tommy from the same stash under Tommy's parents' bed. But Tommy got caught taking some copies from that same stash about six months ago, and Mr. Krasdale went stratospheric with anger.

"He almost killed you last time you took a *Playboy*!" said Billy. "What if he finds out?"

"He has, like, every issue of *Playboy* for the last ten years," said Tommy. "You really think he's gonna notice if three are missing?"

Tommy flipped a magazine each to Robbie and Billy. The stiffening in Robbie's pants increased. He looked at his copy, the November 1976 issue. God, the girl on the cover was hot! There was also an interview with Jimmy Carter, but he didn't care about that. No, he was interested in the cover girl, Patti McGuire.

"What issue did you get?" asked Billy.

"November '76," Robbie replied.

"I got December '76," said Billy.

"I got October," said Tommy.

Billy laughed. "I don't see your dad as the organized type. Who would think that he keeps his dirty magazines in order?"

"You got the gala Christmas issue, Billy. Those are usually the best. I got dibs on it next," said Tommy.

Robbie quickly opened his magazine to the centerfold. Look at her in all her naked glory. Patti McGuire! Yes, Robbie Miller was in love.

"Show me your centerfold, Robbie," said Billy.

Robbie turned the open centerfold toward Billy.

"Holy shit," said Billy. "That's Jimmy Connors's wife!"

"What?" said Robbie.

"Patti McGuire! She's married to Jimmy Connors."

"Lucky son of a bitch!" Tommy said.

"I know," said Billy. "He's the best tennis player in the world, and his wife's a *Playboy* centerfold!"

"McEnroe's the best," said Robbie.

"What?" Billy said. "He hasn't even won anything yet."

"He just won the doubles at Wimbledon," said Robbie.

"Doubles! Who gives a shit about doubles?!"

"Here you guys go again, something new to argue about," said Tommy. "Can't you just enjoy your *Playboy*?"

Just then the warm summer air in the tent was ripped open by loud screams coming from the street.

"What the…" said Tommy.

Chills ran down Robbie's arms. The three boys looked at each other in cold fear. The screams that seemed to be coming from the street got louder. But these weren't normal screams. To Robbie, these were bloodcurdling, late-night-horror-movie screams.

Tommy threw his magazine down and ran out of the tent. Robbie and Billy quickly scrambled to their feet and followed him.

Tommy ran straight to the back screen door and started banging on it. "Dad! Dad!"

Robbie could see Mr. Krasdale sitting on the couch, feet up on the coffee table, a snub-nosed Piels in his hand. Tommy kept banging on the screen door.

"Goddammit, Tommy," said Mr. Krasdale as he put his beer down and slowly lifted himself off the couch. "What the hell is it?" Mr. Krasdale opened the screen door. "I told you, no more shenanigans—"

But then Mr. Krasdale heard the screams. And his face went white. He turned and ran back into the house. Robbie was really scared now. Where the hell was Mr. Krasdale going? Robbie didn't have to wait long to find out. Mr. Krasdale was back at the door in seconds, holding his police revolver in his right hand.

"You three get in the house!"

"But, Dad—"

"Get in the fucking house now, Tommy!"

The boys ran into the house as Mr. Krasdale ran out, gun in hand. They then ran through the den and foyer to the front door. As they peeked out the door, they saw Mr. Krasdale running across the lawn from the backyard. He was heading across the street.

Tommy creaked open the front door so that the boys could get a better look. They could still hear the screams. They seemed to be coming from the woods directly across the street, between the McSorleys' house and the Gayhearts' house. And that's right where Mr. Krasdale was headed.

"Come on," said Tommy as he started quietly opening the door further and stepping outside.

"Tommy, are you crazy? Your father will kill us," said Robbie.

"I can't see from here," Tommy said.

And he walked outside. For once, Robbie and Billy seemed in agreement. They wanted no part of whatever was going on across the street.

"Don't be wimps," said Tommy. "Get out here."

And as there is nothing worse for a twelve-year-old boy to be called than a wimp, Robbie and Billy reluctantly stepped outside onto the porch with Tommy. And Robbie would always remember later that he had wished he had never done so.

Mrs. Gayheart came running out of her backyard—or more like stumbling out of her backyard. "Help me, help me," she cried.

Obviously, it had been her that had been screaming. A man tackled her from behind. He was ramming something into her back, and Robbie didn't need to see the glint of metal to know that it was a knife. She fell to the grass as the man continued stabbing her.

Mr. Krasdale raced across the street in a flash. "Hey! Stop it! Stop it!"

The man didn't look up. He just kept stabbing Mrs. Gayheart, who was no longer screaming.

When Mr. Krasdale got within ten feet of the man, the man suddenly sat up and looked at Mr. Krasdale. Mr. Krasdale got in his NYPD crouch and fired three shots. All three exploded into the man's chest, and Robbie was sickened. This wasn't what it looked like when someone got shot on TV or in the movies. Blood shot out of the man's chest in spurts and splattered over Mrs. Gayheart, who lay still on the grass. The man crumpled on top of her.

Mr. Krasdale turned to the boys and yelled, "Tommy! Call 911."

Tommy ran in the house. Mr. Krasdale pulled the man off Mrs. Gayheart. He pumped her chest, but she wasn't moving.

"Robbie!"

Robbie turned to see his parents on his driveway. He ran to his mother and burst out crying when he got to her. She held him tight, and they cried in each other's arms. His father stoically stared across the street.

Other people started creeping out of their houses to see what had happened. Mr. Krasdale sat on his knees, with his hands on his hips, looking up at the night sky. Mrs. Gayheart and the man who had killed her lay motionless beside him.

Sirens could now be heard.

"Go in the house, Robbie," said Robbie's father.

Robbie ran in the house and ran upstairs to his room. He went to his window and looked outside. Mr. Krasdale was still on his knees on the grass. The sirens grew louder, and Robbie watched as a Suffolk County Police car and an ambulance raced down the street. His room filled with the red lights of the police car and the ambulance, and Robbie started to shake. Five minutes earlier, he had fallen in love with a centerfold. Now, he stood in his room, cold and alone.

The story of what had happened slowly came out over the next couple of days. Mr. Gayheart was a New York City fireman who worked in Queens. He would work three-day shifts—three days sleeping at the firehouse, three days home. He had started a three-day shift at the firehouse on the day his wife was murdered. The prowler turned out to be Mrs. Gayheart's high school boyfriend. He had been stalking her all week, waiting for a night when Mr. Gayheart was away. Saturday was that night. The cops weren't quite sure how the prowler had lured her into the backyard. The two Gayheart kids were toddlers and had been sleeping when everything happened.

The wake was Tuesday and Wednesday. Robbie's parents went on Tuesday night, but Robbie wasn't allowed to go. Not that he wanted to. He was glad to miss that. None of the kids on the block went. The wives on the block made all kinds of food for Mr. Gayheart. Robbie's mom made a meatloaf. She said that Mr. Gayheart was in shock, and she was worried about what would happen to him. Who would take care of those two kids?

Robbie didn't see Tommy or Billy for the next couple of days. The block was quiet. No one wanted to go outside. Robbie tried to lose himself in the Yankees. They won in Chicago on Monday and Tuesday night. That helped a little. But they lost on Wednesday. Maybe Billy was right. Maybe the Yankees weren't going to catch the Orioles.

He tried to sleep, but couldn't. He kept hearing Mrs. Gayheart's screams. And seeing the prowler look up at Mr. Krasdale. And then the blood when the shots hit. He kept seeing the blood. You never saw blood like that when James Bond or Baretta shot someone.

The funeral had been Wednesday. Robbie hoped that with the funeral over, maybe the block would get back to normal. But on Thursday, he still didn't feel like leaving the house. He tried listening to some music. He put on his *52nd Street* album by Billy Joel. But he couldn't get into it. He was sitting in the den in the late afternoon, watching the 4:30 movie on channel 7, when there was a banging at the front screen door.

"Robbie! Robbie!" It was Billy. He was screaming through the screen door.

Robbie jumped up from the couch and ran toward the door.

"Thurman Munson died in a plane crash," Billy yelled.

"What?" said Robbie.

"Put on the TV!" yelled Billy.

Billy came into the house, and he and Robbie ran to the den. The TV was still on the 4:30 movie.

Robbie's mother ran in from the laundry room.

"Thurman Munson died in a plane crash," Billy yelled at her.

Robbie changed the channel to channel 4. Oh God, there it was. A special report.

Yankees Captain Dies in Plane Crash read the heading.

Robbie dropped to the floor. His mother held him as they watched the news report. The pictures showed wreckage near some airport in Ohio. What the hell was Munson doing on a plane in Ohio? The Yankees were in Chicago the night before and were coming home to play Baltimore this weekend. What the hell was going on?

Robbie watched the news for the next two hours. Munson had gotten his pilot's license the year before. Robbie didn't know that. And he knew everything about the Yankees. Munson had been practicing takeoffs and landings at the airport. Two other people in the plane survived. But the Yankees captain was dead.

114

When Robbie's father came home, he tried to console his son. But there was no consoling Robbie. Not after everything that had happened this week. So, Robbie went into the backyard and sat under the tall pine tree.

He looked up at the tree, but there were no streaks of light poking through the branches today. The sky had gone gray. He noticed that the bark was starting to peel on parts of the trunk. And some of the green pine needles had turned brown. The tree was decaying, and from the looks of it, it had been for some time. But Robbie hadn't noticed until just now.

The Last Cheeseburger

(2019)

THE JUICE FROM THE perfectly cooked medium-rare cheeseburger oozed down his cheeks. How did they make these cheeseburgers so damn good? He took another bite and thought about the first time he had been to Corner Bistro years before. It was sometime in the early '90s. He was still living in Manhattan, and his old college buddy Phil had told him about the best burger he had ever eaten—after a night of drinking in the West Village, of course.

At the time, he couldn't believe that there was a great place in the Village that he didn't know about. But in those days, before the internet was at everybody's fingertips, news didn't travel as fast. Things could stay hidden. And Corner Bistro was certainly hidden. It was at the corner of 13th Street and 7th Avenue and was situated in a triangle so that it was almost impossible to find. But find it he did. And never had he tasted a better burger.

He took another bite, and he wondered just how many cheeseburgers he had eaten in his life. He was fifty-two years old, and the number he had eaten was certainly in the hundreds or most likely in the thousands. Even though he had started eating in a healthier way in his forties, the cheeseburger had never been removed from his diet. He didn't eat as many now as he did in his twenties, but he still had to have one every now and then. He wondered just how many more he would eat in his lifetime. Obviously, that would depend to some extent on how long he would live. And how many cheeseburgers he ate might affect how long he lived. When he took the last bite of the last cheeseburger he would ever eat, would he know it? Would he be able to savor it? Of course, if he got hit by a city bus when he left Corner Bistro in a few minutes, this would be the last cheeseburger, and he would have no way of knowing it. But what if he lived to a ripe old age? Would he know when the last one was? Would he be able to linger over the last bite? Or would he be ninety-two years old and eat a cheeseburger for lunch one day, thinking he might have another the next day, or the next week, only there wouldn't be a next day. Maybe he would die in his sleep that night, and that would be it.

That thought made him think about sex. Would a longtime couple married for decades know when the last time was? Would the sex decrease over the years, and as they moved into their seventies and eighties, would it become so infrequent that one day, they would just get to the point that they didn't bother with it anymore? Would the last time be so forgettable or uninspired that they wouldn't care anymore and not even realize it was the last time? Or would their sex life stay robust and frequent? And they would have a great last time together, only they wouldn't know it. The man could die in his sleep that night. And the woman would be left thinking she should have savored it more or whispered something special to her lover of all these years as they finished. If only she had known that would be the last time as they were actually doing it...

He took another bite of the burger and put the theoretical longtime married couple out of his head. But he made a note in his mind to savor it the next time he made love to his wife. Hell, it could be the last. You never knew. One day, it would be.

He went back to thinking about cheeseburgers. He supposed an inmate on death row could choose a cheeseburger as his last meal. He was sure a lot of them had. They would certainly know it was the last one then. Bet your ass they would savor that one! He made another mental note that if he was ever on death row, he would choose a cheeseburger as his last meal, but only if he could get it from Corner Bistro.

He took another bite of the burger and wondered if there was something strange in his coffee that morning. Why was he thinking such odd thoughts? He didn't know. Maybe you reach a certain age, and you realize that there are more years behind you than there are in front of you.

He shoved the last of the cheeseburger in his mouth and savored every last bit of deliciousness as it went down his throat. Damn, it was good. He hoped to have another again soon.

He walked out of the restaurant and thought about his wife and hoped that they would be together tonight. It was a school night, and he hoped that the kids would go to sleep early enough so that something might happen. He hoped—and in the end, that was all anyone could hope for.

"Unfortunately, the clock is ticking, the hours are going by. The past increases, the future recedes. Possibilities decreasing, regrets mounting."

—Haruki Murakami

You Have Memories with Rob Miller to Look Back on Today

(2017)

TOMMY KRASDALE WALKED TO his car outside of the 90th Precinct in the Williamsburg section of Brooklyn. It had been a long shift, and he was exhausted. He hated working night shifts. He knew he would have trouble sleeping when he got home. He could never get used to sleeping in the daytime.

He sat in his car and took a breath. He hesitated before starting the car. He was in no rush to get home, so he took out his iPhone and scrolled the news. Stories about Trump calling the neo-Nazis in Charlottesville "very fine people." Tommy took another deep breath. What was wrong with this guy? His grandfather had fought the Nazis in Europe. And now we have a president who was openly supported by them—and worse, a president who willingly accepted their support. *Very fine people*. How in the world had he ever voted for this guy? It made him sick now. He should have learned his lesson when Trump mocked John McCain's military service.

"I like guys that didn't get captured."

Seriously? A draft dodger said that about John McCain? And yet Tommy had still voted for him. And he couldn't talk about this at work because all the guys loved Trump. At least all the white ones did. He needed to clear his head, and he needed to stop reading and watching the news so much because none of it seemed to be good anymore. So, he scrolled past the news and clicked on Facebook.

You Have Memories with Rob Miller to Look Back on Today, said the blurb on the top of the screen.

He clicked on it, and up popped a picture of Tommy, Robbie Miller, and Billy Cohen. The picture was from 1976 or 1977, he supposed. It showed the three boys holding their baseball gloves and bats, standing in front of the Millers' house. Mrs. Miller probably had taken it. Tommy had his Smithtown Y hat on, Billy wore a faded Mets cap, and Robbie, of course, was in a pristine Yankees cap. Robbie had posted the picture on April 1, 2009, in honor of opening day. Tommy had just joined Facebook at that time. Had it really been forty years since that photo had been taken? Sometimes, his childhood on Victory Lane seemed like yesterday. And sometimes, it seemed like a million fucking years ago. Lately, it had been the latter.

He looked at the photo and focused on Robbie. He hadn't seen or spoken to him in at least fifteen years. Their only communication was a random comment on a Facebook post every now and then. How did that happen? They used to be so close. But Tommy knew why. He thought again about the Trump "very fine people" story. Yes, Tommy Krasdale was pretty sure he knew why he never heard from Robbie Miller anymore.

He had last seen him one St. Patrick's Day twelve or fifteen years ago. He wasn't exactly sure what year, but it was after 9/11 because he remembered talking about it that night with Robbie.

He hadn't seen Robbie in a while and had called him about getting a drink. Robbie had said that would be great, and because it was a few days before St. Paddy's, Tommy suggested getting together then. He and a bunch of the guys at the precinct were going to a bar on the Upper East Side on the holiday. Tommy didn't get to Manhattan very often, so he figured this would be a good time to see Robbie. He knew Robbie was a Wall Street guy, but Tommy didn't think he would mind hanging out with some of New York's finest for a few hours.

Of course, it ended up being a big mistake. Robbie knew Victory Lane Tommy. He knew child Tommy. But Robbie didn't really know cop Tommy. And when Robbie saw cop Tommy in all of his glory that St. Paddy's Day, well, it sort of changed everything.

Tommy couldn't remember if he was the first one to use the N-word that night, but he definitely used it. He remembered that Billy O'Shaughnessy was there, and he, without a doubt, used it. Tommy remembered his father occasionally using the word when he was a kid, and he remembered calling his father out on it. And yet, fifteen years later, he would casually use it with his cop buddies because they all used it. It was a lame excuse, but Tommy had always been something of a follower.

He remembered sitting at a large table that night at Casey's, with Robbie sitting next to him and five or six cops from the precinct sitting with them.

He recalled Billy telling a story about hurting his knee after "chasing this fast little nigger who hopped over a fence" while in pursuit. That opened the floodgates. Soon, every cop at the table started telling their own N-word story. Everyone laughed at each story. Everyone was having a grand old time. Everyone except Robbie. Tommy sensed something was wrong when Robbie went silent. He glanced at him and saw that Robbie's face was white, and he was not smiling. He looked horrified.

Tommy recalled trying to change the conversation, but the beer was flowing, and the boys wanted to boast. More N-words followed. Tommy couldn't look at Robbie. He didn't want to see his face. Robbie finished his beer and told Tommy he had to leave. Tommy didn't even try to stop him. He felt ashamed. He was glad when Robbie left. At least he could relax now. He should have never invited him.

And that was the last Tommy saw of his old friend.

He looked at the Facebook picture again. What had happened to the boy in this picture? He hadn't even wanted to be a cop when he was a kid. He wanted to be the next Evel Knevel. But that, of course, didn't happen. His father was a cop who drank too much and never really seemed happy. So, why would Tommy want that? But when he got older, he realized that college wasn't for him, and he didn't know what to do. His father explained that the benefits were great and you could retire at forty if you wanted, so why not join the academy? So, at nineteen, with no other prospects on the horizon, he did just that. And now, thirty-one years later, he sat alone in his car, divorced, seeing his teenage kid—who barely spoke to him—every other weekend.

He clicked Comment on the Facebook picture and typed, *Love this picture! Victory Lane forever!!!* and shared it. Maybe Robbie would see it and comment. He hated the fact that Robbie probably thought so little of him.

The thought of driving to his apartment in Massapequa depressed him. It had been two years since the divorce, and he still hadn't gotten used to living alone. He missed his wife and kids. He missed his house and his backyard and his pool. When he and Laura had first bought the house, he envisioned that it would be just like the house he had grown up in. But it

123

never was. His street was no Victory Lane. There were never as many kids as when he grew up. You could look out on the street at 2 p.m. on a nice Saturday, and there wouldn't be a kid in sight. His kids grew up playing with other kids only during scheduled playdates. What kind of childhood is that? When he was a kid, if the doorbell rang in the middle of the day, nine times out of ten, it was Robbie Miller or Billy Cohen at the door. But when the doorbell rang at someone's house now, it sent everyone into a panic. Who the hell could possibly be at the door?

Some world we live in, he thought.

People were afraid to answer their door. And the president defends white supremacists and mocks war heroes.

Tommy put his phone down, started the car, and drove away.

He turned the radio to Sirius XM and put on '70s on 7. It was the only station he listened to anymore. He used to listen to WFAN mostly, but he had gotten tired of all the arguing and whining. Everyone liked to argue nowadays. Tommy used to like arguing about sports too. But not anymore. He had no more strength to argue.

"Telephone Line" by ELO was playing. He liked that one. He couldn't sing, but he belted out the words from deep within his soul. Like the song said, he had some dreams, and they had certainly faded out of view.

Then Ringo Starr's "Photograph" came on.

Gotta love '70s on 7, he thought.

He sang along to that one as well. He was happy for a moment, but the song made him think of his wife. She definitely wasn't coming back anymore. His mood went from happy to sad in one lyric. He changed the station to '80s on 8. "The Safety Dance" by Men Without Hats was on.

Fuck that, he thought. He turned the radio off.

When he got home to his apartment, he grabbed a beer and sat at the kitchen counter. No wife to greet him, no kids running down the stairs. Just an empty apartment.

He pulled out his phone and went right to Facebook. Maybe Robbie had commented on the photo. That would lift his spirits. Could he really still be mad at him over a few drunken N-words from fifteen years ago? Did that really negate all the great memories from childhood?

There were seven likes and three comments on the post. Hopefully, one of the comments would be from Robbie.

Great picture, said the first comment from Tommy's sister.

This pic brings me back. Love you guys, said the second comment, this one from Denise Kelly, a girl from Victory Lane.

Nice hat, Krasdale. You look like Bobby Brady's ugly cousin, said the third comment from Ray Cannizzaro, one of the guys from the precinct.

But nothing from Robbie Miller. Tommy's heart sank. Why did he so crave the approval of Robbie? He wasn't even sure it was his approval he craved. He just didn't want Robbie to hate him and think of him as just some racist he used to know. That thought killed him.

He checked the Likes, and Robbie's name was there. I guess that was something. But why couldn't he leave a comment?!

He may not think much of me as an adult, thought Tommy, *but did he have no affection left for Tommy Krasdale the boy?*

A memory of him and Robbie playing *The Six Million Dollar Man* in his backyard flashed across his mind. They used to love playing that game. Sometimes, Robbie would be afraid to jump over the fence in the yard, and Tommy would tease him and tell him that he was really the Bionic Woman.

Tommy put his phone down, walked into his small den, and sat on the couch.

He drank his beer and sat in silence—a fifty-year-old divorced man, alone on his couch, alone with his thoughts.

He picked up the phone again and looked at the picture on Facebook. Two more likes, no more comments.

The Ringo Starr song swirled in his head again as he stared at the picture of himself and the two people who used to be his best friends in the world.

He tossed his phone aside and guzzled the rest of his beer.

Night of the Batboy

(1982)

ROBBIE WAS WORRIED THAT Tommy Krasdale was too pumped up for the night. Sure, they had gone out on Halloween night before to have shaving cream fights with other kids in the surrounding neighborhoods and to throw the occasional egg at a house. But they were fifteen now, and Robbie could see that Tommy wanted to go beyond spraying some shaving cream around. They were teenagers, and Tommy wanted to act like one.

"Don't be a pussy, Miller," said Tommy.

"I'm not a pussy, Tommy," said Robbie.

"Well, you're sure as shit acting like one."

Tommy had a dozen eggs that he had lifted from his kitchen. He wanted to pick one house and pelt it with the whole dozen. Robbie didn't want to throw any eggs at any house. What was the point? But Tommy was obsessed with the idea. To him, it was some sort of rite of passage.

"Why can't we just spray some shaving cream, like we always do?" said Billy Cohen.

"You're a pussy now too, Cohen?" said Tommy.

Robbie didn't like how Tommy always seemed to want to play the tough guy these days. Maybe it was just teenage testosterone. Maybe it was the fact that his father was a tough city cop. But everything lately with him was about who was a pussy and who wasn't. Too often, it seemed that Robbie and Billy were the pussies.

So, they reluctantly followed Tommy around the corner to Plymouth Drive, looking for a house to shower with eggs. Robbie wanted no part of it, but Tommy was his oldest friend, and he didn't want to be called a pussy anymore.

"Maybe we'll get that faggot Kleinman's house," said Tommy.

Of course, thought Robbie.

Tommy had been picking on Howie Kleinman for at least a couple of years now. Robbie didn't understand what Tommy's problem with Howie was. Howie was a nerd for sure. Always had been. He was a nice kid but an easy mark for Tommy. It seemed that Tommy had become the classic bully. Robbie missed the old Tommy. Maybe Robbie was a pussy. But the new Tommy was a dick. And torturing poor Howie Kleinman seemed to be his favorite pastime.

As they approached Howie's house, they saw two things. A group of what had to be ten or twelve girls gathered around in the street halfway down the block. And Evan Kosick and his two lapdogs, Jimmy Tedeschi and John Whitfield, walking toward them.

If Tommy was now a dick, then Evan Kosick was an alpha dick and had been for years. He was a senior and had been making life hell for anyone younger than him for as long as Robbie could remember. He lived a few blocks away on Dearborn Street, so Robbie was disappointed to see that he had ventured to their neck of the woods on Halloween. Nothing good ever happened when Evan was around.

"Look at these little pieces of shit we have here," said Evan, looking at the three boys from Victory Lane.

Here it comes, thought Robbie.

"Little boys looking to cause some trouble?" said Evan.

Robbie and Tommy and Billy said nothing. What could they say? Anything they might say can and would be used against them in the Court of Evan.

"What have you got there, Krasdale?" Evan said, looking at the carton of eggs tucked under Tommy's arm.

"Just some eggs," said Tommy.

"So, the little wimps from Victory Lane want to throw some eggs on Halloween," said Evan.

His lapdogs laughed at that. They laughed at anything he said.

Before Evan could continue making the boys squirm, the growling of a big car engine distracted them all.

Everyone turned toward the sound of the engine.

Back in the middle of the street, parked next to the group of girls, was a muscle car of some kind. It looked like a '72 Buick Skylark to Robbie. Or was it a Pontiac GTO? He wasn't sure, but it looked damn cool, and the engine, even idling, was loud as hell.

The girls that now surrounded the car all looked like seniors. Robbie was surprised to see that many girls out on Halloween night. Were they going egging too?

Evan looked toward the car. "Who the fuck is that?" he said.

Robbie had never seen that car before. Whoever it was wasn't from this neighborhood.

"I don't know who the fuck that is," said Jimmy. "But that's Gina DiStefano leaning into the car window, talking to him."

"And there's Marcy Goldman next to her," said John.

"I hate those sluts," said Evan.

Robbie could sense that something was about to happen, and it wasn't going to be something good. He wanted to grab Billy and Tommy and hightail it back to Victory Lane.

But Evan turned back to Tommy.

"Gimme those eggs, Krasdale."

Tommy hesitated.

"I said, gimme those fucking eggs," said Evan.

Tommy reluctantly handed the carton to Evan. Evan opened the carton and smiled.

"Let's see how those sluts like these," he said.

He grabbed two eggs and handed the carton to Jimmy. Jimmy and John each grabbed two eggs. Jimmy handed the carton back to Tommy.

"Hold on to that, shitbird," he said as Tommy took hold of the now-half-empty egg carton.

Robbie sensed that he and the Victory Lane boys should be leaving just about now. But he was frozen. Part of him wanted to get the hell out of Dodge. And part of him wanted to see what was going to happen.

"OK, boys," Evan said to Tommy and John, "let 'em fly!"

Evan and his lapdogs each flung their two eggs down the block. They threw them high and arching, six eggs soaring through the air, heading right toward the crowd of girls.

When they landed, the boys could immediately hear screams from the girls, and the crowd quickly dispersed.

Evan laughed out loud, but his laughter ended almost as soon as it started.

The engine of the loud Buick roared to life, and the car peeled out down the street, heading straight for the boys.

Everyone froze in the middle of the street as the car raced toward them. In seconds, it was on top of them. Evan and his lapdogs dived to one side of the street. Robbie and Billy dived to the other side. Tommy must have stayed frozen for an extra second because when Robbie turned back to look for him, he saw Tommy jump out of the way of the car at the last moment. The fucking car had almost hit him.

The car screeched to a halt. Out of the passenger car came a kid who looked to be about twenty, and he chased after Evan and his boys.

Out of the driver's side, another twenty-year-old leaped, only he was holding a baseball bat. He had long hair and a bandanna and looked scary as hell.

Robbie saw Tommy—all ninety-five pounds of him—whip by him and hop over the fence of Howie Kleinman's house. He was gone! Billy looked at Robbie, his terrified eyes seeking instruction.

Robbie saw the menacing guy with the bat heading toward them.

"Move your ass, Billy!"

Billy needed no further encouragement. The boys took off toward the corner. They had to get back to Victory Lane and fast.

The kid with the bat tore after them. He was older and faster, and it was clear to Robbie that he wouldn't need long to catch them.

So, why run? thought Robbie.

Running made them look guilty. They had done nothing wrong. That asshole Evan Kosick was the guilty party.

So, Robbie stopped running and started walking casually. He hoped that Billy would follow suit, but Billy kept running.

Robbie looked behind him. The guy with the bat had now stopped running and was walking behind Robbie. Had the ruse worked? Was the kid chasing him now not sure if Robbie was one of the egg throwers?

The kid still looked like he wanted to kill Robbie. And he still had the bat in his hand.

So, Robbie kept walking, and the kid with the bat walked after him. Robbie turned onto Victory Lane. He couldn't see Billy anywhere. He must have made it home already. And no sign of Tommy either. Robbie was on his own.

He tried to keep a steady pace, but was afraid to walk any faster. He was convinced that the kid with the bat would take any hastening as an admission of guilt. And then Robbie would get pummeled.

The last eighty seconds or so that it took Robbie to get to his house seemed like an hour. Batboy kept pace with him the whole time, trailing about twenty yards.

When Robbie got to the foot of his driveway, he saw the garage door open. His father was in the garage, going through his toolbox.

Thank God!

Robbie walked up the driveway to the garage as calmly as he could. He got to his father just as Batboy reached the foot of the driveway.

"What's going on?" Robbie's father asked.

"This guy's been chasing me," said Robbie.

Robbie's father walked out of the garage to the top of the driveway. He saw the kid with the bat standing at the bottom of the driveway.

"That fucking kid threw an egg that hit my sister in the face!"

Robbie's father looked at him.

"It wasn't me!" said Robbie. "It was this kid Evan from Dearborn Street. We were just standing there."

"That's bullshit," said Batboy. "It was him and his friends." And then he took two steps up the driveway toward Robbie and his father.

And that's when Robbie's father took two steps toward Batboy. That made Batboy stop in his tracks.

"My son doesn't lie. He said it wasn't him."

"Fuck that, it was him," said Batboy, pointing the bat toward Mr. Miller's face.

Robbie's father moved two steps closer to Batboy.

"You think you're a tough guy, waving that bat in my face?"

Robbie's father had grown up in Brooklyn, and Robbie had heard many stories of the fights his dad had gotten into when he was a teenager. But he had never seen his dad like this.

Batboy still pointed the bat at Mr. Miller, but Robbie could sense that a modicum of fear had come to him.

"He fucking did it," said Batboy as he inched the bat a couple of inches closer to Mr. Miller's face.

Robbie's father grabbed the fat end of the bat and held it.

"You've got two seconds to get this bat out of my face and get the fuck out of here."

Batboy looked into Mr. Miller's eyes and continued to hold the bat.

"If you don't, I'm going to take the fat end of this bat and shove it so far up your fucking ass that it's going to come out of your throat."

Batboy stared into Mr. Miller's eyes and must not have liked what he saw. He immediately dropped the bat.

He walked away, mumbling, and headed back up the street.

"Robbie!"

Robbie turned to see his mother at the front door. She was frantic.

"Margaret Krasdale just called. She said you and Tommy got chased by some guy with a bat. Tommy didn't know where you were."

"He's fine, honey," said Robbie's father.

"I'm fine, Ma," said Robbie.

"What the hell happened?" Robbie's mother asked.

133

Robbie went inside and told the whole story to his parents. His mother suggested that maybe his days of going out on Halloween should be over. Robbie didn't disagree. He thanked his father for protecting him and went up to his room.

He put on the TV. There was never anything good on Sunday nights. He flipped to channel 2. *Archie Bunker's Place* was just starting. He liked that show, but it wasn't nearly as good as *All in the Family* used to be. He really missed that show. And he missed football. The NFL had been on strike for weeks. So, Sundays sucked lately. Especially this Sunday, with Batboy trying to kill him and everything.

He heard his name being called from outside. He got off his bed and looked out his window.

Tommy was at his parents' bedroom window across the way. Robbie opened his window.

"So, you made it home alive," said Robbie.

"Yeah," said Tommy. "I thought you and Billy were dead. That kid with the bat was crazy."

"I never saw you run so fast," said Robbie.

"I wasn't gonna let him get me," said Tommy.

"Well, thanks a lot for helping me and Billy. I guess we're not pussies anymore."

"I never said you were pussies."

"You did too, asshole."

"All right, I was just busting balls," said Tommy.

Tommy did a lot of ball busting lately. Robbie missed how it was between them when they were younger. There was no ball busting then. Just a pure friendship. Or at least purer than it felt now. Now, it was just different. He liked the old Tommy better than the new one.

They talked for a few more minutes, then said good night. They would see each other at the bus stop in the morning.

Robbie sat back on his bed. He changed the channel. *CHIPs* was on channel 4. He turned off the TV. There was never anything good on anymore. So, he pulled out his box of 45s from his closet. He rifled through the records and picked one out. "It's Too Late" by Carole King. An oldie from when he was little. He liked this one.

He put the record on his turntable, put on his headphones, and lay back on his bed.

Carole sang about things changing, about things that have died and not being able to take it anymore.

He didn't understand what any of that had meant when he was little and the song was new. But now he seemed to understand.

The Popular Table

(1984)

IT WAS THE LAST Saturday of February break, and Robbie wasn't looking forward to going back to school on Monday. It was a wasted week off—he hadn't done anything other than hanging around the house or hanging with Billy. Billy's family usually went to Florida during winter break, but his father couldn't get the time off this year.

So, he ate lunch and went over to Billy's house to see what was going on. Of course, there was nothing going on.

"This time of year stinks," said Billy. "No football to watch, no baseball, nothing."

"What about the Islanders?" asked Robbie.

"Who can get excited about regular-season hockey?" said Billy.

"Not me," said Robbie.

"That's because you're a Rangers fan," said Billy.

"Fuck you, Cohen," said Robbie.

Billy laughed. He and Robbie would argue about the Rangers and Islanders every now and then, but not as passionately as they did the

Yankees and the Mets. It was hockey after all, and even though the Islanders had won four Stanley Cups in a row, New York—and Long Island with it—was still a baseball town.

They sat in the den, watching *Wide World of Sports* on channel 7. Robbie was bored by that too. The only good part of *Wide World of Sports* was the opening credits when the "agony of defeat" guy went flying off the ski jump. The show was already long past that when the front door opened.

It was Billy's younger sister, Mindy. She had stayed over at her friend's house the night before and was just returning home.

"Where are Mom and Dad?" she asked excitedly.

"They're at the mall," said Billy. "What's wrong?"

"You're not going to believe what happened," she said.

"What?" asked Billy.

"Peter Malone got stabbed to death last night!" she said.

"What?" said Robbie. Chills ran down his spine and back up through his stomach. *What did she just say?*

"It's true," she said. "Allison's older sister, Tammy, got a call this morning from Steven Reid. He told her."

Allison was the girl Mindy stayed with the night before. Her sister, Tammy, was in Robbie and Billy's grade. She was a popular kid. So was Steven Reid. So was Peter Malone.

"Wait, back up. What happened?" asked Billy.

"I don't know all the details, but supposedly, Peter Malone and some of the other guys from East went to some bar or club in Kings Park last night, and they got into a fight with some other guys, and Peter got stabbed."

Robbie sat down on the couch. He was stunned and felt a fuzziness in his head. This couldn't be true. He had known Peter Malone since the third grade. They were good friends in elementary school. He had been to Peter's house. No, someone must be playing a prank or something. Peter Malone couldn't be dead. He was only seventeen years old.

"Are you sure about this, Mindy?" asked Robbie.

"That's what Steven Reid told Allison's sister. Why would he make it up?"

Billy looked at Robbie. "Holy shit," he said.

They went next door to tell Tommy. Tommy didn't believe it.

"He's in my English class. I saw him just before break," said Tommy, as if Peter's being in his English class somehow prevented him from dying.

Robbie had hoped that Mr. Krasdale would be home. He was a cop. Maybe he could find out what the hell happened. But he was working a shift in the city this weekend.

"It can't be true," said Robbie. He didn't say it with any kind of certainty. He said it wishfully. But something inside of him told him it was true.

Mindy was right. Who would make up something like this?

Later that night, Robbie lay on his bed, staring at the ceiling. He had spent the whole day in a fog, running over the unbelievable news in his head. But he said nothing to his parents. In his mind, if he didn't say anything about it, then maybe it wouldn't be true. If he didn't speak about it, then maybe the whole thing never happened. But he would know for sure in the morning. If Peter Malone was really murdered last night, it would be in the paper in the morning.

His mom peeked her head into his room.

"Are you OK?" she asked. "You've been acting weird all day."

"I'm fine, Ma, just relaxing."

"OK," she said. "Why don't you put your TV on or something?"

"I will," said Robbie.

He turned on the TV. MTV was on. Duran Duran. They were always on.

That night, Robbie struggled to fall asleep. When he finally did, he dreamed that he was in a field, playing catch with Peter Malone. They threw the ball to each other for a few minutes, but it was uncomfortable. Peter was bleeding through his shirt. As they continued throwing the ball, the bleeding got worse. When his entire shirt was covered in blood, Peter told Robbie that it was time for him to go, and he walked off and disappeared into the woods.

Robbie awoke early, thinking about the newspaper. He knew it was sitting in the mailbox—possibly holding the news that he dreaded. If Peter Malone was dead, it would be in *Newsday*. So, he forced himself out of bed and walked down the stairs. He grabbed his coat and walked out the front door into the frigid February air. He grabbed the paper without looking at it and ran back up the driveway and into the house.

He took off his coat and felt his hands shaking. Not from the cold, but because he was terrified to look at the paper.

He unfolded the paper and looked at the front page. Nothing there. Maybe it wasn't true. Maybe it was a prank after all. But as soon as he opened the paper to page three, there it was.

He didn't read the headline at first because he was jolted by the picture of Peter staring back at him. It was Peter's eighth grade yearbook picture from junior high.

How the hell did Newsday *get that picture?* Robbie thought as his heart nearly stopped.

The headline read "Smithtown Teen Slain in Knife Attack."

He tried to read the article, but the words weren't registering. Then he slammed the paper shut. He couldn't look at Peter's picture anymore. He remembered that picture. His hands started shaking again, and the image of a bloody Peter waking away into the woods from his dream came back to him.

His parents were shocked when he showed them the newspaper.

His mother's big blue eyes teared up. "He was in your class in fifth grade, right?" she said. "You were good friends with him."

His mom had been the class mother that year. And, yes, Robbie and Peter had been great friends that year. But a lot can change between fifth grade and eleventh grade.

"Oh, Robbie, I'm so sorry," she said. "This is too much for you to deal with at your age."

"It happens, Robbie," said his father. "I knew a kid who got killed in a fight when I was around your age."

"But you grew up in Brooklyn," his mother said. "This stuff doesn't happen around here."

Robbie's mind flashed to Mrs. Gayheart for a moment. Maybe his mother meant things like this don't happen to *kids* around here.

"What about those kids who died in that drunk-driving accident a few years ago?" his father said.

"That was an accident," his mother said. "This is murder. But we don't even know what happened. The article tells you nothing."

Robbie would get the details on Monday morning at school.

Robbie had never seen or heard the school so quiet. There were 2,500 kids in his high school, and all of them wandered around that morning in a daze. A group of popular girls cried near the main entrance of the school. Robbie had never seen any of those girls be anything but happy and beaming. Today, they were shattered.

In homeroom, there was a moment of silence in honor of Peter. All the kids were tense and uncomfortable. No one knew what to do or say. His homeroom teacher, Mr. Zielinkski, tried to explain to them that death was a part of life. But he was speaking to sixteen- and seventeen-year-olds. Nothing he said could make any sense to them.

As the day wore on, bits and pieces of what had happened trickled out from those in the know.

It basically had gone like this: Peter and five other popular guys had gone to a club in Kings Park called Late Night. All the guys were guys Robbie had known since at least junior high—a couple he had known all the way back to kindergarten. They went because even though the drinking age in New York was nineteen, this club would let you in if you were seventeen. Nineteen-year-olds got a stamp on their hands, allowing them to drink, and the seventeen- and eighteen-year-olds didn't. Robbie didn't know this. He had never even heard of the place. But there were many things he supposed that the popular kids knew about that he didn't.

When Peter and the boys arrived at the club, there was a group of toughs from Deer Park, drinking in the parking lot. Turns out, they had been turned away from the club because they were in jeans and sneakers. Late Night had a dress code. So, the Deer Park boys decided to hang in the parking lot and cause trouble instead. When the affluent boys from Smithtown showed up, the Deer Park boys decided to give them some shit. Words were exchanged, but nothing came of it. Peter and the Smithtown boys entered the club and stayed there for about two hours.

But when they left, the Deer Park boys were still in the parking lot with two more hours' worth of Budweiser in them. Words were exchanged again.

One of the Smithtown boys was Tony Pasquale. He was a little guy but had always been a hothead. Robbie couldn't remember how many fights

Tony had gotten into in junior high, but it was a lot. It was his thing. Robbie wasn't sure if Tony had started the fight that was about to happen, but Robbie was convinced that Tony had probably added fuel to the fire.

Before long, fists were flying, and soon after that, one of the Deer Park boys pulled out a knife. It struck Robbie as strange. This was Long Island, not Brooklyn. The year was 1984, not 1958. Who heard of kids pulling knives anymore? But this Deer Park kid did. And the tragic part was that it seemed he didn't intend to stab anyone. He just started waving the knife around to scare the Smithtown boys. But he got careless. Because he waved the knife behind him without looking and it ended up in Peter Malone's chest. Not for long. In fact, according to the other Smithtown boys, the knife was in and out of Peter in an instant.

When Peter fell to the ground, the Deer Park boys scrambled into their car and sped away.

Supposedly, Peter got up in an instant and said he was fine. He asked to be driven home. But in the car, he started bleeding profusely and passed out. So, the boys raced to the Smithtown General emergency room. Less than an hour after they got there, Peter was gone.

Robbie was told some version of this story several times that day, and he, in turn, told the story several times. No one talked about anything else.

The wake was scheduled for the next day. Billy Cohen's dad was going to drive Billy, Tommy, and Robbie to the wake.

Robbie had another sleepless night. He thought of how close Peter and he had been in elementary school. And he was reminded of the moment it had all changed.

When they entered sixth grade—junior high—Robbie didn't know that his relationship with Peter would change so quickly. They had been thick as thieves in fifth grade, and everyone in the class looked up to them. Mrs. Schwartz had even chosen Robbie and Peter to be opposing captains for their class during Red and White Day. Robbie captained the White team, Peter the Red.

When sixth grade started, Peter and Robbie sat at the same table in the cafeteria with a group of other boys from their elementary school. This went on for about two weeks. Then Robbie noticed that a table near them started attracting some of the "cool" kids from the other elementary school that had merged into their junior high. Some attractive girls and some confident boys. It was the only table in the sixth grade area of the cafeteria that had boys and girls at it. Robbie sensed that it would probably be a great thing if he could be at that table. The kids there were obviously having a great time. Junior high was going to be great for them.

And then, one day, without warning, Peter was at the cool kids' table. Robbie sat down at his usual table, but Peter wasn't there. A quick glance revealed Peter sitting and laughing with the popular kids. Because that is what they were or would soon be. And somehow, Peter was one of them.

How did it happen? Was he invited? Did one of the popular kids ask him why he was sitting with those losers at the other table? And why didn't Peter invite Robbie over?

Robbie was hoping to catch Peter's eyes. Hoping that Peter would wave him over to the table. But Peter never glanced back at the old table. Peter never waved Robbie over. And Robbie knew in that instant that something had changed in his life. His whole junior high experience—and high school as well—had been determined in that moment. And nothing could change it. The popular kids had established themselves at that moment, and theirs was an exclusive club that had no room for more members. They would have seven years of parties and football games and all-American teenage revelry. Robbie and the rest of them would only be able to watch from afar.

And as Robbie lay in bed, trying to fall asleep, it struck him that if Peter had waved him over that day in sixth grade, Robbie might well have been with Peter and the boys at the Late Night club. Three of the boys who were at that popular table with Peter in sixth grade were with him when he died. Yes, Robbie would have been one of the boys. And, yes, he would have gone to the club with them. It was better than sitting in his room at home, watching *Fantasy Island* and then jerking off to the *Playboy* he had hidden under his bed. And if he had been there, then the wayward knife might have landed in *his* chest.

For years, Robbie wished that Peter had taken him to the popular table with him. And now he wished that Peter had just stayed at the losers table with Robbie. If he had, he would no doubt still be alive.

The wake was at the Branch Funeral Home on Main Street. It was the same place that Robbie's grandfather had his wake ten years earlier. It was Robbie's first time back.

The parking lot was jammed, and it took a while for Mr. Cohen to find a parking spot. When they got out of the car, they all heard a radio blasting from a car that was leaving the parking lot. Robbie thought it wasn't very appropriate to be blasting a car radio in a funeral parlor parking lot. The song was "Here Comes the Rain Again" by the Eurythmics. At least the song was appropriate. Probably some stupid kids from the high school. There were certainly plenty of those.

For years afterward, whenever Robbie would hear that song, it would take him right back to Peter's wake.

The line to the casket was out into the lobby. Robbie remembered what his mother told him when his grandfather died.

"Be here now," she said.

But Robbie wanted to be anywhere but here now.

Mercifully, the casket was closed. At the head of the line was Peter's grandfather, graciously greeting each attendant, saying how he wished he could have met them under better circumstances. Robbie didn't know how the man could even stand, let alone patiently greet everyone who came up to the casket. Robbie glanced over at Peter's shattered parents, but he had to turn away. When it was his turn to kneel and pray at the casket, Robbie tried to think of happy times with Peter from when they were little. But instead, he kept thinking of that fateful day in the sixth-grade cafeteria.

A week after the funeral, Robbie and Billy sat silently in Billy's basement. They were never silent together, but there had not been much talking in the previous week. Stunned silence ruled the day.

"You think the Islanders will win a fifth Cup in a row?" Billy asked, breaking the silence.

"I don't give a fuck, Billy."

"Fair enough."

Billy turned on the old black-and-white TV in the basement. *The Brady Bunch* was on. They sat and watched in silence. Robbie took note of how lame the show was. Why had he loved it so much when he was younger?

"Hey, I was thinking the other day of how we used to play German planes when we were little," said Billy.

"Yeah?" said Robbie.

"I still can't believe that I believed that those planes were really German," Billy said.

"I can't believe that you believed it either," said Robbie. "But that's what made it fun."

Billy laughed, then returned to silence. Then he turned off the TV.

Then Billy said that the week reminded him of when Mrs. Gayheart was killed.

"It's worse," said Robbie.

"Yeah, I know," said Billy.

But Billy was right. Peter's death had brought back memories of Mrs. Gayheart. Robbie loved Victory Lane, but things had always seemed different after she was killed. There was never another block party, and the neighbors never seemed as close as they had been before. He longed for the way it was in the '70s. Everyone on the block had been so close, and all the parents hung out together, and life seemed so much more joyful.

"Be here now, Robbie," he heard his mother say in his head. "Be here now."

But he didn't want to be here now. Now was the '80s, and the '80s sucked. Now was Peter Malone lying in a casket. No, Robbie wished he could go back. But the Victory Lane he loved was gone now too.

Memorial Day

(1985)

CATHY BISHOP DIDN'T ENJOY dwelling on the past. When she did, it never brought her joy or peace of mind. So, she tried to avoid it. But it wasn't in her nature to completely bury the moments in her life that had brought her to her present. Sometimes, she just had to let those memories bubble up from below and break the surface. Now was one of those times.

It was the Friday of Memorial Day weekend, and that holiday had a way of bringing to the forefront things that she spent the rest of the year trying to keep buried.

It was hard to believe that it had been fifteen years since those fateful two weeks when Joey Barone had come home from Vietnam. Those two weeks that were the two best of her life, but had also led to the worst moment of her life.

Memorial Day always made her think of him. Made her think of all the men—no, boys—who were ruined by that war. She never saw Joey again. She had tried to keep in touch with his parents, but they moved away not long after he was committed, and the link was broken. Her family moved away not long after as well. You couldn't be a nineteen-year-old and just have a baby out of wedlock in 1970 on Victory Lane. You probably couldn't get away with it now. So, she and her family had moved back to the anonymity of Queens, and little Joey was born shortly thereafter.

When she was young, she had dreamed of going to school and meeting a nice boy and getting a house in the suburbs—something just like the one they had on Victory Lane—and having two or three kids.

But having little Joey at twenty prevented all of that. They all lived in a small house in Ozone Park. Mom and Dad helped her raise Joey, and she eventually got a job as a receptionist at St. John's University. It wasn't a bad job, but it was nothing that she had ever envisioned for herself.

Meeting a man became an impossibility. What man wanted a single mom who lived with her parents? She went on a few dates, mostly when she was still in her twenties, mostly blind dates that friends at work set her up on. But those led to nothing. Something died in her when Joey went away. Something that never came back.

She recalled seeing the movie *Looking for Mr. Goodbar* when it came out and how it freaked her out when Diane Keaton got murdered at the end. So, she never went to bars or clubs. She didn't want to end up like Diane Keaton in that movie. Not that she had the confidence or the wherewithal to pick up a guy at a bar. She didn't. But that movie ensured that she wouldn't even try.

Little Joey didn't know much about his father because there really wasn't much to tell him. He knew his dad was a Vietnam vet and that he had gotten sick and never recovered. That was all Cathy had told him, and he never asked for any more information than that. If he had, she didn't really know what she would have told him. She wasn't sure if the actual story of his mom and dad was a good story for him to know anyway.

These thoughts roamed through her mind as she sat in her kitchen and drank a glass of iced tea. Friday night at home. There was nothing new about that for her. She was waiting for her son to come home. He had gone to his friend's house after school but was due home any minute. Her parents were out to dinner with their own friends, so it was just going to be Joey and her tonight. She figured they would order a pizza.

Joey walked in and started toward the stairs, ignoring his mother as he went.

"Hello," said Cathy.

"Hi, Ma," said Joey as he continued up the stairs.

"I was going to order a pizza," she said.

"I'm good, Ma," Joey yelled down from his room. "I'm gonna go to the movies with the guys."

"What?" she said.

"We're going to the movies," he yelled down again.

When he came down the stairs, she asked him what he was going to do about dinner.

"We'll grab a slice before the movie," he said.

"What are you seeing?" Cathy asked.

"*Rambo*," he said. "It just opened today."

Cathy frowned, and Joey noticed her disappointment.

"What?" he said.

"You're really going to see that stupid movie?"

"What's stupid about it? Everyone's going."

"What about James Bond? Why don't you go see that?"

"Rambo is cooler than James Bond, Ma."

Rambo: First Blood Part II was opening that day. So was the new Bond film, *A View to a Kill*. Joey had always liked James Bond. He always watched

149

the old ones with her father when they showed them on channel 7. Why couldn't he go see that instead of Rambo?

Joey came back down the stairs with a new shirt on and his hair combed. He was ready for his night out at the movies.

"Can you sit down for a minute before you go?"

"What, Ma?" he said.

"Just sit," she said. "What time does the movie start?"

"Eight o'clock," he said.

"OK, so we have some time," she said.

Joey sulked but sat at the kitchen table across from his mother.

"How was school today?" she asked.

"Fine, Ma," he said.

"You know what happened to your father, right?" she asked.

He rolled his eyes. "Yes, Ma."

"The Vietnam War scarred and destroyed him. It's the reason he's not here. It's the reason you grew up without him."

Joey looked down at the table and said nothing.

"And this movie trivializes all of that. I mean, really, stupid Sylvester Stallone and his muscles going back to Vietnam to re-fight the war. It's an insult to the men who fought there and the men who died there, and it's an insult to your father."

"He's going to rescue POWs," said Joey.

"That's an insult too," she said. "Giving false hope to the families of the guys who are still missing in action. Using their pain to come up with a stupid movie plot. And getting kids like you all excited about it."

"I'm not a kid," he said.

"You're fourteen, Joey," she said. "You're a kid."

"Well, I don't care, Ma. I'm going to see it."

Cathy let out a breath. He was a stubborn boy and always had been.

"Fine," she said. "But just remember when you are watching it that it is bullshit and a fantasy and has nothing to do with what really happened over there."

When her son left, Cathy opened a bottle of red wine, poured herself a glass, walked to the den, and sat on the couch.

Joey never liked when she brought up his father. She understood that. It was as if bringing up his father only served to remind Joey that he didn't have one. So, he never wanted to talk about it.

She sipped her wine and thought about *Rambo*. It just pissed her off! What a stupid movie! Muscle-bound, syllable-challenged Sylvester Stallone wins the war that actual Vietnam vets couldn't! And her son was going to see it and would probably love it.

It reminded her of when Bruce Springsteen's song "Born in the USA" came out the year before. Joey loved that song and was constantly playing it on his stereo and singing it around the house. Cathy didn't mind that. She liked the song too.

But Joey—and it seemed a lot of other people—seemed to think it was this big, patriotic, flag-waving song. She tried to explain to him that it was really about the plight and struggle of Vietnam vets and how they have been mistreated. But he either didn't understand her or he just didn't care. It was strange to her how different the '80s were from the '70s. If that song had come out in the '70s, everyone would have understood its meaning. Today, it seemed that not enough did. And *Rambo? Rambo* would have been laughed at in the '70s.

When Joey returned later that night, his reaction to the movie was predictable. "Oh my God, it was so awesome, ma," he howled.

So, Cathy went to sleep that night, concerned for her son, concerned for the things in his life that were missing and the things he would never have.

151

And she thought again of Memorial Day. Would she watch one of the parades on Monday? She remembered one a few years ago that she watched with her father. First came the WWI vets, followed by the WWII and Korean vets, all clean-cut and in their neatly pressed uniforms. Then came the Vietnam vets.

"Jesus," said her father. "They look like goddamned Hell's Angels. It's disgraceful."

She thought of her son's father. Was Memorial Day for him? She knew Veterans Day was for the guys who fought and survived. And Memorial Day was for the guys who fought and died. Was she supposed to honor Joey on this day? She figured it was OK. He might not have physically died in the war. But by any reasonable metric, the war certainly killed him. So, yes, she would honor him on Monday with the rest of the boys who gave their life. And she would no longer bury his memory. He lived constantly in her thoughts and dreams, and his blood coursed through her son's veins.

So, she chose to remember, not the broken young man who was carted off to the asylum, nor the pained young man whom she so briefly loved after he returned from the war. No, she chose to remember the beautiful teenager she watched cruising to school so many times in his Chevy Biscayne, windows down, with the wind in his hair and not a care in the world.

And she remembered the girl that she was. A girl who had love to give and dreamed of a life that never came to be.

"I have learned that if you must leave a place that you have lived in and loved and where your yesteryears are buried deep, leave it any way except a slow way. Leave it the fastest way you can. Never turn back and never believe that an hour you remember is a better hour because it is dead. Passed years seem safe ones, vanquished ones, while the future lives in a cloud, formidable from a distance."

—Beryl Markham

Snow Angels

(1987)

HE SOMETIMES WONDERED WHY he had gone to college in upstate New York. The winters were brutal in Utica, and this February was worse than the last one. It had snowed in early November, and the snow had never melted. It had just piled up—one storm on top of another—and now there was a foot and a half of snow on the ground. It never got warm enough in Utica to melt.

"Let's go outside," she whispered to him.

"What?" he said. "It's the middle of the night. It's freezing out. It's freezing in here."

"Come on. It will be an adventure, Robbie," she said.

"We'll wake up Ricky," he said.

"No, we won't. He's snoring."

Mary was right. Robbie's roommate was sawing wood pretty hard across the room. He could usually sleep through anything.

She kissed him lightly on the cheek. "I promise it will be an adventure."

All he could think about was the cold. It was 2 in the morning. Was she crazy? No, she wasn't crazy. She just had a healthy appetite for life. Healthier than he had ever had. That was one of the things he loved about her. Why not go out in the snow at 2 a.m.? If he couldn't do that now, at twenty years old and not a care in the world, then when would he?

"You're crazy, Mary," he said. "Just make sure we don't wake up Ricky."

They slid out of Robbie's bed and quietly threw on their clothes and bundled themselves up in jackets and hats. Mary giggled as they got dressed, and Robbie melted inside, like he always did when she laughed. The simplest things in life could bring her so much joy, and her joy was infectious.

They quietly exited the room and quickly made their way to the back door exit of the dorm, and then they were outside in the brutal cold.

"Now what?" Robbie asked.

"The baseball field," she said.

"Why?"

"Have I ever steered you wrong, Mr. Miller?"

"No, you haven't," he said, and he kissed her on her nearly frozen lips.

"Then trust me," she said.

They held hands and trudged through the snow toward the field. This was crazy, but Robbie loved it. This girl could get him to do anything, and he loved her for it. Didn't he come to college to do crazy things like this? He let Mary guide him. He didn't feel the cold anymore.

They got near the field, and Mary fell after getting stuck in a large snowdrift. She laughed her beautiful laugh and wouldn't stop as Robbie pulled her out of the snow. They were near the top of a small hill, and as Mary stood up, she held his hands.

"Lie in front of me and hold my hands," she said.

"Why?"

"We're going to play roly-poly."

"Roly what?"

"You never played roly-poly?"

"Where did you grow up?" he asked.

"Long Island, same as you. Come on. Take my hands and lie down with me."

He laughed. Only Mary! He lay down and grabbed her hands as she lay down in front of him. They leaned toward the edge of the top of the hill.

"Let's go!" she said.

They turned toward the hill and rolled down, arms stretched out, holding hands, rolling fast, spiraling in circles over the icy snow. How crazy was this? In seconds, they were at the bottom. Mary giggled uncontrollably like only she could.

"Wooooh!" Robbie yelled toward the cold black sky above them. "Is this what you used to do as a kid?"

"Yes," she said as if it were a strange question. Didn't everyone play roly-poly as a kid? "Why? What did you play as a kid?"

"Baseball," Robbie answered.

"Then let's go onto the baseball field," she said.

They got up and walked across the field. When they got to the area between where home plate and the pitcher's mound would be, she took his hands again.

"Let's make snow angels," she said.

"What are we, eight?" he said.

"If I tell you it's going to be fun, don't you believe me?"

"Snow angels?"

"Have you ever made one?"

He thought briefly of Tommy and Billy and some of the other boys from the old block. No, they had never made snow angels.

"No."

She smiled. "Then you haven't lived."

They lay on their backs in the snow.

"Now what?" Robbie asked.

"Wave your arms and legs like you're doing jumping jacks."

Robbie and Mary waved their arms and legs with gusto. Mary giggled, and once again, Robbie melted.

They stood up to look at their handiwork.

"Holy shit," said Robbie. "They really look like angels."

"I told you," she said.

Robbie smiled and took her in his arms and kissed her frigid lips, not stopping until those lips were warm. Then he pulled her down into the snow, and she rolled on top of him. He looked up again at the black February sky. It was after 2 in the morning, and maybe it was 15 degrees outside. And yet Robbie felt nothing but warmth. This was how happiness felt. He remembered the feeling from when he was a young boy, frolicking through the neighborhood. Had he ever been happier than he was in this moment? He wasn't sure. He just didn't want the feeling to end.

"OK, I admit it, I'm getting a little cold now. Maybe it's time to go back," said Mary.

Robbie smiled at her. He took a breath and waited a second. He knew he was going to remember this moment. A few more seconds would be okay.

"OK," he said.

They got up and slogged their way back, but not before Robbie glanced behind him to catch one more glimpse of the angels in the snow.

She's Leaving Home

(2019)

SHE WATCHES LUCIA CLAMBER up the steps of the bus. She loses sight of her for a moment, blocked by the other kids. Then she catches her again, through the bus window, making her way slowly toward the back. She moves left to keep track of her daughter and sees her settle in her seat. She sees Lucia peek out the window with her gloriously big smile, and she watches as Lucia waves at her with utter joy. Lucia is not afraid! She is so happy that Lucia is not afraid.

She looks at her husband with relief. She thought they would both be crying. But Lucia is not scared! She is happy!

"I told you she would be fine," her husband says.

The bus pulls away, and Lucia waves at her parents. The first day of kindergarten awaits.

And then the tears come. She told herself she wouldn't cry, but here it is. Seeing her daughter's smile through the window has been at once the happiest and the saddest moment of her life.

"She's going to be fine," her husband says.

She tries to believe it to be true.

The bus turns the corner and disappears. She takes hold of her husband's hand. Her hands are sweaty. She feels as if she is losing something. She sees the image of Lucia smiling again at the bus window, and now the tears become a flood.

"Mom, hello? Are you there?"

She is startled and looks up. She is startled again when, instead of five-year-old Lucia standing in front of her, it is twenty-two-year-old Lucia.

"What? Yes, I'm here," she says.

"You looked like you zoned out for a second," says Lucia.

"No, not at all," she says.

But that is not true. She helps her daughter pack, but her mind is not present. Her anxiety is almost too much to bear. Her daughter has a great opportunity in California. She should be happy. But she feels nothing but dread. Again, she sees five-year-old Lucia waving in the window of the school bus. She wants to go back in time and do it all over. Time has moved too fast. It has run her over.

"Mom?"

"Yes, honey?"

"I lost you there again," Lucia says. "It's like you're not here."

"I'm here," she says.

But Lucia soon won't be, and she feels her knees begin to buckle. She is zoning out again, her mind taking her away.

She watches the hills roll by on the New York State Thruway. The ride from Long Island to Syracuse is seven hours, but she hopes it takes longer. She has dreaded this moment all summer. She had encouraged her daughter to go away to college for her entire life. The moment is here, and she feels queasy in her stomach.

She stands in front of the dorm entrance. She watches her husband hug Lucia. Now it is her turn. Lucia puts her arms around her and squeezes her tight.

"Don't worry, Mom," she says, her voice slightly cracking. "I'll be OK."

She knows at that moment that her daughter will be OK. She's just not sure about herself.

She can't pinpoint what she is feeling. But it feels like a part of her has just died. The seven-hour drive home is torturous. She and her husband hardly speak. It is worse when they get home and walk into their empty house. Another part of her dies then. She wonders how many parts are left.

"Remember this?" Lucia asks.

She looks up and sees her daughter holding an old frame. In it is a photograph of her and Lucia at the beach. Lucia is maybe three years old in the picture. The big smile was there even then. They would go to Montauk every summer when Lucia was little, but they hadn't been in years. She would hold her daughter just above the big ocean waves, and Lucia would cackle with delight as the waves splashed at her feet. Why had it been so long since they had been there? Lucia loved those waves so much. Would they ever go to the beach together again?

"Mom?"

"Yes, of course I remember, honey."

"I was going to take this with me, but maybe you want it?" Lucia asks.

She takes the picture frame from her daughter.

"Yes, I'll keep it," she says.

Lucia watches her mother drift off again.

"We can talk every day, Mom," says Lucia. "And text and FaceTime. It'll be like I'm still here."

But her mother knows it will not be like that. Deep down, Lucia knows this as well.

"You always told me that change is what keeps life exciting," Lucia says.

"Did I?"

"This will be exciting for me."

Her mother knows this is true. And she is happy for her daughter. She is feeling selfish and knows that she shouldn't. She walks toward her daughter and throws her arms around her. She buries her head in Lucia's shoulder. No words are spoken. She just needs to keep her head there for a few moments.

She and her husband sit in traffic outside of JFK. Lucia's jet has already been in the air for twenty minutes—six hours to LA, six hours to a new life, a new world. When she was a child, it seemed everyone wanted to go to California; everyone wanted to go to Hollywood. She wondered why so many people were always so eager to leave home.

At home, her husband makes a sandwich in the kitchen. He asks her if she wants one, but she does not feel like eating. He talks about how much they can get for the house and how maybe it is time to start looking for a smaller place out east. Maybe even Florida. She says nothing.

She goes upstairs and walks into Lucia's empty room. She holds the picture from Montauk and sits on Lucia's bed. She lies down and stares at the ceiling.

And then she is on the beach in Montauk. She holds little Lucia, and they walk toward the waves. She holds her daughter just above the waves, and her daughter howls with laughter as the cold ocean water splashes her little feet. She looks out at the ocean, and the bright sun looks back at them, lying to them, making them believe that things will always be this way and nothing will ever change.

When the Snow Melts

(1987)

RICKY HAD BEEN TRYING his best to get Robbie out of his funk. But a broken heart does not heal quickly or easily.

"Your buddies, alcohol, and music are how you get yourself out of this," Ricky told him.

"I've been getting drunk four times a week for the last three weeks," said Robbie. "Does it look like it's helping?"

"No, you look like shit, Ray," he said, invoking the nickname Robbie's college friends gave him. "Maybe you need to start drinking five days a week."

Robbie laughed. "And the music thing isn't helping either," he said.

"That's because you're not listening to the right music," said Ricky. "Why do you keep listening to the Carpenters? You're supposed to be listening to sad, breakup music."

"Nobody has a sadder voice than Karen Carpenter," said Robbie.

"It's not breakup music, Ray."

"What do you suggest then?" Robbie asked.

"I don't know. Why don't you try that Bruce Hornsby album that you listened to nonstop last semester? There's some sad shit on there."

They were sitting at Spilka's, the dive bar that most of the people at their small college hung out at. It was a Tuesday night, and they pretty much had the place to themselves. The drinking age was upped to twenty-one the previous year, but it didn't matter. Pretty much everyone on campus had a fake ID, and the bartenders at Spilka's didn't care how fake they looked. As long as you showed them something with the right date on it. They were drinking Old Milwaukee on tap. Fifty cents a draft in plastic cups. They were already five drafts in.

Robbie stood up and sauntered over to the jukebox. He popped in a quarter and took Ricky's advice. He selected Bruce Hornsby's "Mandolin Rain" and U2's "With or Without You." Yes, those songs were appropriate for his current state of mind. Would they work? Would they maybe momentarily take away the pain?

He walked back to the bar as the first song came on.

"That's more like it," said Ricky.

Robbie sat down. He listened to the sad Bruce Hornsby song, listened to him sing about his broken heart, about the girl who ran away from him, about tears rolling down his face, and for a moment, it helped. But only for a moment. He drank his beer and looked at Ricky.

"So, I've got my beer, I've got my sad song, and I've got my best buddy with me," Robbie said. "So, why do I still feel like shit?"

Ricky laughed. "It ain't that easy, Ray."

"Yeah, I didn't think so."

He finished his draft and ordered another.

He turned to Ricky. "Who the fuck goes back to their high school boyfriend three years into college? It doesn't make sense, Rick."

"I know," Ricky said. "It's her loss."

"I didn't see it coming. Everything was going so well."

"Nobody sees it coming, Ray."

"I never knew it could feel like this. You see movies and listen to songs about broken hearts, and it just seems like a plot point or something. I didn't know it could feel like this. I'm twenty fucking years old. I'm not supposed to feel like this."

"You'll get over it. Everybody does. It just takes time."

"That sounds like a cliché," said Robbie.

"It is," said Ricky. "But it's also true."

Robbie smiled. Maybe the beer and the music and his best friend were helping. But would they help when he tried to sleep tonight? Would they help when he awoke in the morning? He'd had too many sleepless nights lately. He longed for Mary's warm body next to his. That she would never lie next to him again filled him with dread.

They drank some more, and Ricky tried to make Robbie laugh. He even succeeded occasionally. But they couldn't sit here all night. They would have to leave eventually. And Robbie would try to sleep, try to block out the pain, the pain that the beer and Bruce Hornsby only temporarily numbed.

Back in their room, Ricky was soon snoring. Robbie stared at the ceiling, drunk, but not drunk enough to pass out. His brain would not relent; it would not succumb to the Old Milwaukee, like Robbie had hoped.

Instead, he thought about Mary, like he did every night. He hadn't been looking when he found her. They had become friends, and she had a serious boyfriend back home. He never thought of her as a potential love interest. Maybe that's why he was so relaxed around her. He wasn't trying to impress her, wasn't trying to be something he wasn't. So, maybe she was the first girl to really see the real Robbie. And he was good with her, maybe the best version of himself. At least, that's what he told himself. He liked who he was when he was with her. He wasn't sure if he liked who he was now without her. He thought of Thursday nights at Spilka's, when the drift of the night might take them to opposite sides of the bar. But then they would catch each other's eyes across the room, and they would lock on to each other, and it would feel like coming home, and they would fight their way through the crowded room until they found each other, and everything would instantly be right with the world. Now, when they saw each other across the bar, she would put her head down because she couldn't stand to see the hurt she had put in his eyes.

After about twenty minutes, Robbie had had enough. He was not going to stare at the ceiling anymore. He was not going to torture himself this way. So, he crawled out of bed and threw on his jeans and walked out of the room and out of the dorm and into the night.

It had been a warm spring. It surprised him how cold the winters in Utica were, but for the second year in a row, they were having an early and warm spring.

He needed to walk. He wasn't going anywhere in particular; he just needed to feel the air on his face. Maybe that would help. So, he walked—the only person awake on campus, it seemed.

He walked, and though he tried not to, he, of course, thought of Mary, thought of her head resting on his chest, thought of her giggle and all the silly things they used to do together. He wondered if the joy she had given him had been worth the hell he was now going through.

He walked on, and his brain worked overtime, his memories of Mary running on a constant loop. Pleasure and pain fused together, tormenting him. Damn, he was too young for this! He thought about how Mary and he

166

sort of looked alike and how people sometimes thought they were brother and sister. Mary had even joked that if they had kids together, no one would know which one of them the kids looked like. Suddenly, images of the kids they would never have together flashed across his mind. Yes, he was too young for these thoughts. But the images kept coming.

"I never meant to hurt you," she said to him.

He believed her. He could see it in her eyes. This was hurting her too. But it was no solace to him.

She put his hand on her heart. "A part of you will always be with me," she said.

But what good did that do Robbie? What did it even mean? She was leaving him, and he was lost without her.

Shut off the loop. Enough, he told himself. *Stop thinking about it. Turn off your brain.*

It was like he was watching a movie trailer that he had seen too many times. He didn't want to watch it anymore.

He walked on until he realized that he was on the small hill above the baseball field.

He remembered the time they had come here not too long ago in the freezing cold, rolling down the hill, arm in arm, like a couple of kids. He would always remember this spot. Did he know that this is where he was walking to? The last time he was here, it was freezing, and there was a foot of snow on the ground. On this night, the air was warm, and the grass was bare. And this time, he was alone. It was remarkable how things could change in only a few months.

Tears came to his eyes, and then he broke down. Suddenly, he was the guy in the Bruce Hornsby song. Maybe this is what he needed. Maybe he just needed to cry it out. Yes. Beer, music, your best friend, and a good cry.

He would have to tell Ricky in the morning that a good cry was the missing ingredient in his broken-heart tonic.

But he wasn't sure of that, of course. The release of the tears felt good for a moment. But he saw her face as the tears flowed, and that did not feel as good.

Oh, my sweet Mary, why?

After a minute, the crying stopped. God, he was being such a pussy!

Get ahold of yourself!

How in the hell had he gotten to this point?

He gathered himself and walked down the hill and over to the baseball field. He stood on the grass between home plate and the mound. He and Mary had made snow angels on this very spot just a few months earlier. Wasn't that a glorious moment? It already seemed like a lifetime ago.

Time will heal this, he told himself. Time is supposed to heal everything.

Ricky did say it would take time, and Ricky had never steered him wrong. But he wasn't certain it was true. Maybe it will never heal. Maybe it will always be there, under his skin, like a relentless itch that you can never reach.

But he knew he would have to come to grips with it and accept it. What other choice did he have? Because no matter how much he wanted her back, no matter how much her memory infected his mind, he knew that the snow had melted, and the angels in that snow were gone forever.

He suddenly felt foolish. What was he doing by himself at the baseball field in the middle of the night? He turned around and headed slowly back to the dorm.

The Summer That Came and Went

(2019)

THE RECEPTION AREA OF the Zenith Time Travel Corporation was not at all what Mike Gardner had expected. It was drab and dated and cheap. Could this really be where his time-travel escapade would begin?

"Mr. Brandauer will see you now, Mr. Gardner," the receptionist said.

"Thank you," he said.

"Right through that door," she said.

He stood up and promptly walked through the door.

That's more like it, he thought.

The hallway beyond the door looked like something out of a science fiction movie. If he was going to go time-traveling, he wanted the company that was sending him on his way to look the part.

"Down the hall this way, Mr. Gardner," a voice from nowhere said.

He walked to the end of the hall and opened the door.

"Mr. Gardner, welcome."

"Hello," said Mike.

"Charles Brandauer, Director of Operations," the man said. "Please sit."

Mike sat and took measure of the man before him. Armani suit, silk tie, tanned. He was expecting a scientist of some sort. More of an Albert Einstein type. This guy looked like, well…this guy looked like Mike.

"You work at Goldman downtown, I understand," said Brandauer.

"Yeah, that's right," said Mike.

"You know Bill Wainright?" asked Brandauer.

"Billy? Yeah, I know him. Bit of a prick, but so am I, I suppose," Mike said.

Brandauer laughed.

"You know a lot of Wall Street people, Mr. Brandauer?"

"Some of our best customers are Wall Street people, Mr. Gardner."

"I bet they're all pricks too," said Mike.

"I don't comment on the character of our clients."

"That's probably a good thing," said Mike.

He didn't think much of his own character, and he imagined that most of the rich clients of the Zenith Time Travel Corporation were similarly challenged in that department. His father came from Wall Street, and he himself had worked there his entire adult life. He knew what he and his compatriots of finance were like.

"So, do you have any questions about the process?" Brandauer asked.

"A million," said Mike. "But I have friends who have used this service, and they assure me that it works. So, I wouldn't even know where to start. So, I think I'm good to go."

"And where is it that you would like to go, Mr. Gardner?"

"Montauk, summer of 1989."

"Very good," said Brandauer. "But we'll need a more precise time than just 'summer,' Mr. Gardner. Remember, you can only go back for three hours."

"I'm still working that out," Mike said.

"Of course," said Brandauer. "You have until tomorrow morning to decide."

"I'll be ready. I've only been waiting for this for thirty years."

"Interesting," said Brandauer. "May I ask why Montauk in the summer of 1989?"

"Sure. Why not?" Mike said.

He shifted in his chair. He was surprised that he wanted to tell Brandauer just why. Who the hell was Brandauer to know anything about him or his motivations for undertaking this crazy time-travel adventure? But he wanted to tell someone. It was almost like confession—something he hadn't done since he was a kid.

"I want to go back and see the first and only girl I have ever truly loved," said Mike.

"Very interesting," said Brandauer.

"You see, Mr. Brandauer, you are looking at a twice-married, twice-divorced fifty-two-year-old man who has at various times in his life been a shitty husband, a shitty boyfriend, a shitty friend, and a selfish bastard to boot. My first wife was gorgeous, a beautiful piece of ass that any man would have given his right arm for. And she was a good person too. But I was cheating on her before we even got married, and it got worse after. Why? No real reason why, other than the fact that I was a rich asshole who constantly had women throwing themselves at me and, like a kid in the candy store, I couldn't resist. My second wife wasn't as hot, but she was still damn attractive, and she was a better person than the first one. But old habits die hard, don't they?"

Mr. Brandauer listened intently. He enjoyed listening to clients explain their motivations.

"I wasn't much better with friends either," Mike continued. "Perhaps I picked up some of these things from my father, but it's not entirely fair to blame it all on him. Maybe Wall Street gets some of the blame. But I'm not sure of that either. I mean, does Wall Street turn people into assholes, or does it attract them?"

Mike cleared his throat. This was easier than he thought. "But I wasn't always an asshole. No, there was a time when I was young and pure and kind, and the only thing I wanted was to write a book and sit on a beach and fall in love with a kindred spirit. I didn't give a shit about my father's money and never gave a thought to working on Wall Street. I mean, what could be more boring or soulless than Wall Street? Yes, the asshole sitting before you was a good person once. And I was never better than when I was with her. I've missed her so much these last thirty years, and I've missed the person I was when I was with her."

Thoughts of her danced through his mind. It gave him the chills.

"I first saw her running across Old Montauk Highway with her cousin one morning. I was in my father's Mercedes convertible, driving back to our summer beach house after picking up bagels in town. That road is hilly, and it curves, and I almost drove right off the fucking thing. She was laughing, and her smile was brighter than the fucking ocean sun that she was running toward, and I think I fell in love right at that moment. I stopped the car and watched her and her cousin head over the dunes toward the beach. I wanted to chase after her. I think I would have, too, but a big Cadillac almost rammed me in the ass, so I had to drive on. But I couldn't stop thinking about her."

Just thinking about it again filled him simultaneously with joy and pain.

"I didn't have long to wait to see her again. I cruised that section of the beach for the next two days, but she wasn't there. I was bummed. I figured I would never see her again. That smile she flashed was burned into my brain, and it was killing me that I would never see it again.

"But the next night, my cousin Joe and I went to a little bar at the end of the beach. One of those little fish-and-chip places that there used to be so many of in Montauk. Have you been to Montauk, Mr. Brandauer?"

"No," Brandauer said. "I've been to the Hamptons a few times, but never out to Montauk."

"Well, don't bother. It's just like the Hamptons now. Crowded, with a lot of young, drunk Manhattanites spilling down the road from East Hampton. They've pretty much ruined the place. But back then, back in 1989, it was a nice, little, sleepy seaside town. And it had a lot of these little, casual, waterside restaurants, where the fishing boats would ride right up to the restaurant. It was at one of these places that I saw her next."

Mike cleared his throat and went on.

"My cousin and I walked into the place and sat at a booth. We ordered a pitcher of beer from the waitress, and as I filled my cousin's glass, I saw that smile across the room, and I damn near spilled the whole pitcher of beer. There she was, sitting in a booth across the room with another girl. I must have frozen for a second because Joe asked me what the hell my problem was. I tried to make eye contact with her, but I looked away each time our eyes met. That's how nervous I was. Eventually, I got up and went to the jukebox. And wouldn't you know it? She followed me there. My heart was pounding so hard that I thought she might hear it. She asked what song I played. 'Every Rose Has Its Thorn' by Poison, I told her. She frowned and told me she might dance with me if I picked something better. So, I quickly scanned the jukebox and looked for something more suitable to dance to and, more importantly, something that I thought she might like.

So, I picked 'Goodbye Yellow Brick Road.' Thank God she liked that choice. She told me to meet her in the middle of the room when the song came on."

"Good song," Brandauer said.

"Yeah, so you know how that song starts with those piano chords? As soon as it comes on and I hear that piano, she gets up from her booth and saunters out onto the floor with that smile and bright green eyes looking right through me. So, I get up and meet her on the floor, and we start slow-dancing. Now it's obviously not a dance song, but it's slow enough to slow-dance to. So, she puts her arms over my shoulders, and we're dancing. And I got hard immediately. Like, right away, in a way that's never happened before, and I'm afraid that she's gonna feel it and think I'm some kind of pervert or something. But it's too late. And you know what? She didn't mind because she pulled me closer, and there was no hiding it then. I don't think I've ever been that hard before or since. Then she starts singing the song to me softly, and I swear I never wanted to leave that dance floor, and I never wanted the song to end, and, yes, I wanted my future to lie with her beyond the yellow brick road or anywhere else she wanted to go."

Mike Gardner took a breath. Telling the story had his heart racing. He could have stayed on that dance floor with her forever.

"Her name was Tina Ricci, and she was staying at her cousin's house near Old Montauk Highway for the summer. She was from Westchester and had just finished her junior year at Binghamton. I told her that I had just finished my junior year at NYU and was also here for the summer. She then told me that means we would be seeing a lot of each other this summer. And that was fine with me. The whole time we danced, I couldn't get over her eyes. Yes, my dick was hard, but this was so much more than sexual. It was as if I had been lost at sea my entire life, and when I looked into her eyes, I was finally home.

"She had to leave the bar soon after the song ended to go to dinner with her cousin's family. But she told me that she and her cousin would be at the beach near the Breakers Motel the next morning, the same spot where I first saw her crossing the street. I told her I would see her there. She gave me a quick kiss on the cheek, and I almost buckled at the knees."

Mike crossed his legs. "I'm not boring you, Mr. Brandauer, am I?" he asked.

"Not at all, Mr. Gardner. You're quite the raconteur. Please continue."

"The next morning, my cousin and I hit the beach around 10 a.m., and there she was, lying on a blanket with her cousin. I was worried that I was being too zealous by showing up so early, but she was happy to see me, which put me at ease. She looked beautiful again, of course. She had on a string bikini, like the kind you used to see in those days. Not a thong or anything like that, but it was sexy as hell. But she was so much more than that.

"We walked and talked on the beach. She was an English major and loved to read books. I loved that she loved that. I had to tell her that I was a business major. There can't be a major blander than that, but that's what my father insisted on. But I told her that I loved to read and wanted to write a book one day. She asked what I would write about, and I told her I had no idea. She laughed and then asked what I liked to read. I told her that my favorite book was *The Bonfire of the Vanities*, and she said she loved that book! This was great. None of the girls I hung out with at school read anything, let alone something by Tom Wolfe. Then she told me that I hadn't lived long enough yet to have anything significant to write about, and I told her she was probably right."

"We went back to the blanket and continued talking. She liked Duran Duran, and I liked Guns N' Roses. But we found common ground. I told her that I liked 'Hungry Like the Wolf,' and she told me that she liked

'Sweet Child O' Mine.' But we both liked U2. She pulled out a cassette of *The Joshua Tree* and put it in her boom box, and we lay there and listened to the music. When 'I Still Haven't Found What I'm Looking For' came on, I had to disagree with the sentiment of the song. In Tina Ricci, I had found exactly what I was looking for.

"We met the next night for dinner at the Shagwong on Main Street," said Mike.

"The what?" asked Brandauer.

"The Shagwong. It's a restaurant. Don't ask me where it got that name—I don't know—but it's been in Montauk forever. Still there today. She wore a cute sundress and flashed that movie-star smile at me when she arrived. God, when I think of that smile…"

Mike's eyes drifted faraway for a moment. Then he caught himself.

"Sorry," he said. "Sometimes, when I think of her, I get distracted. If you ever saw that smile and those eyes, you'd know what I'm talking about. But I digress.

"We met for dinner at the Shagwong. She had the swordfish. I had steak. Isn't that funny? I can't remember what I had for lunch yesterday, but I can tell you what I ate that night thirty years ago. I drank beer; she drank strawberry daiquiris. We both had fun showing our IDs that had only recently allowed us to drink legally. We talked about school and what we wanted to do in the future. She wanted to be an English professor. I told her I was probably headed to Wall Street, like my dad. She asked why I would do that. Didn't I learn anything reading *The Bonfire of the Vanities*? Did I really want to be one of those arrogant 'masters of the universe' fools from that book? What about the book I wanted to write? 'Maybe I'll write a book about Wall Street,' I told her. She told me I could do better than that. She was probably right. Sometimes, I would get distracted when she spoke to me though. She was so beautiful that I would get lost sometimes in her gaze.

"After dinner, we walked around town and got some ice cream and then went to the bookstore. We browsed the books and decided to pick out a favorite book for the other to read. I picked out *Lonesome Dove* for her, and she chose *The Prince of Tides* for me. I still love that book to this day because it makes me think of her.

"We left the bookstore and walked to the beach. We took off our shoes and walked down to the surf. The water was cold on our feet, but I didn't mind. I was in the perfect place with the only person in the world that I wanted to be with. We held hands, and she looked at me with those damned eyes of hers, and we kissed. And I'm telling you, it was like a movie, like I could hear the music swell up in the background as our lips met for the first time. It was a long kiss, and I'm not sure exactly how long it was, but it felt endless, in a good way. When we stopped, all I wanted was to do it again. I held her in my arms as the waves lapped our feet, and I swear if I had died right at that moment, I would have lived a happy life."

Mike felt his heart racing. Just telling the story and reliving the moments thrilled him.

"After that first kiss, we were inseparable. We would meet every day on the beach and would meet after dinner every night. My father couldn't understand why I was spending so much time with one girl. But even he liked her, and he rarely liked anyone. We did as much as you could do in a small beach town like Montauk. We ate fish and chips at Gosman's Dock, we visited the lighthouse, we played miniature golf. We went to the movies—"

"What movies did you see?" asked Brandauer.

"*Indiana Jones and the Last Crusade*, the one with Sean Connery in it, and *Lethal Weapon 2*. Remember it like it was yesterday."

"Sorry for the interruption," said Brandauer. "Continue."

"Well, whatever we did, we laughed and frolicked like kids. I never felt so carefree in all my life. When I was with her, the rest of the world didn't exist. When I wasn't with her, she was all I could think about.

"One night, we were back at the Shagwong, having drinks. She said we should go to the beach. So, we finished our drinks and walked—no, trotted—to the beach. It was a weeknight, and it was late—maybe 11 p.m.—so no one was around. She started dropping pieces of clothing as she ran toward the waves. I didn't hesitate. I was naked by the time I hit the water, where she was waiting for me, her naked body shining in the moonlight. We embraced and fell into the water. It was freezing, but I didn't care. My beautiful Tina was there with me in all her glory, and, goddammit, it was not possible for anything in the world to be better than this. We eventually made it back to the sand and attempted to make love right there on the beach, like you've seen so many times in the movies. Unfortunately, we found out that movie sex is bullshit. Did you ever try to do it on the beach?"

"No," said Brandauer. "I can't say that I have."

"Well, don't," Mike said. "We tried it, and after getting sand in all kinds of places that you don't want sand, we threw in the towel. But that didn't stop us. The horse was out of the barn, and we needed to consummate this relationship immediately. We scrambled to put our clothes back on and dashed back up the dunes and into the town. Where could we go? We passed a couple of alleyways and gave it some consideration. Isn't that a place that they always do it in movies too? But, really, how are you going to do it, standing up in an alleyway, and actually enjoy it? So, that wasn't an option either. So, we walked down Main Street, and then I saw it. The Memory Motel. Have you ever heard of that place, Mr. Brandauer?"

"I can't say that I have," said Brandauer.

"There's an old Rolling Stones song from the '70s called 'Memory Motel.' The song is about the actual place in Montauk. Mick Jagger had a one-night stand there once and wrote the song about it. It even has a sign outside that says, *The motel that rock 'n' roll made famous*. It's a hole in the wall. I can't believe Jagger went there. But it was perfect for our moment."

Mike reflected on the song for a moment. He sang it in his head. "Memory Motel." Boy, wasn't that the truth?

"So, I took out my new American Express card that my dad signed me up for," Mike continued, "and just like that, we had a room at the Memory Motel. And then we made love, slowly, taking our time, enjoying this gift from God, reveling in the pure pleasure and joy of the moment. I was a whole person now. What's that line from that Tom Cruise movie? 'You complete me'? Well, she did. Tina Ricci made me whole, and I wanted nothing more than to be with her every waking moment of every day.

"The summer rolled along slowly, the days blending into one another. It's tough to remember a time like that, a time without responsibility, a time when your only daily concern was what amusement you might pursue that day. But whatever it was, I knew I would pursue it with her. So, it really didn't matter what we did because as long as I did it with her, I was happy. We were happy.

"You know, she once told me that she didn't know why I liked her so much. She thought that she was too plain or down-to-earth for me. That I needed someone more cosmopolitan than her. And I didn't know what she meant because I thought she was the most cosmopolitan girl I had ever met, and the last thing I thought was that she was plain. I mean, she was so goddamn beautiful. Plain? There was nothing plain about her. I was the plain one.

"So, we lay on the beach, and we read our books and listened to music on her boom box, and we snuck off to make love whenever we could. I wished we could stay there forever. But nothing lasts forever, Mr. Brandauer, and that summer, like all summers, had to come to an end.

"I assumed we were boyfriend and girlfriend. I was already thinking about how many weekends I could get away from NYU in the fall to visit her at Binghamton. But every time I mentioned it, she would change the subject. The fateful moment came in late August, a few days before we were both scheduled to go back to school. We were at the same shack where we first met, eating fish and chips and drinking tap beer. I mentioned coming to visit her on Labor Day weekend. She didn't say anything at first. And then she told me what a great summer she had had and thanked me for being such a great guy and how she would always cherish these memories. Then she put her hand on her heart and told me that a piece of me would always be there."

Mike Gardner sat back in his chair. He felt exhausted after that last part. He didn't like or understand that last part. He certainly had played it over in his mind countless times before and had never reached a satisfactory conclusion as to what exactly had happened.

"That was it?" Brandauer said. "No further explanation?"

"It's hard to remember now," said Mike. "Something about going back to school and focusing on her studies and not being able to be a girlfriend to anyone right now and long-distance relationships don't work, and blah, blah, blah. I was shocked. I couldn't understand what she was saying. What about what we had? What about this wonderful, magical summer that we just spent together? How could it be over just like that?

"You know, I had a roll of film full of pictures that I took of us that I got developed two weeks later, and I cried, looking at them. Cried. Like a baby. They were all I had left of her. I tried to contact her at Binghamton, but I couldn't track her down. It was like she vanished. I kept those pictures. I even kept them after I got married. Maybe that's why my marriage failed. That, and because I could never forget Tina. My wife wasn't Tina. She could never be Tina. And neither could my second wife and all the girls I had before, during, and after my marriages. And I still have those pictures. There's one of us standing by the water on Gosman's Dock. I look at that picture, and I can almost go back and feel like I am still there with her. But I'm not."

"It seemed like you both had something really special," said Brandauer. "But of course, if it had all worked out, you wouldn't be sitting here before me right now. Of course, we can give you the chance to be back with her. Have you decided what moment you would like to go back to?"

"Believe me, I've put a lot of thought into it. At first, I wanted to go back to the moment when she ended it. Just to see if I can somehow figure out what happened. But that would be too painful. I don't want any more pain. No, I want to see her again as she looked when I first met her. I want to feel that rush that I haven't ever felt again. I want to go back to that first moment at the jukebox. I want to see those eyes and that smile the way they looked that day. I want to feel again the way I did at that moment, Mr. Brandauer. I want to go back to Montauk, New York, on June 3, 1989, at 3 p.m."

"And so you shall, Mr. Gardner. Come back tomorrow at 9 a.m., and we'll send you on your way."

Mike Gardner paced around his apartment in Battery Park City in Lower Manhattan. He had lived there only about a year, since the divorce. His wife got the house in Connecticut. Well, she deserved it, didn't she? He looked out the window and saw the lights of the Freedom Tower staring back at him. There's something that wasn't there thirty years ago. He thought about the journey he was about to take. It was still hard to comprehend that he would be back in 1989 in the morning. What a crazy world.

He looked at his bookshelf. Most of his books were still at the house in Connecticut, but he had brought a few with him. There was the old paperback he was looking for—*The Prince of Tides*. It was certainly worn out after thirty years. He read it only the one time—that summer—but just looking at the cover reminded him of her. He remembered how he had always wanted to write a book and how Tina had encouraged him. But he could never figure out what to write about. Then life and Wall Street and wives had gotten in the way. The writing never happened. He wondered if Tina had ever finished *Lonesome Dove*. He wondered so many things about her. He even tried to locate her in recent years on Facebook, but she was nowhere to be found. Was she one of those people who was afraid of Facebook? Or could it be possible that she wasn't even alive? She could have died twenty years ago in an accident or from cancer, and he would have no way of knowing that. For him, she had simply vanished into thin air. But where she was or wasn't at this moment didn't matter to him. What mattered was that he was going to see her tomorrow. His sweet angel, Tina. One more day. How would he sleep?

———————

At 9:15 a.m. on September 19, 2019, Mike Gardner lay in the transportation chair at the Zenith Time Travel Corporation.

Mr. Brandauer had wished him well and said, "Say hi to Tina."

Fuck him. Mike didn't like the guy. This had nothing to do with him. This was about Mike and Tina. Mike and Tina—he liked saying that in his head, like a schoolboy who draws a heart on his notebook cover with his and his sweetheart's names in it.

I will see you soon, my love.

He was handed a red pill. "This is like that movie with Keanu Reeves?" said Mike. "How exactly does this send me back in time?"

"It would take too long to explain it," the technician said. "We've got to get you on your way now."

"Well, here goes nothing," Mike said as he swallowed the pill.

He awoke as if from a deep sleep. He was lying on the grass somewhere.

"A little late in the day to be passed out, dude."

He looked up and saw two teenage boys looking at him and laughing.

Look at those mullets on their heads! Holy shit.

The fucking pill or whatever it was actually worked.

He stood up slowly and tried to get his bearings. He quickly looked around and saw that he was smack dab in the middle of town, right in the middle of the grass roundabout off Main Street. There was the Shagwong off to his left! And in front of him was the corner diner. In 2019, it was a gourmet taco shop. But there were no taco shops or sushi places in 1989 Montauk. Just diners and seafood places. And a big Mercedes drove past him, and he realized that the car looked big to him now. In 1989, that car was considered small.

But he didn't have time to soak in the sights and sounds of 1989. He had to get to the Liars Saloon. He wanted to get there before Tina showed up and before his twenty-one-year-old self arrived as well. He wanted to grab a booth in the back, where he could be inconspicuous and quietly observe his first meeting with his beloved Tina. He was concerned they would recognize him, but only slightly. He had added 30 years of age and about 50 pounds to disguise himself. And a lot less hair. But to be safe, he brought a pair of sunglasses to hide his face.

The Liars Saloon was probably a 20-minute walk north of the town. When he got there, he was a little winded and sweaty. He reminded himself that he probably needed to lose some weight when he got back to the future. Or the present or whatever the hell it was.

He walked in and felt a rush of nostalgia. The Guns N' Roses song "Patience" was playing on the jukebox. He loved that song. And he was going to need some patience now because he was about to jump out of his shoes with excitement. The anticipation was killing him. Tina Ricci was going to walk in this bar with her cousin soon, and he could barely contain himself.

He walked to the bar and ordered a Budweiser on tap. He took notice of the taps behind the bar. Budweiser, Miller Lite, and Busch. Not a Sam Adams or a Blue Moon to be found. This was truly 1989.

He paid for his beer and walked toward the jukebox. There were only a few scattered patrons in the place, mostly local fishermen. It was 3:30 p.m., so most people were still at the beach. He scanned the jukebox. Poison, Guns N' Roses, Ratt, U2, Van Halen, and some older stuff too. Led Zeppelin, the Stones and, yes, there it was—Elton John's "Goodbye Yellow Brick Road." He smiled at that one.

He sat at a booth in the back, sipped his beer, and contemplated his situation. How insane was it that he was sitting here in 1989, waiting to see his love? He decided maybe that Mr. Brandauer wasn't such a bad guy after all. This crazy time-travel thing fucking worked! He decided he would kiss Brandauer when he got back.

He heard laughing and turned toward the door, and there she was. His heart stopped for a moment. Tina Ricci and her cousin came walking in the bar, talking and laughing. Mike was frozen in his chair, instantly enchanted by her smile, just like he had been thirty years earlier.

They sat down in the booth in front of his and continued chattering. Mike told himself to calm down. His heart was going 100 miles per hour. His angel looked as beautiful as he remembered. Streaks of sunlight shone on her light-brown hair, and her green eyes were brilliant in that same light. And of course, that smile. It wasn't hard to remember now why he fell in love with her.

He listened to them chattering about the beach for a while, but it was hard for him to focus on what they were saying. He was just enjoying hearing the sweet music of her voice again. He had never forgotten what she had looked like, but he realized at this moment that he had forgotten what her voice sounded like. But like an old smell from childhood, he recognized it immediately. It felt like coming home.

He heard noise at the door again and looked up to see his next shock of the day. He watched in astonishment as his twenty-one-year-old self came walking into the bar with his cousin Joe. Goose bumps formed on his arms as he gaped at the bizarre spectacle of his younger self walking not more than twenty feet from him.

Young Mike Gardner sat in a booth with his cousin as old Mike Gardner continued to watch in amazement. He knew he was going to see his younger self, but was not prepared for how jarring it would be. He downed half of his beer to calm himself. And he adjusted his sunglasses to make sure they were firmly planted on his face.

And then he watched young Mike Gardner trade glances with Tina Ricci. This made him feel good. The Mike and Tina show, canceled thirty years ago, was about to be renewed.

Young Mike got up and walked to the jukebox, and Tina Ricci soon followed. Old Mike watched intently as the soon-to-be young lovers chatted together. Then they parted and went back to their booths.

But when "Goodbye Yellow Brick Road" came on, the two lovebirds walked to the center of the bar and began their slow dance. This is what Mike Gardner had come to see.

As he watched them dance, he felt as if he was out there with them. Look how his younger self held her! It was obvious that he was already in love with her. And look at her, softly singing the song in his ear. She was already in love with him.

Me, thought old Mike. Oh, this was glorious!

Yes, it was as perfect of a moment as he remembered. Look at the two of them. They were utterly sublime together. Why would she ever leave him?

The dance ended, and the two sweethearts continued talking. Mike watched them raptly. How he wished he could trade places with his younger self. He wished he could relive the entire summer with her. But he would have to content himself with watching them from a distance. He was cognizant that his time here was running out. The three hours would be over soon.

He watched young Mike say goodbye to Tina. They would see each other in the morning on the beach and begin their euphoric summer. He envied them.

Tina walked back to her booth and sat across from her cousin. Mike listened, of course. He wanted to hear what Tina had to say about him.

"So, what was that all about?" asked the cousin.

"What?" said Tina. "He's really cute."

"What about Will?"

"What about him?" said Tina.

"Well, you're practically engaged to him," the cousin said.

"So, I just had one little dance with a cute guy," said Tina.

"One little dance! It looked like you were going to have sex right there on the dance floor."

Mike listened closely. Who the fuck was Will? Almost engaged? What the hell was this?

"He seems really nice. Will is in Europe for the summer. A little summer fling while he's away won't kill anyone," said Tina.

Mike's heart sank, and he felt himself starting to shake.

"Summer fling? You don't seem like the summer-fling type."

"Well, I'm twenty-one, and, yes, I'm probably going to marry Will," said Tina. "So, this is the last time in my life I can be free before I settle down after school. So, what's the harm if I have an innocent summer fling?"

"Well, what if it ends up being more than that?" her cousin said. "What if you end up developing real feelings for this guy?"

"I just met him. Relax," said Tina.

"But I know you. You're not one for casual relationships. I could see you falling for this guy."

"Maybe," said Tina. "But even if I did, the decision has already been made. I'm marrying Will. If I spend the summer with this guy, then so be it. I'll end it when the time comes."

"OK, it's your life," her cousin said.

"I had one dance with him. I'm sure nothing will come of it."

They paid their bill and left. Mike watched as Tina Ricci walked out of his life for the second time.

He sat there, dumbfounded. For thirty years, the memory of Tina and their summer together had haunted and beguiled him. It affected everything that came after. And now he knew that this great love affair was over before it even started. Tina never had any intention of staying with him. He was there to help her pass the summer months while her boyfriend was away.

He finished his beer and staggered outside. The sun was still bright and blinded him for a moment. He walked down to the pier in front of one of the fishing boats. Then he fell to his knees and started to cry. Had she ever loved him? Was it just a game for her? Did she have doubts? Was there a time when she considered ditching the boyfriend to stay with Mike? Had he wasted thirty years on a memory that was a fraud?

"Hey, buddy, you OK?"

It was a young kid, probably college-aged, standing over him.

"Fuck off," said Mike.

"Fuck you, dude," the kid said, and he walked into the saloon.

Mike climbed to his feet and walked to the edge of the pier and looked out over the bay. Then the tears came rolling again, this time in torrents.

"Tina," he said. "My sweet Tina…"

"Mr. Gardner, Mr. Gardner, are you OK?"

Mike Gardner continued to cry uncontrollably, not realizing that he was back in the transportation chair at ZTT.

The technician began to shake him to get him out of his stupor.

"Mr. Gardner…"

And then Mike realized he was back. Holy shit, it had happened just like that. One instant, he was on the pier in 1989, and the next, he was back in 2019.

"I'm OK. I'm OK," Mike said, wiping tears from his face.

"You had me worried there for a second," the technician said. "Everything OK?"

"Fine," said Mike. He stood up from the chair.

"Mr. Brandauer would like to see you now for your exit interview," said the technician.

188

"Tell Mr. Brandauer to go fuck himself."

Mike hastily exited the building and grabbed a cab. He was back in 2019. That was a good thing. He had decided now that 1989 was not as magnificent as he had remembered.

Back at his apartment, Mike poured himself a scotch on the rocks and sat on his couch. He never had a chance with her. All these years, he wondered why she had ended it and what he could have done differently. But he'd never had a chance. She was the love of his life, and he was her summer fling. But he couldn't accept that.

He drank his scotch slowly. He refused to believe that she didn't love him. She had to have *felt something*. What they had that summer was magical. There was no way what he felt could have been one-sided. No, he would not let himself believe it. She loved him. *She loved him.*

He put his drink down and walked over to the bookcase. He pulled out the copy of *The Prince of Tides* and looked at the creased spine of the book. It was all he had left of her.

Maybe it was time to write that book he had always wanted to write. Maybe he would write about the summer that came and went and the girl who went away with it.

Touch My Cheek Before You Leave Me

(1994)

THE WAVES CRASH, AND she thinks that it is the greatest sound she has ever heard. Is there anything better than waking up by the sea and hearing the ocean outside of the window? Maybe when he lies his head on her shoulder and breathes softly.

Yes, that is better.

She looks at his face and wonders how she ever got on before there was him. She wonders if happiness is something she is allowed. Good things do not happen to her. They happen to her friends. They happen to people in the movies. But not to her.

He shifts his head and opens his eyes. She looks in those eyes and fades into them.

Isn't that a song? She thinks so, but can't remember it. No matter.

It only matters that those eyes are looking at her and she feels there is love in them. Yes, it must be. She is sure of it. But when has she ever been sure of these things?

"Morning," he says.

She kisses him on the forehead and holds her lips there for a moment, perhaps a moment too long. But she has waited to get to this moment and feels she must savor it.

"You won't leave me, Jake, will you?"

"No."

She hears the waves crashing again. It is a beautiful sound, but it also scares her. Doesn't everything have a dark side?

"No, of course not," she says.

They ran down to the seaside a few days ago, and she never wants to leave. It is perfect here. She is perfect here. Or at least, she feels that way. And he is perfect too. The waves crash again, and she knows they will eventually have to leave.

She kisses his forehead again. Then he kisses her softly on the lips, and for the moment, there is no world but this one. They should never leave. Life should be waking up next to him every morning and hearing the waves. She could live to a hundred this way.

"How many bottles of wine did we drink?" he asks.

"Two, I think."

"I thought it was more."

"My head hurts a little."

"Mine too."

He sits up and rubs his eyes. "The waves sound nice," he says.

"We should walk on the beach," she says.

"We will."

And then we must go back? At some point, they'll have to go back. And the melancholy washes over her. Why can't she enjoy the moment as it happens? Why must she make the present past?

They walk on the beach. It is early, and no one is there. The beach is theirs. The waves crash, and the tide washes their feet. If she closes her eyes, maybe this moment will never end. It is here, it is now, it is happening.

Tell me you'll never leave me, Jake. She doesn't actually say it again, but she thinks it. Why does she think it? Why must she be this way? She worries that this is one of those dreams that is too wonderful to be true and will crush your heart when you wake and realize it was just a dream.

She mustn't think these things. She should think of the things they have done in the past few days. Yes, think of those things. They watched the boats come in from the sea and danced on the dock. They had clams and beer at Gosman's. They saw *Speed* with a packed house, and she gripped Jake's hand so tightly every time she thought the bus was going to explode. And they made love. And it was a dream. She does not want to wake up.

Our greatest hopes and our worst nightmares are seldom realized. Where did she hear that saying? She can't remember. She isn't good with things like that. But the sentiment works. She shouldn't worry so much.

A mother and her two toddlers come down the dune. The kids howl and laugh, and their mother tells them to calm down.

The beach is theirs no longer.

"We should eat something," he says.

"Yes."

They eat at the diner in town. He eats his eggs and does not say much. She watches his face, and she thinks of the first time she saw him. She had gone to Mustang Sally's near the Garden with some friends after the Rangers parade. There had been a rumor that the Stanley Cup was going to be brought to the bar. It wasn't. But she saw him at the end of the bar with his friends, and she no longer cared about the Stanley Cup. They cut into the Knicks–Rockets game to show OJ in the white Bronco. His friends were loud and yelling at the TV, but he was quiet and cool. He looked at her, and she looked at him. It was like something out of a movie. Or a dream. But dreams end, and you wake.

"How are your eggs?" she asks.

"Good."

"Good," she says.

"I'm not looking forward to going back to the city," he says.

Then don't! Let's stay here forever.

She isn't any good in the city. But she's perfect out here. Why can't they stay a little longer?

"I know. Me neither," she says.

He reaches out and touches her cheek softly.

"We'll come back someday," he says.

She holds his hand against her cheek. She knows they must leave. But she is happy for the moment. She keeps his hand on her cheek. At least, he touched her cheek before they had to leave. She thinks that is from a song, but she can't remember. She's not good like that.

They leave the diner, and it is cloudy and looks like rain. She dreads the walk back to the motel. She wishes they could watch the sunset one more time, but it is rainy, and they must go.

By the end of the day, they will be back in the city, and they will go their separate ways. She will go to sleep, and then she will awaken, and it will all feel like it was only a dream.

You Can't Put Your Arms Around a Memory

(1997)

FOR A MOMENT, ROBBIE couldn't remember what bar they were in. He gazed across the room, looking for Sean, and couldn't find him. No, wait, there he was, behind the pool table, talking with two girls. Sean caught his eye and waved Robbie over.

Great, thought Robbie. Two drunk girls he didn't want to meet, he would never see again, girls he didn't have the strength to strike up a meaningless conversation with.

But Sean kept waving at him. He needed a wingman. Robbie was almost thirty and wanted his wingman days to be over. But Sean was persistent. He lived for this.

What bar were they in again? Robbie cleared his head. Upper East Side. OK. Ninety-Second Street. Yes, they were at The Tavern. They always seemed to end up at The Tavern on Saturday nights.

The bartender handed Robbie two Bud Lights. He would have to head over to Sean now and play his part when what he really wanted to do was grab a cab and head home.

"Millerewski, my man!" Sean said as Robbie handed him his beer. "Meet Amanda and…" Sean stammered, trying unsuccessfully to remember the second girl's name.

"Patty," said the second girl.

"Right, Amanda and Patty," said Sean.

It was immediately clear to Robbie that Sean was homing in on Amanda and needed Robbie to occupy Patty for a while as Sean moved in for the kill.

"Patty," said Robbie, "what brings you to this fine establishment?" It wasn't much of an opening line and wasn't intended to be. It was just the first thing that popped into Robbie's inebriated mind.

"Oh, we love The Tavern," said Patty. "We always come here."

So did Robbie and Sean, and he wondered if there was a chance that they had already met Amanda and Patty at some point. The girls in these bars had all started to look the same a long time ago. What was he still doing here? His friends from college were pretty much all married now. Wait, wasn't that a line from a song? Carly Simon? He tried to sing it in his head, but the song wouldn't come to him.

"How about you guys?" Patty asked.

"We do too," said Robbie. "Although I'm not really sure why anymore."

Patty frowned at that. Robbie could sense what she was thinking. *Should I waste my time with this sad sack?*

"But I do love the jukebox," said Robbie.

That perked Patty up. "I do too!"

Smashing Pumpkins were playing. "Tonight, Tonight." Robbie liked that song and started singing along with it.

"Oh, I love this song too!" Patty said as she hooked her arm around Robbie and sang along with him.

She looked into his eyes and immediately gave Robbie her *fuck me* stare. He had seen that stare before.

Robbie noticed Sean peering over at him, a shit-eating grin on his face. Sean winked at Robbie. He lived for this shit.

Patty slowly rocked to the music and kept her eyes locked on to Robbie's. They were pretty eyes, and if Robbie were twenty-four, he might be getting turned on right now. But all he really wanted to do was crawl into a hole somewhere and hide. Sean would think he was certifiable if Robbie told him how he felt. Robbie wished sometimes that he could think like Sean. It seemed like such an easier way to go through life. But it just wasn't in him.

The song ended, and a new one came on. "Ordinary World" by Duran Duran. Robbie liked that one too. So did Patty, evidently, as she grabbed his hands and started singing the song to him, never taking her pretty eyes off his, telling him with those eyes exactly what she wanted.

Robbie swayed along with her and watched her sing. He didn't want to cry for yesterday, but the lyrics to the song sort of made it impossible not to think that he should. The song made him think of college and the one who got away. Which he thought was lame all these years later, but that's what a song could do sometimes. Especially if you were pushing thirty, wasting time in a bar on the Upper East Side late on a Saturday night, dancing with a strange girl you didn't want to be around.

None of this was Patty's fault, of course. Maybe she had some yesterdays she needed to cry for as well. Didn't everyone?

You're not so special, Robbie silently said to himself.

196

He just never imagined that he would still be going to bars at this age. In his imaginary life, he had long settled down by now. Maybe there was something wrong with him. Most single guys in New York City would love to be dancing with Patty and her pretty eyes and *fuck me* stare. But Robbie's brain would rather long for a girl he hadn't seen in ten years instead of enjoying the beautiful girl in front of him.

When the Duran Duran song ended, a song by the Dave Matthews Band came on. Patty frowned and stopped dancing. Robbie frowned with her.

"I need a drink," she said.

They walked over to the bar. Robbie ordered two more Bud Lights.

"I was getting into a groove there," Patty said. "But you can't dance to Dave Matthews."

The bartender delivered their beers. They clinked glasses, and Robbie wondered what to say.

"Yeah, I'm not a Dave Matthews fan either," he said. "But overall, I like '90s rock much better than '80s rock." It wasn't a bold statement or even an interesting one. But it was the only thing that popped into his head.

"I agree," she said. "I like everything about the '90s more than the '80s."

Robbie pondered her statement. The movies had been better, the music was better, the Yankees were better. She was right.

"Me too," he said. "You can't argue with peace and prosperity and good music."

"And the city is safer than ever," she said.

"Safest big city in America," he said. "Who would have thunk it?"

They sipped their beers. What should he say next?

"But I guess a lot of fucked-up stuff has happened too," he said.

"Really? Like what?" she asked.

"Wow, where do I start?" he said. "JonBenét, Tonya Harding, the Menendez brothers, OJ—am I missing anything?"

She laughed while Robbie thought.

"Oh yeah, Waco, Oklahoma City, and…Princess Di dying, trying to evade the paparazzi," he said.

"Well, crazy shit happens in every decade," she said.

"Maybe," he said. "But now the crazy shit is a form of entertainment. I mean, how much shit on JonBenét and Tonya and OJ did we all watch? I'm sure some shit like that happened in the '70s and '80s, but maybe we don't remember because it wasn't on TV 24/7."

"So, you don't really like the '90s," she said.

"No, I do," he said. "But I wonder where we are headed if the weird shit keeps happening." He thought that maybe that was a profound statement, and he wondered if she might be impressed with his sociological observation. But he was drunk. Everything sounded profound when you were drunk.

"Don't worry," she said. "The stock market is booming, the city is safe, everything will be fine."

"You're probably right," he said. "But every time I see a commercial for the next episode of *Inside Edition*, I unfortunately can't help but worry about the future."

"You're funny," she said.

Funny? Actually, he was lonely. He loved being single in Manhattan in his early twenties, even in his mid-twenties. His late twenties, not so much. He couldn't shake the feeling that perhaps he had overstayed his welcome.

And the pretty girl in front of him with the *fuck me* eyes still held no allure for him. He had seen girls like her so many times before. He couldn't even tell how old she was. She could be twenty-three or twenty-nine, like him. It didn't matter. He just couldn't imagine telling his kids that he had met their mother while drunk in a bar at 1 a.m. on the Upper East Side. And if he couldn't imagine that, then what the hell was he doing here? Why waste another minute talking to her? For his sake and for hers?

"Where do you live?" she asked.

"On 19th Street, near Gramercy Park."

"Well, I'm right down the street from here on 89th," she said.

His drunken mind flashed to a night the previous summer when he was standing in this same spot, looking at the TV over the bar, and the Olympics were on, but there were no events showing. Instead, there were flashing lights and police cars, and no one in the bar knew what the hell was happening. The bartender eventually climbed onto the bar and reached up to turn up the sound on the TV. Turned out, a bomb had gone off. It was another fucked-up '90s moment that he had already forgotten about until his brain had just reminded him.

"Hey there," Patty said. "Did you hear what I said?"

"Sorry, what?"

"I was just telling you that I live a few blocks from here," she said.

"Right, sorry. I was just thinking about the Olympics bombing," he said.

"The what?" she asked.

"The bombing in Atlanta last year. I was standing right here when it happened. I can't believe that was already a year ago."

She took regard of him, and Robbie again bounced into where he figured her mind was going. Maybe this was a waste of her time. No doubt, when she told a guy she lived a few blocks away, their reaction was usually different. They almost certainly didn't talk about Olympics bombings.

"I have to go to the ladies' room," she said.

Robbie watched the attractive girl he wasn't interested in walk away. He guessed she didn't understand his Olympics comment. He didn't either.

He just was momentarily bewildered that a year had gone by so fast. And where was he? In the same fucking bar, in the same fucking spot, having a conversation about nothing with a strange girl who now thought he was odd. And she was probably right.

How many girls had he met like her in the city of all different shapes and sizes and colors? Many of them would be considered great catches for a guy like Robbie. And some of them probably were. But they all had something in common. They weren't Mary. But it had been long enough, and in the end, Mary didn't want him, so why should he give her another thought?

He was suddenly mad at himself. He had wasted too much time on a memory, and you can't put your arm around a memory.

He had a successful career, and Patty was right; the '90s were pretty awesome despite the weird shit that kept happening. Why should he be the only one not enjoying them? Fuck Mary. She was off living her life, probably not giving Robbie a second thought. So, why should he give her any more of his time?

He decided he would leave before Patty came back from the bathroom. He had decided right then and there that he would have no more pointless conversations in bars. He tried to get Sean's attention, waving over to him, but Sean was too engrossed with Amanda to notice.

So, Robbie turned and headed for the exit. He didn't want to stay a second longer.

The warm summer air hit his face as he stepped out onto 2nd Avenue. He would normally grab a taxi immediately and head downtown. But he decided tonight that he would walk a little first.

At first, he thought he would walk to 86th Street and get a taxi there. But the air felt good on his face, so he kept walking. He was a lonely guy who, at this very moment, didn't mind being alone. The walk was strangely invigorating and gave him the space he needed to clear his mind.

Loneliness can have its advantages. Being alone with his thoughts was what he needed. No Sean talking nonsense to him. No girl trying to get picked up. No one from work bothering him. Just some strangers passing him on the street and the light Saturday night traffic whizzing on by. It's not where he imagined himself being ten years ago. But whose plans ever really work out?

Soon, he was at 72nd Street. He passed a young couple not much younger than he was, stepping out of a diner, arm in arm. They were obviously in love. He felt envious of them and remembered when he felt like they did. He needed to feel that way again and hoped it would be soon. Enough time had been wasted. Some memories need to be forgotten. It was time to look forward, not backward.

A taxi pulled up at the curb, and two people got out. He took a pass on the cab and decided to keep walking. There was no rush to get home. An empty apartment and an empty bed were the only things waiting for him.

It was almost 3 a.m. when he got home. He tried to sleep, but his mind would not allow it. A car alarm blared from the street below. Even still, he could hear the stray voices of people on the street. Probably drinkers leaving Pete's Tavern on the corner.

He loved Manhattan, but at times like this, it could feel like the loneliest place in the world.

When the sun began to peek through his window, he was still awake. It had been a few hours since his last drink, and his mind had cleared. He slid out of bed and stood at the window.

Mary was out there somewhere with her husband and her two kids and probably a dog. Maybe she was awake at this moment and looking at the same sun. But that was as close as he would ever get to her. And that was

OK now. Her world was not his anymore and hadn't been for a long time. He was amazed at how fast ten years could get behind you when you weren't paying attention.

He watched a squirrel walking along the ledge of the building across from his. How the hell did he get up there? He watched the animal fritter about, without a care in the world. He was suddenly envious of the squirrel. Clearly, the animal was not trying to bury any unpleasant memories or deal with unresolved issues. He was just trying to figure out a way to get off the ledge. Perhaps Robbie was doing the same.

He glanced up at the morning sun. He could tell it was going to be a hot day. He usually preferred rainy days. But the sun felt good on his face this morning. He thought it was somewhat strange that the sun looked different to him now than it did when he was a boy. He knew that could not be possible. But he also realized that many things looked different to him now.

The Cool Side of the Pillow

(1998)

IT ALWAYS FRUSTRATED ROBBIE how difficult it had been to fall asleep. Once he did drift off, he could sleep well into the next day. It was the drifting-off part that could take hours. He couldn't understand how people could just hit the pillow and be comfortably sawing wood thirty seconds later. His college roommate, Ricky, would say good night and be snoring a minute later. Robbie had always been envious. What could be better than hitting the pillow and falling asleep within a minute?

His problem was, he could never just turn off his mind. Whether it was reviewing the events of the day or reliving moments from his past, there he would lie, night after night, trying to prevent his brain from replaying the memory. It was press play, watch, then hit the rewind button and start over again, like a videotape in his mind.

Then the fumbling of the pillows would start.

Flip the pillow to the cool side, and that will relax me, he thought.

But the pillow wouldn't stay cool for long, and his brain would remind him about that 9 a.m. meeting from this morning, or that time he hit a home run on his street in a downpour when he was nine years old, or his college girlfriend's laugh that time they made snow angels on the baseball field in the middle of the night sophomore year.

Flip the pillow again, but it's too warm. He'll have to wait a while for the other side of the pillow to get cool again.

Don't look at the clock radio to check the time, he reminded himself. *That will just make it tougher.*

Amazingly, Robbie Miller was able to function quite well at work each day despite the lack of sleep. He was a generally happy person and was well liked by those he worked with and those he hung out with after work. But he couldn't deny that he was lonely. As much as he loved Manhattan and as much as he enjoyed being on his own, he was thirty-one years old now, and living the single life in the city wasn't as exhilarating as it had been when he was twenty-four.

It was time to share his life with someone. It had been that time for a while now. But finding a soulmate in the big city turned out to be a greater challenge than he expected. The bar scene wasn't enjoyable anymore and was never a good place to meet someone. You needed a gift of gab that Robbie didn't possess to succeed in that environment. Small talk just wasn't his thing, and without small talk, meeting women in bars was difficult. He didn't trust people who were good at small talk anyway. How could you ever really know someone who was good at it? After all, it was just noise. The city was noisy enough.

Perhaps this loneliness was the reason he couldn't sleep at night. When he was a boy, he imagined himself married with two kids at this age, living on a tree-lined street, like the one where he grew up. Instead, he retired to bed each night by himself, shifting the pillows and waiting for his brain to go to the videotape again.

Even though he was only thirty-one, Robbie Miller had lived long enough to know that a person's life could change in an instant. Was that the reason he had trouble falling asleep? Was he restless, waiting for his life to change?

———

He was in his office at the World Financial Center, overlooking the Hudson. He was reading the *Daily News* when his secretary told him that the designer was here to look at his office.

"Oh shit, that's right," he said.

They were redesigning the office suite that his department was in, and an in-house designer was coming by to review options for his new office.

The designer walked in his office, and Robbie was floored. She had curly, dark hair and big brown eyes, and he had seen her before.

"Hi, I'm Rob Miller," he said as he held out his hand to her.

"Elizabeth Giordano," she said as they shook hands, and she sat in the guest chair in front of his desk.

Two weeks earlier, there had been an ice cream social in the Space Planning department. They had one the last Friday of every month and had invited Robbie and a couple of other executives from his division, as they were in the process of redesigning their office space. Robbie went for no other reason than he liked ice cream. Robbie was not one to pass up free ice cream. They had an ice cream sundae bar set up in the large conference room. Robbie loaded up with some vanilla and hot fudge and settled in at the far end of the table to indulge. He was distracted for a moment by a woman's voice. He looked up and saw who he now knew to be Elizabeth Giordano. She was on the sundae line, talking to the woman next to her.

"I was on a diet," she said. "But forget that. Free chocolate Häagen-Dazs? Are you kidding me? If you told me it was just regular ice cream, OK, maybe I could take a pass. But free Häagen-Dazs? Chocolate Häagen-Dazs? Please," she said.

Robbie thought she was funny. And she was right. Who in their right mind would pass up free Häagen-Dazs? He wondered who she was. He had never seen her before. She looked to be around his age, and he saw no ring on her finger. He decided at that moment that he wanted to know her. But two weeks went by, and their paths had not crossed. And now she was sitting right across from him.

She had a book with fabric samples that she showed him. They would be ordering new couches for the department. She told him one of the options for the pillows on the couches was mohair.

"What about electric boots?" Robbie asked.

"What?"

"You know, Elton John singing about electric boots and a mohair suit."

"OK…" she said as she looked at him quizzically.

"Bennie and the Jets," he said.

You could take Robbie Miller out of 1973, but you could not take 1973 out of Robbie Miller.

She looked at him all businesslike, and Robbie could sense that she didn't understand why he was singing an old song.

"I don't even know what mohair is," he said. "I just know it from the song."

She cracked the slightest of smiles and said, "Good song."

Maybe Robbie wasn't so bad at this small talk stuff after all.

She soon got right back to business, going over furniture and carpet options. Robbie tried to pay attention, but he couldn't. Elizabeth Giordano was too beautiful. He couldn't care less about furniture or carpet. He wanted to see that slight crack of a smile again.

Could he get her to laugh?

He put on his most serious face and said, "We're forgetting the most important thing in this whole office redesign."

She looked at him more intently and businesslike than she had previously. What could be more important than the items she had already shown him?

"The most important thing in all of this is to make sure we find a spot for that," he said, pointing at the framed Bernie Williams poster on his wall.

She looked earnestly at the poster, then back at him. She didn't know he was joking, and it was obvious to Robbie that she was probably wondering what was wrong with this guy.

"I'm just kidding," he said. "It was my dream as a child to be the next great center fielder for the Yankees. But as you can see, Bernie got the job over me. But I do want to make sure the poster hangs somewhere prominently in the new office."

That small crack of a smile flashed at him again, and Robbie felt a little tingle in his stomach.

"I'm sure we can find a place for it," she said. "Luckily for you, I'm a Yankees fan."

Oh God, thank the Lord, thought Robbie.

"That's good news," he said. "I would never let a Mets fan redesign my office."

She smiled again, and Robbie turned to mush.

They met for drinks about a week later after work. They got a table in the lounge area of the Grill Room with a nice view of the river and the Statue of Liberty.

Robbie was usually a beer drinker, but the setting and the beautiful Elizabeth Giordano were too elegant for beer. So, they drank red wine and picked at a cheese plate and talked. Not small talk. This was real, first-date talk.

She was serious, but he could tell that she was a kind soul. And he could tell that she was lonely, like he was.

She lived with her parents on Long Island. East Northport, to be exact, about ten miles west of the house Robbie grew up on Victory Lane. She was familiar with the Smith Haven Mall, where Robbie spent much of his childhood. He mentioned that he liked James Bond movies, and she said that she loved James Bond movies. She said she liked Odd Job and Jaws, and Robbie was hooked. They talked about the trials and tribulations of dating in your twenties, and it was obvious that she was as exhausted by it as he was. Being single in the big city wasn't as glamorous as it was in the movies.

After five glasses of wine, it was time for her to catch her train back to Long Island. So, he rode the 1 train with her to Penn Station. As she fumbled with her bag on the train, he noticed that she had a paperback copy of Caleb Carr's *The Alienist*. He was impressed. He had read that book earlier in the year, and it was so cool to him that she was reading it too! So many of the girls that he had dated didn't read at all. He hated that. But she was reading a cool book like *The Alienist*. He loved that.

A girl who reads!

He suggested she read another book that he loved, *Time and Again*, which took place in the same time period as *The Alienist* and involved time travel. Robbie was a sucker for time-travel stories. She said she was always looking for a good book to read, and Robbie thought that perhaps he should marry her right then and there.

When her train arrived, she surprised Robbie by kissing him on the lips. Nothing major, just a quick meeting of the lips, but he didn't expect it. A peck on the cheek? Yes, he was prepared for that. The lips? No. But he loved it. There was something special about this girl.

Alone in his apartment later that night, Robbie couldn't get the girl from Long Island out of his mind. Yes, he would have trouble falling asleep. But at least, it wouldn't be from endlessly obsessing about the past. Tonight, the promise of the future would keep him awake.

They lunched the next day at Moran's in the Financial Center. Robbie couldn't believe how relaxed he felt with her, like, somehow, he had known her all his life. And it was comforting to know that there was no stress at the end of these "dates" of whether they would see each other again. Of course they would see each other again. And they did. Dinner and drinks at El Teddy's in SoHo. Dinner at Sal Anthony's on Irving Place, down the street from Robbie's apartment. Then a taxi ride to Penn so that Elizabeth could catch the train home. It was all very chaste and old-fashioned, and somehow, it felt like home to Robbie.

She asked him what it was like, living alone in Manhattan, and he asked her what Long Island was like nowadays. Although he thought about Victory Lane frequently, he was a city boy now, and the suburbs seemed distant to him. But something about Elizabeth seemed to be drawing him homeward.

After a few dates, it wasn't hard for him to imagine her as the mother of his children. It wasn't hard for him to imagine sharing a life with her on an imaginary street that, in his mind, looked a lot like Victory Lane.

When he told her he loved her, she teared up and said, "You'd better not be bullshitting me." There was pain in her face when she said it.

"I would never say that to you if I didn't mean it," Robbie told her.

And her tears of anxiety turned into tears of joy. They embraced and held each other. Years of solitude and rejection poured out of their bodies. For both, it felt like the sun coming out after a long rainstorm.

Robbie hadn't been this happy since college. How long had it been since his college girlfriend had broken his heart? About ten years. Ten years of wandering in the wilderness. Ten years of reviewing things in his mind that it was long past time to forget. Ten years of trying to find the cool side of the pillow. And then one random day, Elizabeth walks into his office, and the pain is lifted.

He asked her to marry him one night at the Bubble Lounge in Tribeca while sitting on an ornate red velour couch and drinking expensive champagne.

She cried more tears of joy and said, "Yes," and they both wondered why it had taken so many years to find each other.

They had known each other for three months. She had walked into his office that day, and everything had instantly changed. They had looked for each other their whole lives, and one morning at work, when they weren't looking, they found each other.

She stayed at his apartment that night. She rested her head on his chest and was quickly asleep. Robbie lightly stroked her hair. He shifted the pillow under his head and was amazed at how relaxed he was. He was never relaxed when he went to sleep. But on this night, his brain was at peace. What a nice feeling that was.

It seemed that Robbie's never-ending search for the cool side of the pillow was over. He felt the warmth of Elizabeth's body on his and quickly drifted off to sleep.

Time Capsule

(1999)

ROBBIE LAY ON HIS couch and wondered if he would stay in this position for the whole day. He didn't see a reason to get up, and he wasn't sure if he could do so even if he wanted. Being hungover at age thirty-one had a different feel to it than at age twenty.

He was supposed to be at the stadium with Sean, his work buddy, for the Yankees–Expos game. But his bachelor party the night before had rendered him useless. He had already been to six or seven games this season and would likely go to six or seven more before the season ended. He could afford to miss today's interleague game against the lowly Expos.

He had just bid farewell to Ricky, his college roommate, who was in town for the previous night's festivities. When Ricky departed, Robbie felt a tinge of sadness. Not because Ricky had left. No, it was more that things just didn't feel right between them anymore. Not bad or contentious. Not at all. They'd had their laughs. It had been good to see him, as always. It just felt different. Something of the spark that used to be between them was gone. The man who had just left his apartment seemed more of a stranger than his best friend. How was that possible? He was as close to Ricky as anybody. It had only been ten years since graduation. Was that enough time to drift apart?

He supposed that Elizabeth was his best friend now. Maybe this was just the natural progression of life. Or maybe his head just hurt from his hangover, and it was making him feel melancholy.

In 1989, a few weeks before graduation, the boys had punched a hole in the ceiling in their on-campus apartment. It was Robbie's idea to make a time capsule out of it. They gathered whatever remnants that were scattered around the place and stuffed them in the hole in the ceiling. A *Time* magazine with Ayatollah Khomeini on the cover. A small poster of the Tyson–Spinks fight. A *Playboy* featuring the Girls of the Big East. A *Rolling Stone* with R.E.M. on the cover. A Huey Lewis cassette that nobody listened to. An opened pack of Trojans. A few empty tall-neck Old Milwaukees. And a few photos of the boys in various states of drunkenness.

Everyone agreed that they would inform the school in 1999 that there was an impromptu time capsule hidden in the ceiling of Alumni Hall, apartment D-1, and the school would immediately think how cute that was, and all the boys would return on homecoming weekend to open it with the school's approval. What a cute human-interest story it would be! Robbie and the boys were 100% convinced that it would happen just like that.

But it was 1999 now, and there were no plans to contact Utica College. No plans were made to go back to campus to open the time capsule. No one was going to homecoming.

When Robbie had brought up the time capsule to Ricky the night before, Ricky had smiled. But Robbie could see that Ricky was sad as well. They both knew the time capsule would never be opened.

Robbie knew he would see him again at the wedding. But when would be the next time after that? He had never questioned the closeness of their relationship before, and it bothered him to do so now. He hoped again that it was just his hangover that was giving him this feeling.

But Ricky's wasn't the only friendship that Robbie felt slipping away. His old childhood buddies from Victory Lane, Billy and Tommy, had joined the festivities. As with Ricky, things with his childhood buddies just didn't seem the same. He longed for the boys of his youth and their wonderful memories on Victory Lane. The men who were now before him were, good or bad, shells of their former selves. He supposed he was too.

He shuffled his position on the couch and turned on the game. Enough feeling sad about old friendships. It was normal to feel this way, especially with the pending nuptials. *Just lose yourself in the game and allow some time for these thoughts and the hangover to recede.*

The Yankees scored five runs in the second, and that relaxed Robbie. With David Cone on the mound, the game was in the bag. He slowly drifted off to sleep.

He dreamed of college. He and Ricky in the apartment in Alumni Hall. They were drinking, of course. And laughing. And Robbie felt so good. This was his happy place. It felt so good to be at school again and away from the real world—

He awoke with a start. The phone was ringing. Where was he? Right, he was in the apartment. Hungover. Yankees–Expos. A look at the TV. Still 5–0, Yanks. He reached for the screaming phone.

"Do you have on the news?" It was his mother.

"What?" he asked.

"Put on CNN. JFK is missing!" she said.

"What do you mean, JFK is missing?" he said.

Had his mother gone crazy? JFK had been dead for thirty-something years.

"Junior!" she yelled into the phone. "JFK Jr. is missing!"

214

"What do you mean, he is missing?" Robbie asked as he grabbed the remote and changed the channel to CNN.

"His plane. The plane he was piloting is missing."

"I didn't know he flew planes," said Robbie.

"Neither did I," said his mother. "But it's been missing since last night, and they think the worst has happened."

Robbie turned his attention to CNN. Why the hell was JFK Jr. flying his own plane? Didn't the Kennedys have private jets?

"It doesn't look good," said his mother. She was near tears.

She had always loved Camelot and Jackie, and everybody seemed to love JFK Jr. He had been at the Yankees game only a few nights earlier. Elaine Benes on *Seinfeld* wanted to have sex with him. Hell, he was going to be president one day…

He watched the CNN coverage. Aerial shots of the water around Martha's Vineyard. Photos of the small plane he had been flying.

"At least the Yankees are winning," said his mother. "Cone's got a perfect game going."

Robbie turned the Yankees game back on. Holy shit, she was right. Cone was throwing a perfect game! Robbie's head was spinning now. A hangover, missing American royalty, and a potential perfect game that he was supposed to attend.

"All right, Ma, let me go," he said. "I was supposed to be at this game."

"A perfect game!" she said.

"Don't jinx it!" Robbie said.

He lay back on the couch and watched as the innings went by, going back to CNN during the commercials. Perfect game still intact. No sign of JFK Jr.'s plane.

When Cone got the last out, Robbie couldn't even leap off the couch to celebrate. The hangover still had him in its grip. It was only the sixteenth perfect game in baseball history, and he could have seen it in person. Sean was going to give him hell for missing this.

Oh well, he thought. There are worse things.

JFK Jr. and his wife and her sister are probably dead. Can't really get so upset about a baseball game when something like that has happened. How much hell can one family go through?

He ordered a pizza and watched the postgame revelry, checking back to CNN every ten minutes or so for any updates on the plane.

Eventually, he drifted off to sleep again. He dreamed of college again. He was in the apartment in Alumni Hall, but there was no Ricky with him this time. Robbie was alone. Where was Ricky? He looked up to the ceiling. He decided to punch a hole in it. He wanted to open the time capsule. So, he punched it with everything he had, smashing it, then waited for the contents of the capsule to come tumbling out. But nothing did.

Where is the time capsule? Robbie panicked. *What the fuck? Where is all of the stuff we put in there?*

He reached up, trying to climb into the ceiling. It had to be in there! It had to be—

The phone startled Robbie. He picked it up.

"You asshole, you missed a fucking perfect game!"

"I didn't know it was going to be a perfect fucking game," Robbie said.

Sean wasn't long for talking, which was fine because Robbie didn't want to talk.

After he hung up, Robbie lay back down on the couch. He was sad now. Not because he missed the game. He was sad about JFK Jr. He was sad about the time capsule that would never be opened. He was sad that he couldn't relate to his Victory Lane friends anymore. He was sad that Ricky had left. Why all this sadness? Maybe it was just the hangover.

He told himself to stop worrying about old friends and time capsules. Move on from those things. But he knew he wasn't always very good at moving on. His mother would tell him to "be here now." So, that's what he would try to do.

The phone rang again. It was Elizabeth.

"David Cone pitched a no-game!" she said.

"A perfect game," said Robbie.

"What did I say?"

"I think you mixed up a no-hitter with a perfect game," said Robbie.

"What's the difference?" she asked.

He explained the distinction, and then they talked about the wedding and work and apartment listings, and they laughed. It was good. Robbie needed to hear her voice. Thoughts of old friends, missing planes, and time capsules faded.

"Baseball is the most important thing in the world that doesn't matter."

—Robert B. Parker

Subway Serious

(2000)

ROBBIE MILLER KNEW THAT his Yankees obsession wasn't healthy. He had been living and dying with the team since he was five years old, and while the moments of joy that the team provided him were exhilarating, the moments of pain were excruciating. There was an old saying that he vaguely remembered—something about the pain of failure being so much greater than the pleasure of success. Yes, Robbie certainly agreed with that one. But when it came to the sports he watched, Robbie, like any other fan, had absolutely no control over the outcome. Which made the pain and the pleasure nonsensical. And yet it was an affliction that he couldn't shake.

And now his worst nightmare had come true. The Yankees and the Mets would be facing each other in the 2000 World Series. He had heard from his parents his whole life about the classic Subway Series that the Yankees and the long-since-departed Brooklyn Dodgers had played in the 1940s and 1950s.

But he never thought it would happen in the modern era with the Yankees and Mets. And it couldn't have happened at a worse time. The

Yankees were the two-time defending world champions and had won three of the last four World Series. They were a modern dynasty again, on par with the great Yankees teams of the past. The Mets were the lovable underdogs, a wild-card team that was lucky to even be in the playoffs. There was absolutely no pressure on them. All the pressure was on the Yankees to win. And the nightmarish prospect that they might lose to the Mets, of all teams, was giving Robbie palpitations.

Elizabeth was incredulous. She understandably thought it was crazy for her husband to get like this over a sporting event, one he had no control over. Robbie knew she was right. But his affliction had no cure.

"If you have a heart attack over this, I will kill you," she said.

"If they don't win, I'll probably die anyway, so you won't have to. But let's not be negative," Robbie said. "We need to be positive. The Yankees are the better team. Everyone knows that. But this is baseball. In a short series, the best team doesn't always win."

"Don't kill yourself! This is so stupid!" She then stormed out of the living room of their apartment and into the bedroom.

Ever since the Yankees had beaten the Mariners in the American League Championship Series, the stress had begun for Robbie. He wasn't sleeping well. He was getting emails from Mets fans who were overly excited about the World Series matchup. Of course they were. They and their team faced no pressure. He would normally be listening to sports radio and *Mike and the Mad Dog* and enjoy the buildup to the series. But there was nothing for Robbie to enjoy this time.

It was only last year when the Yankees and Mets were playing a regular-season interleague series that Robbie ended up in the doctor's office with an irregular heartbeat. He was diagnosed with PVC, or pre-mature ventricular contractions. It meant that he was having accelerated or extra heartbeats. Robbie guessed that this was better than not having enough heartbeats. Either way, he was forced to wear a heart monitor for two weeks so that his doctor could record his heartbeats.

Elizabeth was beside herself. To her, it was the damn Yankees–Mets interleague series that had caused the irregular heartbeat. Robbie wasn't sure about that. But he sure as hell hated those interleague series against the Mets, so anything was possible.

And now the World Series loomed.

Robbie sat in the living room of their apartment on the Upper West Side and tried to not think about it. Maybe a walk outside would clear his head. He told Elizabeth he was going out for a walk and headed to the door.

He stepped onto 85th Street and walked toward Broadway. He was surprised to see vendors on the corner selling Subway Series paraphernalia—pennants, hats, T-shirts, and the like.

Great, thought Robbie. Even a walk outside couldn't get him away from it.

He walked into a deli to grab a soda. He tried not to look at the front pages of the *Daily News* and the *Post*—both teeming with more Subway Series stuff. He grabbed a Dr. Pepper at the deli and walked back onto Broadway. The magazine stand on the corner had about a million copies of the new *Sports Illustrated*. One cover had Derek Jeter leaping in front of a subway car. The other cover had Mike Piazza doing the same. There was no way for Robbie to get away.

He crossed Broadway at 84th Street. He looked up at the movie theater. Maybe a movie would take his mind off things for a couple of hours. But a glance at the marquee squashed that. He had already seen *Almost Famous*. He loved that one. Robbie was a sucker for '70s nostalgia. But the rest of the offerings were not worth the trouble. Neither *Meet the Parents* or *Dr. T and the Women* was going to help his current situation.

Maybe a beer or two at a bar would help. So, he kept walking until he reached Amsterdam Avenue. There was a bar called Fred's that he and Elizabeth liked to eat and drink at. Yes, he would stop there for a beer or two. It wasn't really a sports bar, so there wouldn't be a crowd of guys watching college football this Saturday. He didn't want that crowd because all they would be doing is talking Yankees–Mets. Game 1 was tonight, and Robbie could feel the tension building in his body.

The bartender was wearing a Yankees hat. On the walk over, Robbie noted that about every third person was wearing a Yankees or Mets cap. He couldn't escape it. Robbie ordered a Stella on tap and contemplated his predicament.

His parents had given him his Yankees addiction at a young age—so young that he had no memory of not living and dying with them. On the street where he grew up, most of the kids were Mets fans in the early '70s. Robbie was on an island by himself. Then the Yanks won it all in '77 and '78, and it all changed. Robbie thought they would go on winning forever.

Around that time, he also got into the Giants and the Rangers, and it seemed that his entire year, every year, day by day, revolved around the fortunes of the three teams.

He sipped his beer and was brought back to that October day in 1978 when the Yankees and the Red Sox were forced to play a one-game playoff at Fenway at the end of the season to decide the winner of the American League East. The Yankees had fallen 14 games behind the Red Sox that summer and had staged a furious comeback. And now one game would decide who would go on to the playoffs and who would go home.

Robbie's mom signed him out of his sixth-grade class an hour early so that he wouldn't miss the first pitch.

He sat on the couch in the den in front of the TV with his mom to sweat it out. Carl Yastrzemski homered off Ron Guidry in the second inning, and Robbie's heart sank. Soon, it was 2–0, Red Sox, and the innings were starting to run out. Robbie had to do something drastic. So, he started going into the bathroom between each inning, kneeling at the sink, and praying to God to let the Yankees win. He wasn't sure if that would work or if it was even appropriate. But whenever he considered not doing it at the end of the next inning, he would have an image of an eleven-year-old boy like himself praying at his sink in Boston. He had to out pray that kid in Boston. So, the in-between prayers to God continued.

In the top of the seventh, Bucky Dent hit an improbable three-run homer off former Yankee Mike Torrez to give the Yanks a 3–2 lead. Robbie leaped off the couch and screamed like it was New Year's Eve. His mother cautioned him that it wasn't over yet. She was right. The praying must continue.

Soon, it was 4–2, Yanks, and then Reggie hit one out to make it 5–2. The Yanks were six outs away.

But the Red Sox rallied in the bottom of the 8th and closed the gap to 5–4. So, more prayers at the sink were needed at the end of the eighth and again between the top and bottom of the ninth.

Robbie was scared to death. His mother could see it in his eyes. And he could see it in hers. Her blue eyes looked like they were turning gray with the strain. She needed the Yankees to win, too, because she knew how crushed her son was going to be if they didn't.

Robbie hoped for a quick, stress-free one-two-three ninth, but of course it was not to be. The Sox put runners on first and third with two out. Yaz, of all people, was up. Goose Gossage was on the mound for the Yanks.

Robbie rocked back and forth on the couch in terror. *C'mon, Goose. You can get him! Please, God, let Goose get him!*

223

On the 1–0 pitch, Goose fired a 98-miles per hour heater high and tight, and at first, Robbie thought the pitch was going to hit Yaz. But Yastrzemski swung. He got under it and popped it up toward third base. Would it stay fair?

"Stay fair! Stay fair!" Robbie screamed.

His mom put her hand on his shoulder in anticipation. The ball drifted behind third base in foul territory. Then Graig Nettles settled under it. He was going to catch it! And after what seemed like an eternity, he did.

The Yankees had won.

Robbie's mom grabbed him and hugged him as Robbie screamed with joy.

For a few years, Robbie was half convinced that his prayers had made the difference.

He was older now and realized that if there was a god, he probably couldn't care less who won or lost a sporting event. There were things like cancer and world hunger to worry about. That's why he didn't like it when players thanked God for their success at a game. How about praying to cure cancer? So, Robbie stopped praying for his teams.

When the Giants played the Bills in Super Bowl XXV, it all came down to the final kick. Robbie thought about praying to God to make the Bills' Scott Norwood miss the kick. But he no longer thought it appropriate to pray for sports outcomes. So, he just hoped hard that Norwood would miss the kick. When he did miss, the joy Robbie felt was greater than it would have been had he prayed for it. God didn't need to intervene, nor should he. Which made Robbie wonder again if there was a god. Cancer and world hunger are still with us. If he wasn't affecting the outcomes of sporting events, then what the hell was he doing?

Robbie came back to the present and sipped his beer again and cursed himself for caring so damn much about the outcome of a baseball game. It was an affliction, and it was in his blood, and there was nothing he could do about it.

He walked back to the apartment after two beers. Elizabeth suggested they run out and grab a bite before the game started.

"It will take your mind off of it," she said.

So, they walked to Blondie's on 79th Street. It was just the kind of sports bar that Robbie wanted to avoid. But Elizabeth liked the wings there, and Robbie already knew that he was putting her through hell with his Subway Series paranoia, so he couldn't say no.

Sure enough, when they walked in the place, it was decorated with a wide array of Subway Series accoutrements. It seemed like anywhere you looked in the city these days, Derek Jeter or Mike Piazza was staring back at you. And the crowd around the bar was already forming with hooligans in Yankees and Mets jerseys. Robbie couldn't imagine how many bar fights were going to happen over the next week. That's why he had to watch these games at home without distraction.

"Have a beer. We'll eat some nachos and wings and relax," Elizabeth said.

"I'll try, honey," Robbie said.

"Whatever happens tonight happens," she said. "It's only game 1."

"We need game 1," he said. "We can't have them stealing a game at the Stadium."

"I'm sure we'll get it," she said. "Relax. You know the Yankees are the better team."

"That doesn't matter in baseball in a short series," he said. "It's a fucking crapshoot."

"OK, fine, just drink your beer, and don't worry about it. Worry about it at 8:30 p.m. tonight."

GAME ONE

Elizabeth stayed in the bedroom as the game began. She didn't want to watch Robbie stressing out on every pitch and didn't want to sit in the wrong chair or say the wrong thing or lean the wrong way and perhaps lose the game for the Yankees. Robbie might not have believed anymore in praying for his team, but it didn't mean he didn't still have his superstitions. Elizabeth had learned that the hard way.

The game started well for the Yanks, and they held a 2–0 lead, heading into the seventh. But then the Mets jumped on Andy Pettitte for three runs to take the lead.

Fuck no! thought Robbie.

The nightmare scenario might be unfolding.

The Mets took that one-run lead into the bottom of the ninth. Robbie barely sat during the game, wearing out the floor between the couch and the TV. Elizabeth felt for the poor people in the apartment below. The wood floor in their living room was creaking incessantly as Robbie paced back and forth. And now it was the bottom of the ninth, and the Yanks were three outs away from losing game 1.

Elizabeth was now silently praying for them to win. Robbie might not have believed in God's intervention, but Elizabeth didn't want to take any chances. She couldn't imagine what her husband was going to be like if the Yankees didn't win this series.

Paul O'Neill led off the ninth with a walk, after a long at-bat against Mets' closer Armando Benitez. Soon, the Yanks had the bases loaded with one out. Chuck Knoblauch then hit a sacrifice fly to tie the score. Robbie let out a huge sigh of relief. Extra innings were coming. Now they had to win this game.

But the game dragged on. The 10th inning came and went. Then the 11th. Robbie lived and died on each pitch, and poor Elizabeth was doing the same in the bedroom.

The Mets were retired in the top of the 12th as the clock neared 1 a.m. These damn playoff games take forever with all the damn commercials!

In the bottom of the 12th, Elizabeth's prayers were answered. Jose Viscaino lined a single to left field with the bases loaded off Mets' reliever Turk Wendell, and Tino Martinez trotted home with the winning run for the Yanks.

Elizabeth ran out of the bedroom to join her joyous husband. Robbie embraced her and kissed her on the lips.

"How's your heart?" she asked.

"Much better now," he said. "But now we need game 2. We can't let them go back to Shea with a split."

Elizabeth rolled her eyes. Couldn't her husband just enjoy the win and not worry yet about game 2?

"It's one o'clock. I'm going to bed. Are you coming?" she asked.

"Go ahead, honey. I've got to watch the postgame on MSG."

GAME TWO

Robbie stayed up till 2 a.m., watching the postgame coverage. But he couldn't really sleep and was up early. He ran out at 7 a.m. to get bagels as Elizabeth stayed sleeping. Game 2 wasn't till 8:30 that night, so he had a long Sunday until game time. A lot of time to try to occupy his time and then get his game face on.

The pitching matchup was Mike Hampton for the Mets versus Roger Clemens for the Yanks. It was definitely an advantage for the Yankees, but Robbie didn't want to feel overconfident. But he knew the Yankees had a great chance to take a stranglehold on the series. But if the Mets were to win, they would take all the momentum with them, heading into game 3 at Shea. The thought of that would keep Robbie's stress level high throughout the day.

Robbie ate his bagel while Elizabeth slept. The phone rang around 9 a.m. It was his mother, calling from Florida.

"Great game last night," she said.

"The ending was," said Robbie. "The rest of the game almost killed me."

"Me too," said his mother. "I was worried about you the whole time."

"How's Dad?" asked Robbie.

"Still sleeping," she said. "He spent the whole game cursing and screaming. I wanted to kill him."

Robbie laughed. He could easily picture his father doing that. Robbie kept his in-game tension bottled up. His father just let it fly.

"Well, we need game 2 now," said Robbie.

"Can't you enjoy last night?" she said. "Whatever happens tonight happens."

"I know, but we need game 2," he said.

"Don't get yourself sick," she said. "You've been doing this since you were little."

"I'll be OK," said Robbie.

"You'd better, or I'll fly up there and kill you myself," she said.

"Elizabeth said the same thing."

"Listen to your wife then."

It was a quiet day, waiting for game time. Robbie and Elizabeth went for a walk and grabbed a couple of slices at the pizzeria around the corner as Robbie tried to put the impending game out of his mind.

"Just think, Rob, in a week, it will all be over, one way or the other," Elizabeth said.

But Robbie couldn't think that far ahead.

The Yanks scored two runs in the bottom of the first to get game 2 off to a good start.

In the second inning, Mike Piazza fouled off a pitch from Roger Clemens, and his splintered bat flew toward the mound. As Piazza jogged toward first, Clemens picked up the splintered bat and angrily flung it toward the first-base line, narrowly missing Piazza. Piazza, stunned, started toward Clemens, and the dugouts emptied. Clemens had hit Piazza in the head earlier in the season during interleague play, and there was bad blood between the two. Robbie couldn't figure out why the hell Clemens had flung the bat toward Piazza. Robbie always thought Clemens was a little nuts, going all the way back to his Red Sox days, and this moment solidified that assessment. But no punches were thrown, and the game continued.

The Yankees controlled the rest of the game and took a comfortable 6–0 lead into the ninth after Clemens threw eight dominating shutout innings. Robbie was almost relaxed, heading into the ninth. But Robbie was not allowed to relax. Yankees reliever Jeff Nelson imploded and immediately gave up two runs and allowed two more base runners before Joe Torre gave him the hook and brought in Mariano Rivera. Torre, thankfully, was not taking any chances. After getting one out, Mo gave up a three-run homer to make it 6–5. Robbie could not fucking believe it. But before he could start hyperventilating, Mo calmly got the last out.

Would nothing in this series be easy?

Elizabeth eased her way out of the bedroom. "Happy Pappy?" she said, making an obscure *Seinfeld* reference.

"Happy Schmoopie," he said, returning the favor.

Yes, he was happy. But he knew that all the Yankees had done was hold serve. The next three games would be at Shea Stadium, and Robbie tossed and turned all night, worrying about what horrors might befall his team in that grotesque ballpark in Flushing.

GAME THREE

Robbie enjoyed his Monday at work. It was nice to know that there wasn't a game that night, and he hoped to have a stress-free day. Everyone was talking about the series, and some Mets fans were already conceding defeat. Robbie didn't want to hear any of that. It wasn't over till it's over. Just ask Yogi.

He and Elizabeth ate a nice lunch at Moran's in the World Financial Center's Winter Garden. It was a bright day, and Robbie was able to put the series out of his mind for a while. The TV at the bar wasn't even on a sports channel. Instead, CNN was showing clips of the candidates in the upcoming presidential election. Bush and Gore were on a split screen, shaking hands with voters.

"Who do you think is going to win?" Elizabeth asked.

"Tomorrow night?" said Robbie.

"No, stupid," Elizabeth said. "The election."

Maybe the series wasn't completely out of his thoughts.

"Oh," said Robbie, and he laughed. "I think Gore."

"And tomorrow night's game?" she asked.

"Can't we just enjoy lunch and not talk about that?"

They spent a quiet evening at home, watching *The King of Queens* and *Everybody Loves Raymond*. That relaxed Robbie, but also reminded him how much he missed *Seinfeld*, so he watched a rerun of his favorite show at 11 p.m. as Elizabeth slept. He enjoyed the quiet Monday, but tomorrow, it would be time to get his game face back on.

It was El Duque on the mound for the Yanks and Rick Reed for the Mets. The Yanks held an early 2–1 lead, but the Mets tied the score in the sixth. It stayed that way until the eighth. Robbie was, of course, on pins and needles. If the Yanks could just push across a run, Mo would come in to close it, and the Mets would be buried in a three-games-to-none hole that they would not be able to climb out of. But it was not to be. The Mets pushed two runs across in the eighth and held on for a 4–2 win.

Robbie's hopes for a quick end to the series were dashed. The New York media would love this. They didn't want a short series. All the talk tomorrow would be about how the Mets had made a stand. The Mets would make a comeback. The underdogs now had life. Robbie didn't want to hear any of it.

GAME FOUR

Robbie's mother called him at work on Wednesday. "You're OK, right? It's just one game," she said.

"I'm all right," Robbie said. "We just need tonight's game, and we'll be in good shape."

He was still tense but overall was feeling OK. After all, he never expected to sweep the Mets. So, they got a game. Good for them. Now it was back to business for the Yanks.

"OK," said his mother. "Be positive."

"I will, Mom."

Part of being positive was avoiding all media. On his way to the subway, he noticed the local papers at the newsstand. The front page of the *Daily News* showed a photo of Mets outfielder Benny Agbayani getting the game-winning hit in game 3 under the headline "MET LIFE!"

Fuck that, Robbie thought.

The Yanks needed to nip this Mets' momentum in the bud.

"Be confident," Elizabeth told him right before game time.

But Robbie was too nervous to be confident. So, Elizabeth retired to the bedroom to give her unhinged husband the space he needed.

It would be hard for Robbie to estimate just how important Derek Jeter was to the Yankees. Some people foolishly thought he was overrated. People like Robbie, who watched every game, knew otherwise, and Jeter proved the point by promptly depositing the first pitch of game 4 into the left-field stands. To Robbie, it did more than just give the Yankees a 1–0 lead. No, it was Derek's way of saying to Robbie and all Yankees fans, *Don't worry; I got this.* The Mets won the night before and thus had some momentum—but Jeter just let the world know on the first pitch of the game that the momentum had been stopped.

That lead extended to 3-0 by the top of the third, but the Mets scored two runs in the bottom of the third to make it 3–2. And it stayed that way. And stayed that way…for the next five excruciating innings, with the

Yankees unable to add an all-important insurance run. Luckily, the Yankees' bullpen kept the Mets at bay. When the bottom of the eighth rolled around, Joe Torre was not taking any chances, bringing Mariano Rivera in for the six-out save. Robbie's knuckles were white the whole time, of course, but Mo did the job, freezing Matt Franco for a called strike three to end the game to give the Yankees a 3–1 series advantage.

Robbie raised his fists in the air as Elizabeth came out of the bedroom to embrace him. Just one more to go, and the nightmare of this series would be over.

GAME FIVE

Robbie struggled to focus at work. He didn't want to get overconfident, but it was hard not to be excited. The Yankees were one victory away from avoiding an unthinkable World Series loss to the Mets. One win away from avoiding Robbie's worst nightmare. One win away from avoiding that horrible pain of failure. And it wouldn't be the pleasure of success that Robbie would celebrate as much as it would be just an enormous sigh of relief.

Robbie pondered what was wrong with him. All this stress and nail-biting for nothing more than a sigh of relief? Was it worth all of this?

Robbie caught himself. Nothing was over until it was over. The Mets were not going to lie down and die. Stop thinking about the end of the series. Just focus on tonight's game. Al Leiter versus Andy Pettitte. One more win.

Bernie Williams homered to left in the top of the second, but the Mets answered with two in the bottom of the inning to take the lead. Robbie's thoughts shifted to a possible game 6—or, God forbid, a game 7 back at Yankee Stadium—if the Yankees' fortune did not turn in this game. Surely, the Yankees would win one back in the Bronx if it came to that? But Robbie stopped those thoughts in their tracks. There was still time to end the series tonight.

As if on cue, Derek Jeter homered in the sixth to tie the score.

Okay, thought Robbie, *we're back in business. We can end it tonight. Let's just get the lead and turn it over to Mariano, and we'll be on our way.*

But the score stayed tied through the seventh and eighth innings. Before the start of the ninth inning, Elizabeth came out of the bedroom to offer support.

"You don't look good," she said to her husband. "Don't worry. They're gonna do it this inning."

Robbie wanted to believe his wife, but he didn't dare share her optimism. That could jinx things.

As Elizabeth retired to the bedroom, Robbie sat for once on the couch. His legs were exhausted from all the pacing he had done over five games.

With one out, Jorge Posada walked, followed by a Scott Brosius single. That brought up light-hitting reserve infielder Luis Sojo with the runners on first and second. Robbie rocked back and forth on the couch in nervous anticipation. Could this be it?

Al Leiter was nearing 140 pitches thrown and looked physically and mentally exhausted, which Robbie could certainly relate to. But Mets manager Bobby Valentine stuck with him.

Thankfully, Robbie did not have to wait for an outcome. On the first pitch, Sojo scratched a ground ball up the middle, just under Leiter's glove. It squeaked its way into center field for a single. Mets center fielder Jay Payton raced in to pick it up and flung the ball toward home plate as the slow-footed Jorge Posada raced around third base. Robbie almost fell off the edge of the couch as the ball and Posada arrived home at the same time. Mike Piazza reached out to catch the throw, but the ball hit Posada as he slid across the plate. The ball caromed off Posada and landed in the Mets' dugout, which allowed Scott Brosius to score as well. 4–2, Yanks!

Robbie screamed in joy and leaped off the couch. Elizabeth ran out of the bedroom.

"We still have to get three more outs," he yelled, and Elizabeth quickly retreated.

As always, Robbie just wanted a quick, stress-free bottom of the ninth. But it was not to be.

Rivera got a strike out for the first out, then issued a four-pitch walk—something he never does. Robbie worried that Mo might be gassed after throwing two innings the night before. But he got Edgardo Alfonzo to fly out to left next for the second out. Robbie couldn't believe that they were now so close, just one out away. But Mike Piazza, of all people, was coming up as the potential tying run. Of course, it had to come down to Rivera and Piazza.

Robbie swallowed hard. He didn't know if he could take it.

Piazza took the first pitch for a strike. On the second pitch, he swung mightily and lofted a drive to deep center field.

Robbie's heart stopped. *Had Piazza just tied the fucking game?*

Robbie held his breath as Bernie Williams drifted back and back. But then he stopped just short of the warning track and looked straight up. He was going to catch it.

"He's got it! He's got it!" exclaimed Robbie.

The ball drifted into Bernie's glove, and it was over. Williams got down on one knee for a second, then raced toward the infield, where a pile of Yankees had already piled onto Mariano. The Yankees had just won their third world championship in a row, and Robbie collapsed to the floor and cried.

Elizabeth came out to join him, and Robbie hugged her and continued crying. He could finally enjoy the 2000 World Series.

The next few days were filled with joy. Robbie gobbled up all the newspapers to save. The *Daily News* headline read "Yanks Rule!" The *Post* headline simply read "Dynasty!" He and Elizabeth went to the ticker-tape parade on Broadway and took pictures. And Robbie anxiously awaited the release of the World Series highlight DVD so that he could relive the glory over and over with none of the real-time stress that had almost killed him.

In their apartment a few days later, Elizabeth asked her husband if life could get back to normal now. Robbie apologized to her for being such a crazy person regarding the Yankees and thanked her for helping him through the series.

"Hopefully, you won't be like this next time," she said.

"Hopefully, there won't be a next time," he said.

One Subway Series was more than enough for Robbie.

Robbie again questioned the sanity of sports fandom. It was all so ultimately unimportant. It was supposed to be a form of entertainment. Instead, it was a constant torment. But he guessed it was better than being an alcoholic or a drug addict.

With the series over, Robbie could go back to worrying about the important things in the world, like cancer, world hunger and the upcoming presidential election. The Yankees and Mets could now fade into the rearview mirror for at least a few months.

Robbie hoped he could look back one day on the last week and be happy. The city had really come alive for the Subway Series. It had been a great time.

Unfortunately for New York, it wouldn't stay that way for long.

"If time is anything akin to God, I suppose that memory must be the devil."

—Diana Gabaldon

Vanish by Dawn

(1999)

HE WASN'T SURE HOW many hours he had spent in this place over the years, but it was more than he probably should have. But there was something about Live Bait that always drew him back. Maybe it was the Caribbean flavor of the place. He was always a sucker for those kinds of places. There was something to be said about walking around a cold Manhattan street at night, then popping your head into a place with pastel colors, palm trees painted on the walls, and Bob Marley playing on the jukebox. It was like going on vacation for a couple of hours. That's why Greg liked Live Bait. It made him feel like he was in Key West or Jamaica or some such place. One minute, you were tripping on a cracked sidewalk on 23rd Street; the next, you were drinking a piña colada and joining a group sing-along of "No Woman, No Cry."

There used to be a bar a couple of doors down, called Bar X, that he and his buddies used to hang out in, and it was fine, but Greg always made it a point to get the boys over to Live Bait before the night ended. But the boys were married now, and Bar X was gone.

"Hey, are you there, man? I think you drifted off there for a second."

"What? No, I'm here," said Greg.

He had been sitting and talking to John for the last hour, and it was true; he had drifted. What had they been talking about?

"I'm going to head out anyway," John said. "Early meeting tomorrow."

" 'Kay, dude," said Greg. "I'll call you later in the week. Maybe we'll do Down the Hatch on Saturday."

They shook hands.

"Don't stay out too late," said John.

"One more drink," Greg said.

"You and your piña coladas."

Greg raised his drink and watched his friend exit the bar. It was 10 p.m. on a Wednesday, and the place was thinning out. But Greg didn't want to go back to his apartment yet. Yes, one more piña colada. Then he would go back home, watch the news, jerk off, and fall asleep.

Maybe he would skip watching the news tonight. It was nothing but impeachment and presidential blow jobs now. He fantasized about not watching the news for an extended period and wondered if that would make him a happier person. Maybe all the happy people were the ones who didn't read and watch the news. Maybe there was something to be said about being blissfully unaware. But he knew that wasn't him. He knew he needed to know what was going on in the world. So, he would continue to watch the news and be stressed. There was no escaping it for him.

The bartender handed him another piña colada.

He wasn't sure if he was seeing things at first and did a double take. But, no, he wasn't seeing things. Vanessa Fields had just walked past him. Vanessa Fields, whom he had dated for a year back in the early '90s. Vanessa Fields, the girl he had once loved. Whom he had drank piña coladas with in this very bar on many occasions.

240

She was with two other girls.

What was she doing here? Last he heard, she was living on the Upper East Side.

His eyes followed her and her friends as they made their way to the back of the bar and grabbed a table. Should he go over there and say hi? Should he try to make eye contact? She sat with her back to the bar, so eye contact was out of the question.

What a turn of events! He hadn't seen her in, what, three or four years? They were together in '93, but things petered out sometime in '94.

He remembered being in a bar with her and a group of their friends, watching the World Cup final. They had a fight, and he really couldn't remember what it was about. Probably something to do with the fact that he didn't like soccer or something meaningless like that. The last argument of a relationship is usually over something inconsequential.

She still looked good. He wasn't sure if he could say the same about himself five years later. But looking good was never a problem for Vanessa. He sipped his drink.

Should he go over there? Or take a walk to the men's room and accidentally pass her table and make eye contact? He was suddenly self-conscious. What if she wasn't happy to see him? What if she gave him the brush-off? So, he sat at the bar and drank his drink and continually glanced over at her table, wondering what to do.

"Fuck it," he muttered to himself, and he hopped off the stool and walked past her table and to the men's room.

She didn't see him as he walked past her table with his back to her. But she would see him on the way back. So, he took a piss and walked back toward her table. He did his best to act as casually as possible, and his eyes met hers at the same moment. Shock, surprise, and then a big smile came over her face. He feigned shock as well.

"Holy shit!" he said.

"Holy shit is right," she said, and she stood up.

"You look familiar. Do we know each other?" he said.

She laughed and threw her arms around him.

"Oh my God, Greg, what are you doing here?"

"Oh, I've been coming here every night for the last five years on the off chance that I might run into you. It finally paid off," he said.

She laughed again. Then she turned to her two friends. "Carly, Amanda, this is Greg. We used to be a thing."

"A thing? That's what we were?" he said.

"You know what I mean," Vanessa said.

"Hi, Carly and Amanda. I'm sure she's told you nothing about me," Greg said.

"I actually have," said Vanessa. "He's the guy that used to take me to all the Rangers games and the one who got me into R.E.M."

"The piña colada guy!" said Carly.

Greg laughed. "I guess there are worse things to be known as," he said.

"He's also the CD guy," said Vanessa.

"Oh, right. You've got, like, 9,000 CDs or something," said Amanda.

"Well, not quite 9,000, but maybe 900, give or take," said Greg.

"Who are you here with?" asked Vanessa.

"Right now, just me. I was here with my friend from work, but he just left. I was going to have one for the road and then head out," said Greg.

"Well, sit and join us," said Vanessa.

So, Greg sat with his old girlfriend and her friends. He had loved this girl once. He had played over in his head how he would react and what he would say if he ever ran into her again. And now here she was. He thought it funny that Manhattan can seem like a small town sometimes. You were always running into someone.

So, he sat, and the four of them talked and laughed and drank. He tried to play in his head again just why they had broken up, and he couldn't really remember. Maybe they had just gotten bored with each other. Maybe they weren't mature enough to make a real commitment. Maybe they were afraid. But he was definitely happy to see her, and he was pleasantly surprised that she seemed genuinely happy to see him as well. She kept touching his arm every time he said something funny or even when she told the girls a story about him. He was surprised at how comfortable he felt around her after so much time.

When Carly and Amanda said it was time to call it a night, Vanessa said, "I'm going to stay. I need to do more catching up with Greg."

What an unbelievable turn of events, thought Greg. *Was something happening here?*

When the girls left, Greg and Vanessa grabbed a couple of stools at the bar.

"So, we're both still single," Vanessa said.

"It appears so," said Greg.

"Why did we break up?" she asked.

"I was going to ask you that," he said.

"Maybe we were young and foolish," she said, smiling.

"That would make us old and wise now," he said.

"I don't know if I'm wise, but bite your tongue about me being old," she said.

"Well, young or old, you are still beautiful," he said.

She blushed and looked down. Then she looked up and kissed him quickly on the lips. He pulled her closer and kissed her softly, slowly.

They pulled away and looked into each other's eyes.

"Why did we break up?" he said.

Within minutes, they were at the door of his apartment on 21st Street. He had lived there since '92, not long before he had first met Vanessa. Now, five years later, he figured that the place probably didn't look much different than it did then.

He opened the door, and they walked in.

Vanessa looked around the small apartment. "This is like going back in time," she said. "You even still have that Mark Messier poster hanging in the same spot."

"Yeah, I don't think I've done much redecorating since you were last here," he said, wondering if it was still appropriate for a thirty-two-year-old man to have a sports poster hanging on his wall.

"Oh, but that's new," she said, pointing at a small *Sex and the City* poster on the other wall.

"Yeah, do you watch that show?" he asked.

"Oh my God, I love it," she said. "It's like watching my own life."

"I ordered HBO just to watch it," said Greg.

They stood in the small apartment and took a breath. Was the apartment a mess? Were there dishes in the sink? How odd it was to have Vanessa back in his apartment. He hoped she wouldn't be turned off. He had gotten messier as he had gotten older.

"Something to drink?" he asked.

"Well, I'm already a little drunk, so what the hell?" she said.

He had some vodka in the kitchen cabinet and some orange juice in the fridge. "Vodka and orange juice OK?" he asked.

"Sure," she said as she sat on his couch.

She looked at his wall of CDs. It had grown since she had been here last.

"What are you listening to these days?"

"Nothing new," he said. "Rock is kind of dead."

She got off the couch and walked over to the wall shelf that housed the CD collection. She knew they were stacked alphabetically and went over to the R's and pulled out a disc.

"This was our album, remember?" she said.

"*Automatic for the People?*" he said.

She nodded.

"My favorite R.E.M. album," he said.

He came into the living room, drinks in hand.

She handed him the CD. "Put it on," she said.

He handed her a drink and took the CD case. He pulled out the disc and popped it into the CD player on the floor.

"I haven't heard this album in ages," she said.

"Yeah, I haven't listened to it in a while either," he said as he joined her on the couch.

"Cheers," she said.

"Cheers," he said, and they each sipped their drinks.

He looked into her eyes and listened to the music, and a wave of familiarity came over him. Had it really been five years? This seemed so normal, so natural, so comfortable. He remembered this.

He leaned in close and kissed her softly on the lips. Yes, he definitely remembered those lips. He missed this. He wanted more of this. He wanted more of Vanessa, and from the way she responded to his lips, she wanted more too.

The music played, and they lost themselves in the moment. It was 1999, but it could have easily been 1994. They had been in this apartment, sharing a moment just like this one many times before.

He pulled away for a moment and sang along to the music.

She looked into those eyes and grabbed his face and kissed him deeply.

Then they rolled off of the couch and fell to the floor.

They eventually took the festivities to the bedroom, where they learned that *five years without seeing you sex* was better than makeup sex.

When it was over, they held each other. She brushed his hair. He ran his fingers lightly over her back.

"So, that was fun," she said.

He laughed. "Yeah, I guess you could say that."

"I can't say I imagined being here when I woke up this morning," she said.

"It has been a rather surprising turn of events," he said.

"So, what exactly have you been doing for the last five years?" she asked.

"Unfortunately, I think I was doing the same stuff the last five years as I did the five years before that," he said. "But in my twenties, whatever I was doing was fun. I'm thirty-two now. It's not as fun anymore."

"I hear you," she said.

"Sometimes, I fantasize about just leaving the city and going to an island somewhere and just leaving it all behind," he said.

"Oh my God, yes," she said. "Just pack a suitcase and go to the airport and be done with it all."

"Exactly," he said.

His mind wandered to an imaginary Caribbean island somewhere. He sat on the beach with a frosty drink in his hand. Vanessa sat next to him, looking tanned and beautiful. Now that was a wonderful image. He could almost taste it. Wouldn't it be wonderful if that was life? Sitting on a beach with a drink in hand and a beautiful woman at your side? No impeachment, no Israeli-Palestinian conflict, no embassy bombings, weapons inspectors, no Jesse Ventura, no no-fly zones. Just a beach, a drink, and a beautiful girl.

"Why don't we do it?" he said.

"Do what?" she said.

"Pack a suitcase and get the fuck out of here," he said. "Fly to a beach somewhere and never come back."

"Yeah, that would be nice," she said.

"No, I'm serious," he said. "I'm sick of Monica Lewinsky and Linda Tripp and Yasser Arafat and all of the rest of them. And I hate my job, and I'm tired of the subway, and I'm tired of drinking piña coladas in the concrete jungle with palm trees painted on the wall. I want to drink them under real palm trees on a real beach. I don't care anymore if the president got blown in the Oval Office or anywhere else."

"You're serious?" she said.

"Dead serious," he said. "I have some money tucked away. We can pack a bag and head to JFK in the morning and catch a flight to the Bahamas. Grab a room at some small hotel and then spend a few days looking for a small hut or a house or any damn thing with a roof on it near the beach."

"And then what do we do?"

"We open a little beach bar and serve piña coladas all day. And we never read a newspaper again. We just enjoy each other and let the rest of the world worry about all the other bullshit."

"It would be nice," she said.

"Nice? It would be fucking paradise," he said.

"Hmmm," she said as she rested her head on his chest.

"Do you like your job?" he asked.

"I used to," she said. "But, no, not really."

"And would you really miss going out to bars in the city three nights a week and going home alone? And then getting up to go to work at a job you don't like, working for a boss you probably don't like? I mean, would you really be upset if you never saw your boss again?"

"No, I suppose not," she said.

"So, why don't we do it?"

She contemplated his question. Was there really anything in her life right now that she would miss if it were gone tomorrow? Was her present life anywhere near where she imagined it would be at age thirty? If she stayed in her current situation, would anything in her life ever change? In the blink of an eye, she would wake up one day and be thirty-five. What if when that time came, she was still in the same apartment, in the same job? The thought of that suddenly terrified her. Maybe Greg was right. Why couldn't they just go?

"Let's do it," she said.

Greg shot up. "You're serious? Because I'm fucking serious," he said.

"Let's go to the airport in the morning and say *fuck you* to it all," she said.

He grabbed her and kissed her. Then they fell back on the bed and made love with more passion than ever before.

When they were finished, they lay in each other's arms and listened to the sounds of the city. It was almost 2 a.m., but there was always noise. A car alarm going off in the distance. A truck of some kind rumbling down Sixth Avenue. Someone laughing on the street down below. Greg had always enjoyed the city's background noise. But he was ready for something different now.

"I'll run to the bank first thing and get some cash," he said. "Then a quick email to work, telling them that I'm not coming in. You go to your apartment and pack a suitcase. I'll meet you there, and we'll grab a cab to JFK."

She smiled. "OK," she said, and she closed her eyes and nuzzled herself into his shoulder. In a few moments, she was snoring.

Greg was too excited to sleep. What a turn of events this had all been! But he was ready. He had wanted to make a change in his life for longer than he could remember. He held Vanessa tightly and closed his eyes and imagined the two of them sitting on a sandy beach with a warm breeze soothing their restless souls. It was a comforting picture that gave his active mind some much-needed calm. He slowly drifted off to sleep.

He awoke with a start a few hours later. A car alarm was going off in the distance. He glanced at his clock radio—6:34 a.m. His head hurt. Well, they did drink quite a bit last night. A little hangover was to be expected.

Where was Vanessa?

He got up and walked into the living room, but she wasn't there. She wasn't in the bathroom either. He noticed her coat wasn't on the couch where she left it. She must have already left to go to her apartment. Lots to be done, of course. Even though she would only be packing a suitcase or two, he suspected that she would need some time to decide what to take.

He needed to do the same. He trudged over to the fridge and guzzled some flat Diet Coke to combat the hangover. Then he jumped into the shower. He could hardly contain himself as he quickly washed. Later today, he and Vanessa would be in the Bahamas together.

He quickly dried off and then ran into the living room, naked, where he dialed the airport. There was a 12:01 p.m. flight to Nassau. That's the one they would be on. He bought the two one-way tickets, then got dressed and packed a suitcase.

He hit the street and walked briskly to the Chase bank down the street. He needed to get some cash. It was freezing out, but he didn't care. It was eighty degrees in the Bahamas, and he would be there later today. No need to worry about cold New York winters anymore.

He took out $1,000 in cash and headed back toward his apartment. He realized he should call Vanessa and tell her about the flight and what time he should be at her apartment to pick her up.

Back upstairs, he picked up the phone and dialed her number. Three rings and then an answer.

"Hello?"

"Vanessa?"

"No, it's her roommate, Carly."

"Oh, hi. Can I speak to her, please?"

"She's not here," Carly said.

"Oh, she must have run out. She should be back in a minute, right?" he said.

"Um, no, she's at work," Carly said. "Is this the piña colada guy from last night?"

"Yeah," he said.

A sinking feeling started to develop in Greg's stomach. She must have run into the office to tie up some loose ends and maybe pick up a few things, right? No reason to be concerned…

"You wouldn't happen to have her work number, would you?"

Carly gave Greg the number and hung up. Greg took a deep breath and called the number. It rang twice.

"Vanessa Fields, marketing," she said.

"Hey, you. What are you doing at the office?"

"Working," she said.

It wasn't the greeting he wanted or was hoping for. He could do nothing but press ahead now.

"I got two tickets on the 12:01 to Nassau out of JFK. I'm packed and ready."

"Yeah…" she said, then trailed off.

"You do remember what we talked about last night?" he said.

"Um, vaguely," she said. "I was pretty drunk."

"Nothing about getting on a plane this morning…" he said, and he now realized what a fool he had been.

There was silence on the other end of the phone.

"OK then," he said.

"I'm pretty busy at work right now and supremely hungover," she said. "Call me later in the week. Maybe we'll get a drink."

He felt like a kid in a dream, standing naked in front of the whole class. He had reached new depths of embarrassment. What was he thinking? What was he fucking thinking?

"Sure," he said. "We'll get a drink."

He hung up the phone and felt chills run through his body. How could he have been so stupid?

The phone rang. Did she change her mind? His heart leaped for a moment. He picked up the phone.

"Dude, where are you?" said the voice on the other end.

"Hey," Greg said.

It was Mike Reid from the office.

"Where are you? You missed the 9:30 Wilkerson meeting. What the fuck?"

"Sorry. You won't believe it, but there was no hot water in my building this morning. I couldn't take a shower. They just fixed it. I'll be there in a half hour," said Greg.

"You'd better be, dude. Fuck!"

Greg put down the phone and stared out the window for a moment. It was a raw January day outside. His mood now matched the weather.

By rote, without thinking, he methodically put on his suit and tied his tie. He grabbed his briefcase and walked out the door.

He walked toward the subway at Union Square. He passed the newsstand and glanced down at the headline of the *New York Post.* "Prez

251

Posts 850G Paula Payoff!" the headline screamed. Under that, it read, "US Bombs Iraq Missile Sites as Kuwait Goes on Full Alert."

His gloom deepened.

He rode the subway silently. He glanced at the subway ads, stopping when he saw the *Come Back to Jamaica* ad. Sun, palm trees, and a beautiful girl in a bikini. He laughed to himself. But he wanted to cry.

After work, he didn't want to go back to the apartment right away. So, he stopped off at Live Bait. He sat at the bar and sipped from his piña colada and stared silently at the painted palm trees on the wall. He heard a car alarm go off in the distance. Back to reality.

It all had been a silly dream. And like most nighttime dreams, it had vanished by dawn.

Fighter Jets over Manhattan

(2001)

"A PLANE HIT ONE of the Twin Towers."

"What?" said Robbie Miller.

"A plane hit one of the towers!"

It was his wife, Elizabeth, on the phone. They worked for Merrill Lynch in the World Financial Center, right across the street from the World Trade Center. She worked on the 12th floor. Robbie was on the fifth floor.

"Everyone is leaving the building. We're going outside."

Robbie tried to process what she had told him. Must have been a small plane that lost its way or something. What a start to the morning. He had been preparing for a 10 a.m. meeting.

"Meet me outside on Liberty Street," she said.

"OK," he said. "See you in a minute."

"Something happen?"

It was his coworker Jean, who was returning from the pantry with a cup of coffee.

"A plane hit one of the Twin Towers or something. That was my wife on twelve. The whole floor is leaving the building."

"Really?" she said.

"Really."

Robbie rode down the elevator and exited in the lobby. He immediately saw two police officers run past him. It was about 8:55 a.m. Normally, there would be droves of people filling the Winter Garden or heading to elevators. But there were only scattered people dithering around, looking bewildered.

Robbie walked briskly to the escalator that would take him down to Liberty Street.

He raced down the escalator, pushed through the revolving doors, and walked into hell.

He was hoping to immediately see Elizabeth and her coworkers, but he didn't. Everyone on the street was looking up. Robbie followed their gaze.

He saw the North Tower of the World Trade Center burning near the top of the building. The hole where the plane hit looked like a crack in an eggshell. The flames coming out of the crack were red, not orange. Black smoke billowed from the crack. Debris, what looked like paper, rained down. And panicked people craned their necks upward to watch in consternation.

But where was Elizabeth? She should have been down here by now. Robbie walked onto Liberty Street and turned around in a full spin, but she was nowhere. Then he heard screams. He looked up and saw a body falling from above. It landed on the other side of the West Side Highway. A woman next to him started crying hysterically. People started to scatter.

Robbie looked up again at the cracked eggshell. Still burning bright red. No more bodies falling. Where the hell was his wife?

A woman ran into him, stumbled, then kept going. Everyone else was still looking upward. Robbie scanned the street again for Elizabeth. Maybe her group changed their minds? Maybe they stayed upstairs?

He raced back toward the building entrance.

When he reached Elizabeth's floor, he at first saw no one. Had they all left, as Elizabeth said they would? He ran toward her cubicle, then saw some people. Then he heard noise coming from the large corner conference room. Yes, the room was full of people. He ran toward the room. Inside, everyone was crowded at the window, watching the North Tower of the World Trade Center—which looked so close that you could touch it—burn.

He saw his wife near the window. "Elizabeth!" he called.

She turned and came to him, fighting her way through the crowded room.

"Why didn't you go to the street?" he asked. "I was looking for you everywhere. It's chaos out there."

"We were going to—"

But her voice was drowned out by the noise of a jetliner. Everyone turned toward the southern window. And there it was before them. A fucking jet! An airline jet seemingly headed right toward them. But it wasn't. It crashed into the South Tower of the World Trade Center, and a huge orange explosion—the kind you only saw in a summer action movie—burst from the building, along with the ear-splitting crack of the blast.

In an instant, Robbie—and everyone in the room—knew this was no accident. This was a terrorist attack. Someone was trying to kill them.

Robbie grabbed Elizabeth, and they hightailed it out of the conference room with everyone else.

Someone yelled not to go to the elevators. That made sense to Robbie. The next plane could be headed to their building. So, the group headed to the stairs. Robbie held Elizabeth's hand, and they started the trek down twelve flights. No one said anything. Everyone was just determined to get down the stairs and out of the building as quickly as possible.

They exited the building on the west side, right in front of the Hudson River. It was pandemonium—cops everywhere, trying to make sense of the situation, and people running to and fro. Robbie glanced backward to stare at the unbelievable sight of the towers burning. But he turned away quickly. He didn't want to see any more people jumping from the buildings.

"Let's go north," Robbie said to Elizabeth.

It was the only sensible thing to do. Put as much distance as possible between themselves and the Towers. They ran aside the World Financial Center yacht basin and headed to the sidewalk that hugged the bank of the Hudson.

And then they heard a jet. And collectively, hundreds of people looked up in fear. The sound came from the north. Robbie looked up the river and saw them. It wasn't another commercial airliner. It was two fighter jets! As they streaked southward down the Hudson, Robbie could see that they were F-16s. He let out a sigh of relief. But other people around him were panicked.

"They're ours!" Robbie yelled. "They're ours! They're F-16s!"

It was such a strange feeling for him to be shouting such words on a random Tuesday morning, and he thought how ridiculous he must have sounded. He felt for a moment that he was in a movie. How many movies had he seen in which a soldier had shouted out a similar line? He then briefly had a flashback to childhood, playing German planes with his friend Billy Cohen. This was German planes come to life. But this was no game.

The F-16s zoomed past the Statue of Liberty, then turned and headed back over Lower Manhattan, disappearing out of view to the east. But there were no other planes in the sky. That threat, it appeared, was gone.

So, Robbie and Elizabeth continued north up the pathway, along with hundreds of other bewildered citizens.

Elizabeth looked back at the Towers. The flames still raged. The billowing black smoke reached into the sky and trailed off toward Brooklyn.

"This is unbelievable," she said.

"I know," said Robbie.

The pathway soon turned away from the Hudson and curled east toward the West Side Highway. As hundreds and what now looked like thousands of people walked north along the side of the highway, fire trucks, police cars, and ambulances raced past them in the opposite direction.

"I think we should stop at 570," said Elizabeth. "Maybe we can find out what the hell is going on."

"Good idea," said Robbie.

Merrill Lynch had a building at 570 Washington Street, right off the West Side Highway, about a mile up the road. They knew people there. Maybe they could get some information about what was happening.

So, they continued north, trudging along the side of the highway with all the others, as more emergency vehicles whipped past them in the opposite direction. And every few seconds, it seemed, everyone in the procession would glance back at the Towers, watching them continue to burn, watching history unfold.

It took Robbie and Elizabeth about twenty minutes to get to 570 Washington Street. When they arrived, they walked into the crowded lobby and took a breath. Robbie soon ran into a coworker, Chris Molloy.

"A plane just hit the Pentagon," Chris said. "It's fucking insane."

Robbie contemplated the shocking news. *We are at war*, he thought. He guessed it was with Islamic terrorists. Osama bin Laden, he supposed. He had a flashback to an interview he had seen on TV a couple of years ago with Bin Laden promising attacks on America. But no one took it seriously enough.

Screams were heard coming from the street.

Robbie looked at Elizabeth's panicked face. "Come on," he said.

He grabbed her by the hand, and they headed for the door. They stepped outside and saw everyone looking south. There was a large, curling cloud of dust where one of the Towers had been.

"It collapsed," said a man next to Robbie. "The whole fucking building collapsed."

Robbie couldn't believe it. In all the bedlam of the last hour, Robbie had in the back of his mind that the Towers might end up burning for a day or two. But collapsing? He didn't conceive that such a thing was possible.

"Oh my God," said Elizabeth. "How many people just died?"

Robbie didn't want to think about it because the answer just might be too staggering to contemplate. He knew people in those buildings. Elizabeth's cousin worked in the South Tower. The one that just collapsed.

"Time to go home," said Robbie.

"We shouldn't take the subway," Elizabeth said. "They might attack that next."

"You're right," said Robbie. "Let's walk."

Their apartment was on the Upper West Side. That would be a long walk, probably six or seven miles, but they had all the time in the world. The key was putting distance between themselves and the horror downtown. The key was getting to the safety of home. But was anywhere truly safe now?

They walked back toward the West Side Highway and headed uptown, rejoining the throngs of people moving away from downtown. Along the way, they heard snippets of conversations from their fellow pedestrians—of more planes hitting elsewhere—but who knew if any of it was true?

Robbie tried to block out the noise. Just keep moving north, keep heading home, keep putting distance between themselves and the hell that was unfolding downtown.

Elizabeth has been trying to get her parents on her cell phone and finally had gotten through to them. They, of course, were watching the events unfold live on TV and were freaking out accordingly.

Robbie overheard his father-in-law yell, "Get the hell outta there."

"We are," yelled Elizabeth into her phone. "We're a couple of miles away already."

More emergency vehicles whizzed past them, and Robbie wondered about the carnage those vehicles were racing toward. How many people were in those fucking Towers? How many had gotten out?

He was jolted out of his thoughts by an, "Oh my God," from a woman walking near them.

He turned around in time to see the remaining Tower collapse into a cloud of dust. A horrible day just got unimaginably worse. Inside, he was scared. Inside, he was angry. Inside, he was crying. On the outside, he steeled himself to show calm when most of the people around him were panicking.

Nothing to do but keep moving forward. Nothing to do but get home.

An hour later, they had reached the Upper West Side. The crowds had thinned out, and Robbie and Elizabeth were surprised to see a sense of normalcy on the streets.

"Do these people not realize what the hell is going on?" Elizabeth said.

It did seem strange. People were walking about and sitting in the cafés and restaurants as if nothing had happened.

Whatever, thought Robbie. He wanted to get home and turn on the TV and get some real news.

When they reached their apartment on 86th Street, they both felt a sense of relief. They collapsed on the couch, relieved to finally be safely away from the carnage and chaos downtown. Robbie immediately grabbed the remote and turned on the TV.

They repeatedly watched the video of the planes hitting the Towers, sparking their shared memory from the morning of watching from the conference room when the second plane hit. Elizabeth eventually went into the bedroom, unable to watch the coverage anymore, but Robbie stayed glued to the television.

He was angered when Dan Rather came on and wondered if this attack would precipitate an end to New York's cultural and financial preeminence.

Fuck him, Robbie thought. He loved his city, and he didn't want to hear anyone throwing dirt on the grave of his town. This wouldn't be the end of New York. It couldn't be.

He was able to get ahold of his parents in Florida and was able to assure them that he was safe. His father wondered if they would hit the Empire State Building next.

"They'd better fucking not," said Robbie.

He loved the Manhattan skyline, and it was already killing him that the Twin Towers were gone. They would have to rebuild! But who in their right mind would venture back into a skyscraper after today? Anyway, rebuilding was a thought for another day. CNN was saying that there could be as many as 50,000 dead. Robbie struggled to wrap his head around that number.

He lay down on the couch. He was exhausted.

He eventually turned off the TV. Hours of watching the news and the constant replays of the Towers being hit, of the Towers falling, had worn Robbie out.

He went to the bedroom and got into bed. Elizabeth was already asleep.

He rested his head on the pillow, but sleep would not come. Not tonight. There would be no way for Robbie to turn off his brain. There were too many uncomfortable thoughts swirling around it.

Then he heard jets flying overhead. He knew from the news that the airspace in the entire country was closed. No, the sound he heard was not from any commercial plane. The noise came from fighter jets. They were obviously patrolling the airspace over Manhattan. In a day filled with unbelievable moments and events, this might have been the strangest. Who could have ever imagined that there would ever be fighter jets over Manhattan?

Shooting Stars

(2001)

ROBBIE ALWAYS LIKED RIDING on trains. He liked staring out the window and watching the landscape whiz past him—taking him somewhere new or somewhere old and comforting. The steady rumbling relaxed him, slowed things down, calmed his nerves.

Today, he didn't feel any of those things. He was traveling out of the city on the Long Island Railroad to meet Elizabeth at her parents' house in Huntington. He hadn't been out of the city since 9/11, and he had to admit that the constant terror warnings and scares had taken a toll on him. Maybe getting away for a couple of days would restore some normalcy to his brain.

The train exited the East River tunnel on the Queens side, and Robbie looked out the window at the drab, warehouse-laden landscape of Long Island City. He turned to his right to look back at Manhattan and was struck by the hole in the sky. Where the Twin Towers once stood, there was now only emptiness. When he was a boy and would sometimes take the train in with his dad, he knew they were close to Manhattan when he would see the Towers rising in the sky to his left. It pained him that he and his future kids or anyone else for that matter would never see that view again.

It had been two months since the attack, but it felt longer than that to Robbie. The "new normal" seemed to have been around forever.

He thought back to his first day back downtown six days after 9/11. He rode the 1 train downtown in fear, waiting for some crazed Jihadi to pull out a canister of poison gas or whip out an Uzi and waste the whole train. The news was full of supposed terrorist sightings and plots. Everyone was waiting for the next shoe to drop.

He remembered heading to 222 Broadway—Merrill Lynch's building that was one block south of Ground Zero, as it was now referred to. For three decades, it was the World Trade Center. And yet almost instantly after the attack, it was Ground Zero.

He emerged from the subway a couple of blocks from 222 Broadway, and the first thing that hit him was the smell. That burned-out smell you sense when there has been a fire nearby, only this was the most intense version of that Robbie had ever experienced. He coughed and grabbed the face mask in his pocket and put it on. There was concern about toxins in the air—another thing to worry about in addition to the Jihadis.

The next thing he noticed was paper—office paper—everywhere. It hung on the trees, on the windowsills of buildings, and littered the streets. It reminded him a little bit of what the streets down here looked like in the aftermath of a Yankees World Series parade. But these papers came from the desks of people who worked in the Twin Towers. Some of these people were dead. At this point in the aftermath, they were estimating that there could be anywhere from 10,000 to 20,000 dead.

And that was the next thing Robbie noticed. Signs on the lampposts and street signs with the names of missing people on them. The signs all had a photo of the missing person and a phone number to call with any information. It was six days since the attack, and the local newscasts were full of stories of relatives coming to Ground Zero and holding photos of their missing loved ones and encouraging the firemen to somehow find them. Robbie assumed at this point that none of these people would be found. He tried to bury the thought. He didn't know if he could move forward if he kept his thoughts at the surface.

He glanced at one of the signs. *John Gallagher, 34 years old, Marsh & McClennan, 92nd floor, Tower 1. Please call (201) 656-3534.* Robbie was thirty-four years old. And it seemed like most of the other missing people on the signs were young too.

The last jolting thing in this horrible landscape was the sight of the soldiers. American soldiers in their green camouflage smocks, patrolling the streets like they would in a Godzilla movie or something. But this was no movie.

He passed through the revolving glass doors of 222 Broadway, walking onto the marble-floored lobby, finally free of the horrible smell that lingered outside. Right behind him came a coworker of his, Cindy Manning. She collapsed to the floor, her hands slapping the marble.

"Noooo," she screamed. "Nooooo." Then wails of tears, uncontrollable, unrestrained.

Robbie froze. He looked up and saw the maintenance supervisor, Carlos Ruiz, staring at him, fear in his eyes. They both moved toward Cindy and attempted to lift her off the floor.

"Noooo," she screamed again, followed by tears and sobbing. She was losing her breath.

Robbie and Carlos looked at each other again. Neither knew what to do. So, they stood over her.

Carlos patted her on the back. "It's OK. It's OK," he said.

Her sobs started to slow, and the air started to go back into her lungs. They let her lie there for a minute, and then they lifted her up. Two security guards came over and took her from them. They walked her into the security office and set her down on the couch.

Robbie and Carlos looked at each other again, but said nothing. There was nothing to say. This was the world that they were living in now. As for Cindy Manning, she was only doing what everyone wanted to do. Robbie guessed that her walk from the subway—past the debris, the paper, the soldiers, the faces of the missing, and that horrible stench—had just been too much for her. The lobby of 222 Broadway looked normal. But right outside, it was Berlin in 1945.

In the office that day, it was quiet. There wasn't much talk about work. All the talk was of the aftermath outside the window or the latest terrorist rumors swirling around the city and the country. The police chased a suspicious vehicle across the Williamsburg Bridge. Terrorists might be using crop dusters to spread poison gas.

Well, at least we didn't have to worry about that one in New York, Robbie thought. *Or did we?* That's how fucked up it was.

Robbie was on the 19th floor. He peered out the window and looked down at the carnage and rubble that was Ground Zero. It really looked like Godzilla had come through and just stomped on the World Trade Center. He watched as rescuers and machines picked through the rubble. It was obvious to anyone looking at this scene from Robbie's vantage point that there was no one left alive in that pit. Despite reports to the contrary, this was not a rescue operation anymore.

Then the smell came wafting down the hall.

Fuck, thought Robbie.

It must be coming in through the outside air intake. He went back to his desk and put his mask on. He wouldn't be able to escape the hell outside that easily.

When he left to go home later that afternoon, it was another walk past soldiers and missing person signs. On the subway, he sat alert and with clenched teeth, waiting for his imaginary jihadi to spring into action. He feared that the last words that he would hear on this earth would be *Alluhu Akbar.*

"Jamaica Station," the conductor said over the intercom.

Robbie was momentarily taken away from Ground Zero and brought back to the present. He would reach Wyandanch Station in about forty minutes, where Elizabeth would be waiting to pick him up. He rested his head back and attempted to clear his head. But Ground Zero crept back in.

Each day, he would look out the window of his office and look at the pile of rubble below. In the early days, it didn't change much, and he wondered how in the hell they would ever clean up the mess. One day, a soldier came by his office. Merrill Lynch was allowing the soldiers and rescue workers into the building to use the bathrooms or to get coffee from the pantry. Robbie was shocked to learn that the soldier's unit had been redeployed to here from Germany.

As the weeks went by, the other parts of Manhattan tried to regain a sense of normalcy. And in some sense, they did—but it was clear that most people were on edge. Everyone was still waiting for what would happen next.

In late October, Robbie and Elizabeth tried to do something normal. Elizabeth—like a lot of people who worked downtown—had been laid off on 9/12. She hadn't been out of the Upper West Side since. So, they headed down to the West Village one Saturday to walk around the neighborhood. This was something they did frequently in the pre-9/11 world, and Robbie figured this would cheer them both up. There was this nice little Belgian café on West Third that served the best Belgian fries in the city. So, they ate fries with dipping sauce and drank Hoegaarden on tap and felt normal for an hour. Then they walked outside onto Sixth Avenue and looked downtown at the hole in the sky where the Towers no longer stood. And then the smell came. Where they were standing was about a mile or two from Ground Zero.

"You smell that?" Robbie asked Elizabeth.

"Yeah," she said. "What is it?"

"Ground Zero," said Robbie.

"Oh no," she said, and she put her hand on her stomach. "I think I'm going to be sick."

Their one hour of bliss in the Belgian café was over, and now they were back in reality.

Elizabeth didn't want to return downtown after that, and Robbie didn't blame her. Being down there every day was taking its toll on him. Everyone in the office tried for normalcy, but it was not achievable with hell right across the street. The noise of jackhammers, the occasional soldier coming in for coffee, and the smell that always wafted into the building whenever the horror of 9/11 faded out of consciousness for a moment kept the horror present in everyone's mind. The smell would come back to remind you that there were dead people—lots of them—somewhere in the pile right across the street.

Robbie's train continued its slow rumble east. He flipped through the *Daily News*. The news seemed to get worse every day. It had been five days since an American Airlines flight out of JFK crashed just after takeoff, killing all 260 aboard, as well as five on the ground in the Rockaways in Queens. Everyone assumed this was another attack. Minutes after the crash, the Empire State Building and the United Nations were evacuated. But five days later, they still didn't know what caused the crash.

Robbie wondered how much the city could take. He flipped to the Sports section, but he didn't want to read about the Yankees. It had been two weeks since they had lost the World Series in Arizona in the bottom of the ninth of game 7. Normally, that would have crushed Robbie. But the events of this fall had put sports in perspective. The morning after game 7, Robbie rode the subway, replaying the bottom of the ninth in his head. He was upset but numb. In the end, it was a baseball game. He had terrorists to watch out for.

So, he skipped over the Sports section and flipped past the Ground Zero news and the plane crash news. He saw an article about the Leonid meteor shower that was peaking in the night sky tonight. Supposedly, this meteor shower happened every year at this time, but he had never heard about it before. What a quaint, pre-9/11 idea meteor shower watching was. It sounded interesting to Robbie, but who could get excited about anything these days?

He folded the newspaper and looked forward to seeing his wife. Maybe a weekend out of the city would calm his nerves.

The train pulled into the Wyandanch station. He could see Elizabeth standing in the parking lot in front of her mother's car. It pleased Robbie to see her. Not much pleased him these days, but seeing his wife did. He waved to her as he exited the train. Maybe there was still some normalcy to be had in this world.

They embraced and kissed.

"Missed you," he said.

"Missed you too," she said.

He got in the passenger seat. Elizabeth started the car, and they pulled away.

"How's the city?" she asked.

"Well, it's still there," he said.

"And the smell at Ground Zero?"

"It's still there too," he said.

At dinner, Elizabeth's parents tried to persuade them to move to Long Island, to move away from the terror threat.

"We would still work there. We would still have to commute there," Elizabeth said.

Robbie couldn't think of abandoning the city. Not now. The city needed him. He needed the city.

"We can't leave now," he said. "Maybe when things get back to normal, we could consider it. But not now."

Later that night, neither could sleep. Robbie had spent years struggling to fall asleep, but since he had found Elizabeth, the problem had gone away. But since 9/11, his sleep problems had returned.

"What's wrong?" Elizabeth whispered.

"Nothing," Robbie said. "The usual. What about you?"

"I can't sleep because I know you can't sleep," she said.

He rolled over and stared at the ceiling. "What a world we live in," he said.

She rested her head on his chest. He stroked her hair. And then he remembered the meteor shower.

"Hey, let's go outside," he said.

"What?"

"There's a big meteor shower tonight. I read it in the paper. It's supposed to be happening right now."

"A meteor shower? It's probably freezing outside. Are you crazy?"

"No. Come on. I've never seen one before."

"We'll wake up my parents."

"We'll be quiet."

They got out of bed, threw on some clothes, tiptoed down the stairs, slipped on their coats, and quietly let themselves out of the house and into the backyard.

"There's supposed to be, like, forty or fifty an hour," Robbie said.

"I don't see anything," said Elizabeth as she looked up at the sky.

"They said you need a few minutes to let your eyes adjust to the night sky," he said.

So, they looked at the blackness of the sky and waited.

And then they saw a streak of light shoot across the sky. And then they saw another. And another.

"Holy shit," Elizabeth said.

Soon, the sky was filled with streaks of lights. It was a heavenly sight that neither of them had ever experienced.

Elizabeth held Robbie, and he began to cry. Elizabeth held his face, and she began to cry too. Robbie wasn't sure why he was crying. The last two months had been tough on everyone. Maybe it was just time.

He stayed looking at the sky and wondered what the shooting stars were thinking. They had been revealing themselves at this time each year since the dawn of time. Dinosaurs had looked up and seen these same meteors. Cavemen had looked up and seen them. And it occurred to Robbie that the meteors didn't care much about what was happening down below them. They didn't care about 9/11 or Ground Zero. A hundred years from now, a thousand years from now, a million years from now, they would still be appearing, and every living thing that ever looked up at them now—Robbie and Elizabeth included—would be long gone. 9/11 meant nothing. The trials and tribulations of every person on the planet ultimately meant nothing. We would all be gone. The comets would remain.

"You OK?" Elizabeth asked.

"Yeah," Robbie lied.

"They're so beautiful," she said.

"They are," said Robbie.

They stayed for a few more minutes, then went back inside.

"Hopefully, we can get some sleep now," Elizabeth said.

"Hopefully," Robbie said.

But he knew that sleep would not come tonight. And he wondered if it would ever come again.

Moonlight Mile

(2007)

"ROOM 515, FIFTH FLOOR," said the desk attendant. "Thank you for your continued support of Marriott, Mr. Miller."

"Thank you," Robbie said.

He had never liked hotel rooms, especially when he was away on business and alone. He could never fall asleep and would spend most nights away from home wrestling with himself in his bed.

He just didn't like being away from Elizabeth. It had taken him so many years to find her, and any night away from her reminded him too much of the lonely days before she came into his life. Unfortunately, work took him away from her more than he could stand sometimes. Tonight was one of those nights. He had spent two nights in Chicago and now was in a Marriott somewhere in Indiana.

In his room, he flicked through the TV channels, trying to find something to take his mind off his present situation. He tried CNN, but the news from Iraq was too depressing.

So, he found a rerun of *Seinfeld* and stuck with that. It was the one about the marble rye. He always liked that one. It had always surprised him that a show about neurotic New Yorkers had found such a following with the rest of the country. He guessed that he was something of a neurotic New Yorker as well, and of course he got the humor. The fact that people in the Midwest or the other hinterlands found it funny made him feel good for some reason.

Maybe people really are the same wherever you go, he thought.

Watching the show would occupy his mind for a little and help fight his coming bout of loneliness. But it also made him miss home a little bit more. There were a lot of TV shows that got the essence of New York right, but perhaps none did it better than *Seinfeld*.

He never felt completely comfortable outside of New York. Things just moved differently. Being away from New York made him feel out of sync.

When the show ended, he turned off the TV and tried to sleep. He hugged the pillow next to him and thought of Elizabeth and the kids and wished that he were home. In moments like this, his brain could almost scarily fool himself into thinking that his family didn't exist and never had. That his whole life back in New York was a dream. How could he possibly sleep with strange thoughts like that running through his head?

He hated it when this happened. He knew it would be a long night. It made him think of those days in his small apartment in the city when he was single and alone and he would wonder if he would always be that way.

And then one day, he wasn't. One day Elizabeth appeared, and all was good in the world.

And yet here he was, years later, alone in a hotel room and feeling the same fear he had felt back then. It wasn't rational fear, of course. He wasn't actually alone. He was just away on business. His family would be waiting for him when he got home.

But a man's soul doesn't soon forget the pain of the past. Like an old smell or an old song can stir up the past and bring you momentarily back in time, the empty bed Robbie was lying in took him back to times he didn't want to see again. It was as if the bed was trying to swallow him whole and suck him back into his former life.

So, he got up. Why stay in bed and torture himself? He grabbed a pair of jeans out of his luggage and threw on a T-shirt. Then he opened the door and headed down the hall to the elevator.

He exited the elevator and walked through the silent, empty hotel lobby.

It was quiet in Munster, Indiana—not a car on the road or any signs of life anywhere. He would be home in two days. Two more days. That wasn't so long, right? Then he would hold Elizabeth in his arms, and the kids would run to hug him, and all would be OK. Two days and then a two-hour flight from Midway to LaGuardia.

That's nothing, he told himself.

Why did he struggle with this? Other guys he knew loved being away from their wives and kids. But here was Robbie, in a dark parking lot in Indiana, unable to sleep, unable to quell his uneasiness.

It was a warm night, but Robbie suddenly felt a chill. A pickup truck drove past, momentarily breaking the late-night silence.

He thought of Elizabeth's face. She was waiting for him back home. No reason to feel lonely. No reason to feel dread or isolation. It's just that this desolate spot in Indiana, of all places, seemed so damn far away from her.

It made him think of a recurring dream that he had been having lately. In the dream, he was back at Merrill Lynch in the late '90s, hanging out with the gang after work, and Elizabeth was there. But in the dream, they weren't together. Somehow, in the dream, they had broken up and did not end up together. He would tell himself that something was wrong—he had married her, and they were living happily ever after!—so why was she standing at the other side of the bar at Minter's, ignoring him? Something was wrong.

And then he would wake up in a cold sweat and realize that Elizabeth was lying next to him. It had just been a dream. All was right with the world.

He dreaded what it would feel like if he ever had the dream when he was away on business and he would wake up to find she wasn't there. Maybe that's why he had trouble falling asleep on the road.

He looked up and noticed the bright full moon lighting up the night sky. It was so clear and bright, and he felt like he could reach out and touch it. It felt like the moon was there just for him. But he realized that it wasn't just for him. Half the damn planet could see it. And that included Elizabeth. Maybe she was looking out of their window at home right now, looking at the same moon. If they both could be looking at the same thing at the same moment, then how far away from each other could they really be? He suddenly felt close to her. She was only a moonlight mile away from him.

He stayed outside for another minute, looking up at their moon, imagining Elizabeth in his arms. *Not long now, my sweet.*

Two days, two hours, and a moonlight mile away from home.

A Dish Served Cold

(2011)

ROBBIE WAS STARTING TO doze off. He was watching the Yankees postgame show, enjoying the highlights of their victory over the Tigers. Still, he was tired and wanted to go to sleep. But he saw a news update earlier that President Obama was going to address the nation. It was almost 11:30 p.m. When was there ever a presidential address at this time of night? Robbie had a thought of what it could be, but he was afraid to get his hopes up. But he had to be right. What else could it be?

He switched over to channel 4 and nudged Elizabeth, who was sleeping next to him.

"What?" she grumbled.

"Obama's about to address the nation."

The local news cut away, and there was the president walking toward a podium in the East Room. Robbie felt a swirl in his stomach, and goose bumps started sprouting on his arms.

"Good evening," said President Obama. "Tonight, I can report to the American people and to the world that the United States has conducted an operation that killed Osama bin Laden, the leader of Al Qaeda and a terrorist who's responsible for the murder of thousands of innocent men, women, and children…"

Robbie knew it. *Bin Laden! They got him. They got him!*

"They killed Bin Laden!" He shook Elizabeth awake.

Elizabeth rubbed at her sleepy eyes and focused on the TV. "Holy shit," she said.

Robbie leaned his head back on his headboard. *Ten years,* he thought. For ten years, he had thought about that day every night before he went to bed. For ten years, he thought about those who weren't as fortunate and he and Elizabeth had been on that horrible day. And now Bin Laden was dead. And he was happy, right? But somehow not as happy as he had always dreamed he would be.

They watched the news into the wee hours. People were in front of the White House, celebrating. Someone held up a sign that read *Obama got Osama!* It seemed people everywhere were celebrating. He surmised that revenge feels good for a moment. But when the moment passes, you are still in the same place. Is that why he felt so strange?

They watched for a little while longer, then went to sleep. Or at least Robbie tried to. His brain sometimes had a hard time turning itself off. Bin Laden was dead.

In Lower Manhattan, a new skyscraper was rising at Ground Zero. The Freedom Tower, they called it. Robbie was glad that the skyline would be restored, and he hoped that his city was beyond the terror scares that had hung over it for the last decade.

But he still longed for the days prior to 9/11. The city was different to him now. So was the country.

Killing Bin Laden probably wasn't going to change that. He had often wondered and fantasized about how he would feel when they finally got him. He didn't know if he would pump his fist in joy or shed a tear for everyone and everything that was lost that day.

And now the moment was here, and he did neither.

Maybe too much time had passed. Somehow, he had become numb to all of it. What was that saying about revenge? That it was a dish best served cold. And now he knew what that meant. Because it was exactly how he felt. Cold. He wanted to feel the elation that the people in front of the White House seemed to be feeling. But he didn't feel anything.

He shuffled the pillows and tried to find sleep.

"Scars have the strange power to remind us that the past is real."

—*Cormac McCarthy*

The Fate of Glass

(2016)

Manhattan Investor Monthly, February 12, 2016

The following essay was written by Wall Street financier Robert Miller about his college roommate. Click here to read the full story.

I WOULD OFTEN DREAM of Ricky in the years after college. And while the dream wasn't always the same, the basic premise usually was. We were back at school, setting up our dorm room for the new semester. Sometimes, school looked exactly as it had; sometimes, it looked oddly different. It didn't matter either way. It was school! We were back! The excitement was real. It was palpable.

I don't know if I ever felt more excited in my life than I did on the first day of a new semester. The hope and promise of a new year. Was there anything better? The parties, the friends, the girls, the pranks, all of it...

Whenever I had the dream, it was a wonderful feeling. Ricky and I were back. We were still in school, ready to rule the world—or at least our small portion of it—once again. The dream would never last much past that point. But it was always great when the dream did come.

Waking up would change that. As soon as I would awake from the dream, a profound feeling of loss and regret would come over me. Reality would set in. College was over and had been for a long time. I was in the real world now, and so was he.

In the early years after college, I think I had the dream at least once a week. But as the years went by and the echo of college began to fade, I had the dream less often. But it never stopped coming completely. Twenty-five years after graduation, I still had the dream three or four times a year. But the dream was less exciting in these later years because my subconscious self would realize that it was only a dream.

At one point in these later dreams, I would look at Ricky in the dream and say something to the effect of, "What are we doing here? We graduated years ago! We're not supposed to be here anymore."

And then I would awake.

The dream is all I have left of Ricky now. When it comes now, it hurts. But I cherish it anyway and always look forward to the next one.

I first took notice of Ricky on my first day of college in 1985. They had herded all the freshmen into the student center and broke us out into groups of six. They asked each of us in the group to introduce ourselves to the other five and say a few things about ourselves. Everyone was somewhat shy, including me. I was a wide-eyed seventeen-year-old, away from home for the first time. I didn't know what to say. I certainly didn't have anything interesting to say. After I and four other kids fumbled through our introductions, Ricky jumped in like a game show host.

"My name is Ricky Macfarland, and I'm from Toronto, Canada, and I am pumped to be in college, and I can't wait to have some fun. The next four years are going to be awesome."

281

He had bleached-blond hair and looked like a model in a catalog. And he spoke with incredible confidence. He looked right at the girl next to me and told her that she had beautiful eyes. I certainly didn't have the confidence to say something like that. But this guy did. I immediately made the decision that I needed to befriend this kid. If I hung around with him, I would have all the fun at college that I had been dreaming about.

We were at Utica College of Syracuse University in the Mohawk Valley of upstate New York. It was a small campus, with maybe 2,000 kids, and half of those were commuters. I think I related to Ricky because he was from a major metropolis like me. We were surrounded by kids from small towns in upstate New York.

So, even though he was Canadian, I felt a closer connection to him than to the other kids. He was also older. He was twenty, almost twenty-one. In Canada, the kids go to grade thirteen. That took him to age nineteen. Then he—well, I never found out exactly what he did for the next two years before going to college. I guess he took a couple of gap years before anyone knew what a gap year was. Yes, Ricky always liked to do things first.

It also helped our budding friendship that not only did he live right next door to me, but also neither one of us got along with our roommates. Ricky's roommate, Tim, was an OK guy. But he missed home and his high school girlfriend, and since he lived only an hour away from campus, he went home every weekend.

My roommate, Pete, was a different story. Even though he was initially excited about college, he was a kid wholly unsuited to being away at college. Especially on the floor that we lived on. Our floor had a bunch of loud, rowdy young men looking to have an *Animal House* experience. Ricky was at the forefront of that. But Pete didn't go for loud and rowdy. He seemed very excited to be at college and gave lip service to wanting to have fun. But he soon got into a bad habit of "telling" on the other guys on the floor who were being loud during quiet hours. He started making regular trips to our floor RA with incriminating evidence. I told him to back off a little. I told him he was going to ostracize himself. He didn't listen. It made living with him rather difficult. And it pushed me toward Ricky.

Being older than me, Ricky would teach me things about girls, sex, and drinking. But initially, he taught me how to prank.

There was a rainy day early in our freshman year when I left our dorm to go to a morning class. There was a stray dog milling about the walkway. Now, I've never been a dog person, and dogs have never seemed to like me. And this particular dog was eyeing me as soon as I left the dorm. I tried to ignore him, but he made a run at me as soon as I got near him. He was a somewhat-large dog, a mutt of some kind, and he was wet from the rain. I tried to avoid him, but he was too fast. He leaped at me, and his wet paws scraped me from my waist all the way down past my knees. My pants were now covered in mud. I couldn't go to class like that. So, I hustled back into the dorm to quickly get changed. Pete was already at class, but Ricky was just getting out of the shower.

"What are you doing back from class already?" he asked.

I told him what had happened and pointed out my window to show him the stray dog who had soiled me. Ricky howled with laughter. This is what he lived for.

I hastily changed my pants and raced to class, narrowly avoiding the dog on my second pass.

I returned an hour later and opened the door to my room. Staring me in the face in the center of the room was the dog.

"What the hell?" I said.

The dog panicked at the sight of me and went berserk, bouncing all over the small dorm room. I yelled for him to get out, but that just made him crazier. He eventually jumped on Pete's bed, scrambling the bedspread, which he then dragged to the floor.

I ran out of the room, and the dog followed me. When I opened the back exit door to the dorm, he ran out.

Then I heard the loud laughter coming from Ricky's room. I turned and saw him exit his room.

"That was classic, Rob," he said, still laughing.

How the hell did he pull this off?

Turns out, he grabbed our RA and told him what the dog had done to my pants. Then he went outside and coaxed the dog into the dorm and persuaded the RA to use his master key to open my door.

I had to admit, it was damn funny. But the dog had messed up and stained Pete's sheets, and he was livid.

It was the second prank Ricky had pulled on me.

A week earlier, he had emptied the large garbage can in the hallway and filled it with water in the bathroom. Then he lugged it out of the bathroom and tipped it against my front door. When I opened the door, it tipped over, and all the water came rushing into the room. But my room was a corner room, shaped like a right-angled triangle. When the water came rushing in, it all went to Pete's side of the space.

The dog incident put him over the edge, and he went to the Residence Life office to report that our RA had illegally entered our room. This further put Pete in the crosshairs. All the guys on the floor loved our RA and had grown to dislike Pete.

Luckily, our RA and Ricky got off with a polite reprimand. Pete sulked and further withdrew from the goings-on around him. He couldn't adapt to living in a dorm full of unruly young men. But I took to it. The wacky stuff Ricky pulled made me laugh. I had some wild oats to sow, and Ricky was the perfect partner to sow them with.

Our roommates transferred to different schools after freshman year, so Ricky and I gladly became roommates in our sophomore year.

When his parents dropped him off, I had to remember to refer to Ricky as Richard. His mother had made it clear the year before that she hated Rick or Ricky. His name was Richard. She also got visibly perturbed if anyone mispronounced their last name. It was Mac-Farland, not Mick-Farland. The room also had to be kept spotless. Ricky referred to his mother as inspector 12.

This wasn't a problem on the first day of a new semester. But it was a problem on subsequent visits. I was the messy one, and Ricky tried to keep me in line, but he lost the battle. By senior year, he was as messy as me. It always necessitated a hasty cleanup whenever his parents were coming to visit.

The first thing Ricky put up was a Canadian flag in the window. He also had a T-shirt that was emblazoned with *Proud to be Canadian*. He had been a serious hockey player in high school, and he had that polite but firm way of speaking that all Canadian hockey players seemed to have. Ever see a Canadian hockey player getting interviewed between periods of an NHL game? That's how Ricky spoke. Polite, respectful, but you knew he could pop you in the mouth—or "drop the gloves," as Ricky would say—at a moment's notice.

After putting up the flag, he turned to me and yelled, "You'd better get a Yank flag in here and soon, for fuck's sake."

He wanted to make sure I was as proud to be a Yank as he was to be a Canuck, and he thought it was only fair that we each had our respective flags hanging in the room.

A short time later, the Stars and Stripes were hanging from the ceiling above my bed while the red and white maple leaf hung in the window. That flag ended up being a marker for us. We were on the first floor, and you could see the flag from all over campus. It was a small campus, and Ricky and I spent so much time together that people would refer to us as Ricky and Rob, or Rob and Ricky.

Someone might say, "Do you know Rob—you know, of Ricky and Rob?" like we were morning radio hosts.

And everyone knew that the room with the maple leaf in the window was ours.

Soon, Ricky would stop calling me Rob. Soon, I would be known as Ray.

There was a local TV and appliance store owner in Utica named Ray Seakan. He constantly ran these cheap commercials on the local Utica stations, in which he would scream and wave his arms at the screen, telling you about his discounted prices and shouting, "See me today! Today! Today!" at the screen. You couldn't have a commercial break in Utica in 1985 or 1986 and not see this commercial. He also weighed well over 400 pounds and wore a tuxedo with an enormous cummerbund around his waist. It was quite the sight to see this large man in the giant cummerbund screaming at you every time you turned on the television.

So, when Utica College announced that it was having a Jell-O wrestling contest, I knew that I would sign up for it. I came to college to do things like that. And I knew what character I would dress up as. The surprise was that Ricky, of all people, was too afraid or shy to do it with me. He had already helped me come out of my shell so much in the little over a year that I had known him. He was the one who would stand up at parties and do something outrageous to make everyone laugh. He was the one who would rip his clothes off and run down the hall of the dorm. He was the one who would walk up to any girl he wanted without fear or hesitation and "chat her up," as he liked to call it. And now he was afraid to join me in a staged Jell-O wresting match in the gymnasium in front of the whole school. But it didn't stop me. So, I got one of our other buddies to join me. I dressed up as Ray Seakan by stuffing my shirt with two pillows and wearing a black robe, dressed up to look like a tuxedo jacket, and a large red towel wrapped around me to look like a cummerbund. My partner, Justin, wore a yellow spandex bodysuit and called himself Chubber Lang—a nod to Mr. T's character in *Rocky III*.

There were eight other acts in the Jell-O wrestling event, but Justin and I stole the show. Everyone instantly recognized me as Ray Seakan, and as Ricky would tell me after the show, watching me flail about in the Jell-O was the funniest thing he had ever seen. It was like I had earned his respect in a way that I hadn't before. I had done something funnier and more outrageous than he had ever done. And from that moment on, I was Ray.

Our room was decorated, so it was easy for visitors to tell who lived on which side of the room. I had posters of The Beatles, Pink Floyd, the Stones, the Yankees, the Giants, and Manhattan. Ricky had a Canada tourism poster, that *Study Hard* poster with the picture of some woman's breasts on it that seemed to be in every other room in the dorm, skiing posters, and a Toronto Blue Jays poster.

Of course, the Yankees and Blue Jays were rivals in the American League East, giving Ricky and me something to argue about each day. The Blue Jays had edged out the Yankees in '85, and they were battling it out again in '86. There was a big September series between the two starting on a Tuesday night that we desperately needed to watch. But the first game was the same night as our English History class, which was a once-a-week, three-hour night class. It wasn't normally a big deal to miss a college class, but it was when it was a once-a-week class. But Ricky wanted to watch that game.

So, he decided to go see the professor, Mr. Rogers, that afternoon and proceeded to tell him that his grandfather had been killed in a home invasion back in Toronto and he was so distraught over the circumstances of the death that not only was he leaving later that day to take an Amtrak to Toronto, but also that he needed me to go with him to provide comfort. Mr. Rogers bought it and offered his condolences and told Ricky that we could see him early before next week's class to go over what we missed.

Ricky was ecstatic that we wouldn't miss the game. I was dumbstruck by the lie he told to give us this opportunity. Ricky explained that the lie had to be a little outrageous to make it believable. Simply telling Mr. Rogers that his grandfather died would sound too much like *the dog ate my homework*. Telling Mr. Rogers that his grandfather was murdered in a home invasion had to be believed because who the hell would make up something like that? Well, the answer was that Ricky would.

"Relax, Ray," he told me. "This is college. We can do whatever we want and get away with it. And because of me, we're going to watch the Yankees–Blue Jays game."

I couldn't argue with the logic. And I wanted to watch the game too. English History could wait a week.

Our room always had a steady stream of visitors and became a hangout for everyone that we knew. It seemed everyone always wanted to see what Ricky and Ray were up to.

I got to know my first real girlfriend in college this way. Helen was going out with our good friend Tom, who lived down the hall from us. She got in the habit of coming back from class every day with her roommate, Mary, and coming through our floor to see her boyfriend. Soon, she and Mary would stop by our room first to hang out and many days would never make it down the hall to Tom's room, making it necessary for poor Tom to come down to our room to see his girlfriend.

Mary was from Long Island, like me, and maybe that's why we made a connection. There was something comfortable about her. But I saw her only as a friend in the beginning. It was Ricky who pointed out to me that it was obvious that all the joking that Mary and I did every day was more than friends goofing around.

"You're crazy about her, Ray," he said. "And she's crazy about you. I thought you downstate New Yorkers are supposed to be smart. Don't miss your chance. She's great, and you're a bloody fool if you don't do something."

And he was right. I was still only nineteen years old, and I guess I couldn't see what was right in front of me. But my brother Ricky could. He really had become my brother. And his prodding brought the first love of my life into my arms.

Living with Ricky brought his idiosyncrasies to the forefront. He would grind his teeth at night, which freaked me out at first. It sounded like he was rolling marbles around in his mouth. I had never heard that noise before and have never heard it since. Ricky would also take forever to get ready to go out for the night. A long shower, followed by going through his closet ad infinitum, trying to find something to wear. And he would always blast Tears for Fears' "Everybody Wants to Rule the World" as he got dressed, as it got him pumped up and ready to go. Of course, when he sang Tears for Fears' "Shout," we would both laugh because even he thought he sounded funny, singing that song with his Canadian accent.

Ricky also had a nickname for his manhood. He called it the Cobra, and he even had a T-shirt that said *The Cobra* on it. He told me that my manhood needed a good name too. I didn't agree and didn't know what to call it even if I did. Not to worry; Ricky took care of that. He called it Clint the Bush Pilot, which was mildly amusing, if not entirely accurate, new girlfriend or not. But Ricky liked it enough that he changed the message on our phone's answering machine.

Our message, in Ricky's voice, now said, "You've reached the room of every woman's fantasy, but unfortunately, Ricky and Rob are out with their pals, the Cobra and Clint the Bush Pilot, and are unable to come to the phone right now. However, if you leave your name and number—and your measurements if you are a female—we will get back to you as soon as possible."

Now I realize that something like that wouldn't play well nowadays, but in 1986, everyone, including the girls we knew, thought it was hilarious, and more than a few of them left a message with their measurements on it. Even my mother thought it was funny. Ricky's mother? Not as much. But Ricky didn't care. It was funny to him. His mother would have to get used to it or not leave messages.

Ricky and I both also snored a lot. We soon came up with a system where we would throw stuffed animals—given to me by Mary, who sometimes got caught in the cross fire—across the room, hoping to land them on the other's noses to stamp out the wood sawing. If that didn't work, we would snap our fingers, which had a fairly high success rate. I still use that trick today with my wife when needed.

Sometimes, I would have to sleep at Mary's if Ricky was bringing a girl back to the room, which happened somewhat frequently, especially in the spring semester, when the sun would come out and, as Ricky would say, "The blond locks become golden. The birds can't resist the golden locks, Ray."

Neither the Yankees nor the Blue Jays won the division in '86. The Red Sox finished first, with the Yankees in second, and the Blue Jays a few games back in fourth. But the New York football Giants were the dominating team in the NFL in 1986 and cruised their way into their first Super Bowl. I had spent my childhood watching horrible Giants teams, and the thought of them ever reaching a Super Bowl seemed like a distant dream that would never happen. The Super Bowl had seemed like a game that was reserved for Dallas and Pittsburgh.

But now the Giants were there, and it was like a dream come true. Ricky had been telling me for almost two years that the Giants would never win a Super Bowl with Phil Simms as quarterback, but here they were. And they were the heavy favorites to beat the Denver Broncos. And although Ricky didn't like the Giants, he decided to root for them in the big game because he didn't like John Elway and because he wanted to see how insane I would get if the Giants won.

I parked myself in front of the big screen TV in the dorm lounge early in the day to watch all the pregame shows and to ensure that I got a good seat. The TV room never really filled up, except on Thursday nights, when *Miami Vice* was on, but I was taking no chances.

When the game started, it didn't go exactly as planned. The Broncos were dominating the play and held a 10–7 lead late in the second quarter. I was nervous as hell, and Ricky kept trying to calm me down, but to no avail. But Giants defensive end George Martin sacked Elway in the end zone for a safety, and Ricky and I both leaped up in excitement. I landed on his back piggyback-style, screaming like a lunatic. When I rolled off his back, I mistakenly grabbed on to his gold chain and ripped it right off his neck.

"For fuck's sake, Ray," he yelled. "My grandfather gave me that."

I was too happy to care.

"The grandfather who was murdered?" I said.

That caused him to laugh out loud. "Good one, Ray."

The Giants dominated the second half and cruised to a 39–20 victory. I was beyond ecstatic.

"Congrats, Ray. Phil Simms came through," said Ricky.

He even opened a bottle of Molson Golden that he had brought back from Canada when he returned from Christmas break and proceeded to pour the whole bottle on my head. I loved it.

To this day, when I see a highlight of George Martin sacking John Elway, I think of Ricky and the gold chain and his grandfather.

Ricky occasionally had a hard time falling asleep. He would put the radio on low sometimes to help, but it rarely worked. So, I pulled out my copy of the soundtrack to the Christopher Reeves movie *Somewhere in Time* and put it on the turntable, and Ricky loved the soothing violin music. And it helped him fall asleep. But he could never get the name of the album right.

If he was struggling to fall asleep, he would say, "Put on *Summertime*, Ray."

"It's *Somewhere in Time*," I'd say back to him.

But he could never get it right. So, *Summertime* it was.

We would also talk about our futures during the quiet times when we turned in for the night. Ricky would always talk about the two of us opening a business together. He would even go around telling people this all the time. He would also tell me that we should buy houses next to each other and raise our families together. I wasn't crazy about the idea of going into business together, but I did like the idea of living next to each other. College years were like dog years. After four years with Ricky, three of them spent living in a small room with him, it felt like we had been together for decades. So, the idea of our living next to each other as adults and raising our families together was appealing. I couldn't imagine not being around him. But then Ricky might say in the next sentence that he didn't want kids.

"What do you mean, you don't want kids?" I would ask him.

"They're bloody expensive," he would say. "I mean, look how much we're costing our folks right now."

There Are Places I Remember

I was happier than I had been at any time since I was a little boy. Ricky was one of the coolest kids on campus, and he had chosen me as his best friend and comrade in arms. Kids like Ricky had ignored me in high school. Now I was in the game, and Ricky was my partner in crime and my protector.

Late in my sophomore year, my relationship with Mary collapsed, and Ricky was there to pick up the pieces for me. Whenever I was down, he would pick me up. I wanted to sulk and feel sorry for myself, but he wouldn't let me. If we needed to go out and grab a beer on a Tuesday afternoon, well, Ricky made sure we did so. If he thought pulling a prank would get me out of my doldrums, then we pulled a prank on one of the guys. He was the rock that I leaned on, and I knew he would always be there for me. Ricky was always about doing something fun, and having him around when my heart got broken was a saving grace for me.

In September of '88, the summer Olympics were taking place in Seoul, South Korea. Canada didn't have much going for it in the summer games, but it did have runner Ben Johnson, who was a threat to take the gold from Carl Lewis. None of us had heard of Johnson, so Ricky kept reminding us. Johnson was from Scarborough—via Jamaica—the same section of Toronto as Ricky. In Ricky's mind, he was Ben Johnson, and Ben Johnson was him. He made sure all of us were aware of this and never missed a chance to remind us that Johnson was going to win the gold.

Sure enough, Johnson beat Lewis for the gold and set a world record in the 100-meter dash.

Ricky was beyond ecstatic. He spent the next three days telling everyone, "Call me Ben."

Most people who met Ricky thought he was a great guy, a fun guy, who was always making people laugh and doing something outrageous. He was someone that people wanted to be around. But for some people, Ricky's actions were sometimes obnoxious, and those people reacted differently upon meeting him. The "call me Ben" act was obnoxious, but I still found it funny. He was a rough-and-tumble Canadian kid, surrounded by somewhat arrogant Americans who didn't think much of Canada, and he was happy that his countryman had beaten the great American. He was having a moment, and most people laughed with him.

Of course, the fun ended three days after the race when Johnson tested positive for steroids and was stripped of his gold medal, which now went to America's Lewis.

Now everyone on campus couldn't wait to call Ricky Ben. And they did, relentlessly. To his credit, he took it in stride and, as always, had a good laugh about it. Either way, it brought him attention, and for Ricky, all attention was good.

This was also the year that Ricky almost bought a car. Not just any car, but a brand-new $4,000 Yugo. Remember Yugos? They were the cheap, ugly, boxy cars made behind the Iron Curtain in the former Yugoslavia and sold to consumers in Ronald Reagan's America. It just so happened that at the beginning of the semester, Ricky's father had given him a check for $4,500 to deposit in his local bank account in Utica so that he could pay for the fall semester. Wouldn't it be better if he used the money to buy a brand-new car? In Ricky's mind, it would.

"Are you crazy? What about your tuition?" I asked.

"I'll tell the old man it got stolen," he replied.

"Out of your bank account?" I replied.

"We'll figure it out, Ray," he said. "Bottom line is, we'll have a new car. I can always come up with a story for my dad."

He even started making phone calls to see where in central New York he could buy a Yugo.

"You're crazy," I told him.

"How classic would it be, Ray, if I came cruising onto campus in a shiny red Yugo?" was his answer.

"It would be hilarious," I told him. "But then you would have no money for the semester, and your father would kill you."

"This is college, Ray. We can do whatever we want and get away with it," he replied.

Luckily, cooler heads prevailed, and his desire for the Yugo went away.

Toward the end of junior year, my sister, who was a hotel management major at Cornell, won a trip for two to Hawaii. But she didn't want to go, so she asked me if I wanted the trip. I was hesitant because I had never flown before, was scared at the prospect of doing so, and wasn't sure if I wanted my first flight to be one that would take me halfway around the globe.

"Are you crazy, Ray?" said Ricky. "A free trip to Hawaii. Of course we're going!"

So, Ricky traveled home with me to Long Island when the semester ended. He liked my "folks," as he called them, and they enjoyed his irreverence. Some people loved him; some didn't. My mother was terrified of flying, which was why I had never flown to that point. She wasn't thrilled that we were flying to Hawaii. Ricky calmed her down though. He had made almost annual trips to Florida with his family for years. He said, in Canada, they refer to Florida as the 14th province. He was an experienced flyer.

"Don't worry, Mum Miller," he told my mom. Or mum if you are from Canada. "I'll take care of your boy."

The flight from JFK included a layover in San Francisco, a connecting flight to Honolulu, then another connection to Maui. I was nervous, and the flights were thankfully uneventful, but it helped to have Ricky there with me. If he was calm, I was calm. He was such a confident person that, to me, he was indestructible. I was safe with him.

In Maui, we sunned and drank at the pool and on the beach at the Royal Lahaina Beach Resort, mingling among all the honeymooners. We got more than a few strange looks from the young lovers who were obviously wondering what the two young college guys were doing there. For Ricky, the main goal was to get a "rockin' tan" to go with the soon-to-be bleached-blond locks. He said he was going to be a "bronze goddess."

"God," I told him. "Bronze god."

"That's what I said, Ray," he replied.

But he kept getting it wrong. He had it all planned out. He would start the first two days with fifteen sunscreen "to get my base." Then two days of eight sunscreen, then right to oil. Then he would be a bronze god. I didn't know much about suntanning other than to know that I burned easily. Ricky had obviously put a lot of thought into it and seemed to have it down to a science. So, I didn't pay much attention to his plan. But as we soon found out, the sun in Maui was quite different from the sun at Lake Ontario.

Ricky had fair Scottish skin. I sort of noticed it turning red, but didn't think much of it. After day four in the Hawaiian sun, Ricky was excited to move away from sunscreen and start applying the oil. But it didn't go as planned.

After one day of baking in the sun without sunscreen, Ricky was burned to a crisp. His skin was as red as a boiled lobster. His discomfort was extreme. At our room that night, he was crying out in pain. He begged me to go to the hotel store and buy some Noxzema.

I don't know exactly what I expected to happen on our trip to Hawaii, but I know that rubbing Noxzema cream on Ricky's burned body was not high on the list. We'd had a nice trip so far. We had rented a Jeep and drove on the road to Hana, the island's volcano. We drank frosty tropical beverages on the beach. I even got Ricky to try lobster for the first time, and he loved it. Now he was the lobster, and he could find no relief, no matter how much cream I applied to the burned areas.

So, our last two days in Maui were spent keeping Ricky out of the sun and trying to soothe his burns, but to no avail. The bronze god had turned into rust.

But in Ricky's mind, it was still a great trip. He loved the Hawaiian greeting *mahalo*. He said it incessantly while we were there, and it continued when we returned to campus in the fall for senior year.

He couldn't wait to tell everyone about the trip and how amazing it was, leaving out the sunburn portion of our adventure.

He greeted everyone with, "Mahalo," and said it so often that he soon had half the campus saying it.

Kids who had never been to Hawaii or had ever heard the word were saying it incessantly. I swear Ricky should have gone into politics.

Ricky wasn't done with long trips. The mission during senior year for Ricky was for the gang to go to Daytona Beach for spring break. But not to fly, as that would be too easy. No, he wanted to rent an RV and drive there. It was only 1,180 miles or so from Utica to Daytona Beach, so why not, right?

He worked out all of the arrangements for us to rent our 27-foot Southwind Winnebago. There would be eight of us going, and it was around $150 a man to rent it for a week. The plan was to drive it straight down, with only a few rest stops along the way.

Ricky volunteered to drive first because Ricky liked to do everything first. I wanted no part of driving that monster, so I was glad when it was decided that the driving would be split four ways, not eight. Ricky took the first five-hour driving shift. He sang most of the way, which was amusing and annoying at the same time. We blasted Guns N' Roses' *Appetite for Destruction* and Van Halen's *OU812* on the tape deck to drown him out. It took 21 hours, but we made it to Daytona safely.

We, of course, made no arrangements to park the Winnebago at an RV park because we didn't have the money for that. The plan was to park it on the beach every day and then find a spot somewhere in town to park it at night. Problem was, the bathroom septic tank in the Winnebago was full by the time we got to Florida.

Having the camper bake in the Florida sun every day did not help the matter. And we certainly could no longer use the bathroom anymore. We solved the bathroom problem by showering and using the toilet in the hotel room of some girls from our school who were staying right on the beach. But the problem of the full septic tank was another matter. The back of the camper was starting to stink. Ricky had an idea to solve the problem. We had been parking and sleeping in a McDonald's parking lot each night, and it was here that Ricky came up with a plan.

We would drive the Winnebago over the bridge, away from Daytona Beach and into residential Daytona. There, we hoped to find a nice, quiet street with a sewer to dump the contents of the tank.

So, we drove the monster over the bridge to look for a suitable sewer. We had been getting up at 6 every morning, driving out of the McDonald's parking lot, and getting a good spot on the beach. On this morning, we got up at 4 and started rolling before the sun came up.

After driving around a nice middle-class neighborhood for ten minutes, Ricky pulled up at the curb and parked the Winnebago so that the main of the septic tank was right over the sewer.

"Ray, get out and pull the cap off of the main," he said.

"No way," I replied. There was excrement dripping from that main, some of which had been in that tank since shortly after we left Utica. "It was your idea to get a Winnebago. You pull the cap," I said.

"OK, Ray, don't get your panties in a bunch," he said.

Ricky exited the vehicle, and I and the rest of the guys followed him, quietly tiptoeing our way to the back of the camper. Everyone wanted to see what was going to happen when Ricky pulled the cap. Everyone, except our friend Steve, who was still passed out drunk and couldn't move.

The neighborhood was silent and still, the first rays of sunlight just peeking over the horizon.

We all crowded behind Ricky as he inched his way toward the septic tank. But before he could pull the cap, we were startled by the sound of a man heaving. Who was it? Where was it? I peeked around the front of the camper, and there he was. Steve was on the front lawn of the house across the street, puking his brains out. He must have quietly slipped out of the vehicle while we were waiting for Ricky to pull the cap. And he wasn't being quiet about it. He was puking loudly. Now there were lights on in the house. Then lights on in the house next door.

"Pull the fucking cap. We have to get out of here," I said as loudly as I could without further alerting the whole street.

Ricky pulled the cap. A stream of shit poured out into the sewer. The rest of us ran across the street and pulled Steve off the grass and dragged him back to the camper. Unfortunately, he didn't come with us quietly. More lights went on in the neighborhood. The front door of the house in front of us opened, and a man in a robe stood, gaping at us. Being that we were in the South, this New Yorker was relieved to see that the man wasn't holding a shotgun.

Ricky hastily put the cap back on the septic tank, and we all piled back into the Winnebago.

"Hit the gas, Rick," I yelled, and the monster tore out of the neighborhood and headed back toward Daytona Beach.

The next day, Ricky and I sat atop the Winnebago, drinking a beer, watching the girls, and looking out into the Atlantic. We were so lucky to be there. So lucky to be in college. So lucky to have a partner in crime to have adventures with. So lucky not to have a care in the world.

On our last night at college, Ricky and I sat on the lawn in front of our dorm until the sun came up. We got drunk with the boys and gave ourselves a great send-off, capping four years of laughs, hijinks, and camaraderie. I was a boy when I met Ricky, and although I wouldn't say that I was a man yet at this point, I was at least on my way.

He raised his beer to mine and said, "Ray, we'll never have a day like this again."

"What are you talking about?" I said. "Of course we will."

My immediate concern after college, other than finding a job, was how Ricky and I were going to manage to see each other enough. You don't spend four years a few feet apart from someone and then just walk away and get on with your life.

The first thing we did was speak on the phone a couple of times a week. But that was difficult in those pre–cell phone days. Long-distance calls between New York and Toronto were not cheap. And these were not quick calls. We would sometimes talk for an hour, like a couple of adolescent schoolgirls. And what did we talk about? Anything and everything, just like we always had. I think we just needed to hear each other's voice on a regular basis.

Work on Wall Street wasn't much fun. I wasn't ready for it mainly because my heart and my head were stuck in Utica. When would I go back for a visit? Was Ricky coming down to New York? Should I plan a trip to Toronto? Remember that time Ricky and I did this or the time Ricky and I did that? It was hard to focus on work when my mind was looking backward.

Then we got in the habit of making drunken phone calls to each other in the middle of the night. Our parents were not amused. I think this was the main reason I moved out of my parents' house as soon as I did. Ricky wouldn't stop making drunken phone calls at 2 a.m. every weekend.

There were visits, of course, especially in the early years after college. I spent a weekend in Toronto sometime in the spring or summer of '90. He came to Manhattan for a visit sometime later that year. We had some good laughs, and things seemed as normal as ever.

We went to a reunion weekend back in Utica in '91 or '92. He had asked me before we went up for the weekend if I could loan him $400. He wouldn't tell me what it was for, and I didn't ask. He just said that things were bad with him and his father now, and he couldn't hit up the old man for the money. I didn't hesitate to give it to him. He was my brother, and saying no wasn't an option. I was just happy to see him.

As time went on, the once-a-week phone calls slowed down to every other week. There's not as much to talk about when you don't see someone that often. Suddenly, you each have a daily life that doesn't include the other. And then telling the old stories isn't as fresh as it used to be.

Before you know it, it's five years after graduation, and you haven't seen each other in a year. Has it been that long? We've got to get together soon. And then you do, and for the first time, it doesn't feel the way it used to. Something has changed.

But you have dreams, and Ricky always seemed to be in them. It always seemed to be a dream about the first day back at school, and we would be setting up the room for the new semester. I loved those dreams. College was so much better than the real world.

In 1995, Ricky got married. He and his fiancée had thrown a big engagement party six months prior that I had attended with a few of the college gang. We had fun at the party, and Ricky was the same as ever. At the wedding, he even provided the congregation with some laughs.

During the ceremony, the minister came to the fateful moment and asked Ricky if he took Claudia to be his lawfully wedded "husband."

Ricky started repeating the vow but stopped short when he realized the minister's error. He then took a breath, turned to the congregation, and deadpanned, "Is there a minister in the house?"

Everyone in the church, the minister included, broke into laughter. Typical Ricky.

Two years later, his first son was born. Richard Macfarland Junior. He was excited when he called me to tell me the news. "Let me tell you, Ray, this boy is going to make his mark on this world."

I didn't see him again until my own bachelor party and wedding two years later. We had some fun, but something was missing between us. Either he had changed, or I had changed, or we both had changed. It was ten years since school had ended, and there was suddenly a lot of time and space between us.

Soon, Ricky had another child, and I had my first. The phone calls between us became less and less frequent. I still thought of him regularly and often told my wife stories about him that she always found amusing. But the days and the weeks and the months passed with me living my life in New York and Ricky living his in Toronto.

His was one of the first calls I received after the 9/11 attacks, checking in to see if I was OK, but I didn't see him again until 2004.

He was coming to Manhattan on business. Amazingly, I hadn't seen him since my wedding five years prior. It was astonishing to me how fast five years could go by as you got older. He wanted me to hit the town with him and spend the night with him at his hotel. I was hesitant. I had a wife and a two-year-old at home. Couldn't we just go out and then I can go home? But Ricky insisted. We hadn't seen each other in five years. My wife was OK with it. It was just one night. So, I met Ricky at the W Hotel in Times Square after work.

As always, the initial sight of him gave me a thrill. Seeing him was like coming home. We hugged and went down to the hotel bar for a drink.

"Looking good, Ray," he said.

"You too, my friend," I said.

Looking at him was like looking at an old picture, but a picture that had come to life.

We went to Bobby Van's steak house for dinner. Over the course of the meal, we caught up with what was going on in each other's life and asked about friends from school we had recently seen or spoken to, and we, of course, also recounted a few stories from the good old days.

Then we went to the Playwright Tavern to have a few more drinks. And it was here that I realized that we had nothing left to talk about. The hour and a half we spent at dinner talking about our current lives and our old friends and memories had exhausted our conversation. At dinner, we were two old friends catching up. At the bar, we were two married fathers in our late thirties who really didn't know one another. And that realization made me incredibly sad.

We went back to the hotel and went to sleep, sleeping across from each other like we had done hundreds—more than hundreds—of times. But I couldn't really sleep. I knew I should be home with my wife and baby daughter. Ricky even started snoring, which gave me a chuckle. But snapping my fingers did not get him to stop.

We said our goodbyes in the morning, and I was relieved. I wanted to get back home. I had no idea that this would be the last time I would ever see him.

Life marched on. My wife and I added another daughter. Work became more intense. Even with email and then texting, Ricky and I didn't communicate often, although he was never far from my mind. As my kids got older, I would frequently regale them with stories of Ricky that made them laugh. I even taught them some Ricky-isms. Ricky would always refer to underwear as *gotchies*, and the term always stuck with me, so much so that my daughters now say it. I'll also greet them with the occasional *mahalo*, and they give it to me right back and can explain the story behind it.

In 2006 or 2007, Ricky organized a golf weekend with some of the boys from school. But I couldn't go. Not that I didn't want to see him and the gang. I did. But I was almost forty years old and didn't want to spend a weekend getting drunk and pretending I was nineteen again. Not when I had a wife and kids at home who I didn't see enough as it is because of the hours I spent at work.

"Couldn't we do a weekend together with our wives?" I asked him. That I could go for.

"Why the hell would we do that, Ray?" was the answer Ricky gave me.

So, I didn't go. They had the boys' weekend without me. But I did get a drunken phone call from them at 1 a.m.

He organized another get-together with the boys a few years later, and it was the same thing. I couldn't bring myself to leave my family for a weekend to get drunk. Again, I suggested having a weekend with our wives. Something where we could relax, enjoy each other's company, reminisce a little, and act our age. Maybe our wives would even become friends. But the suggestion was shot down. So, Ricky and the boys had another weekend together, and my house received another drunken phone call in the middle of the night. My wife was a good sport about it and even said I should go to the next one. But it just didn't feel right to me. Yes, I wanted to see Ricky and the boys. But at my age, I didn't want to pretend to be in college again for three days.

In the fall of 2013, Ricky sent out an email to the boys, trying to organize the next boys' weekend. Should I go to this one? I still wished we could bring our wives and have more of an adult weekend. But before I was forced to decide, Ricky sent another email out, saying that something had come up at work and the weekend was off for now.

About a month later, he sent out an email, saying that his cell number and email address had changed. I saved the information and made a mental note to call or text him soon. It had been too long.

In early 2014, I did just that. A quick text, telling him that I was thinking about him and how I had told my kids the day before about the time he let the stray dog in my room and how my kids thought that was hysterical. But I received no response. So, I sent an email to him, saying the same thing.

It was a day later that the email was answered. But it wasn't from Ricky. It was from his wife, Claudia. She said she had some bad news. Ricky had recently been diagnosed with skin cancer. Melanoma, to be more precise. He was presently taking part in clinical trials and wasn't taking calls or emails. She would let him know that I had reached out to him. She also provided a link to a website that had been set up for him.

I was knocked to the floor by the news. Skin cancer. OK, that usually wasn't too bad, right? A lot of people got skin cancer and beat it, right? But why was he in a clinical trial? That didn't sound too good. My heart was racing, so I took a few deep breaths to calm myself. I clicked on the link to his website, and my mood worsened. This wasn't a website for someone with a minor bout of skin cancer. It was the website of someone fighting for his life. Turns out, melanoma is the deadliest form of skin cancer, and if it isn't caught early, it is almost always fatal.

As my heart continued to race, I replied to Claudia's email and asked her to tell Ricky that I loved him and was praying for him. On the website, there was a forum to leave messages for Ricky, and I quickly typed my love and support. My hands were shaking as I typed.

It became difficult to focus on work over the next weeks and months because Ricky's plight was constantly on my mind. Ricky was a star. He was a rock. He was the last person I could ever imagine something like this happening to. I couldn't imagine what he was going through. He was only forty-nine years old. He had a wife and two teenage sons. How the hell did this happen?

And then, of course, I remembered Maui. The rockin' tan that became a horrible sunburn. Is this where the first seeds of his skin cancer had sprouted? It made my heart stop. He was always so fucking concerned with getting a good tan! My reading on melanoma informed me that blond-haired people of Northern European descent with pale skin were the most susceptible to this disease. That was Ricky.

His wife posted frequent updates on the website on Ricky's situation and treatments. She put up a brave face, but it was becoming clearer that things weren't going well. She asked for people to post messages on the forum to lift his spirits.

So, I wrote a long post, reminding Ricky of all of the crazy shit we did at school, highlighting the stories I previously wrote about here and a bunch more that I didn't.

In her next update, Claudia explained that Ricky had read my post with her and their sons, and Ricky had laughed so hard that he was brought to tears. Their boys had listened raptly and were amazed at our "devilish" acts, as she called them. It warmed my heart to know that I had made him laugh. It was our last laugh together.

Ricky hadn't called me, and I understood why. He had been my big brother, my protector, the guy I looked up to. I knew him. I knew he couldn't face talking to me in his current condition. I knew, and I understood.

So, I emailed him and told him to stay strong and to keep the faith, knowing that those were hollow words. What else could I say? I told him that my mother asked the pastor at her church to say a prayer in his honor. I told him again that I loved him.

He wrote back the following: *Thanks, Ray. Finished the latest round of treatments and getting stronger. Say thanks to your folks. I miss them. My boys loved the stories you wrote, and I told them a few more, but I had to tell them the PG versions, of course. Talk to you soon.*

It wasn't a long message, but it warmed my heart. I was glad that I made him and his boys laugh. But the credit really went to Ricky. He was the one who had made me laugh more than I could have ever dreamed of. He was the one who had made most of those stories possible.

Not long after that email, I sat at my desk in my office one late October morning and saw an email from Claudia . It was short and to the point.

Ricky passed away over the weekend at home. Details on the website.

I started shaking and for some reason left my office and walked into the hallway. I think I felt the need to move. I called my wife and told her the news and then started crying. I quickly ran into the men's room and sat in a stall so as not to make a scene.

When I composed myself, I went back to my desk and read the email again, half hoping that I had imagined it. I went to the website. He had died Saturday, and the funeral was today, Monday, in Toronto. When I came out of my fog, I remembered with a shock that I had had a dream about Ricky the night before.

In the dream, we were sitting in a room somewhere, and he looked frail. He told me that he was finished with all his treatments and there was nothing more that the doctors could do. He was going to die. He told me not to be upset. He said it was OK. He said he was OK.

He was already dead when I had the dream. It was chilling. My wife said it was his spirit visiting me. I didn't believe it. But who knows?

I spent the next few weeks in a bit of daze, still not truly believing what had happened. I went to a movie by myself one Saturday morning to clear my head. *Interstellar*, it was. At the end of the movie, Anne Hathaway is stranded by herself on a distant planet. Matthew McConaughey is trying to find her. For some strange reason, this made me think of Ricky. I imagined him stranded by himself somewhere, alone. The way the music swelled as the movie faded out and the credits rolled, I was overcome. I held it in as I made my way to the car, but I cried like a baby on the drive home. I couldn't get the image of Ricky being stranded all alone out of my head.

The next year was tough. I couldn't get thoughts of him out of my head. I couldn't believe that his visit to New York in 2004 was the last time I saw him. I occasionally posted pictures of him on Facebook, and I would get lots of comments from people who missed him and couldn't believe he was gone.

In November, I went to see the new James Bond movie, *Spectre*.

In it, 007's boss, M, says the following at one point in the movie: "The French have an old saying—it is the fate of glass to break."

And it hit me hard. Of course, all glass in the world will ultimately break. People are glass. All people will eventually break. Ricky had just broken sooner than expected. That son of a bitch. He always wanted to be first at everything. I smiled a little. Maybe he was off somewhere, waiting for me. And when I get there, the party will start again.

I always thought that our relationship would rekindle when we got older. Once our kids were older and we had more time, we would reconnect as middle-aged men. But you know what they say about the best-laid plans.

Even now, as I type these words, I can't truly believe that he is gone. But the fact that I am typing them reinforces the reality. So, I will stop typing and hope that in doing so, it will somehow become unreal. And I can pretend that nothing has changed and that Ricky is just off living his life, happy and alive as ever. Surely, we'll get together soon, and won't it be great?

And then I will go to sleep and hope to dream. And in the dream, it will be Ricky and me, on the first day of a new semester, setting up our room, having a laugh, with a new school year and the whole world in front of us…

Alternate Realities

(2019)

TINA RICCI-GRAYSON SAT at the bar at Del Frisco's and sipped her drink. It was a VIP, which the bartender had told her was the most popular drink at the place. He told her the sole ingredient was pineapple-infused vodka, hence the name VIP.

"Shouldn't it be called a PIV?" she asked.

"I guess," said the bartender. "But what would you rather drink, a VIP or a PIV?"

"Point taken," she said.

Whatever it was called, it was delicious, and at $18 a drink, she supposed it should be. She sipped the drink and pondered how long it had been since she had been in Manhattan. She and Will had come in to see *The Book of Mormon*, and that had to have been at least two years ago. Was that the last time? They used to take the kids in every year at Christmastime to see the tree at Rockefeller Center, but they didn't do it last year. The girls were in their twenties now and didn't care about that stuff anymore. So, she guessed it had been two years. She and Will used to always go to Manhattan at least three or four times a year. But that had stopped too.

She also wondered why Claire had chosen Del Frisco's to meet for lunch. It was a loud, cavernous steak house, which seemed to her to be an odd place to meet her old college friend on a Wednesday afternoon. But Claire worked in the neighborhood and said she sometimes sees celebrities from NBC eating there because 30 Rock was right across the street.

Tina was fifteen minutes early, and she knew Claire usually ran late. The VIP was going down easy, and she wondered if she would have to order another one before Claire arrived. She wasn't one to drink this early in the day. But things in her life hadn't been very stable lately. Actually, it was longer than lately. Her relationship with Will had been deteriorating for several years. The girls had gone off to college, and instead of the passion reigniting, they realized that they really didn't know each other anymore. They were alone together for the first time in twenty-something years, and all it showed them was that they were alone. Happy hour and then dinner at the club every Friday night became more of a chore than a release. And then there were the weird dreams she had been having recently.

She hadn't thought of Mike Gardner in years. And yet he made a random appearance in a dream a few weeks back. She didn't think much of it at the time. It certainly wasn't unheard of for a random person from the past to appear in a dream. But that appearance got her thinking about him. And that led to his appearance in another dream. In both cases, the dreams were set in modern times. In the first one, he appeared at a backyard barbecue at Tina's house, and they spoke to each other in a casual manner, as if they had seen each other recently. She couldn't recall in the morning what they spoke about. But it was friendly. In the second dream, she was at a party somewhere, and there he was again. But this time, after a short conversation, they started kissing with abandon, right in the middle of the

311

party as people watched. And as people are wont to do in a dream, Tina didn't care that people were watching and didn't care that she was married. She just desperately wanted to kiss Mike Gardner, like she had done so many times before one summer long ago.

This second dream led her to reminisce about the summer she had spent with him. Oh, to be that young and carefree again! What year was it? It was the summer before senior year of college, so that made it 1988, right? No, it was 1989. Though she had been back to the Hamptons a few times since, she had never made it back to Montauk. What was the name of that restaurant with the funny name where they had eaten? The Shagston? No, that wasn't it—

"Are you going to order one of those for me?"

Tina snapped out of her daydream to see Claire standing in front of her.

"Hey," said Tina as she put her drink down and hugged her friend. Then she turned to the bartender. "Two more VIPs," she said.

They took their drinks to their table by the window, where they could watch the people walking across Sixth Avenue.

"So, talk to me. What's happening, girl?" Claire asked.

Claire was her friend from college. They had been in the same sorority and had stayed in touch on and off for the past thirty years. Usually, they met for lunch in the city, as they were doing now, but they hadn't seen each other in a few years.

"Nothing really," Tina said. "Same old boring life, I guess."

"How are Will and the girls?"

"The girls are great. Out of the house. Katie has a serious boyfriend, so we'll see what happens."

"And Will?"

Tina hesitated and sipped her VIP. "These are really good," Tina said.

Claire regarded her friend. She could see a certain sadness in her face. "Everything OK?" Claire asked.

"I'm sorry," said Tina. "I think it's the VIP. These are really strong."

"Yes, they are," said Claire. "You look like you need one."

"Yeah," said Tina. "I probably do."

"Is it something with Will?" Claire asked.

Claire knew Will all the way back to their college days. Could they be having trouble? Claire always thought they were the perfect couple.

"It's nothing, really," said Tina. She sipped her drink again. "Things are just...I don't know."

"Well, you've been married for twenty-something years. That's the way it is sometimes when you've been married that long," said Claire.

"I've been having these dreams lately," said Tina.

Was she really going to get into this with Claire? She wouldn't normally open up with someone about something so private. But those VIPs...

"What kind of dreams?"

Tina laughed. She was flustered. *But what the hell?* she thought. She needed to talk to someone.

"I've been having dreams about this guy I dated back in college."

"Oh, that sounds interesting," said Claire. "Someone I know?"

"No, it's not a guy from college. It's a guy I met one summer between junior and senior year."

"I only know you with Will. I don't remember you with anyone else," said Claire.

"I wasn't," said Tina. "Except for this guy that one summer."

"And now you're dreaming about him. Please, do tell," said Claire.

Tina took another sip from the VIP. It was still so odd to her that she was thinking about Mike after not thinking about him for years.

"My aunt and uncle had a summer place in Montauk near the beach, and they invited me to stay with them for the summer. My cousin was the same age as me, and I figured, why not? There are worse ways to spend a summer. Will was in Europe for the summer anyway, so it was a no-brainer.

"So, I met this guy one afternoon at a dive bar near the water. We flirted at the jukebox, and then we danced—"

"What song did you dance to?" Claire asked.

"I don't remember," said Tina. "But we danced, and it was nice, and I think we ran into each other a few days later on the beach, and it took off from there."

The waiter came to the table to take their lunch order. Tina ordered a Caesar salad. Claire ordered the $20 cheeseburger. They each ordered another VIP.

"So, where was I?" Tina said.

"You met again on the beach, and it took off from there."

"Right," said Tina. "It did take off from there. I remember we went skinny-dipping in the ocean one night, and then we ended up at some seedy motel in town. And then we spent every day together. I didn't think much of it. I was with Will, and that was that for me. I was just having fun. But it was obvious that it meant more to him. I should have slowed it down. But I was flattered at how much he liked me. And I did like him. He wanted to be a writer."

"So, what happened?"

"I broke it off when the summer ended," said Tina.

"And that was it?"

"Well, he didn't take it well. I guess I can't blame him. But I was twenty years old. I'm sure he got over it."

"But thirty years later, you're dreaming about him."

"Yeah," said Tina.

"And you never saw or heard from him again?" Claire asked.

"No."

"I'd tell you to look him up on Facebook, but I know you're not on it."

"No," said Tina. "Will thinks social media is evil, so neither one of us is on it."

"Well, it is kind of evil," said Claire. "But not being on Facebook in 2019 is like not having a TV in 1960."

"Well, it's not like I want to or would ever contact him," said Tina. "These dreams I've been having have just been making me wonder how my life would have been so different if I had made a different decision thirty years ago."

"We all make decisions that affect our future. I try not to dwell on it though," said Claire.

"I try not to either," said Tina. "But with things the way they've been with Will…"

The next round of VIPs landed at the table.

"Just in time," said Claire.

"Just in time," said Tina.

Later, on the way back to Westchester, Tina sat and looked out of the window as the train lumbered out of Manhattan. Her mind drifted back to Montauk. Back to the summer of '89. She replayed images of Mike Gardner in her head. Images of him walking with her on the beach. Images of him kissing her in the back seat of his car. Images of him eating with her at that restaurant.

What the hell was that restaurant called? She took out her iPhone and googled *restaurants in Montauk*. And there it was! The Shagwong! What a ridiculous name! And then she thought about all the times they had sex that summer. How many times? She didn't know, but it was a lot. And it was good. Why did she go back to Will? What was so special about him? She really couldn't remember what drove her decision.

She allowed herself to imagine an alternate reality. One where she stayed with Mike and broke up with Will. Where would they be living now? What would their kids look like? Would they still have the passion that they had thirty years ago? Would they sit on the back porch and read together? Of course, if she had married Mike, she wouldn't have had her daughters. No sense playing what-if. You could drive yourself crazy doing that. She had to deal with her actual reality, not any alternatives.

At home, Will and Tina ate a quiet dinner together. She was still a little tipsy from the VIPs and tried to flirt with her husband after dinner. But he didn't respond in the way she wanted.

She thought the VIPs would help her fall asleep quickly, but they did not. Her mind was still buzzing. Will had given her a quick kiss good night and then turned away from her and fell asleep. Tina turned toward her side of the bed and closed her eyes, but sleep would not come.

She wondered where Mike Gardner was at this very moment. Probably happily married, probably lying in bed with his wife.

What's done is done, she thought.

She yawned. Maybe sleep would come soon. And maybe, just maybe, she would see Mike Gardner again in her dreams.

Just Another Movie

(2020)

HIS MIND THOUGHT BACK to 9/11. He remembered walking along the West Side Highway toward Vesey Street when the first plane hit the North Tower. He heard the jet approaching, but didn't think much of it. Noise was part of life in Manhattan, and the sound of the jet caused only a minor uptick in his senses. It was 8:46 a.m., and his mind was elsewhere.

When the plane hit the building, he, of course, looked up. His reaction was one of momentary shock, of course, but he also was in awe of the sight. He had seen explosions like that only in the movies. He stopped and watched the top of the building burn and noticed people on the street scurrying about. But he did not feel any fear. Of course, his brain told him that something horrific had just occurred, but he instinctively knew that he was in no immediate danger. However horrible the sight unfolding before him was, he was comfortably at a safe distance. It was like watching a movie.

This is what he thought as he heard the clanging and shouting outside of his apartment. It was 7 p.m., and it had been several days now that the people in Manhattan—those who had stayed—had been opening their windows to cheer and clap in support of the hospital workers who were working nonstop, treating COVID-19 patients. He opened his window as well to look at the people in the building across the street, who were leaning out of their windows.

He noticed a woman across the way who had been at her window every night, seemingly yelling louder than anyone. She certainly had gusto. He wasn't making any noise. But he did enjoy watching the people who did.

There were signs that things might be getting better. Cuomo said in his daily press conference that 422 New Yorkers had died the previous day. Which came across as good news, given that, only two weeks earlier, the state was averaging 700 dead a day.

But at his own daily briefing later that same day, the president suggested to Americans that injecting disinfectant into people might cure them of COVID-19. Dr. Birx looked at him like she had just gotten hit in the head with a rock as the president waited for her to confirm his suggestion. He had previously suggested to her that light could somehow be injected into the body as another possible cure. She quietly and tepidly disagreed with him. But not strongly enough. She certainly was no profile in courage. So, perhaps things weren't getting better. The president's daily press briefings had become a bad reality TV show that had stayed on two or three seasons longer than it should have.

The people across the way started singing "New York, New York." The night before, it was "Lean on Me." He felt some New York pride as his neighbors belted out the Sinatra tune. But he didn't join in. He was content to watch and listen.

The buzzer to his apartment rang. His Chinese food had arrived. He would have to go downstairs to pick it up as deliverymen were not allowed in his building's elevator during the pandemic.

There Are Places I Remember

The deliveryman recognized him, as this was the third time this week he had ordered from the Chinese place on the corner. When his mother had called to check on him earlier in the week, he casually mentioned that he had been ordering a lot of Chinese takeout. She reacted with alarm, convinced that the food was contaminated with the coronavirus. She was also worried that the delivery boy would have it as well. He wondered now if she might be considering injecting bleach into her body.

He ate his sesame noodles on the couch. Time to turn off the news. How much depressing news could one take? Too much news about death, too much news about people fighting about wearing masks or social distancing. These were not issues for him. He had no problem hiding his face and no problem keeping socially distant. He was way ahead of the curve on that front, as he had, for all purposes, been socially distancing himself for years. He couldn't understand why some people had a problem with it. He enjoyed being away from people.

He switched the TV to Netflix. He had gotten it only a few weeks ago. But he had been working from home since March 13, and with the entire city on lockdown, there was nothing much to do but watch TV. There were no sports to watch, no movie theaters open, so Netflix it was.

He had watched all three seasons of *Ozark* in four days and had recently started watching *Orange Is the New Black*. He had also watched the Scorsese movie *The Irishman*—all three and a half hours of it. That one had made him sad. The movie ends with Robert DeNiro as a lonely old man in a nursing home. It made him feel that he might end up the same way. He realized that much of his own life was like watching a movie.

He had watched 9/11 happen in front of his eyes from a close but safe distance. He was now doing the same with the pandemic. The hospital workers and essential workers were putting themselves in harm's way every day, and he was fifteen floors above them, safely eating Chinese food and watching Netflix, while the horror unfolded within shouting distance of him on the streets below. It really was like watching a movie. It was as if he was binge-watching the pandemic in real time. Like 9/11, the pandemic was just another movie for him. He was right there for both, but in the end, he was as safe as a moviegoer watching a disaster movie in a theater.

It dawned on him that he had been watching—and not doing—his whole life. That was probably why he was alone. And that was probably why DeNiro in the nursing room had unnerved him. He saw it as a glimpse into the future, and he obviously did not like what he saw.

Maybe he should run outside without his mask on and roll the dice. That wouldn't be a passive act, would it? He would be in the movie then, not just watching it.

But of course, he would not do that. It had been a long time since he had truly engaged with the world around him. He tried to bury the thought of DeNiro and the nursing home. No use worrying about the future. The emptiness of what may lay ahead for him was too daunting to think about.

So, into the TV he dived. Maybe he'd find an old movie on Netflix tonight instead of bingeing a new series. Something from the past, something from when he was a kid. He was happier and less alone back then.

He grabbed the remote and flicked through the seemingly endless possibilities.

"The present changes the past. Looking back, you do not find what you left behind."

—*Kiran Desai*

Goodbye Wonderland

(2041)

THE CAR DROVE ONTO the Long Island Expressway at Exit 70, heading west back toward the city. Robbie enjoyed the quiet of the car, interrupted only sporadically by some conversation with his driver, Jonathan. Many people were using driverless cars now, but Robbie wasn't comfortable with those. Of course, he had the money now to fly back to the city in a helicopter, but alas, he was afraid of those too. He had seen too many James Bond movies in his day. There was always a helicopter exploding in a Bond movie.

He scrolled through the news on the screen on the back of the passenger seat. He skipped over the national news. It usually depressed him. He knew he should read the business news, but he was bored with that. He saw something pop up on the screen about local Long Island news. He touched that. Maybe there would be something of interest. He saw something about a rare whale sighting off Smith's Point. A story about overcrowded schools in Nassau County. Another about noise from airliners disturbing the occupants of apartments near MacArthur Airport. And then he saw it in the bottom-right corner of the screen.

Smith Haven Mall Demolition Begins This Week.

His heart sank immediately. He knew people didn't go to malls anymore, and there were only a couple of them left on Long Island. But that was his mall. It was the anchor of his neighborhood, the center of so much of his childhood. How many hours had he spent there as a young boy with his mother? How many hours had he spent hanging out there as a teenager with his buddies? How many movies had he seen there? And now it was being torn down to build apartments.

Long Island was overcrowded, and apartment space was desperately needed. The mall was built in 1969 on an old farm. That was considered progress back then. Now it was being torn down in 2041 to make room for apartments. He supposed that would now be considered progress.

Memories of the mall's early '70s heyday flooded his brain. He thought he should listen to some music from the era to accompany his thoughts. Who should he listen to? Elton John was an obvious choice. Maybe Stevie Wonder or the Carpenters? Three Dog Night? Where did that thought come from?

"Play Three Dog Night," he said.

His earbuds replied, "Playing Three Dog Night."

"Shambala" came on. Robbie smiled. He had forgotten all about this song. How many years had it been since he had heard it? Fifty maybe? He settled back to enjoy it. Robbie found himself singing along and was surprised that he remembered the lyrics. He was seventy-four years old, and he was singing a song that came out when he was five and one he hadn't heard in decades. It still surprised him, the things he could remember from those days when so much of the more recent past was lost to him. The song momentarily made him feel that he *was* on the road to the Shambala.

He noticed Jonathan peek in the rearview mirror, no doubt alarmed by Robbie's atrocious singing. Robbie chuckled and closed his eyes, happily lost on his way to Shambala.

When the song ended, he said to Jonathan, "We're going to take a detour, Jonathan. I need you to get off at Exit 58 and head north."

"Of course, Mr. Miller."

What was he hoping to see? What was the point of seeing the mall one last time? He couldn't say. But given the choice of seeing it one more time versus not, well, that was an easy choice for him to make.

As the car headed west, Robbie's thinking of the mall made him think of his mother. She always loved that mall. His thoughts drifted to one of the last times he saw her.

It was almost twenty years earlier. She had caught COVID-19 in late 2020, and although it put her in the hospital, she beat it. But that virus did something to her. She was never the same after that. A year and a half later, she was gone from cancer.

On one of his last visits to her in the hospital, they had a conversation that he frequently replayed in his head.

He told her that he was going to swing by Victory Lane after his visit with her and visit the old house. She frowned at that.

"Why are you going to do that?" she asked.

"Because I'm here. Why wouldn't I want to see it? You know how I feel about the old house."

"It won't look the same, Robbie. It won't feel the same," she said. "It will only upset you. Nothing is ever as good as you remember it to be."

"I just want to see it," he said.

"And what will that do?"

"Maybe it will make me feel good for a few minutes."

"Maybe," she said. "And then maybe it will make you feel bad after the thrill of seeing it fades. You look back too much, Robbie. You always have. Don't let nostalgia kill you. Haven't I always told you to be here now? Be happy for now."

"Now sucks," he said.

"Maybe. But it's really all you have. It's all any of us have."

He looked at her and tried to hold back the tears.

"And *now* doesn't suck," she said. "You have a wonderful wife and three great kids."

"I know," he said. "But the rest of the world is just insane right now."

"The world is always insane, Robbie. It always has been, and it always will be."

He knew she was right. But he also knew he couldn't change who he was. "I know, Ma," he said. "Don't be too hard on me. I know you are just like me."

"I know," she said. "So, I can tell you that fretting about the past doesn't do you any good. You can't go back. All you have is the road in front of you."

And that road eventually ends, he thought now.

He looked out of the window of the car. There was the sign for Exit 58.

"Get off here and make a right, Jonathan. Then head about three miles north."

The car cruised along Alexander Avenue—past streets that Robbie played on as a boy—then crossed Middle Country Road, and there it was before him. The Smith Haven Mall, the place where he had sat on Santa's lap, where he had seen *Rocky* and *The Spy Who Loved Me* and countless other movies. The place he had spent hours playing Space Invaders and Pac-Man. The place he and his buddies had ogled pretty "mall chicks" as they cruised the suburban bazaar. The place his mother referred to as Wonderland. She would ask him if he wanted to go to Wonderland, and of course, he always said yes. A trip to Wonderland could mean an ice cream cone, a ride on the carousel, and if he was good, maybe a toy from McCrory's.

He got out of the car and watched cranes and dump trucks ferry about the empty parking lot. The mall was still there, but it was vacant and cold and lifeless. He wondered how fickle a thing time was. How at the same moment he could feel as if the mall had opened ages ago—which it had—and feel like it had opened yesterday and seventy-plus years had somehow evaporated in a minute.

It was then that he decided that he didn't want to linger here. He didn't want to see the mall this way. He wanted to remember it as it was. He wanted it to remain Wonderland.

He'd also had in the back of his mind that he would have Jonathan swing the car around and cruise by Victory Lane to see the old house. But he remembered his mother's words. It wouldn't look the same. She was right. Better to remember it the way it was when he was a kid.

He glanced at the mall one more time and got back in the car.

"Sorry for the detour, Jonathan," he said. "Back to the city."

Robbie closed his eyes. As the car sped away, he thought of his mother and of ice cream cones and pretty girls and carousels.

"You only live as long as the last person who remembers you."

—*Akecheta from* Westworld

Tomorrow

(2019)

STREAKS OF SUNLIGHT POURED into the bedroom and flooded the room with light. He had to hold his hand up to his eyebrows to block out the sun, but he didn't mind. He liked the warm sun on his face. Somehow, it made him feel alive even though the truth was that he had very little life left in him. Yes, sunlight on his face was a good thing. Maybe the only good thing left.

When the doctors informed Charlie Dunn that his cancer was terminal, he had been surprised. He had always been an optimist, and when he was diagnosed, he was sure he would beat it. But the chemo, radiation, and drugs had all failed to slow the spread. Still, he had still held out hope. Surely, he would beat it, right? He never envisioned that this would be the way it would end.

It wasn't that he never feared getting cancer. He did. He supposed everyone did to some degree. But he was born in 1941. He had always assumed that a cure would be found in his lifetime. Hell, they had cured polio and smallpox and found treatments to control HIV. But cancer still lumbered on, virtually unimpeded. A friend of his had speculated that "they" had a cure years earlier, but the drug companies and the oncologists wouldn't let it out. Cancer treatment was a billion-dollar business. Too many doctors and drug company executives and salesmen had been getting rich off the disease for decades. They weren't going to kill their cash cow. But Charlie wasn't that cynical. Yet he still couldn't believe that they hadn't found a cure in the nearly eighty years he'd been alive.

Now he was at the point where the doctors told him he had days or maybe a couple of weeks left at best. He could stay in the hospital or go home and spend his final days with family. He chose home.

Not his home, but his daughter's. He was a widower, and he couldn't be alone in his house in his condition. His daughter and the kids would have to look after him in her home until the end came. He didn't want to burden them, and he didn't really want to interact with them either. That would be painful for him and everyone involved. So, Charlie Dunn the optimist wanted the end to come quickly now.

His daughter made him as comfortable as possible in the guest room, and the kids would check in occasionally to see how he was doing. But he could barely talk and felt guilty that they all had to see him like this.

After several days, Charlie found himself sleeping most of the day. He dreamed a lot. With his future bleak and term limited, he dreamed exclusively of the past. Mostly, in the dreams, he was a boy again or a young man with his life still in front of him. In one dream, he was on the beach in Montauk with his parents and siblings. They used to go there when he was a boy. In another dream, he was in his office on 23rd Street, the first job he had after college. But he couldn't remember the names of the people in the office. He also dreamed about a girl in college that he had a crush on. God, she was beautiful! Or at least he remembered her that way. What was her name again? And then a dream where he was sitting in a café in Paris. That one wasn't about the past because he had never been to Paris.

In fact, he had never visited most of the places in the world that he had wanted to see when he was younger. There was never the time or the money or the will to do so. And yet he always thought that he would visit these places at some point. But he thought they would cure cancer too. Now, of course, he would visit none of them. His life now—his whole world—was the guest room in his daughter's house on Long Island.

He had fallen asleep the night before while watching the Yankees game. He wasn't sure if they had won or lost. They were in first place and were pretty much assured of another postseason appearance, and yet he realized that he would not be around in October to watch the playoffs. He had seen every World Series the Yankees had played in since 1949, and it made him sad that he would see no more. He wondered if there was a heaven. If there was, could he still watch the World Series? And if there was no heaven, then it didn't matter if the Yankees made the World Series or not. It didn't matter if they had won or lost the night before. None of it mattered.

He lay in his bed in the guest room and stared at the ceiling. He could hear his daughter milling about in the kitchen downstairs. He had heard the kids leave the house for school in the morning. But he was drugged up on painkillers and wasn't sure if they had left twenty minutes ago or hours ago.

He noticed a fly zip across the room and land on the wall near the window. Before the cancer, he would have grabbed a magazine and hunted the fly. But he couldn't move now. He watched the fly as it banged into the closed window, trying to escape, lured by the bright sunshine. He wasn't sure how many flies or insects or spiders he had killed in his life, but it was certainly a lot. And now he would soon be joining them. He was now the fly, and cancer was the magazine that would soon smash him. The difference was, all the flies and insects he had killed did not know it was coming. And they were blessed in not knowing that death was even a thing. Only humans carried that knowledge. Humans were the only species in the history of the world that lived their lives, knowing that they would die. The fly, with its tiny brain, lived in blissful ignorance. People did not.

Maybe that is why he was dreaming about the past. Maybe that is why he spent too much of his life dwelling on the past. Because he—like all people—knows exactly what the future ultimately holds. That is the price we pay for our big brains. We wake up every day, knowing that we are one day closer to the end. He was suddenly envious of the fly.

He was certain that when he fell asleep tonight that he would not wake in the morning.

He wished he could go back in time and hug his children, his grandchildren, his wife. He wished he could feel young again and run along the beach and feel the air in his lungs and the wind in his hair. But those were impossibilities.

And although he wanted the end to come quickly, something in his soul still yearned. Yes, he would never see Paris or Rome or Rio. He had accepted that. All he really wanted now was to drift off to sleep one more time, but not to dream.

He suddenly just wanted desperately to wake up in the morning once more. And when he would awake, he would somehow crawl out of bed. And he would walk outside and feel the crisp air on his face and feel a breeze through his hair and look up at the blue sky and feel the warm sunlight on his face. My God, wouldn't the sunlight on his face—not through the window, but on his face—feel wonderful? Yes, he wanted just one more tomorrow. Was that too much to ask? One more tomorrow to have the sunshine on his face.

He unsuccessfully tried to ignore the pain, but eventually, he drifted off to sleep. And soon, he was dreaming. In the dream, it was the present day.

But instead of being old and cancer-ridden, he was pain-free and young. He hopped out of bed and scampered down the stairs, full of life and vim and vigor. He ran outside, but he wasn't outside of his daughter's house. No, he was on a wide boulevard, and there before him stood the Eiffel Tower.

My God, he thought, *I'm in Paris!*

He had made it to Paris. He felt a warm breeze run through his hair. It felt wonderful.

Then he looked up at the bright blue sky, and Charlie Dunn—forever the optimist—raced toward the warm, shining sun.

There Used to Be Stars in the Sky

(2020)

SHE WAS NEVER REALLY a baseball fan and admittedly never quite understood the subtleties of the game. She never understood why so many people in the city argued over the Yankees or Mets and seemed to care so deeply about their fates. When she was a child, her father would drone on endlessly about the Brooklyn Dodgers and how horrible it had been when they left for California. It never made sense to her.

So, it was strange to her that perhaps her happiest memory was of that time in the Catskills, when her father hit the big home run to win the fathers softball game when she was five years old. She could still remember him rounding third base and her mother jumping up and down and everyone celebrating at home plate. And then her father lifting her up to what felt like the sky. Her mother was happier than she had ever seen her. Her father, the hero.

Chills had run through young Cathy Bishop's body. Yes, this was the happiest memory that she could think of, the only one that stood on its own and had no dark side hiding under the joy. Was it pathetic that this was the happiest memory of her life? Maybe all memories of five-year-olds are the happiest? When Daddy is always the hero and Mommy is god? She wondered exactly when this memory happened. It must have been 1955 or '56. Long before Kennedy or Vietnam. Long before her life went adrift.

She had been in the hospital for just over a week now and had been getting progressively worse. Her lungs were hurting, and breathing was increasingly labored. She had begun hallucinating as well—or at least, she thought she was. How does one know? The doctor said she might need to soon go on a ventilator and that they would have to induce a coma in her to intubate her. Maybe she was already in a coma? Maybe that's why she was hallucinating? The doctor was in a hazmat suit—or at least, that's what it looked like to her. Or maybe that was part of her hallucination?

Daddy rounded third base, and she jumped for joy. She ran to home plate, and he lifted her to the sky.

Oh, how she loved the Catskills. They would sit on the porch of the cabin at night and look at the stars, and they were always the brightest stars in the universe. Why were the stars never as bright as they were then?

She sat next to Daddy, and they toasted marshmallows while Mommy read a paperback. The stars seemed so close that Cathy thought that she could reach out and touch them.

"You can't see the stars like this back home in the city," Daddy said. "The city lights block out the view."

The doctor in the hazmat suit appeared at her side. She could hear some mumbled conversation, but she could not make out any of the words. If she was in a coma, would she be able to see and hear?

She peeked out of the dining room window of the house on Victory Lane. She watched Joey Barone washing his Chevy Biscayne. Had there ever been a more beautiful sight? If Daddy hitting the home run was her happiest memory, then watching beautiful Joey Barone wash his car was a close second. If this was a hallucination, she prayed that it would last longer. There was a song playing on the transistor radio of Joey's porch. Something by The Rolling Stones, but her mind wandered before she could remember the song.

She felt pain in her lungs again.

"You may have to go on a ventilator," she heard the doctor say again. "We may have to induce a coma."

She sat on the porch in Queens with Daddy, and they looked at the sky. It looked like the Fourth of July. There was red, white, and blue everywhere, and Mommy held a sparkler. She looked up and realized that Daddy was right. You can't see the stars in the city.

She sat in the passenger seat of the Chevy Biscayne. Joey was driving her home from the mall. The mall is the most wonderful place she had ever seen, but being in a car like this with Joey was better. She reached out and touched his hand and wanted to stay in the car with him forever. If they could stay in the car and never leave, nothing bad will ever happen.

Do you love me, Joey? Tell me that you love me...

She had a moment of clarity and deep down realized that she hasn't seen Joey Barone in fifty years. This was a dream, and she wondered if it was all a dream. She struggled to breathe, and this, she sensed, was not a dream. Something terrible was happening to her.

"When can we go to the Catskills again?" she asked her father. "I want to see the stars again, Daddy."

"We'll see, honey," he said. "Maybe next summer."

Her son loaded her into the car to take her to the hospital. Her fever was 103, and the coughing was worse. Breathing had become difficult. Her sense of smell was gone. She didn't want to be a bother. She asked him if she should get tested before going to the hospital. Her son told her it is too late for that. She struggled to hear him through his mask.

She held her baby grandson and kissed his forehead, but the baby was crying. Her son took him away from her. Breathing was becoming difficult again. Was she still hallucinating? She suddenly remembered that her grandson was a teenager now. She hadn't hugged him since the pandemic started.

That's right. We're in a pandemic.

She was in the hospital, right?

Daddy was rounding third base again, and everyone cheered. Mommy jumped for joy.

She watched her father walk through a field at night. He walked into the woods and disappeared. She called out after him, but he did not answer. She followed into the field and edged closer to the woods, but Daddy was nowhere to be found. She looked up at the sky and saw nothing but blackness. There used to be stars in the sky, didn't there? She called out to her father, but he did not answer.

We're not in the city anymore, Daddy. Where are the stars? I want to sit on the porch and look up at the bright stars. I want to see the stars again, Daddy! I want to see the stars.

The doctor told the nurse that they needed this bed and the ventilator turned over as soon as possible. The nurse removed the tube that ran down Cathy Bishop's throat and then disconnected it from the ventilator.

"Time of death: 3:03 p.m., December 3rd, 2020."

Everybody Has a Once Upon a Time

(2043)

HE LOOKED AT HIS grandson and could see that the young man was a lot like he was at the same age. Unsure of himself, perhaps even a little timid. Fifteen was an awkward age, but he guessed all ages after ten and into the early twenties are awkward. The world never ceases to be a mystery, and just when you think you have it all figured out, it can slap you in the face. The boy had everything he needed, perhaps more than that. But he seemed adrift. Weren't all fifteen-year-olds? Robbie sure was at that age—or at least, that's what his memory told him.

"You look lost, Michael," Robbie said to his grandson.

"I'm not lost, Pops," Michael said. "Just bored."

They were sitting on the porch of Robbie's beach house out east. The boy loved coming here when he was younger, playing in the sand or rushing into the waves. Now he stared blankly at the ocean.

"Why do all kids today seem bored?" Robbie asked.

"Because we are. There's nothing ever going on."

Robbie laughed. He figured that all teenagers feel that way at some point.

"Well, I wish I could bring some excitement into your life. You kids today don't seem to know how to have any fun," said Robbie.

He laughed to himself after he said it. All parents or grandparents have probably said the same thing at one time or another. He didn't like sounding like a cliché.

"You're probably right, Pops," said Michael. "I think your generation had all the fun. That's why I always like listening to your stories."

Robbie liked telling his grandson stories. Hell, he liked telling anybody stories. Anything that allowed him to relive the old days. He guessed that was another cliché. He was just another old man hung up on the good old days.

"So, do you want to hear any stories?" Robbie asked.

"Tell me one about your mother," Michael said. "I always like those."

Robbie thought for a moment. What was a good Mom story? Something lighthearted that would make Michael laugh? Robbie's mother could be a serious, pensive woman. But she was also a class-A neurotic, which often led to some funny moments. He thought of one that always made him crack up.

"Did I ever tell you the pee story?" Robbie asked.

"The what?"

"The pee story."

Michael laughed. "Um, no, Pops, I don't think I've heard that one."

"OK, good then," said Robbie. "You're going to enjoy this."

"A story about pee?"

"Well, sort of."

"OK, this ought to be good," said Michael.

"I was in fourth grade," said Robbie. "I guess the year would have been 1976, the year of the Bicentennial."

"The what?" Michael asked.

"The Bicentennial, the 200th birthday of America. It was a big deal at the time. You'll see. You'll get to celebrate the Tricentennial when you're older."

"So, what does any of that have to do with pee?" Michael asked.

"I'm getting to that," said Robbie.

He shifted in his chair. He did indeed like telling stories.

"So, as I was saying, I was in fourth grade, and it's just a typical Tuesday or Wednesday at Nesconset Elementary School. School started in those days around 9 a.m., so it must have been around 10 a.m. when there was a knock on the classroom door. So, Mrs. Buckley walks over to answer it. A woman from the main office is there, and she whispers something to Mrs. Buckley."

"How do you remember the name of your fourth-grade teacher? I'm fifteen, and I can barely remember the name of mine," said Michael.

Robbie laughed. "Well, for better or worse, your grandfather remembers a lot of stuff."

"Apparently," said Michael.

"So," said Robbie, "the woman from the main office is whispering to Mrs. Buckley. And then to my surprise, Mrs. Buckley turns to me and says, 'Robbie, your mother is here to see you.'

"I was shocked. What the hell was my mother doing here? The other twenty-five kids in the class were sort of shocked too. They were all looking at me, wondering what was going on. So, I get up and walk to the door and step out into the hallway as Mrs. Buckley closes the door behind me. The woman from the office walks away, and there is my mother, standing there.

I got nervous for a second. Did something terrible happen? Why else could she possibly be here?

" 'What's the matter?' I asked her.

"And I'll never forget how she looked down at me and pointed her finger at me and asked me, 'Did you pee before you left the house this morning?' "

"What?" said Michael, incredulous.

"That's exactly what I said to her," said Robbie. "So, she looked down at me again and asked again if I had peed this morning. I was bewildered and was racking my brain, trying to figure out why in the world she had come all the way to school to ask me that."

"And what did she say?" Michael asked.

Thinking about it made Robbie laugh. "She told me that she had cleaned the toilet in the morning and the water was a bright blue from the toilet cleaner. But then she noticed after I had gotten on the bus that the toilet water was still bright blue. 'If you had peed, the water would have turned yellow and then clear after you flushed,' she said to me. 'So, did you pee or not?' I told her I didn't remember. And she tells me that I didn't, and she's worried that my bladder is going to burst."

"Oh my God, that's crazy," said Michael.

"I know," said Robbie. "But that's not the funny part."

"How could that not be the funny part?"

"Well, after I promised her that I would ask Mrs. Buckley for a hall pass so that I could relieve my bladder before it burst, I turned to go back into the class. But she stopped me. 'What's wrong?' I asked. And she pulls out a comb from her pocketbook and tells me that my hair is a mess and proceeds to comb my hair."

"OK…" said Michael.

"So, my mother leaves, and I walk back into the classroom with my freshly combed hair, and immediately, every kid in the class wants to know why my mother came. Twenty-five kids are asking me why she came. And of course, I don't know what to say. And then one kid, noticing my hair, blurts out, 'She came to comb his hair!' and the whole class bursts out in laughter. So, I immediately tell everyone that is not why she came. 'So, why did she come?' asks another kid. And there was the problem. No way in hell I could tell them why she actually came. Could you imagine that? So, I just kept saying that she didn't come to comb my hair. But nobody believed it. So, there it was. I was now the kid whose mother came to school and interrupted class to comb his hair."

"That is unbelievably crazy," said Michael. "I would have died."

Robbie chuckled. "That was your great-grandmother. She was unique."

He thought of how he would remind his mother of this story when he was older and how she would laugh hysterically and say, "I don't know what I was thinking."

And then his mind flashed to the last time he saw her in the hospital, and a momentary sadness came over him.

"What about your father? You have some good stories about him too. I like the one where the kid chased you with a bat and your father threatened him," Michael said.

"Yeah, that was a good one. Did I ever tell you about the time he was forced to umpire my Little League game?"

"No, I don't think so," said Michael.

"I was ten or eleven years old. My weekly Little League baseball games were always played on Sundays at noon. So, one Sunday, we get to the field for the game, and we find out that neither umpire has shown up. Back then, we had two umps for a game, usually a couple of high school kids who got paid five or 10 bucks a game."

"That's it?" Michael said.

"This was 1978 or '79. That was a lot of money for a high school kid back then," said Robbie.

"So, where were they?" Michael asked.

"Who knows?" Robbie said. "They were high school kids. They probably stayed out too late the night before. So, the problem now is, what do we do? Does the game get canceled and everyone goes home?"

"So, what happened?"

"Well, the coaches of each team commiserated. They obviously didn't want to disappoint the kids, so they decided to see if one or two of the parents would be willing to step in and umpire the game."

"And this is where great-grandpa comes in, right?"

"Right," said Robbie. "They ask if any of the parents want to ump, and my dad is the only one who volunteers. But that leads to a new problem. How the hell is one person going to umpire a game? In the major leagues, you have four, in Little League two. How would one person be able to cover all the bases?"

"So, what did they do?"

"They asked my dad if he *could* cover all the bases. He didn't want to disappoint the kids, so he said, yes, he would do his best. So, they decide to have him ump behind home plate so he can call balls and strikes with the understanding that he will have to run out from behind the plate to call all the plays at the other bases as best as he can. With a heavy chest protector and a catcher's mask on. In ninety-degree heat, which was hot back then."

"I take it, things didn't go well?" Michael asked.

"At first, it was fine," said Robbie. "We were the road team that day, and I was batting leadoff. If anyone thought my dad wasn't going to be impartial, he disproved that notion right away when I came up to bat to open the game. On the first pitch, I got an inside fastball, and I ripped a

342

line drive down the left-field line that just landed foul by a foot. It would have been an easy double or triple. Second pitch, same thing—another inside fastball that I ripped down the line again, and this time, it was foul by about three inches. Man, I was frustrated. So, I stand back in the box, looking for another inside fastball, and, man, this time, I'm going to keep it fair. The only problem was, the third pitch was a fastball on the outside corner, and I froze. When I heard the ball hit the catcher's mitt, I knew I was out. And sure enough, my dad called out strike three. And he was right. And that right there should have prevented what happened after from ever happening. I mean, how could anyone accuse my dad of favoritism when he rings up his son on strikes in the first at-bat of the game?"

"But they did," said Michael.

"Not immediately," said Robbie. "But as the game progressed, yes. You see, these stupid Little League parents start bitching and moaning on every ball or strike call that didn't go their way. Not just the close pitches, but every freaking pitch. And childish comments, like, 'Oh, he just wants his son's team to win,' and nonsense like that."

"At the guy who called out his son on the first play of the game," said Michael.

"Yes, and it kept getting worse," said Robbie. "My poor father is running around like a chicken with his head cut off, trying to cover all the bases and make the calls as best as he can, but the parents of the other team just won't stop. Now I can see my dad doesn't want to make a scene, but I also know that he is from Brooklyn, and he is not gonna take this shit much longer."

"This sounds like it's going to get good," said Michael.

"Oh, it did," said Robbie. "I'm playing short, and around the third or fourth inning, the guy on first tries to steal second. Now this is the first year that we are playing on a major-league-sized field, and it was almost impossible for most of the eleven-year-old catchers to make that long throw from home to second to throw a runner out. But not our catcher. Our catcher was a kid named Pete Rizzo, and already, he had the body of a 16-year-old. He had no problem making that throw. So, he throws a dart to me covering second, and it was a close play, but I clearly tagged him out. My father dutifully ran from behind the plate and made the right call. And sure enough, those parents went nuts. Yelling, screaming, cursing, you name it—all directed at my father, who was soaked from sweat and now finally out of patience."

"What did he do?"

"He walks toward the first-base line and crosses it in front of the grandstand, where the other team's parents are sitting. He rips off his chest protector and flings it on the grass. Then he takes off his catcher's mask and holds it out, pointing toward the grandstand. Then he walks right up to it. And points the mask in the face of one of the parents. 'You want to ump?' he says. Then he shoves it in the face of the next parent and asks the same question. Of course, he gets no response. I can see the faces of all these parents, and you could see they all had an *oh shit, we pissed off the wrong guy* look on their faces. They were scared. And my dad didn't stop. He went one by one through the front row, shoving the mask in front of each person's face, asking if they wanted to ump and getting stone-faced silence in return. Then he pointed up to the top row and said, 'Anyone up there want to ump in 90-degree heat? No? Then all of you shut the hell up, and if I hear anyone make a sound the rest of the game, I'm going to shove this mask up somebody's ass. Got it?' And no one made a peep."

Michael laughed. "That's awesome. What happened the rest of the game?"

"Nothing," said Robbie. "They didn't make a sound the rest of the game. You've never seen a Little League game this quiet before. And the other team's coach apologized to my dad when the game was over and thanked him for umpiring."

"That's great," said Michael.

"Yeah, it was," said Robbie. "Your great-granddad was great. He didn't take crap from anyone."

Robbie missed him, of course. He wished that he had some of his father's toughness. But Robbie didn't grow up in Brooklyn. Yes, some bad things had happened on the street he grew up on, but most of his childhood was magical—or at least, that's the way he remembered it. He remembered his dad telling him that he was glad he was raising his son in the pristine suburbs, but he also worried that Robbie wouldn't learn the toughness he needed. Either way, Robbie felt that he had made his way in this world just fine. But he still missed that toughness and fearlessness of his father.

"I also like the stories about you and your college roommate. What was his name?" Michael asked.

Robbie immediately brightened up. "Ricky," he said.

"Yes, Ricky," said Michael. "I always liked the one about the time he let that stray dog in your room. And when you drove that truck thing down to spring break."

"I'll try to think of one you haven't heard," said Robbie.

If he had all the time in the world, he could probably never tell all of the Ricky stories. What was a good one he could tell now? He rewound the videotape in his brain and stopped on something suitable.

"I never told you the Pictionary story, did I?" Robbie asked.

"What's Pictionary?" Michael asked.

"It was an annoying board game that people played back in the '80s and '90s. But it was also the focal point of one of my favorite Ricky stories."

"What's a board game?" Michael asked.

"You've never seen Monopoly or checkers? I'm sure they still make them."

"Oh, OK, I think I've seen those," Michael said.

"It was like charades, only you draw on a big pad to see if your teammate can guess the word or phrase you are trying to describe," Robbie said.

"Doesn't sound like much fun," said Michael.

"It wasn't," said Robbie. "But it's the key to this story."

"OK, let's hear it," Michael said.

"OK, so it was the beginning of my senior year in college, and I had started dating this girl named Debbie Mandaro. She had big blue eyes that reminded me of my mother, and even though we were in the early stages, I thought maybe she could be the one," said Robbie. "She also was a great cook and had made me a lasagna that was almost as good as my mother's.

"She lived in the same apartment complex on campus as I did. So, she invites me over one Saturday night to hang out with her and her roommate, Maria, and Maria's boyfriend and tells me that we are going to play Pictionary. Now, that was not my idea of a fun Saturday night at college. But the relationship was new, and I liked her, and if that's what she wanted to do, then so be it. I was game.

"So, I head over to her apartment on Saturday night, and she explains that we will be playing Pictionary, and it will be the boys against the girls. So, I'm like, OK, whatever. Debbie and Maria versus me and Maria's boyfriend, who I had just met. Fine, let's go. But before we begin, she explains that she is, like, the best Pictionary player ever. And I'm like, OK, I didn't know there was such a thing. I mean, how good can anyone be at Pictionary? But she insists she is the best. Didn't matter to me. I just wanted the game over and done with so I could spend Saturday night with my girlfriend.

"So, the game starts, and I'll be damned if she wasn't right. They blew our doors off. She was phenomenal. Whatever she drew, Maria guessed it almost immediately. Whatever Maria drew, Debbie knew the answer right away. It was maybe the quickest game of Pictionary ever."

"OK, so what happened?" asked Michael.

"Well, that should have been the end of the story," said Robbie. "But it wasn't."

"I didn't think so."

"The next day, I'm with Ricky, telling him the story of the Pictionary game and how Debbie was the greatest Pictionary player ever. Of course, his response was, 'How can anyone be that good at Pictionary?' I told him, I know. It sounds crazy, but it's true. She's, like, the Babe Ruth of Pictionary.' And that should have been the end of the story."

"But it wasn't," said Michael.

"No," said Robbie. "The day after that, unbeknownst to me, Ricky is sitting in our room when he notices Debbie walking back from class. Now we lived on the first floor, so Ricky slides the window open and peeks his head out. 'Hey, Debbie, Ray tells me you are one hell of a Pictionary player.' Ray was my college nickname."

"I remember you telling me that," said Michael. "Why was that again?"

"It's too long a story to tell now," said Robbie. "Another time."

"OK, so Ricky tells her she's one hell of a Pictionary player," said Michael.

"Right," said Robbie. "And then he says, 'How about Ray and I challenge you and Maria to a Pictionary game? If you win, we'll take you girls out to dinner at the Aylesbury Inn.' That was the most expensive restaurant in Utica. 'But if we win,' he says, 'you have to cook us a five-course dinner.'

"Now, of course, Debbie immediately accepts the challenge. This is going to be the easiest win of her life. I mean, she's the greatest Pictionary player ever. And for a free dinner at the Aylesbury Inn!

"When Ricky told me what he had done, I freaked out. 'She's the greatest Pictionary player ever!' I yelled. 'How the hell are we going to pay for a dinner for four at the friggin' Aylesbury Inn?' "

Michael laughed. "What did Ricky say?"

"He said, 'Don't worry, Ray; we're gonna win.' And not only that. He got her to agree to the menu items he wanted in case we were to win. Lasagna, chicken cutlets Parmigiana, garlic bread, a Caesar salad, and a chocolate layer cake. And she told him, 'Sure, no problem. Whatever you want,' because she knew there was no way that her and her roommate could lose.

"So, we head over to Debbie's apartment on Saturday night, and the game begins. They went first, and of course Debbie guesses Maria's first drawing right away. I thought to myself that this is going to be over quickly, right? But she couldn't get the second one, and now it was our turn.

"And I get the first one right. And Ricky gets the second one right. And then I get the third one right. And we're getting them right quickly, like without even thinking. And we get the next one and the next one. And we start realizing that living four feet apart from each other for almost four years had had an effect. We basically knew what the other one was thinking before we even thought it. It's like our minds had melded together without us even realizing it.

"And now I can see Debbie squirming. And Ricky isn't being shy about hiding his excitement. Every time we get another one right, he's hooting and hollering, and I can see Debbie turning white. I mean, she's the greatest Pictionary player in the history of the world, and here we are, blowing her doors off.

"Before you know it, we're almost all the way across the board, needing only one more right answer to win the game. And we got it, just like that. I couldn't believe it. It was exhilarating. We went around the whole damn board without getting one wrong. They never even got another chance to go. I can honestly say it was probably the greatest performance in the history of Pictionary, if such a history actually existed.

"So, we high-fived and hooted and hollered some more, and Debbie's face went cold. I think those blue eyes I told you about went black. 'It's just a game, so don't be upset,' I said. But she was upset. And it didn't help that Ricky immediately started telling her just the way he likes his garlic bread and how much frosting he likes on his chocolate cake."

"Sounds like she was pretty upset," said Michael. "Did she get over it?"

"No, not really," said Robbie. "The next day, she was cold and aloof toward me. And it got worse as the week went on. By the next Friday, she wasn't speaking to me. All because of Pictionary! And the capper is, the following Saturday, we're supposed to go back to her apartment for the big five-course dinner. Now I'm thinking it's never gonna happen. Our relationship is dead. But Ricky wants his dinner. And sure enough, Debbie has Maria call our apartment on Saturday morning to ask if we're still coming for the dinner. Ricky tells her, 'Damn straight we are.'

"So, we go over that night, and to her credit, she went all out and made a spectacular meal. But it was eaten in silence. She still wasn't talking to me. You could cut the tension with a knife. But we were a couple of hungry college boys and chowed down like there was no tomorrow. We even took home all the leftovers."

"And what happened with you and Debbie?" Michael asked.

"Nothing," said Robbie. "It was done. Our relationship ended as soon as Ricky and I completed our whirlwind tour around the Pictionary board."

"I'm telling you, Pops, you have the best stories," said Michael.

"Well, when you're as old as I am, you're bound to have a few funny stories," said Robbie.

"Yeah, but all these stories took place when you were a kid. I don't have any stories like these."

"I'm sure you have some good stories of your own," said Robbie. "You just have to get out there. At any moment, something might happen that you'll remember the rest of your life."

"I don't know, Pops," said Michael. "My life is pretty boring."

"Everybody has a once upon a time, Michael," said Robbie. "Stories happen to you every day. You just have to open your eyes and see them."

Elizabeth walked onto the porch and handed Robbie and Michael each a glass of iced tea. "Is he keeping you entertained?" Elizabeth asked Michael.

"Yes, as always, Grandma," said Michael.

"Well, you know your grandfather," said Elizabeth. "He'll talk about the old days all day if you let him."

Robbie eyed a large seagull that had landed on the beach in front of them.

"Hey, Liz, remember that time the seagull stole your sandwich?" Robbie asked.

"How could I not?" Elizabeth said. "I still miss that sandwich."

"What happened?" Michael asked.

"Oh, your grandfather and I were on the beach. I think it was in Montauk not long after we got married. And we got some great hero sandwiches at a deli and brought them to the beach. Sure enough, I took one bite, and a seagull swooped down and snatched the whole sandwich right out of my hands."

Robbie laughed. "See, Michael? A random moment, and here we are, talking about it forty-something years later."

Elizabeth sat down with them, and they chatted and told a few more stories, Michael listening and still wondering why nothing interesting or funny ever seemed to happen to him. As the sun started to set, Michael and Elizabeth retired to the house. Robbie stayed outside to watch the sunset.

He had enjoyed telling Michael the stories, but of course he now couldn't stop thinking about his mother and his father and Ricky. God, how he missed them! He shifted in his chair and tried to get them out of his head, but it was a losing battle. He decided to stop fighting it and let the melancholy wash over him.

Telling the stories felt good. Telling the stories kept the people in those stories alive. And perhaps they kept him alive as well. He reckoned that we are all just a composite of our stories. We collect them throughout our lives like souvenirs and pull them out every now and then to validate our own existence, to somehow convince ourselves that it all wasn't a dream.

The sun went down below the horizon, and Robbie walked slowly back into the house.

2020 Visions

(2020)

THE REGULAR SIGHT OF kids riding their bikes around the neighborhood was one of the remarkable visions of the pandemic. He and his family had lived on Victory Lane for almost twenty years. He had raised his kids here.

His kids had nice bikes of different shapes and sizes since they were six years old, but they had mainly sat unused in the garage. Kids from their generation rarely rode their bikes, it seemed. When he was a kid, his bike was part of his identity. He never went anywhere without it. Same for his friends. Today's kids seemingly couldn't care less. But then the pandemic hit, and the world came to a stop. And then the bikes came out. Kids and even some of their parents had suddenly come out of hiding and were leisurely pedaling around the neighborhood.

And John Borelli found himself sitting on his porch each day at 14 Victory Lane, watching these people, his neighbors, riding their bikes. He found it peaceful and relaxing. And anything peaceful and relaxing right now was welcome.

There Are Places I Remember

The world John and everyone else knew had pretty much ended on March 13. That was John's last day in the office in the city. The same day that the NBA announced the postponement of the rest of the season and the same day that the world found out that Tom Hanks had COVID-19. It was early May now, and John had been home almost seven weeks, and there was still no telling when he might go back to the office.

The first two weeks were unsettling. His body kept waking up at 5:15 a.m., as it had for years, even though there was no reason to be up. The alarm clock was off. There was no reason to be upright, except for the occasional 9 a.m. Zoom call for work. He was already tired of those. But after a couple of weeks, his body stopped waking up. He was slowly adjusting to being a person with no good reason to get up in the morning other than to smell the roses. And he was starting to enjoy it.

Of course, when he turned on the news and saw the latest death tallies, frustration and some fear would set in. The governor was a calming influence, and his daily press conferences were not to be missed. But sometimes, John had to turn off the TV and clear his mind. So, out on the front porch he would go and wait for the kids and their bikes to calm him.

"You and your bikes."

John turned to see Sally exit the house and hand him a glass of wine.

He took the wine and thanked her. "I like watching the kids on their bikes. Certainly, there are stranger things than that in the world right now."

His wife sat down next to him with a glass of her own in hand. "You are right about that," she said. "Have the murder hornets arrived yet?"

He laughed and sipped his wine. They had been drinking quite frequently since the lockdown began. And now, with the weather getting warm, it was becoming a daily practice to sit outside around 4 p.m. every day and throw a couple back. He hadn't drunk this much since before he was married, but what else was there to do? They could worry about masks and ventilators and droplets and surges and bending the curve and the approaching murder hornets. Or they could sip some wine and watch the kids. And breathe in the clean air. There were few cars on the roads and virtually no planes in the sky. Just a warm breeze and a nice Chardonnay.

Other than watching the news, the only real stress was their weekly visit to ShopRite to get food. The fear of being around people, of making sure that you are six feet away from everyone else and getting anxious when someone gets too close. And then furiously wiping down the shopping cart. And then wiping down the door handles of the car and the steering wheel before driving home. And then wiping down the handle of the front door after entering the house. And then unloading all the canned goods you had stocked up on in anticipation of the coming apocalypse. Meat plants had been shutting down around the country due to outbreaks. Must make sure you have enough food in the freezer and in the pantry just in case the whole damn system collapses. Then taking the mask off and breathing again.

"One of my high school friend's father died," said Sally. "She just posted it on Facebook."

"COVID?" he asked.

"Yep."

"How old?"

"Seventy-eight."

"Underlying conditions?"

"She didn't say."

How many people now had they known had died in the pandemic? At least three. All of them old. That made it a little easier. But on the news last night, there was a story about a 36-year-old father of three in Queens who caught COVID-19 and was dead four days later, with no underlying conditions. So, what do you do? You take another sip of the Chardonnay—that's what you do.

There Are Places I Remember

John noticed an Amazon truck turn onto the block. In addition to kids riding bikes, the sight of an Amazon truck coming down the block was part of the new normal. He hoped it would stop at their house. He had ordered another old Elton John CD and was eager to start listening to it. Yes, he still collected CDs. Not that he played them. No, he would give them to his wife so that she could download them onto his iPhone. He was terrible with technology. This would be the fourth old CD he had bought on Amazon since the pandemic started.

Something about the current state of the world had him drifting back to his childhood, seeking out the music of those seemingly innocent times. He thought it strange because he was not usually someone who spent his time looking back. But he guessed the uncertain future had something to do with it. With the world turned upside down, it was hard to look a year or two ahead. Heck, it was hard right now to look a week or two ahead. So, maybe there was nothing to do but look back.

The truck stopped in front of the house, and the Amazon driver got out. John met him halfway down the driveway.

"You can leave it right there," John said.

The driver placed the small package on the driveway about twenty feet from John. Social distancing at its finest. John waited for the truck to pull away before retrieving the package.

On the porch, Sally grabbed the package and quickly worked it over with a wet wipe. John opened it. *Honky Chateau.*

"Ah," he said, and he studied the album cover. "Now I can listen to 'Rocketman' and 'Mona Lisas and Mad Hatters' whenever I want."

"You could already do that on Amazon Music," Sally reminded him.

"I like to have the album in my hands," he replied.

"Then you should have ordered the vinyl," she said.

Sally sipped her wine as John studied the back of the CD.

"When do you think it's going to end?" Sally asked.

"Not anytime soon."

"I wonder if things will ever go back to normal."

"Maybe," he said. "Maybe not. Maybe it's a good thing if they don't."

"Yeah, I know what you mean," she said.

"I don't miss it," he said.

"Miss what?" she asked.

"Work, the commute, getting up at 5 o'clock—all of it. I like sitting here with you and drinking wine and watching bicycles."

"I know," she said. "I like having you here."

"We're lucky," he said. "Think of all the hospital workers going through hell and the grocery store workers getting paid shit and putting themselves at risk so that we can sit on the porch every day and drink wine. Makes me feel guilty."

"I know," she said. "Me too."

They stared out toward the street. Two more kids whizzed by on their bikes, laughing as they went.

The world had stopped, and people were dying, and people were wearing out, but John and Sally had been spared so far. Yes, they felt guilty, but what could they do? They could wear their masks, keep their distance, stay home, and hope that, in doing so, they were in some small way a part of the solution and not part of the problem.

Sally's iPhone bleeped. She looked at her screen.

"Look at this. Murder hornets spotted in Washington state," she said.

John laughed. "2020," he said.

"2020," said Sally.

They both drank some more from their glasses.

"Hey, why don't we get on the kids' bikes?" Sally asked.

"Are you kidding?" John said. "When was the last time you were on a bike?"

"I can't remember," she said. "Let's do it! We could catch COVID next week or get bitten by murder hornets at any moment. So, let's ride the fucking bikes."

John contemplated his wife's suggestion for a moment. He hadn't been on a bike in years. But she had a point. What the fuck, right? Why not ride a bike? When he was a kid, it was his favorite thing to do. The world as they knew it might be ending. So, why not go bike riding with his wife?

"Let's do it," he said.

"For real?" she said.

"If a murder hornet is going to kill me, I might as well ride a bike one last time."

They put down their wineglasses and leaped off the porch and went into the garage. Their kids' bikes, looking as new as the day they bought them, awaited.

Each hopped on a bike, which fit them uncomfortably, but they got the hang of it as they slowly rolled out of the garage and down the driveway. They picked it up quickly. It was true that riding a bike was like, well, riding a bike.

Down the street they went, laughing like the kids who rode past their house minutes earlier.

They neared the top of the hill at the end of the street, and John peered ahead. They couldn't see the future; they couldn't see how the pandemic would end, and they couldn't see what the world was going to be. The only vision they had was the fifty feet of street in front of them. That was the new world of 2020. They reached the crest of the hill, then sped down as fast as they could.

The Christmas Present

(2060)

THE OLD MAN LEANED forward in his wheelchair. He was trying desperately for his hands to reach his feet. He didn't wear shoes anymore because they hurt his feet and because he hadn't walked in at least two years. No need for shoes. But his feet were freezing. He just wanted to rub his feet and keep them warm. He didn't own a pair of good socks anymore. The pairs he had were thin, and some had holes. If his hands could just reach his feet…

He was sitting in the TV lounge of the Sunnyside Rest Home. Not many people watched television anymore, not even most of the old people at Sunnyside. But the old man grew up with television and still liked it. Loved it really. Sunnyside set up the room for guests who were nostalgic for the old days. The TV was only used to show old movies.

Today, they were showing *Raiders of the Lost Ark*. He remembered seeing it as a teenager in 1981 and thinking that it was the greatest movie he had ever seen. So much so that he went back to see it three times that summer. He was surprised that he could remember the year that it had come out. He couldn't remember the dates of much of anything that had happened in the past fifty years or so. But he could remember the year of a movie that came out seventy-nine years earlier. Funny how someone can remember exactly when the moments of youth occurred while the rest of life's timeline becomes a blur.

When the movie was over, Nurse Wenda checked in on him. He liked Nurse Wenda very much, although when he first arrived at Sunnyside, he called her Wanda until he found out it was Wenda. These new-style names! Wenda? So be it. But she was the nicest and most attentive of all the Sunnyside workers, and the minutes he spent with her each day were the only real nice minutes of the day.

"How was the movie?" she asked.

"Great," he said. "Made me think of my older sister. She had a huge crush on Harrison Ford back in the day. He played Han Solo too, you know."

It was clear to him that Nurse Wenda hadn't a clue who Han Solo was, but he didn't have the energy to explain it to her.

"Everything else OK?" she asked.

"Well, my feet are freezing again," he said. "These damn socks just aren't cutting it."

"I'm sorry," she said. "The socks they provide here aren't high-quality, are they? Let me fix your blanket."

She rewrapped the blanket around his feet, and it helped a little. Then she wheeled him back toward his room.

It was December 20th, and holiday decorations were all around. As they passed the Christmas tree in the hallway, the old man was jolted by memories of Christmases past. Something about the lights on the tree brought him back to childhood and the big tree that would sprout in the living room every December. His brother and sister would be there and his parents. His grandmother too. But they were all gone now.

Nurse Wenda wheeled him into his room. He groaned.

"Are you OK?" she asked.

"Just my damn feet," he said.

"Here, let me help," she said.

Nurse Wenda removed his socks and slowly rubbed his feet.

"Does that help?"

"Yes," he said. And it did.

But when she put his socks back on and left the room, his feet were soon cold again.

He dreamed that night of Christmas. In the dream, he was a child. He ran down the stairs with his older brother. There was the beautiful Christmas tree, with wrapped presents flowing out from underneath it. Santa had come. Was there ever a greater joy in life than coming down the stairs as a child on Christmas morning? He grabbed a present and tore off the wrapping paper. Rock 'em Sock 'em Robots! Oh, yes, he had wanted nothing more in the world.

When he awoke the next morning, he had the usual aches and pains, but his cold feet got his attention first. The planet had warmed considerably over his lifetime, and it was a balmy sixty degrees out seemingly every day this December. But still, he couldn't get his damned feet warm.

After breakfast, he was wheeled into the TV room. *Dances with Wolves* was playing. That was a good one. He thought maybe it had won the Oscar back in the day, but he wasn't sure. Either way, he wasn't paying much attention to the movie. He was still thinking about the dream. About Christmas morning and Rock 'em Sock 'em Robots. Oh, how he loved that game! And Christmas as a child. The wonder of waiting for Santa and opening your presents. How long had it been since he had felt such joy?

What other great presents had he opened on Christmas morning?

There was that great *Guns of Navarone* mountain playset that he got when he was seven or eight. He loved that one. It came with a full set of American and German soldiers and a working elevator so that you could ferry troops to the top of the mountain, where the two big guns were. He spent untold hours playing with that one.

And he remembered getting one of those race car sets. One of those where the cars never stayed on the tracks for more than five or ten seconds. In the TV commercials, they went round and round the track endlessly. The reality was different. But it was a great present nonetheless.

When he was a little older, he got one of those handheld Mattel electronic football games and played it every day for months. Who would have thought that a game featuring little red dots on a tiny handheld screen could be so much fun?

But probably the greatest Christmas gift he ever received was the Atari console when he was fourteen. Yes, nothing beat that one. He could still close his eyes and hear the noises that the Space Invaders game made.

He couldn't think of any gifts he had received as an adult. In fact, he couldn't remember when he last received a Christmas gift at all. He hadn't seen his son in at least a year. Maybe longer. His son had probably given him a Christmas gift at some point in the previous years, but he couldn't remember any of them. Certainly, his wife had gotten him something, but she was gone ten years now.

He just missed Christmas the way it used to be. He always loved decorating the house and the tree. And he loved all the houses in the neighborhood covered in Christmas lights. He even loved the nonstop Christmas songs played on the radio. And the Christmas specials on TV, like *Rudolph* and that one where Fred Astaire sang the theme song. The whole season had always filled him with hope and something to look forward to.

Doesn't everyone need something to look forward to? Something so that when you wake up in the morning, you have a reason to get out of bed.

But as an old man, all alone in a nursing home, he had nothing to look forward to. And with nothing to look forward to, life bordered on being unbearable. And his cold-as-hell feet weren't making it any better.

"Which one are you watching today?"

It was Nurse Wenda.

"*Dances with Wolves* with Kevin Costner," he replied.

"Don't think I know that one," she said.

"He was once voted the Sexiest Man Alive," he said. God only knows how or why he remembered that.

"The what?"

"Never mind," he said.

"How are those feet today?" she asked.

"Freezing."

She promptly put her hands under his blanket and rubbed his feet. It felt good, but the old man was embarrassed. How pathetic that this is what his life had come to.

Dreams came to him again that night. Once again, he dreamed of Christmas morning. This time, he and his brother were playing with the Rock 'em Sock 'em Robots. But his brother's face was vague. Did he not remember what his brother looked like as a child? No matter. He was just enjoying playing the game and being in his childhood living room on Christmas.

When Christmas morning came a few days later, he was wheeled into the TV room. *Miracle on 34th Street* was playing. Not the original black-and-white version, but the color version from the '90s. He knew the actors' faces, but he couldn't remember their names. The original, with Natalie Wood, was better.

He tried to concentrate on the movie, but his mind wandered. So, is this how it ends? He was once a man with an important job. People reported to him and depended on him and took directions from him. He had a wife and a child and a house, and he was liked. He had friends. People knew who he was. But all that was long gone. He was just an old man sitting alone in a wheelchair on Christmas morning. And of course, his feet were still freezing.

"Merry Christmas, Mr. Tate."

He turned to see Nurse Wenda. "What are you doing here on Christmas?" he asked. "Shouldn't you be home with your family?"

"I'll be home later," she said. "I didn't want you to be all alone on Christmas."

She held a box in her hands. It was wrapped in red-and-green paper with cartoon Santas on it.

"Besides," she said, "I have a little present for you."

He looked at the present and felt a momentary rush of excitement and anticipation. When was the last time he had felt that way?

She handed him the gift, and he held it in his hands and stared at it for a moment. A Christmas present on Christmas. He certainly wasn't expecting that.

"Here, let me help you," she said. She ripped open the wrapping paper and opened the top of the box inside.

He looked in the box and saw a pile of thick wool socks. All different colors.

"I know how cold your feet have been lately," she said. "I figured you could use a few of these."

He held one of the thick wool socks in his hand, and he was damned if this wasn't the softest thing he had ever felt.

"Let's get one of those pairs on your feet," Wenda said.

She removed his old, worn-out socks and gently put a pair of the new ones on.

His feet felt a warmth that he could not remember ever feeling before. And he felt pleasure. And joy. He couldn't believe how the warming of his feet could feel so good. And then he started to cry.

"What's wrong?" asked Nurse Wenda.

"Th-thank you," he said, barely getting the words out as he fought the tears. "These socks are the greatest Christmas present I've ever received. Thank you, Nurse Wenda. Thank you."

"Oh, it was nothing," she said. "I just knew how much you needed some good socks. It's Christmas. Everyone should open at least one present, right?"

"Yes," he said. "You are right."

"What's the movie today?"

"*Miracle on 34th Street,*" he said.

"Don't think I know that one," she said. "Is that 34th Street in the city?"

"Yes," he said. "It's where Macy's used to be."

"What's Macy's?"

"An old store," he said. "The little girl in the movie is trying to prove that the man dressed as Santa at Macy's is actually the real Santa."

"And does she?"

"She does," he said.

"That sounds cute," she said.

Today, it felt more than cute to the old man. It seemed real.

"I'll check on you later, Mr. Tate. Enjoy the movie and enjoy those socks."

The old man settled back in his wheelchair and was content. His feet were warm, and nothing else mattered. It was Christmas, and he was happy.

Atari? No, these socks were far better than Atari or Rock 'em Sock 'em Robots. They were unquestionably the greatest Christmas present that he had ever received.

He rested comfortably in his wheelchair and enjoyed the movie. He even looked forward to tomorrow's movie, whatever it may be. He hoped it would be a slapstick comedy or something like that. They hadn't shown one of those in a while. *He hoped*. Wasn't that something?

That night, he dreamed of Christmas again. But it wasn't a Christmas from the past. It was a Christmas in the future. In the dream, he sat in the wheelchair in the TV room. Nurse Wenda handed him a present, wrapped beautifully in shiny red-and-green wrapping paper. His excitement was palpable. He awoke before he could open it. But he awoke happy for the first time in years.

"The past beats inside me like a second heart."

—John Banville

When the Evening Comes

(2062)

"Mr. Robert Miller, so nice to finally meet you."

"And you, Mr. Gundersen."

Mr. Gundersen regarded the old man sitting before him. He looked spry for a man of 95. And he seemed rather humble for a Wall Street titan. Gundersen had seen photos and video of this man over the years, and he was always dressed to the nines. But the Robert Miller sitting across from him in the guest chair of the Zenith Time Travel Corporation was dressed for a stroll in the park.

"I will tell you that you are the oldest person to ever use the services of the Zenith Time Travel Corporation."

"And is that a problem of some sort?"

"Not at all, Mr. Miller," said Gundersen. "Just curious. It's 2062. We've been in business for forty-five years. The average age of one of our patrons is fifty-five. I believe the oldest before you was seventy-one or seventy-two."

"I guess that makes me a trailblazer for the over-ninety set."

Gundersen chuckled.

"So, where does a ninety-five-year-old man who has done and seen so many things want to go back to?"

"Victory Lane, Long Island, July 16th, 1973."

"I'm pretty well versed in my history. I'm trying to think of something significant that was going on at that time," said Gundersen. "Watergate?"

"No, nothing like that," said Miller. "The politics of that time hold no interest to me now."

"Just curious," said Gundersen. "Why you want to go there is your business."

"Well, if you'll indulge an old man, I'll try to satisfy your curiosity."

Mr. Gundersen shifted in his chair. Not all clients told him why they wanted to go back to a certain time, but it always fascinated him when they did. It was the best part of his job.

"How old are you, Mr. Gundersen, if I may ask?"

"You may," said Gundersen. "Fifty-three."

"So, you're old enough to have some regrets, but perhaps still too young to look inside of yourself and see your true self, to see when in your life you were truly happy."

Gundersen pondered that. "Perhaps you are right. Certainly, a man of your age and experience has more insight into that sort of thing than I do."

"You're right about that, Mr. Gundersen," said Miller. "That's why I don't want to go back to see the Civil War, or the Kennedy assassination, or the birth of Jesus, or any other event in history. Those things hold no meaning for me now."

"What do you want to see?"

"The world the way it looked when I was six years old."

"Interesting," said Gundersen.

"At fifty-three, maybe you are old enough to understand what I am about to tell you, or maybe not. Maybe I'm the only one who thinks like this. What did John Lennon sing? 'No one I know is in my tree'? Maybe I'm like him."

Now Miller shifted in his seat. He wasn't sure if Gundersen would understand his motivations, but he wanted to tell him anyway. He wanted to express it to another soul, regardless of whether that soul would understand.

"You see, Mr. Gundersen, things in this world don't look and smell to me the way they did when I was a boy. And I don't mean since I'm an old man. I mean, since I'm a teenager. Now, that could just mean that I remember things from my early days through the rose-colored glasses of youth. Or it could just mean that a child sees and senses things differently than an adult. But whatever the reason, I have spent the better part of the last eighty or so years yearning for the world of my youth. So, I want to go back to 1973 and look at the sky and see the sun the way it looked then because I swear to you it looked different than it does today, or twenty years ago, or even sixty years ago."

Mr. Gundersen listened intently. Obviously, the old man was longing for the innocence of youth. Hell, everyone could relate to that.

"And I want to smell the freshly cut grass," Miller continued. "The smell of a lawn that has just been mowed has never smelled to me the way it did then. And the sound of a plane in the sky. I've been on planes all around the world, but the sight and sound of one in the summer sky in 1973 is something I haven't experienced since then."

Robbie paused a moment. "You think I'm a crazy old man, don't you, Mr. Gundersen?"

"Not at all," Gundersen lied. "This is very interesting."

Robbie closed his eyes for a moment and imagined Victory Lane in 1973. An image of a plane in the sky seeped into his mind.

"My friend Billy Cohen and I would see a plane in the sky, and I would tell him if it was German or not. If I said it was German, we would dive for cover under the nearest tree."

Gundersen looked quizzically at the old man.

"We grew up watching World War II movies on TV. German planes was a game we played."

"Sounds like fun," said Gundersen.

"Oh, it was, Mr. Gundersen," said Miller. "More fun than anything I've ever done in my life."

"So, you'll be taking a nice stroll through the old neighborhood, as it were," said Gundersen. "I think I can relate to that. And as we've extended the time one can spend in the past from three hours to eight, you'll get the chance to spend a nice day there."

"There is one more reason I want to go back, if you'll indulge me, Mr. Gundersen."

"Of course, Mr. Miller."

"I want to go back and look into my mother's eyes one last time before I die," said Miller. "My mother had the most beautiful eyes anyone has ever seen, and to see them again will make this old man before you die happy."

"Well, that is especially interesting, Mr. Miller," said Gundersen. "And I can certainly understand the sentiment."

Robbie Miller wasn't convinced that Mr. Gundersen truly understood anything he had just told him. He wasn't sure he understood it himself. But it did feel good to express it to another human being. Just saying his motivations out loud made them seem less crazy. Hell, the whole idea of time travel was insane in and of itself. What did it matter where you wanted to go back to and why? Going back in time anywhere was crazy enough.

There Are Places I Remember

Wanting to see his old neighborhood, wanting to see his mother—wasn't that a more valid reason than to see some historical event?

Robbie lay awake in his bed on the 80th floor of his 57th Street luxury apartment. His bedroom window faced east. If he stood up, he could look ahead for miles. Not far enough to see Victory Lane, but it was out there, about fifty miles to the east. He hadn't been back there in decades.

His last visit upset him too much. The large, leafy oak trees that had lined the sidewalks were long gone. The woods behind the houses on the east side of the street were gone as well, cut down to make room for apartment buildings. But the thing that had upset him the most was that he couldn't recognize the house that he had grown up in. It was still there all right. All the houses were. But everything else about the front of the house and the front lawn was so different that he could get no sense that he was standing in front of *his* house. So, he peeked into the backyard to look at the tall pine tree that he loved so much as a boy. Seeing that tree would give him a sense of place and make everything else on his old property fall into place for him. It would tell him that he was home. But the tree was no longer there. And that had filled him with dread.

But tomorrow, through the miracle of science or whatever the hell you called what they did at the Zenith Time Travel Corporation, he would see Victory Lane in all its youthful splendor, before the march of time and the sorrows of its inhabitants wore her down.

And, by God, he would see his mother! Chills ran through his old body, just thinking of it. His glorious young mother, before age and illness destroyed her, with her soulful blue eyes that momentarily eased the burdens of life for every person who ever looked into them.

I'm coming home, Ma.

He awoke with a start. He was lying on his back in what appeared to be tall grass. They told him he might experience some disorientation, and, boy, were they right. Where was he? He lurched up off the ground and got his head above the grass. He saw some slabs of cement strewn about the field around him. Why were there cement slabs in a field? He slowly got to his feet. He was in an open field, surrounded by woods. He could hear traffic to his left. So, he walked toward the traffic. He clawed his way through the tall grass, and after a small rise, the grass cleared away, and there was road in front of him, and instantly, he knew he was home.

It was Middle Country Road. Look at the cars! He marveled as a shiny mint-green '72 Pontiac Grand Prix went racing by. Then what looked like a '67 Plymouth Barracuda. And then a big, boxy station wagon. God, remember station wagons?

And on the other side of the road, in all of its new suburban splendor, stood the sprawling Smith Haven Mall. He felt a lump in his throat. There were few places he loved as a child more than that mall. He remembered watching Santa land via helicopter in the parking lot and waiting patiently in line at Abraham & Strauss to sit on his lap. His father buying him soft-serve ice cream at Barricini Candy. His mother getting him something from the toy aisle at McCrory's. Or when he got older, playing Space Invaders with his friends at the Time-Out Arcade. And then eyeballing the mall chicks! Were there ever hotter girls anywhere than mall chicks? And of course, there was the mall movie theater. Was there ever a grander movie theater anywhere? With its giant single screen and plush red velvet seats. He had gone back once in the late 90s to visit, and they had turned that beautiful theater into a six-screen multiplex, and, by God, it almost made him cry.

He walked closer to the edge of the road. He could see the movie sign now. *Live and Let Die* was playing! Of course! It opened in July of '73. Holy shit, this time-travel thing actually worked! He was literally standing and breathing in 1973. He saw that movie with his parents when it first opened some ninety-odd years ago. Or in this case, a couple of weeks ago...

And in all his excitement at seeing the mall, he almost forgot what it meant. It meant that the field with the tall grass that he "landed" in was the field he and his friends used to play in, the field behind the woods of Victory Lane...

Now a chill went through him. It was there. A scant walk through the field, then the woods, maybe 500 feet. Living and breathing. Victory Lane.

He glanced back at the mall one last time, then turned back toward the field.

And then he noticed the sun. It was warm and welcoming. It was like running into an old friend he hadn't seen in years. It truly did look different and better and captivating. That was the sun he remembered! He stared up at it as he walked again through the tall grass and past the stone slabs—surely from construction debris from when the mall was built a few years earlier.

He made his way through the grass and into the woods. He picked up one of the foot trails that zigzagged through these woods, the woods that he used to play Cowboys and Indians in. As he waded deeper into the woods, he could see the backs of houses coming into view through the trees. Victory Lane.

His heart started to beat faster as he edged closer to the houses. Was this unreal? How he had yearned for so long to be back at this place and time! And through the miracle of the Zenith Time Travel Corporation, here he was.

He came to the end of the woods. To his right was the back of the Rosellis' house. He could tell by the new in-ground pool in the backyard. They were the first family on the block to get one. That meant the house to the left was the Huertgens.' He walked to the left of the Rosellis' backyard fence and into the unfenced yard of the Huertgens'.

He walked through the backyard, into the front, and there before him was his first view of Victory Lane in decades. It was just after 2 p.m. on a Monday. He could hear the welcoming sound of a lawn being mowed, which was odd because most dads in the neighborhood mowed their lawns on the weekend. He could also smell freshly cut grass, and it smelled as good as apple pie warming in the oven on Thanksgiving. He walked across the Huertgens' front lawn to the sidewalk and peered left down the street. Look how small and young the oak trees along the sidewalk were! Those beautiful trees that were now long gone.

The rest of the street was as beautiful as he remembered. He caught a glimpse of his house, across the street, three houses down. He chose this day and time to come back to because he knew that he and his sister would be away, staying for a week at his grandparents' house in Brooklyn, as they did every year at this time. Although the Zenith Time Travel Corporation assured him that it was perfectly safe for him to run into his past self, the idea weirded him out. No, he was here to see his beloved street and, most of all, his mother.

He noticed that there was not a soul on the street. He thought that was a little odd, but then he realized that it was ninety-plus degrees. Most of the moms and the kids, the ones who weren't at camp, were probably inside, trying to stay cool. Of course, in 2062, ninety-plus days were the norm. But for 1973, it was hot.

There Are Places I Remember

He walked across the street toward his house. He was delighted at how everything looked, as if he had been here yesterday. On his last visit, in the 2030s, everything had looked so different. But this was the Victory Lane he knew and loved. He couldn't remember what he ate for lunch yesterday, but he immediately remembered the '72 Delta 88 parked on the driveway as he walked past the Bishops' house. It was a boat, but he loved that car. And the wind chimes that hung from the Rosenbergs' porch. He hadn't thought of them in about eighty years, but now that they were before his eyes again, it was as if he had heard them chiming this morning. The memory of them was clear and instantaneous. He still easily remembered the names of the families in each house. Marsh, Bishop, Rosenberg…

And then he came upon his house. His heart raced, and he felt as if he might fall. The beautiful house that he had grown up in now stood before him. The wood shakes that fronted the house were clean and new. He loved those shakes. They were so much better than the aluminum siding that would be installed on the house in the late 1980s. And the bright red window shutters. Only in the '70s would you see those! But he loved them.

As he stood at the foot of the driveway, he noticed a transistor radio sitting on the porch. That meant his mother had been sitting on the porch, listening to music, as she always loved to do. So, where was she now?

He didn't have to wait to find out. The screen door swung open, and out walked his mother, holding a glass of iced tea.

It felt like his heart stopped for a moment. His mother stood before him, looking more radiant and beautiful than he remembered. And so young! He had forgotten how she looked at this age. What age was she? Yes, she would be 31 years old in the summer of '73. She was a kid! Oh, what a wonder the Zenith Time Travel Corporation had created!

"Hello?" his mother asked the question curiously, but with a gentle smile, as was her wont.

He realized how strange it must be for her to see this ninety-five-year-old man standing at the foot of her driveway.

"Good afternoon, ma'am," he said.

Still smiling, she said, "Can I help you?"

"I'm sorry," he said. "It's just that I used to live here…"

She looked at him quizzically, and he realized his mistake. The damn street and house didn't exist until five years earlier. How could he have lived here? Stupid old man! He had to recover quickly!

"Well, not right here exactly, but around here," he said. "Many years ago."

"Oh," she said.

"I was at the mall and decided to take a walk over here. This all used to be woods when I was a boy. I used to play here."

"Really?" she said. "That must have been at the turn of the century or more. I didn't even know there were houses around here at that time."

He was glad that she seemed to be friendly and not at all alarmed by the strange old man in front of her house. *Their* house, but he didn't need to remind himself.

"Yes, there were a few houses in the area," he answered. He then wiped his brow as that beautiful 1973 sun beat down on him.

"Would you like some iced tea?" she asked.

Just like his mother to notice someone's discomfort and try to alleviate it.

"That would be wonderful," he replied.

He walked up the driveway toward the porch. His mother handed him her glass of tea, and he looked into her eyes for the first time over 40 years. He stood frozen for a moment, holding the glass, looking at her. She let go.

"Just give me a second to grab a glass for myself." She headed back inside.

He sat on the wooden porch chair next to the milk box. He certainly remembered the silver tin milk box. But even that was gone by the mid '70s, replaced by supermarket milk in plastic containers.

His mother returned with her glass of iced tea and sat in the chair next to him.

On the radio, he heard the opening strains of Seals and Crofts' "Summer Breeze." How many decades had it been since he had heard that song? He loved it when he was little.

Without thinking, he looked at his mother and said, "Seals and Crofts, 'Summer Breeze.' "

His mother looked at him incredulously. "What an interesting old man you are. How do you know that song? My husband probably doesn't even know who sings that song, and he's more than half your age!"

He cursed his faux pas. He can't keep making mistakes like that. Not that it was even remotely possible for her to ever guess the truth. But he didn't want to push his luck.

"My granddaughter likes that song," he lied.

He sipped his tea and stared at his mother. He could feel tears welling up inside, and he fought hard to hold them back.

"You have beautiful blue eyes," he said.

"Oh, that's so sweet," she said.

"My mother had eyes just like yours."

She regarded the old man before her. Something about him was familiar, but she couldn't put her finger on it.

"There's something about you," she said. "Have we met before?"

"Maybe in another lifetime," he said.

She laughed. "Maybe," she said. "I just realized I haven't even introduced myself. I'm Barbara."

"Robert," he said.

"Another Robert!" she said. "My husband and son are Roberts too."

He almost replied, "I know," but caught himself at the last moment.

"Actually, my son is Robbie. He and my daughter are at my parents' house in the city, but they'll be home in a few hours. My husband is picking them up on his way home from work."

"How old are your children?"

"Debbie is eight, and Robbie is six."

Of course, he knew that, but he was so enraptured by the fact that he was talking to his thirty-one-year-old mother, here on their porch, in 1973...well, he had to keep talking to keep himself from grabbing her in his arms and crying. How many times did he sit on this porch and these chairs with her when he was a boy?

"And your boy, Robbie—Yankees or Mets?"

"Oh, Yankees, like his dad," she said. "But it's tough for him now because everyone likes the Mets now. You know, Tom Seaver and everything, although the Mets are having a lousy year."

"You never know," he said. "They might make the World Series this year." He was old, but he still remembered his baseball history. A memory then flashed in his head—sitting on the floor in front of the TV in the den, watching Wayne Garret of the Mets make the last out of the 1973 World Series against the A's. In the den, right inside the front door they were sitting in front of. The first World Series he could remember.

"Tell your son not to worry and to stick with the Yankees," he said. "I think they have a bright future."

"I hope so," she said. "He's six years old, and he absolutely lives and dies with them. In fact, we're taking him to his first game next week. He can't wait."

He remembered that too. He met Bobby Murcer at that game and got his autograph. It was like meeting God himself.

"I bet he loves Bobby Murcer."

"Oh, please," she said. "You have no idea."

His mind then flashed to 1974, when he heard that Bobby Murcer had been traded and how he cried and cried.

She wiped some sweat from her brow. "It's getting really hot out here. Would you like to come inside?"

He supposed it was hot, but he didn't feel it. This wasn't hot to him anymore. 2062? Now that was hot. Way back in 1973, not so much.

They walked in the house, and the smell of home filled his body. He again felt a little weak in the knees at what he was experiencing. He was home. *Home.*

He noticed the red-orange shag carpet in the foyer. Oh, the '70s! Always the middle child, stuck between the '60s and the '80s, but oh, how he loved them. But the carpet in his house didn't smell. Unlike the shag carpets in all his friends' houses, which smelled like cigarette smoke. But his parents thankfully never smoked. And yet cancer would get his mother anyway...

She led him into the kitchen. Avocado, of course. He noticed a box of Devil Dogs and a box of Hostess Big Wheels on the counter. How many of those had he eaten back in the day? And that bright yellow box with the Indian chief on it. He always loved that box.

"I haven't had lunch yet," she said. "Would you like something to eat?"

"I wouldn't want to impose," he said.

"No bother. I have some bologna and cheese in the fridge. I can make a couple of sandwiches."

Bologna and cheese. On Wonder Bread with mayo, no doubt. His go-to lunch as a boy. And pretty much everyone's go-to lunch in 1973.

"If it's not too much trouble," he said.

Of course it wasn't. She went to the bread drawer and pulled out the Wonder Bread in its bright-colored polka-dotted packaging. It didn't matter if it was the carpet, or the Hostess box, or the Wonder Bread. Everything in 1973 was colorful and bright, and he loved it.

The sandwich was wonderful, even the gluey Wonder Bread.

She watched him as he ate and said, "You do look familiar to me. Are you sure we haven't met before?"

"You look familiar to me too," he said. "Maybe we did know each other in another lifetime."

She laughed. "Maybe." She could hear the radio still playing outside. "I left the radio outside. I'll be right back." She left the kitchen table and walked to the front door to grab the radio from the porch.

Robert Miller continued eating his sandwich, hoping this day would not end. How he had missed his mother all these years! But this day would end—and end soon. He didn't want to still be here when his father arrived home with his younger self and his sister. That would be too much.

His mother returned to the kitchen, holding the transistor radio. She switched it off and sat across from him.

"Oh, turn that back on if you can," he said. "I love that song."

"You love that song?" she asked. "What an interesting old man. How do you know these current pop songs?" She switched the radio back on. The Carpenters' "We've Only Just Begun" came on.

He was amazed at how sad Karen Carpenter's voice was. Even when she sang a song like this, one that was supposed to be this happy song about a young couple starting their lives together, her voice was filled with sadness. At least, that's the way he always heard it. He looked at his mother, and his eyes filled with tears.

"Are you OK?" she asked as she reached out to him.

Karen Carpenter kept singing—about when the evening comes, about there being so much of life ahead.

He broke down in tears, looking into his mother's eyes, trying to hold back, then not caring. He let it out.

She got up and came over to him. "It's OK. It's OK," she said as she put her arm around him.

He took hold of her arm and held it there. He lost himself for a moment in her warmth and smell.

"I'm sorry," he said. "I've just always found that song incredibly sad."

"I know what you mean," she said. "I play that song for my son, Robbie, all the time. We have the record. He loves it."

Yes, he does, Robert Miller thought. *Yes, he does.*

"I'm sorry again," he said. "You must be wondering how this crazy, strange old man ended up in your kitchen, crying his eyes out."

"It's OK, really. You're a very sweet man."

He stood up and walked toward the front door. She followed right behind him.

"Are you sure you're OK?" she asked. "Do you need me to drive you somewhere?"

"No, thank you. I'm fine," he said. "I'm going to walk back to the mall. My daughter will be picking me up."

He reached the door and turned toward his mother.

"Before I go, let me give you some old-man wisdom," he said. "Actually, it's a couple of pearls of wisdom that my mother used to give me."

He looked straight into his mother's big blue eyes. "First, she used to say, 'Always remember where you came from.' I've always adhered to that one."

"And the other one?"

"Be here now," he said. "Unfortunately, I've struggled mightily with that one. But she was right. Beautiful young Barbara Miller, don't look back. The past is just that—past. And the future is not guaranteed. So, try to forget the past and live in the present."

He took his mother in his arms and held her tight. At first, she was taken aback, but there was something about him. She hugged him back, and she meant it. She felt it.

The old man stepped out the door and slowly walked away.

Robert Miller exited the woods behind Victory Lane and once again was in the tall grass where his time-traveling adventure had begun.

Had it been worth it? Oh, yes, it most definitely had. He had been haunted most of his life by nostalgia, and this was the final scratch of that itch. But it felt good. It made him think back to that time fifty or so years ago, when those scientists first approached him, looking for seed money, telling him they had found a way to make time travel possible. And how he had given them the money, not because he wanted to see or experience something historical. But because he wanted to see his mother one more time.

Of course, Mr. Gundersen didn't know any of that. Robbie's majority ownership of the Zenith Time Travel Corporation had always been kept a secret. It didn't matter anyway because he wasn't going back. He had said his goodbyes to his children and grandchildren and settled his affairs. His illness was beyond repair. It was time.

He lay down in the tall grass and looked up at that 1973 sun that was just starting to go down. He thought of the Carpenters song again and sang it in his head. Yes, evening had finally come for Robert Miller. He stared at the sun and noticed a jet flying overhead. Looks like a 747, probably out of JFK, heading for Europe. On a different day, he and Billy Cohen might be ducking from it right now.

He closed his eyes and hoped to drift off to sleep. He hoped that Elizabeth and Ricky and his mom and dad were waiting for him. Ninety-five years had passed, and it startled him to realize that it had all seemed to go by so quickly. He opened his eyes and looked at the setting sun one more time. Then there was nothing.

As ninety-five-year-old Robert Miller lay dead in the grass, back at 16 Victory Lane, six-year-old Robbie Miller listened intently as his mother told the story of the strange old man who had visited her that day.

She told them the advice the old man had given her. *Always remember where you came from and don't look back.* Robbie wasn't quite sure what either one meant, but his father took this as an opportunity to remind them that he wanted to sell the house one day after Robbie and his sister had grown up so that he and his mother could move closer to the city and shorten his commute.

Robbie desperately hoped they would never sell the house. They couldn't! Robbie wanted his parents to always be in this house. He wanted to visit when he was an adult. He wanted his kids to visit the house he grew up in. He wanted the house to always be there. He wanted Victory Lane to always be there, just as it was now.

"You can't sell the house!" he said.

"Don't worry, Robbie," said his mother. "If we sell the house, it won't be for years."

"Yes," his father said. "Don't worry about something that's years away. Worry about something fun. Worry about which Yankee shirt you're going to wear next week at Yankee Stadium."

Yes! Yankee Stadium. They were all going to Yankee Stadium next week! What could be better than that?

Later that night, Robbie Miller rested his head on his pillow. Just thinking about Yankee Stadium filled him with more excitement than he could stand. Would he meet Bobby Murcer? He thought of the line of great Yankee center fielders—DiMaggio, Mantle, Murcer…Miller? Yes, he would be the next great Yankees center fielder. He was certain of it. Thoughts of his parents selling the house had moved out of his mind. He could worry about that another day.

He flipped the pillow to the cool side, closed his eyes, and dreamed of running down flyballs in the great baseball cathedral, with the brilliant sun in his eyes and the rest of his life staring back at him.

Acknowledgments

THANKS, AS ALWAYS, TO my parents, John and Vera, who inspired some of the stories in this book and especially to my mother who—for better or worse!—passed on the nostalgia bug to me.

To my brother, John, who read the first draft of this book and provided valuable insights.

To my editor, Craig Lancaster, for his yeoman's efforts and suggestions.

To Stuart James Macpherson, for pulling me out of my shell so many years ago.

To my daughter Gianna, the next beneficiary of the nostalgia bug.

To my daughter Andrea, who helped me design the back cover of this book.

And most importantly, to my wife, Elisa, my biggest champion and the person who read the first stories in this book and encouraged me to keep going.

During the early days of the pandemic, Elisa and I got in the habit of sitting on the porch each afternoon, drinking a glass of wine. I used these afternoons to bounce story ideas off her, and this back-and-forth led to some of the stories in this book. In fact, the story "2020 Visions" was a direct result of one of these sessions.

Thank you, Schmoopie!

About the Author

MICHAEL DI LEO IS the author of *The Spy Who Thrilled Us: A Guide to the Best of Cinematic James Bond* and *Images of Broken Light*. He grew up on Long Island and is a 1989 graduate of Utica College of Syracuse University. He works as a project manager in Manhattan and lives on Long Island with his wife and two daughters.

michaeldileoauthor.com

Follow on Instagram at michaeldileo.author